COURTNEY MILAN

the Heiress Effect

This is a work of fiction. Names, characters, places, and incidents are the product of the author's imagination or are used fictitiously. Any resemblance to actual events, locales, or persons, living or dead, is purely coincidental.

For Bajeeny.

I've waited and waited for a book to dedicate to you, my nearest sister. I wanted one that was perfect. I'm settling for one where I didn't accidentally name the heroine after you. Now look at the date—Bump.

Chapter One

Cambridgeshire, England, January 1867

MOST OF THE NUMBERS THAT Miss Jane Victoria Fairfield had encountered in her life had proven harmless. For instance, the seamstress fitting her gown had poked her seven times while placing forty-three straight pins—but the pain had vanished quickly enough. The twelve holes in Jane's corset were an evil, true, but a necessary one; without them, she would never have reduced her waist from its unfashionable thirty-seven inch span down to the still unfashionable girth of thirty-one inches.

Two was not a terrible numeral, even when it described the number of Johnson sisters that stood behind her, watching the seamstress pin the gown against her less-than-fashionable form.

Not even when said sisters had tittered no fewer than six times in the past half hour. These numbers were annoyances—mere flies that could be waved away with one gilt-covered fan.

No, all Jane's problems could be blamed on two numbers. *One hundred thousand* was the first one, and it was absolute poison.

Jane took as deep a breath as she could manage in her corset and inclined her head to Miss Geraldine and Miss Genevieve Johnson. The two young ladies could do no wrong in the eyes of society. They wore almost identical day gowns—one of pale blue muslin, the other of pale green. They wielded identical fans, both covered with painted scenes of bucolic idleness. They were both beautiful in the most clichéd, china-doll fashion: Wedgwood-blue eyes and pale blond hair that curled in fat, shining ringlets. Their waists came in well under twenty inches. The only way to distinguish between the sisters was that Geraldine Johnson had a perfectly placed, perfectly natural beauty mark on her right cheek, while Genevieve had an equally perfect mark on her left.

They had been kind to Jane the first few weeks they'd known her.

She suspected they were actually pleasant when they were not pushed to their extreme limits. Jane, as it turned out, had a talent for pushing even very nice girls into unkindness.

The seamstress placed one last pin. "There," the woman said. "Now take a look in the mirror and tell me if you want me to change anything out—move some of the lace, mayhap, or use less of it."

Poor Mrs. Sandeston. She said those words the way a man scheduled to be hanged this afternoon might talk about the weather on the morrow—wistfully, as if the thought of less lace were a luxury, something that would be experienced only by an extraordinary and unlikely act of executive clemency.

Jane sashayed forward and took in the effect of her new gown. She didn't even have to pretend to smile—the expression spread across her face like melted butter on warm bread. God, the gown was hideous. So *utterly* hideous. Never before had so much money been put in the service of so little taste. She batted her eyes at the mirror in glee; her reflection flirted back with her: dark-haired, dark-eyed, coquettish and mysterious.

"What do you ladies think?" she asked, turning about. "Ought I have more lace?"

At her feet, the beleaguered Mrs. Sandeston let out a whimper.

As well she should. The gown already overflowed with three different kinds of lace. Thick waves of blue *point de gaze* had been wrapped, yard after obnoxiously expensive yard, around the skirt. A filmy piece of *duchesse* lace from Belgium marked her décolletage, and a black Chantilly in a clashing flowered pattern made dark slashes down the sleeves of her gown. The fabric was a lovely patterned silk. Not that anyone would be able to see it under its burden of lace frosting.

This gown was an abomination of lace, and Jane loved it.

A real friend, Jane supposed, would have told her to get rid of the lace, all of it.

Genevieve nodded. "More lace. I definitely think it needs more lace. A fourth kind, perhaps?"

Good God. Where she was to put more lace, she didn't know.

"A cunning belt, worked of lace?" Geraldine offered.

It was a curious sort of friendship, the one she shared with the Johnson twins. They were known for their unerring taste; consequently, they never failed to steer Jane wrong. But they did it so nicely, it was almost a pleasure to be laughed at by them.

As Jane wanted to be steered astray, she welcomed their efforts.

They lied to her; she lied to them. Since Jane wanted to be an object of ridicule, it worked out delightfully for all concerned.

Sometimes, Jane wondered what it would be like if they were ever honest with each other. If maybe the Johnsons might have become real friends instead of lovely, polite enemies.

Geraldine eyed Jane's gown and gave a decisive nod. "I absolutely support the notion of a lace belt. It would give this gown that certain air of indefinable dignity that it currently lacks."

Mrs. Sandeston made a strangled sound.

It was only sometimes that Jane wondered if they could have been friends. Usually, she remembered the reasons she couldn't *have* real friends. All one hundred thousand of them.

So she simply nodded at the Johnsons' horrific suggestions. "What think you two of that clever strip of Maltese that we saw earlier—the gold one, the one with the rosettes?"

"Absolutely," Geraldine said, nodding her head. "The Maltese."

The sisters cast each other looks above their fans—an exchange of sly smiles saying, clear as day: *Let's see what we can get the Feather Heiress to do today.*

"Miss Fairfield." Mrs. Sandeston put her hands together in an unthinking imitation of prayer. "I beg you. Keep in mind that one can achieve a far superior effect by employing fewer furbelows. A lovely piece of lace, now, that's the centerpiece of a beautiful gown, dazzling in its simplicity. Too much, and…" She trailed off with a suggestive twirl of her finger.

"Too *little*," Genevieve said calmly, "and nobody will know what you have to offer. Geraldine and I—well, we have only a mere ten thousand apiece, so our gowns must reflect that."

Geraldine gripped her fan. "Alas," she intoned.

"But you—Miss Fairfield, *you* have a dowry of one hundred thousand pounds. You have to make sure that people know it. Nothing says wealth like lace."

"And nothing says lace like…more lace," Geraldine added.

They exchanged another set of looks.

Jane smiled. "Thank you," she said. "I don't know what I would do without the two of you. You've been so good to me, tutoring me in all things. I have no notion of what's fashionable, nor of what message my clothing sends. Without you to guide me, who knows how I might blunder?"

Mrs. Sandeston made a choking noise in her throat, but said nothing more.

One hundred thousand pounds. One of the reasons Jane was here, watching these lovely, perfect women exchange wicked smiles that they didn't think Jane could understand. They leaned toward one another and whispered—mouths hidden demurely behind fans—and then, glancing her way, let out a collective giggle. They thought her a complete buffoon, devoid of taste and sense and reason.

It didn't hurt, not one bit.

It didn't hurt to know that they called her friend to her face and sought to expose her foolishness to everyone they saw. It didn't hurt that they egged her on to more—more lace, more jewels, more beads—simply so they might fuel their amusement. It didn't hurt that the entire population of Cambridge laughed at her.

It couldn't hurt. After all, Jane had chosen this for herself.

She smiled at them as if their giggles were the sincerest token of friendship. "The Maltese it is."

One hundred thousand pounds. There were more crushing burdens than the weight of one hundred thousand pounds.

"You'll want to be wearing that gown Wednesday next," Geraldine suggested. "You've been invited to the Marquess of Bradenton's dinner party, have you not? We insisted." Those fans worked their way up and down, up and down.

Jane smiled. "Of course. I wouldn't miss it, not for the world."

"There will be a new fellow there. A duke's son. Born on the other side of the blanket, unfortunately—but acknowledged nonetheless. Almost as good as the real thing."

Damn. Jane hated meeting new men, and a duke's bastard sounded like the most dangerous kind of all. He would have a high opinion of himself and a low opinion of his pocketbook. It was precisely that sort of man who would see Jane's one hundred thousand pounds and decide that he might be able to overlook the lace dripping off her. That kind of man would overlook a great many defects if it would put her dowry in his bank account.

"Oh?" she said noncommittally.

"Mr. Oliver Marshall," Genevieve said. "I saw him on the street. He doesn't—"

Her sister gave her a gentle nudge, and Genevieve cleared her throat.

"I mean, he looks quite elegant. His spectacles are very distinguished. And his hair is quite…bright and…coppery."

Jane could just imagine this specimen of thwarted dukehood in her mind's eye. He would be paunchy. He would wear ridiculous waistcoats, and he'd have a fob watch that he checked incessantly. He'd be proud of his prerogatives and bitter of a world that had led him to be born outside of wedlock.

"He would be utterly perfect for you, Jane," Geraldine said. "Of course, with our lesser dowries, he would find us quite…uninteresting."

Jane made herself smile. "I don't know what I would do without you two," she said, quite sincerely. "If I didn't have you to look out for me, why, I might…"

If she didn't have them trying to set her up as a laughingstock, she might one day—despite her best efforts—manage to impress a man. And *that* would be a disaster.

"I feel that you two are like my sisters, given the care you take for me," she said. Maybe like stepsisters in a blood-curdling fairy tale.

"We feel the same," Geraldine smiled at her. "As if you were our sister."

There were almost as many smiles in that room as there was lace on her gown. Jane offered up a silent apology for her lie.

These women were *nothing* like her sister. To say as much was to insult the name of sisterhood, and if anything was sacred to Jane, it was that. She had a sister—a sister she would do anything for. For Emily, she would lie, cheat, buy a dress with four different kinds of lace…

One hundred thousand pounds was not much of a burden to carry. But if a young lady wanted to remain unmarried—if she *needed* to stay with her sister until said sister was of age and could leave their guardian's home—that same number became an impossibility.

Almost as impossible as four hundred and eighty—the number of days that Jane had to stay unmarried.

Four hundred and eighty days until her sister attained her majority. In four hundred and eighty days, her sister could leave their guardian, and Jane—Jane who was allowed to stay in the household on the condition that she marry the first eligible man who offered—would be able to dispense with all this pretending. She and Emily would finally be free.

Jane would smile, wear ells of lace, and call Napoleon Bonaparte himself her sister if it would keep Emily safe.

Instead, all she had to do for the next four hundred and eighty days was to look for a husband—to look assiduously, and not marry.

Four hundred and eighty days in which she dared not marry, and one hundred thousand pounds to the man who would marry her.

Those two numbers described the dimensions of her prison.

And so Jane smiled at Geraldine once again, grateful for her advice, grateful to be steered wrong once again. She smiled, and she even meant it.

⌘ ⌘ ⌘

A few days later

MR. OLIVER MARSHALL WAS ALMOST LOATHE to relinquish his coat when first he entered the Marquess of Bradenton's home. He could feel the chill biting through his gloves, the draft of a winter wind rattling the windowpanes. The wire frame of his spectacles felt like ice against his ears. But it was too late.

Bradenton, his host, stepped forward. "Marshall," he said pleasantly. "How good to see you again."

Oliver handed off his own gloves and heavy greatcoat and shook the marquess's extended hand.

"Good to see you as well, my lord. It's been too long."

Bradenton's hands were cold, too. He'd grown paunchier these last years, and his thin, dark hair had receded up his forehead, but the smile he gave Oliver was still the same: friendly and yet cold.

Oliver suppressed a shiver. It didn't matter how high the servants piled the coal, how merry the blaze they set. These fine, old houses always seemed to be inhabited by a wintry chill. The ceilings stretched too high; the marble on the floors seemed icy even through the soles of his shoes. Everywhere Oliver looked he saw mirror-glass and metal and stone—cold surfaces made colder still by the vast, empty expanses that surrounded them.

It would warm up when they moved out of the entry, Oliver told himself. When more people arrived. For now, it was just Bradenton, Oliver, and two younger men. Bradenton motioned them forward.

"Hapford, Whitting, this is Oliver Marshall. An old school friend. Marshall, this is my nephew, John Bloom, newly the Earl of Hapford." The Marquess of Bradenton gestured to a man at his side, earnest and pale. "And Mr. George Whitting, my other nephew." He indicated a fellow with a shock of sandy hair and matching, untamed sideburns. "Gentlemen, this is Oliver Marshall. I've invited him to assist in completing your education, as it were."

Oliver inclined his head in greeting.

"I've been tasked with seeing to Hapford's introduction," Bradenton explained. "He'll be sitting with the Lords next month, and none of us were expecting that."

Hapford had a black band around his arm; his clothing was dark. Maybe there was a reason the house seemed cold and somber after all.

"I'm sorry to hear of it," Oliver said.

The new earl straightened and glanced over at Bradenton before responding. "Thank you. I intend to do my best."

That glance, that deference paid to the other man… *That* was why Oliver was here. Not to recall school-era friendships that had gone tepid over the years. Bradenton was the sort of man who nurtured new entrants to Parliament. Nurtured them, and then did his best to keep them as part of his coterie. He had quite a collection now.

"I'd wish for a little more time to prepare you, but you're coming along." Bradenton gave his nephew an approving clout on the shoulder. "And Cambridge isn't a bad place to conduct the exercise. It's a microcosm of the world out there. You'll see; Parliament is not so different."

"A microcosm of the world?" Oliver was dubious. He'd never met a coal miner at Cambridge.

But Bradenton didn't take his meaning. "Yes, there is rather a bit of the riffraff here." He glanced over at Oliver.

Oliver didn't say anything. To a man like Bradenton, he *was* riffraff.

"But the riffraff usually manage themselves," Bradenton continued. "That's the point of an institution like Cambridge. *Anyone* can aspire to a Cambridge education, so everyone who aspires chooses to start here. If you do it right, by the time they've finished their degrees, the most ambitious ones have become just like us. Or at least, they want to enter our ranks so badly that the next thing you know, all their ambition has been subsumed into the greater glory."

He gave Oliver a pointed nod.

Once, Oliver would have been annoyed by such a speech. The sly implication that Oliver didn't belong, the even slyer one that he'd been *subsumed* into Bradenton's goals instead of being a person in his own right…

When he was thirteen, he'd knocked Bradenton down for committing precisely that sin. But now he understood. Bradenton reminded him of an old farmer, walking the perimeter of his property every day, testing the fences and peering suspiciously at his neighbors, making sure that *his side* and *their side* were clearly delineated.

It had taken Oliver years to learn his lesson: keep quiet and let men like Bradenton test the fences. It wouldn't do them any good, and if you were careful, one day you'd be in a position to buy their whole damned farm.

And so Oliver held his tongue and smiled.

"The ladies will be arriving shortly," Bradenton said, "so if you'd like to start with a brandy…" He gestured off the entryway.

"Brandy," Whitting said decisively, and the party moved to a side room.

Bradenton had an entire room reserved for nothing more than this—a sideboard with glasses, a decanter of amber liquid. But at least the chamber was smaller and therefore warmer. The marquess poured generous splashes into tumblers. "You'll need this," he said, passing glasses to his nephews first and then to Oliver.

Oliver took the spirits. "Many thanks, Bradenton. Speaking of this coming February. There is something I wanted to talk to you about. The voting reform act, in this coming parliamentary session—"

Bradenton laughed and tipped up his glass. "No, no," he said. "We are *not* going to discuss politics yet, Marshall."

"Well, then. If not now, perhaps we might speak later. Tomorrow, or—"

"Or the next day or the one after that," Bradenton finished with a gleam in his eye. "We have to teach Hapford *how* to get on before we teach him what to get on about. Now is not the time."

That, apparently, was not an attitude shared by all. Hapford had looked up with interest when Oliver started speaking; at this, he frowned and turned away.

Oliver could have argued. But then…

"As you say," he said mildly. "Later."

A man like Bradenton needed to receive deference. He needed a neighbor who stopped five feet from the fence instead of challenging the property lines. Oliver had swayed the man before, and he knew how it was done. Bradenton could be directed, so long as nobody penetrated the illusion that he was in charge.

Instead, Oliver let the conversation meander to the subject of mutual friends, the health of Oliver's brother and his wife. For a few moments, they could pretend there was nothing to this but a cozy, intimate environment. But then Bradenton, who stood by the window, raised his hand once more.

"Drink up," he said. "The first lady has arrived."

Whitting looked out the window and let out a whimper. "Oh, God, please no. Never tell me you invited the Feather Heiress."

"Blame your cousin." Bradenton lifted an eyebrow. "Hapford wants a few minutes in the corner with his fiancée. And for whatever reason, Miss Johnson insists on having her invited."

"Speaking of whom," Hapford said, with a quiet dignity that looked out of place on his boyish features, "I would prefer that we not slander my fiancée's friends."

Whitting let out a puff of air. By the grim look on his face, Oliver would have imagined that he had just been sentenced to three years of hard labor. "Spoilsport," he muttered, and then edged up to Oliver. "Someone should warn you," he muttered.

"Warn me about what?"

The man leaned forward and whispered dramatically. "The Feather Heiress."

"Her wealth comes from…goose down?"

"No." Whitting didn't look at him. "It's originally from transcontinental steamers, if you must know. She's called the Feather Heiress because being around her is like being beaten to death by feathers."

He looked utterly serious. Oliver shook his head in exasperation. "You can't beat someone to death with a feather."

"You're an expert on it, are you?" Whitting raised his chin. "Shows how much you know. Imagine someone starts beating you with a feather. Imagine that they never stop, until one day, the constant annoyance of goose feathers pushes you over the edge. In a fury you strangle the person who has been beating you." He demonstrated this with a wrench of his hands. "Then you hang for murder. You, my friend, have been beaten to death by feathers."

Oliver snorted. "Nobody is that bad."

Whitting put his hand to his head and rubbed at the furrows on his brow. "She's worse."

"Ah, ah," Bradenton said, lifting a finger. "She's almost here. That's not how it's done, *gentlemen.*" He emphasized the last word and then set down his glass. A gesture, and his young nephews followed him back to the entry. Oliver trailed after.

Yes, Oliver knew how it was done. He'd been on the receiving end of those almost-insults all too often. Upper-class politeness counted off cruelty not by the words that were spoken, but by the length of the silence that passed.

A servant opened the door and two women passed into the entry. One, swathed in folds of dark wool dotted with snow, was clearly a chaperone. She took down the heavy hood from her face, revealing gray, curling hair and a pinched mouth.

The other…

If ever a woman had wanted to announce that she was an heiress, this one did. She had made every effort to flaunt her wealth. She wore a fur-lined cloak, white and soft, and kid gloves with ermine showing at the cuffs. She gave a shake of her head and then undid the clasp at her neck—a clasp that shone with a golden gleam. As she moved, Oliver caught a sparkle at her ears, the glitter of diamonds and silver.

As one, the men stepped forward to greet her.

"Miss Fairfield," the Marquess of Bradenton said. He had a pleasant tone in his voice, a convivial friendliness as he dipped his head to her.

"My lord," she responded.

Oliver moved closer with the rest of the group, but stopped in his tracks when she took off her cloak. She was…

He stared and shook his head. She *should* have been pretty. Her eyes were dark and shiny; her hair was up, with a glossy riot of curls pulled out and artfully arranged about her shoulders. Her lips were pink and full, poised in a demure half smile, and her figure—what he could see of it—was precisely the sort he liked, soft and full, made up of curves that even the most determined corset could not hide. Under any other circumstances, he'd have found himself stealing glances all evening.

But looking at her was like picking up a luxurious peach and discovering it half-taken over by mold.

Her gown was ghastly. There was no other word for it, and even that one scarcely did justice to the thrill of helpless horror that traveled through him.

A little lace was in fashion. Falls at the cuffs, perhaps, or a few inches at the hem. But Miss Fairfield's gown was lace all over—layer upon layer of the most intricate hand-knit stuff available. Black lace. Blue lace. Gold lace trim. It was as if someone had swept into a store, ordered three hundred yards of each of the most expensive kinds of lace, and then crammed every ell on one dress

This wasn't a case of gilding the lily. If there was a lily underneath all that, it had long since been crushed to a pulp.

The party stopped in its tracks as she took off her cloak, frozen in wordless contemplation of a wardrobe that made the word "gaudy" sound sweet and demure by contrast.

Bradenton recovered first. "Miss Fairfield," he repeated.

"Yes, you did already greet me." She had a very pretty voice. If Oliver could shut his eyes—or perhaps look at her from above the neck—

She swept forward, too far forward, advancing on Bradenton until he actually took two steps back. This brought her earrings—heavy diamond stones clasped in silver—to dangle a few feet from Oliver's eyes.

One of those earrings would buy his parents' farm three times over.

"Thank you so much for the invitation," she said. As she spoke, she folded her cloak.

One of the gray-liveried servants should have stepped forward and relieved her of the burden. But they, like everyone else, had been momentarily stunned by the hideousness of her apparel.

Miss Fairfield didn't seem to notice. Without once looking to her side—without even glancing at Oliver—she handed him her cloak. His fingers took hold of it before he could register what she'd done. She turned away from him, greeted Hapford and Whitting, her voice pleasant, the back of her neck taunting him with little curls.

She'd handed him her cloak. As if he were a servant. A footman came up to Oliver, apologetically taking the unwanted burden from him, but it was too late. He could see the horrified smile on Whitting's face, the one he didn't quite seem able to repress. Bradenton, too, gave Oliver a too-amused smile.

He was long past the point of getting angry at little slights, and this one hadn't even been intentional. But God, she was a disaster. He almost felt sorry for her.

Bradenton gestured behind Oliver. "Miss Fairfield," he said, "there is another man here to whom you have not yet been introduced."

"There is?" Miss Fairfield turned and finally set eyes on Oliver. "Goodness. I didn't even see you when I came in."

She'd seen him. She'd just thought he was a servant. A simple mistake; nothing more.

"Miss Fairfield," Oliver said smoothly. "A pleasure."

"Miss Jane Fairfield, this is Mr. Oliver Marshall," Bradenton said.

She put her head to one side and looked at him. She *was* pretty. That annoying part of his brain couldn't stop noticing it in spite of the garish way she'd rigged herself out. Pretty, if you liked the healthy glowing English rose sort of woman. Normally, Oliver did.

He wondered when she was going to realize her error. Her eyes narrowed in concentration, and a frown left a furrow on her chin.

"But we've met," she said.

This was not what he had expected her to realize. Oliver blinked uncertainly.

"I'm sure we've met," she continued. "You look familiar. There's something about you, something…" Miss Fairfield tapped her lip with a finger, shaking her head as she did. "No," she concluded sadly. "No. I am wrong. It's simply that you look so common with that hair and those glasses that I mistook you."

He looked *common?*

Another woman delivering an insult of that magnitude would have emphasized the word just to be sure that her intent was not mistaken. Miss Fairfield, though, didn't act as if she was delivering a set-down. She sounded as if she were remarking on the number of pups in a litter.

"I beg your pardon." He found himself standing just a little taller, looking at her with a hint of frost in his expression.

"Oh, no need to beg my anything," she said with a smile. "You can't help your looks, I'm sure. I would never hold them against you." She nodded at him, as graciously as a queen, as if she were doing him a tremendous favor. And then she frowned. "I'm so sorry, but would you repeat your name again?"

Oliver gave her his stiffest bow. "Mr. Oliver Marshall. At your service." *Don't take that literally,* he almost added.

Her eyes widened. "Oliver. Were you named, perchance, after Oliver Cromwell?"

That was definitely *not* a genuine smile on his lips. His forgery nearly cracked under the strain. "No, Miss Fairfield. I wasn't."

"You weren't named after the one-time Lord Protector of England? Why, I should have thought that he would be an example that your parents would have wished you to emulate. He started out common like you, didn't he?"

"The name implies nothing so grand," he managed to get out. "My mother's father was named Oliver."

"Perhaps *he* was named—"

"No," Oliver interrupted. "Nobody in my family had hopes for my posthumous execution, I assure you."

He almost thought she smiled at that, but the twitch at the corner of her lips disappeared before he was even sure it was there. There the conversation ground to a halt.

One, two, three...

As a boy, Oliver had gone back and forth between two worlds— between the heights of the upper class, so freezingly polite, and the more cheerful working class world that his parents inhabited. There was a frozen silence that Oliver associated with these moments of upper-class awkwardness. It was that moment when every man around made a calculation based on manners, and decided to hold his thoughts to himself rather than speak aloud and risk rudeness. He'd been on the receiving end of that silence all too often as a boy: when he'd admitted that he'd spent a summer in manual labor, when he'd referred to his father's former occupation as a pugilist... In fact, for those first years until he'd learned the rules, silence had followed just about every time he had opened his mouth.

For all that it was supposedly born of manners, that silence could cut. Oliver had been on the outside of it often enough to know precisely how deeply. He glanced over at Miss Fairfield.

...four, five, six...

Her lips were smoothed into placid acceptance. Her smile was open and honest. There was no sign that she even noticed the tension.

"Who else will be joining us this evening?" she asked. "Cadford? Willton?"

"Not, uh—" Hapford glanced around. "Not Willton, he's...indisposed."

"Is that one of those—what do you call that thing, that thing someone says in order to avoid telling the truth?" Miss Fairfield shook her head, her diamond earbobs shaking. "The word for it is on the tip of my tongue. I can feel it. It's a...a..." She raised her chin, her eyes suddenly bright. "Euphemism!" She snapped her fingers. "That's a euphemism, isn't it? Tell me, is he really just bosky from last night?"

The men exchanged glances. "Right," Hapford said slowly. "Miss Fairfield, if you'll take my arm..." He led her away.

"Poor man," Whitting said. "He used to make fun, until Miss Johnson made him stop. He's no fun now that he's besotted."

Oliver didn't generally approve of mocking people behind their backs. It was cowardly and cruel, and he knew from personal experience that it was never as unobserved as the mockers supposed.

Poor Miss Fairfield. She had the opposite of conversation, the opposite of taste. They were going to rip her to shreds, and Oliver was going to have to watch.

Chapter Two

DINNER PROVED TO BE MORE PAINFUL than Oliver had imagined.

Miss Fairfield talked too loudly, and what she said…

She asked Whitting about his studies, and when he made a wry comment about preferring to concentrate his efforts on the study of liquids, she stared at him.

"How surprising." Her eyes were very round. "I had not thought you to have the capacity of intellect to read physics!"

Whitting stared at her. "Did you—" The man seemed to grasp hold of his amazement with a visible struggle. A gentleman would never ask a lady if she had intended to call him stupid. Whitting took several deep breaths and addressed Miss Fairfield once more. "Yes. I do not have the sort of personality to enjoy the study of physics. As to my capacity…" He shrugged, and gave her a forced smile. "I must have misunderstood you."

In the lexicon of English gentlemen—a language of euphemism and false politeness—this was one of the more stinging insults. "I must have misunderstood you" usually translated into, "Hold your tongue." Oliver steepled his fingers and tried to look anywhere but at the two.

Miss Fairfield didn't seem the least troubled. "Did you misunderstand me?" she asked in tones of solicitousness. "I am *so* sorry. I should have realized the sentence construction was too complex for your capacity." She leaned toward him and spoke again, this time raising her voice and slowing her words as if she were talking to an aging grandfather. "What I meant was that I had not thought that you were intelligent. That would make the study of the physical world difficult."

Whitting turned red. "But—that is—"

"Perhaps I am wrong," she said cheerily. "*Do* you enjoy the study of the physical world?"

"Well, no, but—"

She patted his hand comfortingly. "There's no need to worry," she confided. "Not everyone has that capability. You make up for any lack of intellect by being so kind."

Whitting sat back in his chair, his mouth working.

From another woman, that would have been an unforgivable insult. If Miss Fairfield had shown the slightest indication that she was being devastatingly awful on purpose, she would have been ostracized. As it was, when she patted Whitting's hand, comforting him on his stupidity, she seemed actually to feel sorry for him.

She asked Hapford if he was going to take elocution lessons, and when he said no, hastened to assure him that nobody worth knowing would hold the quietness of his speech against him.

"Lemon juice," she said, speaking to Oliver across the table, "would do wonders for your freckles. Have you considered it?"

"Would you know, my aunt says the same thing?" he murmured. "And I have yet to try it."

"Oh, of course." She looked stricken. "How thoughtless of me! I suppose it would be difficult to obtain enough lemons, especially for one in your position."

Oliver didn't ask what his position was supposed to be.

After that, she complimented the Marquess of Bradenton on the cut of his coat, assuring him that his unfortunate slope-shoulders were "almost unnoticeable."

And when he sputtered in response and turned away, she set down her serviette.

"Don't feel embarrassed," she said. "It's acceptable to lose the flow of conversation. Not everyone is clever enough to think of something to say immediately."

Bradenton's lips thinned.

"And you're a marquess," she added. "Maybe there *are* deficiencies in your understanding, but nobody will ever notice them so long as you make absolutely certain to introduce yourself as a marquess first."

Bradenton's nostrils flared, but she was already turning back to address Oliver.

"Mr. Cromwell," she said, "do tell me how you spend your days. You're an…accountant, if that's what I recall hearing."

The truth was far more complicated. Besides, no matter what he said in reply, a woman who confused him with the long-dead Oliver Cromwell was unlikely to care about details. "I studied law at Cambridge," he finally said. "But I have no need to practice, so I—"

"Oh, so you're something like a solicitor, then? Perhaps you could explain something for me. How does a solicitor differ from an accountant? I had always thought they were cut from the same cloth."

No, he wasn't going to react. "A solicitor—"

"Because that's all my solicitor ever does," she said innocently. "Send me accounts. Do you do things besides send accounts, Mr. Cromwell?"

Oliver looked down the table at Miss Fairfield's earnest face, her diamond earbobs flashing in the lamplight, and admitted defeat. There was no way to explain even the basics of the world to someone who was impervious to reality, and he had no wish to insult her while trying. "No, Miss Fairfield," he said politely. "I think you have the general idea." He looked away.

But she must have seen him grimace. She leaned forward. "Oh, poor Mr. Cromwell," she said in kindly tones. "Are you in pain?"

He almost couldn't make himself look back at her—but it would be impolite to ignore her. He turned, slowly, wondering what she was about to say.

She was looking at him with deep concern.

"That noise you just made. It reminded me of our gardener. He has lumbago. There's a poultice I make for him when he's at his worst. Would you like the receipt?"

"I don't have lumbago." The words came out of his mouth a little too curtly.

"That's precisely what our gardener says, but after the poultice, he always feels so much better. Do let me send it to you, Mr. Cromwell. It will be no trouble at all. You seem rather young for lumbago, but since you're in service, such afflictions must come on early."

He swallowed. He thought of telling her that his father didn't suffer from lumbago despite years spent farming. He thought of explaining. He might even have burst into laughter, but that would have embarrassed her.

Instead, he inclined his head. "I'd be delighted to receive it, Miss Fairfield. Send it to my London address—Oliver Cromwell, care of the Tower, London, England."

For a bare moment, she paused. Her hand froze in the middle of reaching for her spoon. She looked over at him, her eyes wide—and then she looked away. "Well," she said. "It would be improper to correspond with a gentleman. Perhaps you are right. Not such a good idea after all."

Dinner with Miss Fairfield was like—he hated to admit it—being beaten to death by feathers. He hoped, for her sake, that her dowry was truly massive and that somewhere in England, there was a man in need of a fortune. Someone who was going deaf and wouldn't have to listen to her.

It was extraordinary. She obviously meant well, and still…

Dinner ended; the gentlemen slunk off to port and cigars, grateful for at least this temporary reprieve.

There were no awkward pauses once they were established in the library together.

"She is," Whitting said to Oliver, "precisely as bad as I said. Wasn't she?"

"Really," Bradenton said, with a shake of his head, "gentlemen. It's unbecoming to insult a lady."

"Indeed," Hapford echoed.

Whitting turned, a protest on his lips—and saw that the marquess was smiling, a hard, evil smile. "Good one," Whitting said. "God, if we couldn't insult her, there'd be no fun to be had at all."

Hapford sighed and looked away.

Oliver held his tongue. She *was* awful. But…he didn't think she could help it.

And there had been a time when he'd been the one saying all the wrong things. Speaking when he should keep quiet. Telling men like Bradenton that he only received respect because of his title—God, that was almost the worst thing she could have said to the marquess. If Bradenton zealously checked the fences of his prerogatives, Miss Fairfield had leaped over his efforts and trampled his fields.

"She's so irritating," Whitting was saying, "that I can almost feel myself breaking out in a rash in her presence."

It didn't matter how irritating Miss Fairfield was. Oliver had been on the receiving end of those snide comments one too many times to rejoice in making them.

Instead, he poured himself a glass of brandy and stood at the window.

He didn't listen. He didn't laugh. He didn't join in, even though Bradenton tossed a few sentences in his direction.

In the end, he was actually glad to rejoin the ladies.

But it didn't get better. Whitting glanced at Oliver after every one of her telling remarks, expecting him to join in his derision. The other men took turns standing next to her, drawing her fire in little batches. It bothered Oliver. It bothered him exceedingly.

There was a small supply of little cakes on the back table; Oliver put several on his plate and wandered off to look out the window. But there was no escape; she left the other men and came to stand by him.

"Mr. Cromwell," she said warmly.

He nodded at her, and she started speaking.

It wasn't that bad if he just listened to the sound of her voice. If he avoided parsing it out into individual words. She had a pleasant intonation—warm and musical—and a lovely laugh.

She called him Mr. Cromwell. She commiserated with him on the difficulty of accounting. She mentioned—three times—how much respect she had for people like him, people who had to work for their living. It wasn't bad at all, now that he'd prepared himself for the cyclone-force devastation of her conversation.

And then, as he stood next to her, smiling and trying to be polite, she reached out and took one of the cakes off his plate. She didn't even seem aware that she'd done so. She smiled, holding his cake in her fingers, waving it about as she gestured during the conversation.

That only meant that everyone could see what she had done.

Behind her, the others were grinning. Whitting made a loud remark about pigs feeding from any trough. Oliver gritted his teeth and smiled politely. He was *not* going to break. They'd laughed at him, too.

"So," Miss Fairfield was saying, "I'm sure you're most proficient with numbers. That's an excellent talent to have—one that will serve you in good stead in the future. I'm certain any employer would think of you so."

She took another cake as she spoke.

"It's a wonder that they found enough lace to wrap all the way around her," Whitting said behind her.

If Oliver could hear it, so could she. But she didn't react. Not so much as a flicker of pain crossed her eyes.

He'd been wrong. She *was* going to break him. Not because she was so awful; she meant well, at least, and that made up for a great deal. She was going to break him because he couldn't stand beside her and listen.

It reminded Oliver of an afternoon twenty years ago, back when he'd still been at home. A pair of boys had called his next-youngest sister, Laura, a plump little calf. They'd followed her home making mooing sounds. That was back when Oliver could solve problems with his fists.

Miss Fairfield wasn't his sister. She didn't seem to notice. But she might be *someone's* sister, and he didn't like what was happening to her.

He'd come here to try and talk to Bradenton of reform. He'd come here to change minds. He hadn't come here to see anyone mocked.

So he kept silent.

And when she reached out for another cake, he handed her his entire plate instead.

Her eyes widened for a moment. She stood in place, looking at him, and he was reminded—temporarily—that when Miss Fairfield held her tongue, when he was able to forget the monstrosity that she was wearing, she was actually quite lovely. There was a dimple in her upper arm, the kind that made him want to reach out and explore its dimensions. She looked up at him with eyes that were adorably brilliant.

"I beg your pardon," he said. "I've been holding these for you, but I must go…talk to a man."

She blinked. He inclined his head and left her.

"What is it with him?" he heard Whitting wonder.

It was simple. He didn't like to laugh at anyone. He could find too much of himself in the object of their amusement. And while much had changed since his childhood, that never would.

⌘ ⌘ ⌘

JANE SHUT THE DOOR to her sister's room and let out her breath in one great whoosh. Her face hurt from the effort of smiling. She set her cloak atop a clothespress and worked her shoulders back and forth, relaxing muscles that were frozen to tenseness. It was as if she were becoming a real person once more, one with feelings and desires all of her own instead of a simulacrum, spouting whatever nonsense was necessary.

It was nice to be able to have feelings again. Especially when the reason for this desperate charade was sitting on the edge of the bed in front of her, dressed in a nightgown.

"Well?" Emily asked. "How did it go? What happened?"

Somehow, returning her sister's welcoming smile didn't seem to use the same muscles that she'd employed all evening.

They didn't look like sisters. Emily had soft, blond hair that fell in natural curls; Jane's hair was dark brown. Emily's features were delicate—an artist's application of thin, arching eyebrows and fine lashes. Jane—well, there had never been anything *delicate* about her. She wasn't the sort of woman that one typically called plain. She was pretty enough, she supposed, in a plump way.

Nonetheless, when she and her sister stood side by side, Jane felt as if she were a draft horse. The kind of horse that people on the street eyeballed as it clopped past, whispering to one another. *That beast is nineteen hands at the shoulder, I'd warrant. At least one hundred and fifty stone.*

Jane supposed they took after their respective fathers. And *that* was part of Jane's problem.

"Well?" Emily demanded again. "What did the new fellow think of you?"

Some people confused Emily's energy with childlike enthusiasm. Jane knew her sister better. She was always in motion—running when it was allowed, walking when it wasn't. When she was forced to sit, she jiggled her leg impatiently.

She jiggled her leg constantly these days.

Jane contemplated her answer. "He's tall, at least," she finally managed. He was tall—maybe an inch taller than Jane in heeled shoes, which was a rare feat in a man. "And clever." He hadn't even paused to deliver that quip about the Tower of London. "Luckily, I managed to wear him down in the end."

She smiled faintly at the door as she spoke. Ah, the bittersweet taste of victory. He'd been impressive, really. He had tried so hard to be nice to her and her money.

"How did you do it?"

"I had to eat off his plate," Jane admitted.

"How perfectly lovely. You used my trick." Emily glowed with a smile, jiggling her leg against the pink of her coverlet. "I thought you said you were holding it in reserve. I'll have to think of another good one."

"I *was* holding it in reserve." Jane blinked. "He was quite determined to be kind to me, and he was funny to boot. If I'd let him talk to me much longer, he would have made me laugh. I had to break him before that happened."

He'd had the strangest expression on his face near the end, solemn and brooding, as if he wanted desperately to like her and was upset at his own failure. His complexion was so fair, she wouldn't have thought he'd have been able to brood. His eyes had managed the trick—those pale, troubled eyes, masked slightly by the glass of his spectacles.

"We'll need a new reserve trick." Emily rubbed her chin.

Indeed. Jane wouldn't feel safe until Marshall was actually laughing with the others. She was almost going to regret breaking him. He'd been *nice.*

But she'd given him no reason to be kind to her. No reason except the hundred thousand reasons that any man had, and that made him not nice at all. She shook her head, dispelling all thoughts of kind-eyed, bright-haired men, and turned back to her sister.

"I have something for you." She turned back to the cloak she'd tossed aside and rummaged through the pockets until she found the gift.

"Oh!" Emily was sitting up straight now. "Oh, it has been forever since the last one."

"I found it this afternoon, but Titus said you were not to be disturbed during your nap, so…"

She held out the volume.

Emily's face lit and she reached out eagerly, taking the book with a reverent sigh. "Thank you, thank you, thank you. I love you forever." She brushed one hand gently down the cover. "I hope that Mrs. Blickstall didn't raise too much trouble over it?"

Jane waved a hand dismissively. She had an understanding with her chaperone. Their uncle had chosen Mrs. Blickstall to accompany Jane, but it was Jane's fortune that paid her salary. So long as Jane augmented the woman's quarterly payments, Mrs. Blickstall was willing to alter the reports she delivered to their uncle…and to allow a little contraband from time to time.

Contraband like novels. In Emily's case, *dreadful* novels.

"*Mrs. Larriger and the Inhabitants of Victoria Land,*" Jane said. "Really, Emily. Where is Victoria Land?"

A dreamy look stole into her sister's eyes, and she clutched the book closer. "It is the land of ice and snow at the South Pole. At the end of the last volume—the one where Mrs. Larriger was kidnapped by Portuguese whalers and held for ransom—she talked them into letting her go. The whaler captain, in a fit of spite, deposited her on the icy shores of Victoria Land."

"I see," Jane said dubiously.

"I have had to wait two entire months to find out what happened to her."

Jane simply shook her head. "I didn't know there were inhabitants of Victoria Land. I had thought that a land without soil would be a harsh environment to support human life."

"There are penguins and seals and who knows who else? It is *Mrs. Larriger* we're talking about. She escaped execution in Russia after proving herself innocent of the murder of the Czarina's pet wolfhound. She singlehandedly put down an armed revolt in India. She foiled the combined armies of Japan and China, and only then was she captured by whalers."

"All those governments around the world," Jane mused. "All wanting to execute the same woman. Surely they can't *all* be wrong."

Emily laughed. "You just don't like her because she's too much like you."

"Oh, I'm like a fifty-eight year old woman?" Jane put her hand to her hip in mock disgust.

"No," Emily said cheekily. "But you're bossy and argumentative."

"I am not."

"Mm hmm." Emily lifted the book to smell the fresh-cut pages. As she did, the sleeve of her night rail slipped to her elbow, exposing two round, shiny scars.

"Bossy or not, that book is tripe," Jane said. But her throat felt too tight, and her fingers curled into a ball. She didn't think she could ever forgive Titus for those scars.

If Emily took note of her altered tone, she didn't remark on it. "There's no smell quite so good as a newly printed, unread book. As for this one... It's educational. How else am I to learn about other countries?"

There was nothing to be said about Emily's scars, and the fact that she had them was no reason to stop teasing her. So Jane bumped her sister's shoulder and adopted a severe tone. "You realize these books are fiction? That each separate volume is probably written by a different man, one who has likely never left London? They're not *educational*. They're *made up,* and I imagine that the actual residents of Russia, China, and Japan would be quite disturbed to hear what the supposed Mrs. Larriger says of them."

"Yes, but—"

The door to the room opened without warning, interrupting the argument. Emily jumped and jammed the book under her skirts. Jane stepped in front of her sister. But the damage was already done.

Titus Fairfield looked from Jane to Emily and then back again, more slowly. He shook his head sadly.

"Oh, girls," he said.

Their uncle Titus was balding and had heavy jowls. That, combined with his deep, somber voice, made him appear perpetually dour and disapproving—an appearance that he no doubt rejoiced in. Jane suspected that he practiced that glum expression in the mirror.

He probably thought an air of moroseness made him seem more intelligent.

"I am not fooled," he said.

Jane looked at Emily. Emily looked back at Jane.

"Uncle Titus!" Emily said. "How lovely to see you."

Their uncle held out one hand and tapped the finger of the other against his palm. Emily heaved a sigh. Slowly, she stood and pulled the book out from underneath her. Uncle Titus strode forward and took it from her.

"It's an improving work," Emily told him. "A very moral tale, about..."

"Mrs. Larriger and..." A sad sound escaped him. "Victoria Land." He spoke those last words as if he were reluctantly reciting the name of a brothel. "Jane, my dear, what have I told you about leading your younger sister astray with novels?"

Jane would have been delighted to have Emily give up Mrs. Larriger and her string of unlikely, ridiculous exploits. It wouldn't take much to divert her attention—just allowing her out in company. Even letting her outside for longer than ten minutes at a time might do the trick.

She'd tried to argue that point too many times.

"Oh, but Uncle," Emily said, "it's an educational tale, replete with...geographical features of interest."

"A novel."

Emily set her jaw determinedly. "A true story, covered with the thin veil of fiction to protect the identities of the innocent."

Titus Fairfield opened the book, turned a handful of pages, and began reading aloud. "'Having convinced the seals to pull my raft and catch my fish, it only remained for me to find some way to train the voices of the penguins.'" He looked up. "A true story, covered by the thin veil of fiction?"

No. Even Titus wasn't that gullible.

Emily clapped her hands to her ears. "You're ruining it. Don't tell me what happens."

Titus looked at her. "If that is what it will take to stop this. You've disobeyed me, and disobedience has consequences." So saying, he shuffled slowly to the end of the book. "You should not be allowed to take pleasure in your willfulness. If you do not want to hear the ending, then…" He bent his head and began to read. 'Chapter Twenty-Seven. After the sharks had come—'"

"La la la," Emily sang, drowning out his words. "*La la la la.*"

He stopped and closed the book, his expression even more grim. "Emily, my dear. Who taught you to tell untruths? To flout the authority of your elders? To speak as your guardian is speaking?"

You, Jane thought. *Necessity.*

But her uncle, apparently, had a different thought. His eyes traveled to Jane.

He didn't look at her with accusation in his eyes. There wasn't a cruel bone in his body. His expression was just pathetically, droopingly sad. He sat gingerly next to Emily and patted her shoulder.

"Now, Emily," he said quietly. "I know you to be a truthful girl. And I know that you feel a great affection for your sister."

He didn't know Emily at all. He'd never bothered to know either of them.

"It's quite natural," Titus said, as if Jane were not in the room. "But you need to keep in mind that your sister is lacking in moral character."

Jane refused to react. It never did any good to argue or scream or cry—any response on her part only reinforced his poor opinion of her.

But Emily shook her head. "I don't like what you're saying. It's not true."

"I understand, I understand," their uncle said, in his slow, sad voice. "I won't ask you to hate your sister—that would be unnatural for any girl, let alone one of your frailties."

Jane could see Emily's fist clenching in her skirts. They might not have looked like sisters, but looks were deceptive. And Emily was incapable of letting an insult to Jane go by.

Don't fight it, Emily. Just nod your head and let him maunder on.

"You're wrong," Emily said.

"You're overly emotional." Titus picked up the offending novel and slipped it into one of his voluminous pockets. "And I think I can identify the culprit. If you need anything to read, dear Emily, there's material aplenty already in my study. You need only ask."

Emily stared directly at her uncle. "Material in your study? But it's all old law books."

"Very improving," Titus said.

"Which should I read tonight, then? *A Treatise on the Art of Conveyancing* sounds so promising, but how could I read that, when *The Legal Relations of Infants, Parents, and Child* is available?"

Jane made a little motion with her hands. *Stop, please stop.* But Emily wasn't done.

"Oh, now I recall," she said. "I've read them all. Because I'm trapped in my room, not allowed to go out in company, not allowed to even read of real people—"

Or invented ones.

Titus stood. "Miss Emily," he said, "you're overwrought. You attend church, as any good young woman should. And Mrs. Blickstall accompanies you on walks appropriate to your physical wellbeing every morning." He frowned at her. "It's not like you to be so emotional. Was there...an occurrence today?"

"An occurrence?" Emily echoed. "Why, yes. The first thing that occurred was that I woke up."

Titus frowned. "Dear child. You know I did not mean the word in that sense."

Emily glared at the man. "Then say what you really mean."

"Did you have—that is, did you have the misfortune of—of falling victim to—"

Emily set her jaw. "I had a seizure."

The concern on his face was real. He placed one hand on Emily's shoulder. "Poor, dear child," he whispered. "No wonder you are overwrought. You should sleep."

"But Jane hasn't told me about her evening yet."

Titus looked up from Emily to contemplate Jane. Jane wished she could hate him. She wished she could hate his good wishes and his assumptions and his single-minded determination to cure her sister. But he wasn't a bad man. He was just a tired, lazy one.

He heaved another, horrible sigh. "Emily, your sister…"

Emily patted his hand. "How can I encourage her to do what is right if I am never allowed to speak with her?"

Titus sighed. "Very well. You may speak with your sister a little while longer. But Emily…encourage her to marry. It would be the best thing for all of us."

He wanted Jane out of his life. It was, Jane supposed, partially her fault. Her choices. It wasn't surprising he thought her a bad influence on her sister. But there was nothing she could do now to change his mind. Her uncle knew that she wasn't really her father's child, and that, *that* made everything about her unforgivable. She could break her heart trying to change his mind, but she had to keep that safe for Emily.

"I will, Uncle," Emily promised.

"You are an inspiration to us all, my dear," Titus said, and with another sad smile, he left the room.

Emily waited until his footsteps had disappeared down the hall before she balled her hands. "I hate him," she said, standing up and turning back to her bed. "I hate him. I hate him. I hate him." With every sentence, she drove her fist into her pillow. "I hate his sorrowful face and his wide concerned eyes. I hate him."

Jane went to her sister, put her arm around her. "I know."

"At least *you* get to go out in company," Emily said. "I'm nineteen, and for God's sake, he won't let me go anywhere—for fear that I might suffer from an *occurrence* if I did. Does he really think that I'm better off languishing in my room like a storybook princess with nothing to read but moral philosophy and legal tracts?"

Jane had long since given up wondering what Titus really thought. He *intended* to do what was right. A doctor had once told him that her sister's fits were exacerbated by exercise and excitement, and so Titus had put Emily on a regimen of bland languishment. The fact that Emily was so often confined to her rooms meant that *he* saw her seizures less often, and so nothing could convince him that this dictum hadn't worked.

The last thing Titus had wanted was to become the guardian of two girls. Especially when one of them wasn't his blood relation, and the other suffered from inexplicable fits.

Jane sighed and pulled her sister close. "Fifteen more months," she said. "Then you'll be twenty-one and free of him. We can leave him and live off my money, and I promise you, you will have every novel you want. You'll dance at every dance. Nobody will stop you. Nobody will dare."

Emily heaved a sigh. "I want to know how Mrs. Larriger escapes Victoria Land."

Jane thought—briefly—about teasing her sister some more. But there'd been enough heartache that night. Instead, she crossed back to her cloak and pulled out a second slim volume. "As he keeps finding them... I got two copies."

Emily made a little noise in her throat and grabbed the book. "I love you." She opened the cover, ran her fingers tenderly down the elaborate frontispiece. "I don't know what I would do without you."

Jane didn't know, either. It wasn't that Emily needed a guardian—quite the contrary. She needed the opposite of a guardian, someone who kept Titus from interfering with her too badly. She needed someone to fend off the endless stream of physicians. She needed someone to bleed the edge off of her unbearable frustration. Someone to give her something to do, even if it was only to smuggle terrible novels for her to read.

"Titus would disapprove," Jane said. "You're supposed to be encouraging me in my search for a husband."

Emily shut her eyes. "Never," she said. "Never leave me, Jane."

That was the crux of it all. Jane was the product of her mother's sin. She was argumentative, crude, unmannerly. She was, according to Titus, a poison in their household, one he only tolerated in the name of the duty he owed his dead brother.

And so that was what Jane had made of herself. She was a blight, one that would choke her uncle in return. It didn't matter. He didn't love her, and he had no legal obligation to keep her around. The instant he believed she had a respectable offer, he'd know that he could get rid of her and feel complacent about having done his duty—and her presence would no longer be tolerable.

She put her arms around her sister. She thought of the hard look Bradenton had given her that evening, of the sweet, meaningless smiles that the Johnson twins gave her. She thought of the look on Mr. Marshall's face when she'd taken the cakes off his plate.

Insolence on that level required real effort. She was *exhausted*.

Still, Jane smiled. "Don't worry." Mr. Marshall had seemed like a decent fellow, and she'd managed to disgust even him. "I can safely promise that I am never going to marry."

Chapter Three

LONG AFTER THE LADIES HAD LEFT, the gentlemen stayed. Bradenton had invited Oliver, and Oliver had hoped that the *later* they'd spoken of would come soon—that he'd have the chance to present his argument to Bradenton.

Instead, Bradenton had sat down with his nephew at a table near the brandy decanter. "Watch, Whitting," he had said. "It'll be your turn soon enough."

The process of turning a young man, scarcely twenty-one, into a politician, was fascinating. The marquess had asked Hapford questions. Who had said what? How had they looked as they spoke? What had Hapford thought of them? Bradenton was a good teacher, gentle and kind.

"Good," he finally said to his young nephew. "You've done quite well. You pay attention to the right things, and you listen when you need to. You'll do your family proud."

Hapford ducked his head and flushed faintly. "I'm trying."

That was when Bradenton's eye fell on Oliver, and his smile widened from avuncular indulgence to something altogether sharper.

"What make you of Mr. Marshall?" he asked softly.

Hapford looked at Oliver and swallowed. "I—well—he's...he's..."

"I know. He's sitting right here. But I know Marshall. We're old acquaintances. And he wants a favor of me, so he won't object to a little plain-speaking. Isn't that so, Marshall?"

Oliver had no idea what the man was about, so he simply inclined his head. "Just so, my lord."

"Very well, then," Hapford said. He took a deep breath. "By my observation, Mr. Marshall is—"

"Ah, ah." The marquess held up a finger. "You took me at my word, didn't you?"

Hapford looked about in some confusion. "Shouldn't I have done so?"

"Take nobody at his word. Not me. Not Marshall." He smiled and patted his nephew's shoulder. "Normally, I'd wait a week to introduce this, but you've done so well until now. This is advanced material, so to speak. Marshall, if you'll oblige me, tell my nephew why you really agreed with me."

"I want to know what you're up to," Oliver said in bemusement.

"And if you will, explain why I spoke the way I did in front of you."

Oliver paused, wondering if Bradenton really wished him to explain everything aloud. But the marquess made a little motion with his hand.

"You wanted to demonstrate that you could make me do as you wanted. That you have the upper hand." And Bradenton did, for now.

"Precisely so," Bradenton said. "You see how it is, Hapford. Men like you and me, we have power and information. We can trade that power for other things. Small power gets traded for less important things. Large power, well…" He shrugged. "What do you think that Mr. Marshall wants?"

"He wants your vote on the question of the extension of the franchise," Hapford answered swiftly. "And I wanted to ask him—"

"Later. What else does he want?"

"He wants…" Hapford bit his lip. "He wants your influence on the question as well. You're a powerful man, so your support would likely mean more votes than just your own."

"Well done, indeed. Now let's see if you've mastered the lesson. What else does Mr. Marshall want?" He leaned back in his seat and waited.

The silence stretched; Hapford peered at Oliver, as if he could see into him, and finally shook his head.

"Put yourself in Marshall's place," Bradenton advised. "You grew up on a farm. Your parents scraped together enough to get you into Eton and then Cambridge. By birth, you stand firmly in one world, but you've connections to another one. A better one. Tell me, Hapford. What would *you* want?"

This, Oliver supposed, was the sort of training that men received if they were born into the right families: the beginning of a thousand lessons on the operation of politics, conducted at night, so that the new men would know how to go about. This was how institutions continued for hundreds of years, how wisdom was passed on to the right sort.

He'd remember this.

But now he felt like an insect pinned to a specimen card.

Hapford had a thick ring around one finger. He turned it in place, peering at Oliver, frowning as if trying to recognize what species Oliver was.

"Money?" Hapford guessed.

His uncle nodded.

"Recognition?"

Another nod.

"Um…" The young earl pulled back and shook his head.

"Tell him what you want, Marshall."

Oliver unclenched his jaw. "Everything," he said. And it was the simple truth.

Later, when he was gone, Oliver was sure that Bradenton would tell Hapford even more. He'd explain how Oliver was coming up in influence—a longer path than the one Hapford treaded, one where he had to work harder, with less training. For now, that single word would do. Oliver wanted everything, and Bradenton could speed his way.

"Oh," Hapford said in confusion.

"Speaking of everything," Oliver said. "The bill that—"

"Not yet," Bradenton interrupted. "Tell me, Hapford. What think you of Miss Fairfield?"

Hapford blinked at this sudden change in conversation. "She's a little odd, I grant you, but Geraldine vouches for her..." He trailed off in confusion. "I don't know. I don't like speaking ill of people."

"That," said Bradenton, "is a nicety you'll have to rid yourself of. Tell me, what makes Miss Fairfield so odd?"

Hapford stood and walked to the window. He stared out it a long time. Finally, he turned around. "She doesn't...she doesn't seem to know what's expected of her. What her place is."

Bradenton was usually so good humored. But at that, Oliver caught a look in his eye—a thinning of his lips—and he remembered that in all the nonsense that Miss Fairfield had spouted that evening, she'd told Bradenton that nobody would think anything of him if he hadn't been a marquess.

"Yes," Bradenton said tightly. "She doesn't know her place, and she's too stupid to be taught it by the normal methods. What are we to do about it, Hapford?"

Hapford frowned. "I don't see why we need to do anything. She isn't hurting anyone, and Whitting takes such amusement from her that it would be a shame to deprive him of it."

"There's where you're wrong." Bradenton's voice was quiet. "It harms everyone when people don't know their places. Something should be done about it."

Hapford considered this. "Even if that's true..." He shook his head. "No. Geraldine doesn't let anyone speak ill of her. I don't want to upset her."

"Yes, well," Bradenton said tersely. "In another few years, we'll see if you're so eager to do Miss Johnson's bidding. But never mind. You're right in essentials. A gentleman never hurts a lady; the potential repercussions to his reputation are not worth the risk."

Hapford looked relieved.

Bradenton shook his head and leaned over, tousling his nephew's hair. "Watch, and I'll show you how it's done."

And then he looked over at Oliver. He looked at him as if he'd been planning this moment for hours—and he probably had. Oliver felt a sick pit open up in his stomach. Whatever it was that Bradenton was thinking, he didn't want to hear it.

"Very well, Marshall. It's your turn now. We're going to talk about the vote." His voice was soft once more. "Do you know why I voted against the last bill?"

Oliver had his own suspicions. "I suppose you'll tell me."

"It was too expansive. People need to know their places or there will be chaos. If even Parliament won't hold them to order, we might as well surrender."

Oliver swallowed. "Actually, my lord, the last bill was rather conservative. You see, the—"

"You'll never get my vote on anything more liberal. I ask for so little—just that rate-paying clause I introduced. If they can't afford to pay it, what business do they have offering an opinion?"

Oliver shut his mouth in annoyance. That would only put this same debate off another ten years. But a small step forward would be better than nothing. "Perhaps we could come to an agreement if the rate was low enough."

"Perhaps." Bradenton tapped his fingers against the arm of the chair. "But there is one other thing I need. Hapford, why do you suppose Marshall is so keen on this bill?"

"I had thought his background." He flushed. "My apologies for speaking of it so openly, Marshall."

"Yes. What else?"

"I…" Hapford shook his head, looking at Oliver for some hint. And perhaps he found it because his brow cleared. "Because everyone is talking about the issue," he said. "And if he plays a role in getting it passed, he'll get the credit."

"Precisely," Bradenton said. "It was me and my friends who got the last bill voted down. Think what it will mean if he is the one to broker the compromise. He'll be respected, elevated, talked about for office of his own. It will be a coup."

Oliver's nostrils flared.

"It's one I'm willing to grant him," Bradenton said. "That's what it means to be us, Hapford. We don't just vote. We give power."

Oliver leaned forward, wanting. Wanting so hard that he could almost taste victory in his mouth.

"And so if we're going to be doing it," Bradenton said, "we have to be sure of him."

"We do?" Hapford echoed.

"We do. We need to know that he's going to be part of the proper order. That he'll know his place, and expect everyone to be in theirs."

That taste of victory turned metallic. Oliver didn't know his place. He'd spent too many nights seething at the way of things, too long wanting to rise in power, not just so that he might wield it, but so that he might wrest it from the hands of those who abused it. They'd spent years trying to teach him his place; he'd learned through long, hard experience that the only way forward was to keep quiet until he grew so tall they could no longer shove him down.

But all he said aloud was, "I should think I've proven my discretion over the years."

Bradenton simply smiled. "Didn't you hear me, Marshall? I don't want your words. I have a job that needs doing, and I cannot do it myself."

That sick sensation in Oliver's stomach grew.

"You see, Hapford?" Bradenton said. "He wants. I have. The only way to make a deal is if I want something, too." He leaned forward. "And what I want, Marshall, is Miss Fairfield." There was no masking the venom in his voice. "I don't want to see her or her annoying gowns. I don't want to hear her thoughtless jibes." Bradenton's nostrils flared. "She's the worst of the worst—a woman with no birth to speak of, who thinks that her hundred thousand pounds makes her my equal. A woman like her, running about, spouting her tripe… She does damage to us all, and I want her gone."

"That's not going to happen," Oliver said sharply. "I don't ruin women, no matter how annoying they are."

Hapford was looking between them, his eyes worried. "Well said, Marshall."

Bradenton seemed to come back into himself with one long, slow breath. The hatred in his eyes dimmed to mere amusement. "Oh, look at you two. Ruin her? Goodness, how sordid. I wouldn't ask my worst enemy to kiss her."

"Then what are you asking?"

The marquess leaned back in his seat. "I want her to know her place. Humiliate her. Hurt her. Teach her her lesson. You know how it's done; it took you long enough to learn yours."

For a second, the room seemed to go hazy about Oliver. He'd learned his lesson, all right. He'd learned to keep quiet in public and seethe in private. He'd learned to keep his ambition hidden. To let men like Bradenton see only what he wished to see.

"Don't answer, Marshall. Work it through your principles." Bradenton smiled. "But in the end, we all know how this will work out. It's one annoying girl against your entire future. Against the future of voting rights."

"I say," Hapford muttered.

"It's not pretty," Bradenton said. "And yes, Hapford, there are times when you might not like the details, messy as they are. But this is how things get done. If there's something you can't do, that must nonetheless be done…"

"But—"

"One day, your Miss Johnson will wish she'd cut the acquaintance far sooner. You're doing her a favor, Hapford. You're going to be her husband; it's your duty to do what she needs before she knows it."

Hapford lapsed into silence.

"And as for you, Marshall…" Bradenton looked at Oliver. "Take the time you need to salve your conscience. To tell yourself whatever it is you need to make this palatable. You'll be doing her a favor, you know."

No, Oliver thought. *Not a favor. And I'm not doing it.*

But that sick pit in his stomach felt differently.

Yes, it whispered. *Yes, you are.*

⌘ ⌘ ⌘

IT USUALLY TOOK JANE ONE DAY, at most two, to crush a man's interest in her. Any positive feelings her fortune engendered could be quickly overcome, so long as her first impression was sufficiently negative.

She had assumed that Mr. Oliver Marshall would prove no different.

She had assumed wrongly. The second time they encountered each other was on a street corner. She was going into the modiste for a second fitting with her companion; he was passing by, talking with a male friend.

He stopped on the street, tipping his hat to her. And that was when something awful happened.

She looked into his eyes. They were ice-blue and mobile. In the bright mid-morning, his spectacles made him look sharp and intelligent. He didn't look over her head as if wishing her elsewhere. He didn't curl his lip in disgust or nudge his companion as if to say, *That's her; she's the one I was telling you about.* He looked at her straight on, his eyes flickering over her as if he were wondering what lay beneath the blinding orange-and-green pattern of her day gown. And he smiled at her as if she deserved more than a few scraps of surface civility.

She wasn't in heels any longer, so he had several inches on her now. His hair was a bright copper, and when he lifted his hat at her, the wind caught the ends. He seemed open and uncomplicated—so far from the dark, brooding gothic hero that filled the pages of Emily's novels.

Still, she felt something that she'd only read about in the pages of a book. There was a slow prickle in her throat, a flush of heat that slid over her skin. She felt a sense of pure awareness. A *frisson*. She felt a real live frisson just from looking into his eyes.

How dreadful.

She looked away. "Mr. Cromwell," she said, almost desperate to erase that feeling from her skin. "How lovely to encounter you again."

He didn't seem annoyed at her misidentification. He didn't blink or correct her. "Miss Fairfield," he said, and gave her a smile so friendly that she almost stepped back.

Mr. Marshall's companion was a dark-haired gentleman who would have fit the brooding hero mold rather better. He blinked and looked between the two of them with a curious expression on his face. "Cromwell?" he asked in low tones.

"Yes," Mr. Marshall said. "Did I forget to mention that? I've been politicking under an assumed name. Play along, Sebastian." He turned to Jane and said, "Miss Fairfield, might I introduce my friend? This is Mr. Sebastian—"

The other man took a step forward and took her hand. "Sebastian Brightbuttons." This, with a glance at Mr. Marshall. "If you get to assume a name, I want one, too."

In all the months in which Jane had been operating under a charade, she'd learned to deal with almost every emotional response to her mannerisms. She could manage everything from anger to disbelief.

Playfulness? That was new. She swallowed and tried to do what she always did. She imagined the conversation as a prime coach-and-four. She imagined it racing along a road at top speed, the wheels glinting in the sunlight. And then she imagined driving it straight into a hedge.

"Sebastian," Jane mused. "Like Sebastian Malheur, the famous scientist?" A comparison guaranteed to put this gentleman off. Malheur was a name that one heard around Cambridge a great deal—a man who was known for giving lectures where he openly talked of sexual intercourse under the guise of discussing the inheritance of traits. His name was cursed alongside that of Charles Darwin, and sometimes with greater vituperation.

But instead of flushing, Mr. Marshall and Mr. Brightbuttons exchanged amused glances.

"Very much like him," Mr. Brightbuttons said. "Are you an enthusiast of his work? I am." He leaned in a little closer. "Actually, I think he's brilliant."

Marshall was watching her again, and Jane's skin prickled under his perusal.

That was when Jane realized she'd made a mistake. Those freckles, his background—they'd all misled her into thinking that he was a quiet little rabbit.

He wasn't. He was the wolf that looked as if he were lounging about on the outskirts of the pack, a lone hanger-on, when in truth he had adopted that position simply so that he could see everything that transpired in the fields below. He wasn't solitary; he was waiting for someone to make a mistake.

He looked willing to wait a very long time.

But he hadn't had to. She'd used the wrong-name trick on Marshall the other night, and here she was, repeating it again. Use a stratagem too many times, and people began to be suspicious.

She blamed that damned frisson.

Mr. Brightbuttons, or whatever his name was, was grinning at her, too.

"Tell me," he said, "do you *really* think that I'm like Sebastian Malheur? Because I've heard that he is excruciatingly handsome."

He smiled at her, and Jane realized she'd made another mistake. He wasn't Sebastian some-random-name-that-he-hadn't-admitted-to. He *was* Sebastian Malheur in the flesh.

Mr. Marshall was friends with the infamous Malheur. Jane swallowed.

"You can't be very much like Malheur, then," she managed. "I've been looking at you for a full thirty seconds, and I haven't had a single flutter of interest."

Mr. Marshall let out a crack of laughter.

"Very well, Miss Fairfield," he said. "You've earned it. May I introduce Sebastian Malheur, my friend and cousin. He won't assume you're as dreadful as rumor says, so long as you give him the same credit."

Jane opened her mouth to agree. She almost did, before she realized what he'd said—and what she'd almost assented to. She had to physically yank her hand behind her back to keep from offering it in friendship.

"What are you talking about?" Her voice sounded far too high. "I haven't got a dreadful reputation. And Malheur—isn't he some kind of evolutionist? I have heard that his lectures are entirely wild."

"I'd planned to call the work I'm preparing now 'Orgies of the Peppered Moth,'" Mr. Malheur said brightly. "It's a series of heated interrogations of winged insects, completely unclothed, doing nothing but—"

Mr. Marshall jabbed his friend with an elbow.

"What? Have you got some sort of vendetta against moth-on-moth—"

"Really, Sebastian."

His friend shrugged and then looked back at Jane. "Only one way to find out," he said. "Come to my next lecture in a handful of months. I'll start off with snapdragons and peas. Nobody can object to a discussion of plant reproduction. If they did, we'd require flowers to don petticoats instead of wandering around, showing their reproductive parts to all and sundry."

Jane choked back a laugh. But Mr. Marshall was watching her, a quizzical expression on his face.

She swallowed and looked away.

"Miss Fairfield," Mr. Marshall said, "are you familiar with chameleons?"

"I dare say I was just reading about those," Jane said officiously, trying to regain her balance. "Those are a species of flower?"

Mr. Marshall didn't even twitch at that, and that made Jane feel all the more uneasy. He was supposed to smile at her. Better yet, he was supposed to sneer.

"Or maybe it was a hat," she added.

Not so much as a curl of his lip.

"The chameleon," Mr. Marshall said, "is a species of lizard. It changes its coloration so that it hides in its surroundings. When it darts across the sand, it is sand-colored. When it slips through the forest, it is tree-colored."

His eyes were the color of an unforgiving winter sky, and Jane shifted uneasily in her tracks. "What a curious creature."

"You," he said, with a small gesture of his hand, "are an anti-chameleon."

"I am an ant-eating what?"

"An anti-chameleon. The opposite of a chameleon," he explained. "You change your colors, yes. But when you are in sand, you fashion yourself a bright blue so that the sand knows you are not a part of it. When you are in water, you turn red so that everyone knows you are not liquid. Instead of blending in, you change so that you stand out."

Jane swallowed hard.

"Well, Sebastian," Marshall said, turning back to his friend, "what think you of that sort of adaptation? What kind of creature tries to stand out from its surroundings?"

Mr. Malheur frowned and rubbed his forehead as he considered the question. "Poisonous ones," he finally said. "Butterflies do it all the time. They are brightly colored so that birds cannot confuse them with other creatures. 'Don't eat me,' the color shouts. 'I'll make you vomit.'" He frowned as he said this. "But one ought not apply the principles of evolution to human behavior. Individual choice is not the product of evolution."

And yet the comparison was all too apt. That was precisely what Jane intended, even if she'd never thought of it that way. She *did* want everyone to notice her—and she wanted them to think her poisonous.

"Well, then, Miss Fairfield. You have it yourself, from Mr. Malheur's mouth." He gestured at his friend. "We can conclude nothing."

"Mr. Cromwell…"

Mr. Marshall held up a hand, cutting her off. That frisson went through her again, tingling at the base of her spine.

"It's Mr. Marshall," he said quietly. "But I think you're clever enough to know that."

God, she was in dire straits. *You're intelligent enough to remember two syllables* was hardly a compliment, but she'd not received any praise at all in months. It left her feeling warm and utterly confused.

"I—I'm not sure—" She took a deep breath, tried to gather the shreds of her charade about her. "Was I mistaken then? I'm so sorry, Mr. Crom—I mean, Mr. Marshwell."

"I am not going to lie to you," Mr. Marshall said. "And might I suggest…"

She looked at him, looked up into those eyes like a winter storm. She looked up into a face that should have been ordinary, and Jane felt her whole body come to a standstill. Her heart ceased to beat. Her lungs seized up in her chest. Even her hair felt like a heavy burden. There was nothing but him and his foolish not-even-compliments.

"Might I suggest," he finally said, "that you don't need to lie to me, either."

"I—"

He held up a finger. "Think about it," he said. "Think carefully, Miss Fairfield. And once you're done thinking… Well, the two of us might have a very productive conversation."

She swallowed. "About fashion? You don't appear to be the sort to care."

He smiled, just a curl of his lip. "About a great many things. And yes, Miss Fairfield. About fashion. About the colors you wear, and what they are hiding."

He touched the brim of his hat and gestured to his friend.

"Good day," he said pleasantly, as if he'd not just uttered a horrendous threat, and he walked off.

"Good God," she heard Mr. Malheur say as they walked away. "What was that all about?"

If Mr. Marshall answered, the response was swept away in the clop of horse hooves from a passing omnibus.

Chapter Four

THE THIRD TIME JANE met Mr. Marshall was even worse. She scarcely had a chance to speak with him at the Johnsons' dinner, but she could sense his eyes on her all through the meal. He sat just down the long table from her, close enough to converse with. It didn't matter what she said to him. It didn't matter how she said it. He never gave her that freezing look that suggested that he'd been offended.

Instead, he looked…amused.

She felt wrong the entire evening—as if her shift was too small, as if she no longer fit in the armor of her clothing.

When the gentlemen joined the ladies in the library after, she found herself uncertain, constantly aware of him. Her responses were forced, not flowing. She felt like—what was it he had called her?—an *anti-chameleon*, burning brightly in the middle of the room.

Don't marry me; I'm poison. She was poison. She was a blight. Her gown tonight was a wasteland of red-and-black silk, devoid of good taste and fringed with clattering beads. She loved it almost as much as she loved the band of polished silver on her arm. She'd perfected the art of holding her wrist just so—moving it back and forth so that it reflected light into a gentleman's eyes. But she'd hit Mr. Marshall three times now, and he hadn't so much as grunted.

God, what was she to do?

Mr. Marshall suggested that music might be a good way to spend the evening, and she breathed a sigh of relief. Everyone would be looking at the performers, and they'd never ask her to join in. Jane wouldn't have to be *on*. Being dreadful was such wearying work. The company adjourned to the music room.

Jane stayed in her seat, holding her breath, hoping nobody would notice she wasn't moving.

Nobody did. They all filed out without glancing in her direction. Of course not; they didn't want to see her.

She slumped in relief as the door closed behind the last man. Alone at last. Alone, with no need to pretend. She could *breathe*. She could stop thinking, stop examining every smile, stop worrying about why it was that Mr. Oliver Marshall kept glancing in her direction.

She set her fingers against her temples, wishing all the tension away, letting her eyes drift shut in relief.

Silence. Blessed, blessed silence.

"Thank God," she said aloud.

"I rather think you should thank me."

Her eyes jerked open, and Jane pushed herself to her feet. Her gown caught underfoot, the beads clicking together. She scarcely managed to catch herself from falling—and she swiveled, just in time to see Mr. Marshall. He was still sitting in his chair on the other side of the room. He watched her with a look of amusement, tapping his fingers against the arm of the chair.

Oh, God. Hadn't he left with the others? What had she said aloud?

"Mr. Cromwell!" she blurted out. "I thought you had gone with everyone."

His fingers paused in the middle of a tap. Those blue eyes of his met hers. The dim light made his spectacles into a shield, reflecting her own image back at her.

"There's no need to pretend." He spoke as if he were a mesmerist attempting to send her into a trance. "And you have no cause for worry."

There was nothing common about him, first impressions be damned. Behind those spectacles lurked something feral and untamable. He hadn't moved from his chair, and yet still she felt a little tickle in her palms. A catch in her breath.

His eyes were too sharp, his expression far too even. He set his glass on the side table next to him and leaned back, looking her over as if he were royalty and she the thief who had been caught raiding his larder.

"Worry?" she repeated in her best breathless voice. "Why would I worry? You're a gentleman. I'm a lady." She took a step closer to the door. "I'll join the others after all."

He waved a hand. "Don't bother, Miss Fairfield. I have sisters enough that I can recognize the supposedly innocent act from a half-mile's distance. You're not fooling me."

She blinked. "Why should I not act the innocent? I have no guilt on my conscience."

Mr. Marshall clicked his tongue and stood up. There ought to have been a rule somewhere that men who wore spectacles could not exceed six feet in height, but he was easily that. He should have been a jovial, round-faced clerk. He should have been anywhere else but here.

He shook his head and took a step toward her. "You're wasting your breath. I know your secrets."

"I haven't any secrets. I—"

"Cut line, Miss Fairfield. You are either very, very stupid, or extraordinarily clever. And I, for one, suspect that you fall on the side of cleverness."

She stared at him. "Mr. Cromwell. This is becoming improper."

He shrugged and moved closer to her. "How convenient," he said, "that you notice impropriety when it serves your purposes."

She sucked in her breath as he reached out his hand.

"And when it doesn't..." His fingers were inches from her face. He could have reached out and touched her.

He didn't. He snapped his fingers. She jumped.

"Miss Fairfield," he said quietly, "I am not your enemy. Stop treating me as one."

Her heart slammed in her breast. "I have no enemies."

"That, Miss Fairfield, is bullocks, and you know it. You have only enemies."

"I...I..."

"And I," he said, "know exactly what that feels like. Look at me, Miss Fairfield. Think about what I am. I'm a duke's bastard, raised on a farm. I've never belonged anywhere. I spent my first few months at Eton with these jackasses, getting into fights three times a day because they wanted me to know I didn't belong. There's little love lost between me and Bradenton."

She swallowed and looked at him. There was a proud set to his jaw, a fierce light in his eyes. She knew all too well that a little thing like expression could be falsified, but... She didn't think he'd manufactured that note of anger.

"Bradenton thinks he can dictate what I do," he told her. "So insult him and his ilk all you wish. I'll applaud you every step of the way. Just stop lumping me in with them. I'll tell you my truth, if you'll tell me yours."

She shook her head, not knowing how to answer. Nobody had ever questioned her act. "I don't know what you're talking about."

"Then don't talk," he said. "Sit, and hear me out."

She needed to go. Immediately. She shouldn't listen. She...

"Sit," he repeated.

Perhaps it was because he didn't speak it as a command. He indicated the chair she had recently vacated, and somehow turned a word that would have been a single, solitary demand in another man's throat into a polite gesture.

She sat. Her stomach fluttered. She didn't know what to say to him, how to regain what she had just lost. "I'm not going to marry you," she finally blurted out.

He blinked twice and shook his head. "Is that what this is about? You're trying to avoid marriage? You're doing a good job of it."

She couldn't breathe.

"In fact…" He tilted his head and looked at her. "But I promised you truth, so here is mine. You're the last woman I would marry."

Her breath sucked in.

"I don't need your money. My brother and I are on good terms, and when he reached his majority, he settled a good sum on me. If I needed more for any reason, I would apply to him first." He shrugged. "I want a career in politics, Miss Fairfield. I want to be a Member of Parliament—and not some distant day in the future, either. I need time to gain influence. I want people to listen to me, to respect me. I will be prime minister one day."

Not *I plan to be* or *I want to be*. Not for Mr. Marshall. *I will be.*

He leaned forward, his eyes blazing.

"I want every man who slighted me—everyone who called me bastard behind my back—to bow down and lick my boots for daring to think I was beneath him. I want everyone who tells me to know my place to eat his words."

The air felt heavy and thick between them. His hand was a white-knuckled fist at his side.

"And so the last thing I need is to be tied to you. You'll open no doors for me, bring me no influence. If the rumor is right, you only have a fortune in the first place because you're a bastard like me."

She let out a breath.

"Just like me," he said. "Yes, you legally have parents. But the man who sired you…"

Those damned hundred thousand pounds again. She put her fingers to her forehead. She'd been thirteen when a complete stranger had died and left her a fortune. She'd been fifteen when she finally understood why the man she thought of as her father had abandoned his wife and her children—those two so-different-looking daughters—on a country estate.

She was the bastard, the foul fruit of that imperfect union. She was the one Titus Fairfield disapproved of. She'd never belonged—not here, not in her uncle's home. Not anywhere. And those hundred thousand pounds marked her out.

"I know," he said. "I know what it is like to lie awake at night scarcely able to breathe with the weight of isolation. I know what it's like to want to shout out loud until it all falls to pieces. I know what it's like to be told again and again that you can't belong."

It was too much, too much to hear the words she'd whispered only to herself echoed in the real world. "Why are you saying these things?"

He shrugged. "It's simple, Miss Fairfield. Because I think everyone deserves a chance to breathe."

Breathe? Around him, she could do no such thing. The light of the oil lamp reflected off his glasses, obscuring his eyes, making it almost impossible to divine his intent. But she could feel, rather than see, his gaze on her—a sharp, penetrating look, one that cut straight through the garish pattern of her silk gown. No. He didn't make breathing any easier.

"I have no difficulties drawing air," she said with no regard for the truth.

"Oh?" His eyebrow raised and he tilted his head at her. "That's not what I see. I see shoulders that dare not relax, muscles that dare not twitch, lips that dare not do anything but smile. You're awash in choices, Miss Fairfield, but you know as well as I that the wrong one will bring your carefully husbanded awful reputation to naught."

She swallowed again.

"Don't lie to me," he said. "What is it that you say to yourself in the dead of the night, when nobody is about to hear your words? Do you shut your eyes and look forward to the morrow, eager to greet it, or do you dread each new day and count them off as each one passes?"

He took a few steps toward the door.

"You count," he said softly. "That's what it means, to not belong—it means that you count. It wouldn't be bearable if you didn't know it would end. How many days, Miss Fairfield, until you can drop this illusion? How many days until you can stop pretending?"

"Four hundred and seventy-five." The words escaped her. She raised her fingers to her lips, stricken, but he didn't look at all pleased at having wrested that admission from her.

He shook his head instead. "You have four hundred and seventy-five days of *this* on your shoulders. Miss Fairfield, don't tell me you can breathe."

"I have no difficulties…" The words sounded weak, though. Unconvincing.

"I know that," he said. "If I'd not been here, you'd have kept on. That's what it means to count—that you get through it, no matter how crushing that number is. I know that because I've counted. I counted my way through Eton, through my years when I was a student at Cambridge; I'm counting my way through this particular visit. I know what it's like to count, Miss Fairfield." He took off his glasses and rubbed the lenses against his shirt. "I know it quite well." He looked up.

Without his glasses, she had imagined that he'd be bleary-eyed, unable to see her. But whatever the fault in his vision, his eyes fixed on hers, sharp as ever, blue as the sky.

"You're an intelligent woman," he said. "Logically, if you're pretending to this...whatever it is that you're trying to avoid is awful."

She wanted to speak, wanted to say something, to say *anything*. But all that came out was a little choke, deep in her throat—something guttural and painful, something she hadn't even known was lodged inside her.

So this was why she'd felt that frisson. It wasn't his eyes. It wasn't his height. It wasn't even his shoulders—and she absolutely was *not* going to think of his shoulders. It was simply that he knew what it was like to stand outside everyone else. He knew, and she hadn't even had to tell him.

"That's the truth?" she finally managed to say. "That is the truth you promised me?" It had been more than anyone had given her.

He tilted his head and replaced his spectacles.

"It's ninety-five percent of it," he finally said.

He inclined his head to her, and then—before she could think of anything to say—he tapped his forehead in a sort of salute and left her alone.

⌘ ⌘ ⌘

IT WAS THE MISSING FIVE PERCENT of the truth that rankled Oliver. The air on the verandah was cold against his cheeks; behind him, he could hear the sounds of a piano duet played by the inimitable Johnson sisters.

Nobody had said anything when he'd wandered from the music room out onto the verandah, cold as it was.

They really didn't care about him, and he returned the favor as best as he could.

He didn't want to take Bradenton up on his offer. He'd told himself that he'd find another way to convince the man. Maybe that was why he'd talked to Miss Fairfield the way he had—to prove he wouldn't do it.

But he hadn't said *no* the other night when Bradenton asked.

And Oliver had greeted her on the streets in part because of Bradenton's suggestion. Some part of him—some sick part—had wondered how it might be done. He thought of her eyes just a bit ago, so wide. Her mouth parted ever so slightly, as if to whisper her agreement. Her hands wringing together. He'd hit on the key to Miss Fairfield and he knew it.

Bradenton was right; he could break her. He knew exactly how it was done.

It was that memory—one that made him break out in an uneasy sweat—that had brought him out into the cold. It was possible to break someone who was alone. It was easy to break someone if you gave them a support, allowed them to lean on it...and then swept it all away.

Oliver had no answers, which is why he was standing outside in the middle of a January night. The chill brought no clarity of mind. Cold stone and cold walls surrounded him in the middle of this cold city. The verandah was little more than a square space of outdoors a few paces wide. He'd grown up on a farm; this was hardly any room at all.

Hardly a surprise. Cambridge always made him feel caged.

The outside door opened behind him. He didn't turn.

Miss Fairfield came to stand beside him.

Her beads clacked as she moved, her brocade glittering in the dim light in a garish imitation of military braid. It was the ugliest gown he'd ever seen, and she wore it like the shield that it was. She set her hands on the balustrade, gripping it tightly, not saying a word. Her breath was ragged, as if she had climbed three flights of stairs. As if even the thought of trusting another person had her heart racing.

It should race. She should walk away. But he didn't say that. He just regarded her, watched her watching him back.

"Well, impossible girl?" he asked. "What's it to be?"

She took another breath. "I count," she finally said.

It took him a moment to remember their previous conversation.

She twisted her hands together. "I count every day as it passes."

He didn't say anything. He wanted to comfort her, but that seemed cruel, given the possibilities of what lay between them.

"I am afraid to even speak to you," she said. "If I open my mouth, I'm afraid it will all spill out. I'll talk and talk and talk and never be able to stop it all. There's too much."

He tilted his head and looked at her. "Did I sound like a man with a moderate number of complaints?"

"No. No." She shook her head, and then threw her arms in the air helplessly. "I don't know what you want. I know what everyone else desires, but you… I don't know about you."

Oliver thought of Bradenton, dangling his vote in the Reform Act before him—dangling it like the tempting bait that it was. He thought about what it would mean for his chances at achieving office. He thought about the marquess, believing that Oliver was his for the purchase.

Nobody shoved Oliver around. Nobody.

"I went to school with Bradenton," Oliver finally said. "He was an ass back then, until…" He paused. "He's better at hiding it now, that's all."

She didn't say anything.

"I want him to pay," Oliver said. "For every filthy assumption he's made."

He turned to her. She was watching him, her eyes wide.

"It's that simple," he said. "You're annoying him. Good for you. I don't want you to feel alone."

Her breath caught.

God, that had been a cruel thing to say. The prospect of friendship was a hell of a thing to dangle in front of a woman who felt she had no choice but to drive everyone away. He had no idea what she was facing, but he'd wager that whatever it was, it was a lonely path.

And there was the fact that he *didn't* know his own mind. Maybe he meant every word he was saying. But if he'd wanted to take Bradenton up on his filthy offer, he'd have started this same damned way—by earning her trust.

For all that he rejected the idea of doing Bradenton's bidding, there was a vicious symmetry to using the marquess. To fooling him into thinking that Oliver was complacent, that Oliver would do whatever he wanted. It would mean something, to boost himself with Bradenton's help. To exceed his power and then pay him back years later.

He wanted that so badly he could taste it.

She let out a shaky breath. "Say it again," she said.

It wasn't a lie. Not really. He wouldn't do what Bradenton wanted; there was no need to tell her about it.

And if you do decide to do it, it's best not to mention it. You're just keeping your options open.

Oliver pushed that voice away.

"You're not alone," Oliver said.

It was ninety-five percent of the truth.

⌘ ⌘ ⌘

OLIVER TOOK LEAVE OF THE COMPANY a few minutes after midnight. He was rather surprised when Bradenton followed after him, walking with him to the pavement out front. Instead of ignoring him, though, the marquess called for his carriage and gestured to Oliver. Oliver came—reluctantly—to stand by him.

"You should meet them," Oliver said quietly. "The people who will be most affected by the extension of the franchise. You'll see—"

Bradenton laughed. "Don't be ridiculous, Marshall. I meet them every day. They stitch my shoes and measure me for my trousers. I cannot walk anywhere without tripping over a worker. Showing me yet another one won't help your case."

Oliver contemplated the shapes of the buildings across the way. In the dark, he couldn't make out much more than the silhouette of peaked roofs, rough dark pools of windows with lamplight glimmering from them. The sound of Bradenton's carriage—hoof clops and the creak of leather—drifted to them from the mews behind the building.

"I said *meet* them," Oliver replied. "Not use their services. *Meet* them. Talk with them. See what sort of men they are. My sister-in-law and I are organizing a set of dinners when I return to London, for—"

"You mean I should treat them as my social equals? I do enough charity work, Marshall." He smiled. "Here I am, talking to you."

If this is a sample of your charity, I'm sure you're well-loved on your estate.

But he didn't say it. He held all his complaints in the stillness of his heart, marking them down to accounts earned but not yet repaid.

"You've always been amusing," Oliver said instead. "But there's no need to laugh off what I'm trying to tell you. Which is—"

Bradenton laughed. "Leave off, Marshall. I don't want to talk to you about your precious reform."

The carriage turned the corner, a dark ghost in the mist.

Bradenton turned to Oliver. "You're thinking about my proposition. You cannot know how gratifying I find that, to know I judged you rightly after all."

Oliver's hand tightened, his knuckles whitening.

"So what did you mean with her tonight, then? I suppose if you want to hurt her by making her fall in love with you and then sending her into a decline, it will serve. Still, that seems overly sordid."

"You can't hurt someone you don't know," Oliver said. *And I know you well.* "Sometimes the easiest way to break a person is to make him think you're on his side and then withdraw your support."

He shouldn't have spoken words laden with such double meaning. But Bradenton laughed.

"That is why I need you to do it. I'll pay you no false compliments, Marshall. I admit, I have a personal interest in seeing Miss Fairfield too unhappy to move about in society any longer." His lip curled. "But you're clever and too ambitious by half. I won't allow you a foothold until I'm sure of you."

"One choice on my part will make you sure?"

"No." Bradenton shrugged. "One, you'll dismiss as accident. Two, you'll doubt yourself. Three times…" He paused, as if recalling something. "Three times, and you'll convince yourself you were right to act as you did. Three times doing a thing will change a man's character."

"So there will be other tasks, then." He couldn't do it. Even contemplating this one made him feel sick to his stomach. It brought back old memories, memories he had long since vanquished to their rightful place.

But Bradenton shook his head. His carriage stopped in front of him, and a footman jumped down to open the door. Bradenton advanced forward, "There's no need for anything else," he said airily. "By my count, you're already at two."

Chapter Five

THERE WERE THREE SKILLS that Miss Emily Fairfield had found necessary in her current position in life: lying, smuggling—and most important of all—scaling walls. It was the last she'd put to use at the moment.

After a tepid ten-minute walk around the garden at midday, she'd been put down for a nap in her room as if she were a child of four.

She waited until the house grew quiet, the servants departing to mop floors and go to market. Then she'd hastily changed her clothing and scrambled down the stone wall outside her window. She wanted to go *away*—anywhere, so long as it was not here.

She had an unapproved novel in one cloak pocket, a handkerchief in the other, and a determination to spend all two hours of her ridiculous nap outside.

Titus Fairfield's house sat at the outskirts of Cambridge. It was a sad, two-story affair of graying stone surrounded by drab bushes. She pulled her skirt close to avoid the thorns of the gooseberry bush, squeezed through a narrow gap in the back hedge, and obtained her freedom on the gravel track leading away from town, across fields and over hills.

This was behavior that Uncle Titus would call foolish—setting out on her own, unaccompanied by a chaperone, walking with real strides instead of taking the delicate steps that befitted her status as a supposed invalid. Going out for hours instead of minutes.

And maybe he was right. A little bit. But the alternative—lying in bed when it was light outside, staring at the ceiling, imagining bludgeoning her uncle with one of his law books—was even more ill advised. *That* left her feeling shaky, guilty, and almost feverishly restless. When she felt that way, she'd watch him over breakfast, thinking idly of pulling his bookshelf down around his head.

Not the sort of imagery that made her proud. She held her head high on the main road, nodding at passing farmers. Her gown was a little too fine to make her anything other than a lady escaped from chaperonage, but people saw what they thought would fit in. She marched down the road, brushing the fence posts and stone walls with the tips of her fingers, marveling in the feel of wind on her cheeks, the taste of freedom. It was cold; the wind bit through her gloves, and her cloak wasn't thick enough to keep off the worst of the chill, but she didn't care.

What if something happens? Her uncle's mournful voice seemed to drift to her on a memory. He could have carved it in stone and set it above the mantelpiece, he'd said it so often. *What if something happens?* He'd been worrying about *something happening* to her for years, with the result that nothing happened at all.

Today, she was resolved to walk through Grantchester. She'd seen Grantchester Road half a dozen times in her stolen ramblings, and while a village might not be the stuff of Mrs. Larriger's exploits, it was something more than a handful of goats. She would walk and smile, and nobody would know that she'd escaped from the dreadful clutches of…of…

Not pirates. Not whalers. Not the czar of Russia.

"I've escaped from the dreadful clutches of a nap," she announced to the road.

Emily passed a farmhouse, then another, then—a sign that the village was nearby—a grain mill. Students were working industriously inside a grammar school. She nodded at a smith in his yard as he examined a horse's hooves.

When she reached the main square, she thought about buying an apple from a green grocer, just to prove she could. But it seemed futile to waste her few coins on wizened fruit.

She wanted so little—just the chance to do the things everyone else did. Was it so much to ask?

What if something happens?

A bitter thought, that—that she had to fear *everything,* simply because of what might occur. A bitter thought, indeed.

And at that, Emily realized it wasn't just the thought that was bitter. It was the taste in her mouth.

It wasn't an *actual* taste. Years of experimentation had demonstrated that. It was a growing bitterness that spread through her until she tasted it not just on her tongue, but in her cheeks and stomach—in parts of her body that ought not to have been able to taste at all. The taste fell somewhere between rancid almond and rotting eggs.

Familiar. Annoying. And—as the timing went—completely awful. In a minute, Emily was going to start smelling bad things. Shortly after that…

Something *was* going to happen. The very thing her uncle feared, the reason she wasn't allowed outside.

She didn't have time to make her way out to the indifferent fields outside of town, and if she collapsed in front of the grammar school with her leg spasming, someone would see her for certain. They'd ask to help, insist on seeing her home. Her uncle would find out, and…

And she'd never go out again. There wasn't time to think or time to choose.

Emily crossed the square and ducked into the public house.

Act as if you belong.

She swallowed the taste in her mouth, smiled as the telltale olfactory dysfunction took her senses, masking the scents of baking bread and soup in a foul miasma.

She slid into the nearest bench and tucked her skirts behind the table. Hopefully nobody would look at her. Hopefully, the few minutes of her fit would pass with nobody the wiser. Hopefully—

"Miss," a pleasant voice said from across the table, "please don't sit here."

Emily looked up, and that was when she realized that she wasn't alone at the table. A man sat across from her, wedged against the wall. A book was open before him, and he had half a loaf of bread sitting beside an empty soup bowl.

Her leg had already begun to twitch.

"I'm sorry," she said, gritting her teeth. "I really can't stand up right now."

His accent had been almost too perfect, too studied. His clothing was as English as tea and biscuits. He'd tied his blue cravat in a crisp, formal style, fixed it in place with a gold pin, and laid a very proper hat on the table. The white perfection of his cuffs peeking out from underneath his coat contrasted all the more with the dark brown of his skin.

She looked up into his eyes—almost black—ringed with thick, long eyelashes. His lips pressed together in something that might have been annoyance.

"Miss…" His breath hissed out, and his hands flattened on the table.

He was Indian. She'd seen Indian students before—there were dozens attending Cambridge. Like all of the men in Cambridge, she'd seen them only at a distance from carriage windows or across a green. She doubted her uncle would have let her anywhere near them. Something, after all, might have happened.

He looked at her, more wary of an English miss than any Cambridge student should have been. Maybe he wouldn't turn her in after all.

"I'm sorry," she apologized again. "I don't mean to be making faces at you. I'm about to have a fit. It will pass in a few minutes."

He frowned, but there was no time to explain.

Emily didn't have proper fits. At least, that was what Doctor Russell from London had said. It wasn't really epilepsy, he'd explained, because she never lost her senses. She was always present; she could even speak and move her limbs. It came on her now, the seizure, familiar as a glove.

She'd watched herself in a mirror before. Mostly, her right leg spasmed. But that was not the only effect. Her whole body shivered and her face contorted. Her heart raced, too—heavy, swift erratic beats, like a three-legged horse attempting to gallop.

Her companion at the table stared at her in consternation for a few moments. "Is there anything I can do for you?"

She gritted her teeth. "Don't tell anyone what is happening."

He made a noise that might have been assent.

Sometimes, Emily wished she were not conscious during her fits. She was constantly aware of how she looked, what others would be thinking of her. She wished she could disappear into nothingness and return with no awkward memories. If she had lost consciousness, a doctor had told her, he'd have known it was epilepsy for sure. As it was, she was a special case—not fitting in anywhere. No known treatments. No understood causes.

She focused on the grain of the wooden tabletop in lieu of thinking of what was happening. Someone had carved a set of initials into the corner. She held onto those letters—A+M—repeating them to herself over and over until her spasms faded to twitches, until the twitches faded to the liquid exhaustion of well-used muscles.

It had lasted twenty seconds. Such a short space of time to cause her so much trouble.

She let out a breath.

"Miss," said a voice behind her. "Are you well? Is this man bothering you?"

She turned to see a buxom woman, a towel strapped to her apron strings.

"If he's any trouble at all, I'll have my husband…"

"No," Emily squeaked out. "Not at all. I felt faint, and had to sit down. He has been solicitous. Very solicitous."

"Pushing himself on you?"

"Quite the opposite," Emily said. "I'm afraid I intruded at his table without so much as asking his leave."

He—whoever he was—hadn't said a word in this exchange, as if he were used to not having his opinion consulted. To being discussed as if he were not there. He simply watched Emily with those dark, wary eyes.

"Hmm," the woman said. "Well, he has been quiet thus far, but you never know."

"If you wouldn't mind bringing some tea?" Emily smiled at her. "I would appreciate the refreshment."

"Of course, dearie. And he's truly not bothering you?"

Emily shook her head and the woman left.

The man across from her was silent for a few moments. Finally, he said, "Thank you for not having me thrown out of here. It's the only place within a four-mile walk of Cambridge that serves a vegetable soup, and I get tired of bread and cheese and boiled greens."

"You're studying at Cambridge, then?"

The book in front of him made that much obvious.

She would have thought that the suppers at Cambridge had more lavish offerings than boiled spinach. Little lordlings went there, after all. But he didn't explain further, and she was already imposing on his space.

"I'll be able to stand in a few minutes," she said instead. "I'll vanish as quickly as I came."

"No need to rush on my account," he replied, politely. He looked down at his book and then back up at her. There was still a touch of wariness in his voice—and a hint of something else.

"I do mean it," Emily said sincerely. "I'm so sorry to have imposed. You were here first, so—"

His lip curled up in a half smile, and that last hint of wariness vanished. "I rarely have the chance to sit with pretty girls," he said. "I don't feel imposed upon."

Her heart was still racing. From the fit. Absolutely from the fit. It couldn't be because this man had looked at her. But...he'd made her feel pretty.

She *was* pretty. Emily had always known it, for all the good that it did her. The servants said so. Titus said so. The doctors said so. *A shame, that all this is happening to such a pretty girl. A waste, all that beauty.*

Her looks didn't seem so extravagantly wasteful now, under his polite—but unmistakable—perusal.

"My name is Miss Emily Fairfield," she finally said.

He looked at her for a few moments longer. "A pleasure to meet you, Miss Fairfield," he replied. "I'm Mr. Anjan Bhattacharya." When he spoke his name, the precise tones of his accent altered into something different, no longer English.

Emily bit her lip. "Wait."

His face went blank.

"I'm sorry. Bhatta. Charya?" She felt herself flush.

He sat back in his seat and looked at her. "Yes. That's actually not bad."

"Bhatta. Charya. Bhattacharya." She smiled. "No, it's actually quite easy. I'm just not used to hearing its like. You're from…"

"India, of course. Calcutta, to be exact. My father is in the civil service in the Bengal Presidency. My uncle is…well, never mind. I'm the fourth son, shipped off to obtain a real, solid English education." He shifted, glanced down at his book again.

"And you're studying law."

He raised his eyebrows.

"My uncle is a tutor in law," Emily explained. "When I have no other choice, I read his books. I've read that one."

He smiled at her. "Then I'll ask you if I have any questions."

"You can try," she responded. "I understand a little bit. But I have no formal education. Still, I'd welcome the chance to talk…" Oh, how pathetic that made her sound. She swallowed the rest of her sentence. "But I'm sure you have other people you'd rather talk to. Are you far along in your studies?"

"I'm going out this year." He made a face. "I'm studying for the Law Tripos. Between now and Easter, I suspect I shall be terrible company." A look passed over his face. "I intend to do well."

Emily knew a sign to keep quiet when she heard one, so she stopped talking. Her tea came, and she drank it slowly, trying not to watch him while he read and made notes in a little book. She mostly failed. Her whole skin prickled with awareness.

"Well, Mr. Bhattacharya," she finally said, when she could nurse her tea no longer, "it was lovely meeting you. I suppose I must be going now. I'll leave you to your reading."

He looked up from his book. He blinked at her a few times, as if somehow she'd surprised him. And then—shockingly—he smiled. Not that placid non-smile he'd given her before. This, *this* was what she'd been waiting for. This was what she had left the house to find. His smile was like a sunrise, and it slid over his face with genuine ease. Her pulse beat in anticipation. Of what, she wasn't sure—but she felt on the brink of *something*.

"Miss Fairfield," he said.

"It's Miss Emily," she told him. "I have an older sister."

"I believe," he said, "that the gentlemanly thing to do would be to offer to accompany you back to your home, to make sure you came to no further harm."

"Oh?" She liked the idea. She tried not to let it show how much she liked it.

Something might happen, that voice whispered.

"I don't think I'd get more than a hundred paces with you," he said simply. "In Cambridge, perhaps. Here?" He shook his head. "I have no desire to be pummeled today, so I'll have to do the ungentlemanly thing and wish you farewell."

"I'll be walking this Thursday at one," Emily responded. "And…I don't much like being around throngs of people."

His smile hadn't abated. It was pulling her in. "Oh?"

"There's a path along Bin Brook, where it crosses Wimpole Road."

"I know it," he said softly. "But your parents will object, I'm sure."

"My parents are dead," Emily said. "I live with my uncle." She paused and saw the look on his face. If she told him the truth, he'd never meet her. "Here I am," she said breezily, "out on my own without a chaperone. My uncle isn't conventional, Mr. Bhattacharya. He leaves me to my own devices. So long as we stay to public roads, he won't object."

All true, and yet so misleading.

"But…"

"I have fits," she told him. "My uncle knows that I'm starved for rational conversation."

Still true.

Emily gave him a dazzling smile and was gratified to see him brace his hands against the table, dazzled in spite of himself.

After her implications, a lie could not make it any worse. "He won't begrudge me a walk," she told him. "And it's perfectly acceptable for men and women to walk together so long as they remain in public."

"Is it?"

Emily nodded and held her breath.

"Well." He drew out the syllable slowly, as if contemplating what she'd said. "I suppose. This Thursday."

She smiled back and then stood. Her leg ached, her muscles were sore— but the palms of her hands tingled with excitement, and suddenly, the next few days didn't seem too awful. "Until then."

Something might happen.

She thought of her empty room, of afternoons composed of naps and evenings spent in company with her uncle's solicitous condescension. She thought of how she'd felt slipping out of her room—as if she were on the brink of screaming, and sure that if she shrieked, her uncle would think she'd gone mad. This might have been foolish. It might have been wrong.

But thank God, finally, *finally,* something was happening.

⌘　⌘　⌘

IT HAD BEEN THREE DAYS since Jane's last conversation with Mr. Marshall, and in that time, she had imagined telling him everything a hundred times over. Last night, she had scarcely slept, thinking about what she would say when next she saw him. What it would be like to have someone who understood, who *knew*.

She had a list of things she would say—a calm, precise, rational list. She wouldn't let words tumble out of her like a stream undammed, rushing back to old banks. He wouldn't think her deranged at all.

That delusion lasted up until the moment she saw him again. Jane had just disembarked from the carriage and turned to wait for Mrs. Blickstall, who was right behind her. As she did, she caught sight of him on the other side of her horses.

He was walking on the pavement headed in the direction of the market a few streets over. His stride was determined and swift, his expression abstracted as if his mind were on anything other than her. He didn't see her; he simply kept walking. Five strides, and he was already several yards distant.

She started to wave at him, but he bore a distant expression, one that arrested her hand.

He was a duke's son. A man who, by his own admission, wanted one day to be prime minister. No doubt he had far more pressing problems on his mind than the piddling questions that plagued Jane: accounts of her sister's guardianship and medical treatment. In the time it would take to hash through the sordid, petty details of her life, Mr. Marshall could review the entire text of every act passed by Parliament in their last sitting.

She curled her fingers in an abortive movement and brought her hand back to her side.

He'd been kind. He'd been clever enough to see a great deal about her. But it would be foolish to think that those two things meant that he actually cared about her. He had more important things to deal with than a young lady and her sister.

Jane squared her jaw and crossed the pavement to the bookstore. She wouldn't watch him retreat down the street. She wouldn't relive her stupid fantasies of friendship.

The store was musty and empty; Mrs. Blickstall, bored, took a seat at the front and folded her hands primly while Jane looked through the volumes at the back of the shop. She could hear the bell ring, idly, the murmur of a customer's voice as he spoke with the shopkeeper. Jane picked one book from the shelves and then wandered down the aisle, perusing titles. She heard footsteps behind her.

Instantly her mind went to the man she'd commanded herself to forget. Mr. Marshall. It was him.

No, ridiculous. It wouldn't be. He was already off to a very important meeting. He had no time for stupid girls in small shops buying—

"What is it that you have there?"

She jumped.

God, his voice. She'd never properly imagined his voice when she thought of talking with him. She wouldn't have known how to describe his voice to anyone else. Warm, of course. Such breadth in it. The other night it had hissed with controlled fury. Now it sounded as if he was on the edge of laughter.

She turned, ever so slowly. Oh, God, the frisson was back—a crackling electricity that rushed down her spine. Jane sucked in her breath and dug her nails into her palm, but it didn't help. Before she could help herself, she was smiling—an over-large goofy grin, far too revealing.

He had the kind of looks that improved with familiarity. That brush of freckles across the bridge of his nose invited her touch. As if he were whispering to her. *Come, make yourself comfortable.*

Jane swallowed and pressed her palm against her stomach, lest she do precisely that.

He looked…well, he *looked*. He was looking at her, not at some faraway point. With his attention focused on her, her whole being felt insubstantial. As if she might simply float away.

He was already carrying a book. *A Practical Guide to P—*

She couldn't read the end of the title, as his hand was obscuring it.

"Mr. Marshall," she said with a laugh. *Don't blurt out everything all at once, Jane. Whatever you do, don't blurt out everything all at once.* "How lovely to see you. How do you do?"

She was congratulating herself on her restrained manners when, to her faint horror, she realized that her mouth was still moving.

"I saw you on the street, but you looked busy and I didn't want to interrupt. You were doing something important, no doubt. You probably still are. I should let—ah…"

Shut up, Jane, she commanded her fluttering nerves, and luckily, they obeyed.

He didn't wince at the excessive flow of speech. Instead, he reached out and took the volume she was carrying from her.

"You should let me look at your book," he said, turning the spine so he could read it. His eyebrow rose. "Mrs. Larriger and the Criminals of New South Wales?"

Jane felt her cheeks flush even hotter. He probably read important books, books with sober-sounding names, like *A Practical Guide to Proper Behavior.* That had to be what he was carrying. He no doubt thought her flighty.

"It's not mine," she blurted out. "That is, it's for my younger sister. My sister, Emily."

He looked faintly amused.

She wrinkled her nose at him. "I'm allowed to abuse her taste because she's my sister, but don't you dare."

"I have three sisters," he said mildly. "Four, now, counting my sister-in-law. I would never be so foolish as to speak ill of anyone's sister." He turned the book in his hand. "So, is it any good?"

The question surprised her.

"I haven't read it." She shrugged. "But I did read the first eight of the series. They're awful, but they're also curiously compelling."

"I like curiously compelling. And I love awful. Should I get it?"

She choked, imagining Mrs. Larriger on his bookshelf next to *A Practical Guide to Political Careers.*

But he was flipping through the book as if he were considering the purchase.

"Mrs. Larriger is old, bossy, annoying, and I do believe she isn't in her right mind. You wouldn't…"

"She sounds a great deal like my aunt Freddy." He smiled at her. "Old, bossy, annoying… She never leaves her home any longer, and some people speak ill of her for that. But don't tell me my aunt isn't in her right mind. It's like with your sister. I love her too well to hear your criticism."

She swallowed. "If you're going to do this, you have to start with the first one." She wandered back down the aisle and scanned the titles on the spines. "Here."

She held out *Mrs. Larriger Leaves Home* and waited to see what he would do with it.

He took it without hesitation and opened it up. "Nice frontispiece," he commented. "Do you think the author is really named Mrs. Larriger?"

"No," Jane said baldly. "I do not. The first book was printed two and a half years ago, and since that time, there have been twenty-two more published, practically a book every month. I think Mrs. Larriger is composed by committee. No one person could write so swiftly—not unless she had nothing else to do."

"Mmm, that does seem unlikely." Mr. Marshall turned to the first page. "'For the first fifty-eight years of her life, Mrs. Laura Larriger lived in Portsmouth in sight of the harbor. She never wondered where the ships went, and cared about their return only when one of them happened to bring her husband home from one of his trading voyages. There was never any reason to care. Her house was comfortable, her husband brought in an excellent income, and to her great satisfaction, he was almost never present."' He looked up. "There are worse starting paragraphs, I suppose."

"Do continue on."

"'But one day, on one of those rare occasions when her husband was home, he was struck on the head by a falling anvil. He died instantly.'" Mr. Marshall blinked. He blinked again and set his finger on the text he'd just read. "Wait. I don't understand. How did an anvil fall on her husband while he was at home? Where did it come from? Was he in the habit of suspending anvils from the ceiling?"

"You will have to read and find out," Jane said. "I am not in the habit of telling people what happens in a book. Only brutes disclose what comes next."

He shook his head. "Very well, then. 'That day, Mrs. Larriger sat in her parlor. But the walls seemed thicker. The air felt closer. For almost sixty years, she had never felt the slightest curiosity about the world outside her door. Now, the air beyond her walls seemed to call out to her. *Leave,* it whispered. *Leave. Leave before they conduct the inquest.*'" Mr. Marshall laughed. "Ah, I think I am beginning to understand the anvil—and Mrs. Larriger."

"'She took a deep breath. She packed a satchel. And then, with a great effort, with the effort of a woman uprooting everything she had known, Mrs. Larriger put one foot outside her door into the warm May sunshine. And as she didn't burst into flame, she marched down to the harbor and purchased passage on a vessel that was departing within the next five minutes.'" He closed the book. "Well. I'm getting it."

"It will go well with *A Practical Guide to Plato's Most Important Writings.*"

He frowned. "What's that?"

She gestured. "I can't see the entire title of your book."

"Ah." His grin flashed brilliantly, and he turned the book to face her. *A Practical Guide to Pranks,* it read.

"All nostalgia, I'm afraid. I miss the days when I could respond to ridiculousness with a little mischief, that's all." He sighed. "There was one night when we were students at Trinity... There was a man who had a new phaeton that he was crowing about. So my brother, Sebastian, and I disassembled it and then reconstructed it entirely inside his rooms. We couldn't put the wheels on, you understand, but everything else... He was so violently drunk when he returned that he thought nothing of it, but you should have heard him shout come the morning."

He wasn't anything like she'd imagined, this man who claimed he would be prime minister. He had a sparkle in his eye and an air of mischief about him. Was he pretending at politics, or was he pretending at this?

"And here I had the impression that you were respectable."

He sighed, and the light in his eyes dimmed. "Alas. I *am*." He spoke the words grudgingly. "High spirits are always excused in the young, but I'm well past the age where a good prank can be overlooked. Still, one can imagine."

This felt like a dream—standing next to him, talking about books and pranks.

"Sebastian," she said. "That would be Mr. Malheur, would it not?"

"He's the only one of us who skipped over the respectable phase. He's never stopped being a troublemaker." His eyes abstracted. "In some ways, I envy him. In others, not so much."

"Of us?"

"I forget; you don't know us. My brother, Ro—the Duke of Clermont. Sebastian Malheur. Me. They called us the Brothers Sinister because we were always together, and we are all left-handed."

"Are you sinister?" she asked.

Something flashed in his eyes, a hint of discomfort. "I'll leave you to decide. I can hardly judge for myself."

Her nervousness had faded to a pleasant hum. She was smiling a great deal at him.

"Tell me, Miss Fairfield," he murmured in a low voice. "What do you think? Because I rather get the impression that you're a good judge of sinister behavior."

She could feel the tug of him. She'd dreamed of this—of having a friend, someone she could laugh with. Someone who looked at her and looked again, who looked for the pleasure of looking and not to criticize her deportment or her clothing. If she had dared, she might have dreamed of more.

But the bell rang behind him, and Jane glanced over to see who had entered the shop.

Her breath caught. It was Susan, the upstairs maid, dressed in brown and white. She caught sight of Mrs. Blickstall, still sitting bored at the front of the room; Mrs. Blickstall sat up straighter and pointed at Jane in the back.

Jane took a step forward just as Susan came up to her.

"Miss Fairfield, if you please." The maid's voice was breathy, as if she'd dashed all the way here from the house.

She probably had.

Susan glanced once at Mr. Marshall. "Perhaps we might have a word outside."

"You can speak freely," Jane said. "Mr. Marshall is a friend."

He didn't dispute the label, and her heart thumped once.

"There's another physician come," Susan said. "I got away as soon as I could, but he was just going in with Miss Emily as I left, and that was twenty minutes past."

"Oh, hell. What kind of quackery does this one practice?"

"Galvanics, Miss. That's what he said."

"What the devil are galvanics?"

"Electric current," Mr. Marshall supplied. "Usually stored in some sort of electrical battery, used to deliver shocks as—" He stopped talking.

Jane felt her face go white. She couldn't look at him. She couldn't think of this dream world she was leaving, this place where one might talk of books and laugh about pranks and consider what it meant to be respectable. This was not the world she inhabited.

She fumbled a heavy coin from her pocket and pressed it into Susan's hand. "Thank you," she said.

The household staff no doubt very much appreciated the fact that Jane and her uncle were at odds. It gave them all sorts of ways to supplement their income.

"Miss Fairfield," Mr. Marshall said carefully, "might I accompany you home?"

In her mind, she'd imagined telling him everything. She'd imagined him telling her not to fret, that it would be all right. But he couldn't say that now. After all, he'd told her he wouldn't lie to her.

It wouldn't be all right. The best she could hope for was an uneasy truce—one bought with as many banknotes as she could carry.

Her mind had gone numb. There was no room in her life for a simple friendship.

"No." Her voice was tight. "Don't. You're respectable, see, and you should try to remain that way. I have to go bribe a doctor."

Chapter Six

BY THE TIME SHE REACHED HOME, Jane could scarcely breathe. Her chest heaved uselessly against her corset and spots danced in front of her eyes.

The housekeeper greeted her in the entry, glancing once out the door. But she didn't ask any impertinent questions—questions like, *Where is the carriage?* or *Why are you gasping for air?*

Jane answered those unspoken queries anyway. "I left the carriage behind," she said. "I thought a brisk walk would be nice." In truth, with the market in full force today, it would have taken her forty-five minutes to bring the conveyance around. It had taken her fifteen minutes of quick marching to make her way home.

"Of course," the housekeeper said, as if it made sense for Jane to be heaving in the entryway like a fish landed on the dock.

Jane's hair was falling out of its careful arrangement. The curls at her ears were tilting; the hairpiece of long brown curls pinned to the nape of her neck had come askew. Pins jabbed into her scalp. She reached up a hand, tried to arrange it all into some semblance of order, and gave up when her fingers encountered chaos.

The housekeeper didn't move from her spot. "The exercise has brought color to your complexion."

Ha. Sweat beaded on Jane's forehead. She could feel it trickling down one cheek, tickling her skin as it slid. She didn't need a mirror to tell that her face was bright as brick.

"I'll just go see my sister, then?" She threw this out airily.

Mrs. Blickstall was just turning onto the street behind her, puffing heavily.

"Yes," Jane said. "I'll go talk with Emily. Just like I always do when I return home." *Coming at a dead run, just like I always do.* She clamped her lips together. *Shut up, Jane.*

The housekeeper gave her a pitying look—one that said, *Really, Miss Fairfield, don't bother with the lies. We all know how this is supposed to work.*

Jane sighed and slipped her a coin. It disappeared almost instantly.

"She's in the east parlor, with Alice and Doctor Fallon. I'll see you're not disturbed."

Jane nodded and started grimly down the hall.

She found her sister sitting at a table. One sleeve was rolled up; the arm that was bared had been strapped to the table, exposing the pale skin of her scars.

Strips of white cotton were wound about her wrist and forearm, holding metal plates in place. These were attached to wires, which in turn were attached to some kind of contraption. Jane had no idea what it was. Some evil-looking, foul-smelling collection of jars. *Galvanics. Electrical batteries.*

But at least Emily looked to be bored rather than in pain. She brightened at the sight of her sister.

"Jane!"

"What is this all?" Jane asked.

"We're waiting for a seizure to come on." Emily rolled her eyes.

"Miss Emily," said the man standing by the curtains, "I believe I have told you before. You must not move. When you wiggle your leg like that, you jar the contacts. They might come loose, and if they're slack at the wrong time, I can't complete the circuit."

Emily gave Jane a speaking look of waggling brows and compressed lips. "Yes," Emily said, "Meet Doctor Fallon. He's been hard at work this morning."

Doctor Fallon was a trim man of maybe forty. His chestnut-brown hair had not yet started to gray. He had a curling mustache and brown, bristling sideburns.

Jane strode forward. "I'm Miss Jane Fairfield, Emily's sister. Would you mind explaining your methods?"

He frowned in puzzlement. "But I've already told Mr. Fairfield everything."

"I take an interest in medical advances." Jane settled into a chair next to her sister. "I would like to hear about yours." She made a face at him that she hoped passed for a smile.

He seemed taken aback for a moment and then responded with a rusty smile of his own. "I am a galvanist," he said earnestly. "Which is to say, I practice medicine of the galvanic sort. To wit, I have discovered that passing current through the human body can produce a number of effects, such as numbness, pain, convulsions..."

He glanced down at Emily, whose lips had pressed together into a thin line.

"Ah," he said, "and, ah, I have found a few useful effects as well. For instance, the application of galvanics can cure malingering."

Oh, Jane was sure it did. Delivering an electric shock to a patient who was pretending to be sick would no doubt be very effective. It would probably "cure" lesser illnesses, too.

"That's lovely," Jane said. "Good work, having found that out."

He smiled uncertainly.

"I'm positive," Jane continued, "that there's absolutely nothing at odds with your oath as a physician in delivering—what was it you called it?—galvanic current to your patients."

He flushed. "Ah, well, you see. In my case, *doctor* is something of a courtesy title." He brightened. "A rank bestowed upon me by dozens of grateful patients."

So he was a complete quack. Jane folded her hands and wished, not for the first time, that her uncle was not so dreadfully gullible.

"Interesting," she said. "Have you ever cured anyone with a convulsive disorder?"

"Ah, no. But I have *caused* convulsions, and, ah…" He looked down at Emily, as if not quite sure he should speak on in her presence.

If he could deliver an electric shock to her, he could damned well tell her what he was doing. Jane made a gesture for him to continue.

"It's a theory I have, you see. Galvanic current flows. It has a direction. If current can cause convulsion, flowing in one direction, then when someone is having a convulsion, one ought to be able to stop it by applying an equal and opposite current in the other direction. It's a simple application of Newtonian laws. With sufficient experimentation, I am sure I can calibrate the precise amount to apply."

"You are *sure?*" Jane asked dubiously. "Is *sure* the proper word to use to describe your theory?"

"I am…hopeful," he amended. "Quite hopeful."

Maybe a few years ago, she might have let him try. But Jane had heard a dozen men make equally grandiloquent, equally ridiculous claims about how their particular form of torture would cure her sister's fits. None of their treatments had worked, and they'd all been painful. And there were Emily's burns. She felt the corners of her mouth curl up in a snarl.

"So let me understand. You are proposing to deliver as many electric shocks as you like to my sister, for an indeterminate amount of time, on a theory for which you have no evidence other than a wild guess."

"That hardly seems fair!" he squawked. "I haven't even had a chance—"

"Oh, no," Emily said, speaking up at last. "He's demonstrated that he can cause a convulsion in me with his current. I told him that it wasn't the same *kind* of fit that I have. It doesn't feel the same at all. But it is, after all, only my body. What do I know?"

Jane couldn't speak for the black rage that filled her. She'd wanted to protect Emily. Why did her uncle have to bring in these fools?

"Exactly," the charlatan said. "I am the expert on galvanics. What would she know?"

Jane particularly remembered the man who had insisted that the convulsions were an invention of Emily's mind. Since they were so, he'd insisted that he needed only offer her an incentive to stop. Those burns along her sister's arm—matched by the ones on her thigh—had been his version of an incentive. What did *Emily* know, after all?

"Well." Jane's voice shook. "There's only one way I can think of to find out what Emily knows."

"Your pardon?" The doctor shook his head.

Jane tried not to snarl at him. "I propose to take the radical course of asking her. Emily, what do you think of this course of treatment?"

Only the tremble of Emily's hands really answered that question. Jane swallowed her anger and waited for her sister's reply.

"I would rather have the fits, thank you."

Then Fake Doctor Fallon could go to hell, for all Jane cared. The only difficulty was how to send him there. She turned to him. "Thank you very much," she said, "but your services are no longer needed."

He looked shocked, glancing from his acrid-smelling jars to Emily, and then back to Jane. "You can't discharge me," he finally said. "This is my chance. I could write this up, make my name…"

There was a good reason why Jane always kept a few bills in an inner pocket. She found these now and unfolded them, holding them out. "I am not discharging you, Doctor Fallon. You may have these twenty pounds if you walk away right now. You only need tell my uncle that you have determined that your treatment is ill-suited to my sister's condition. He will pay you. I will pay you. And we will all profit from it."

He scratched his head. "But how can I know if my treatment is ill-suited without further experimentation?"

Sometimes Jane wished she were good at diplomatic speeches. She wished she'd mastered coquettish looks and innocent smiles. But she hadn't. She was singularly bad at those forms of persuasion. She was good at handing out money and opinions.

"You won't know," she told him. "You will have to live in ignorance. That is what it means to accept a bribe. I give you money; you tell what lies you need to tell."

His eyes had widened as she spoke. "But that would be dishonest!" he protested.

God. Her uncle had found an *honest* charlatan this time. The others had all been only too happy to be offered the money.

"Twenty-five pounds," Jane tried. "Twenty for you, five more that you might donate to the parish as a sop to your conscience."

He hesitated.

"Come," Jane said, "do you want the parish poor to suffer simply because you hadn't the bravery to walk away from this house?"

He reached forward, fingers outstretched toward the bills. But before he could take them from her, he snatched his hand away, shaking his head in outrage. "This," he said, his voice shaking, "this is an ungodly household."

Jane could have struck him. He wasn't even a real doctor. He wanted to torture her sister. And *she* was the ungodly one? Maybe she should offer thirty pounds.

But Emily was the one who smiled and peered innocently up at him. "Oh," she said, in a deceptively naive voice, "but it is. It *is*. We all tell lies, all the time. You wouldn't want to stay around here. It might be catching."

Ironically, Jane thought, that was the actual truth.

"You should accept our filthy lucre and be shut of our wretched lies," Emily continued.

He looked between the two sisters.

"Here," Jane said, adding a third bill to the ones she already held. "Have thirty pounds. Leave tonight. You can still catch the six o'clock train."

He hesitated, unspeaking.

"Alice will pack your things for you. Won't you, Alice?" The maid had been sitting at the window—presumably to function as a chaperone for Emily when she had been alone with the doctor. But, like all the servants in the Fairfield household, she recognized an opportunity to earn a little extra when it was presented. She jumped to her feet and came forward. Doctor Fallon made no motion to stop her from wrapping his jars in cotton.

"I'm not sure," he said. "This doesn't seem right."

"Well, if you would like to stay," Emily said, "you are more than welcome to."

Jane sent her sister a surprised look.

Alice undid the wires attached to her sister and Emily stood. She took a swishing step toward the doctor. Jane would have admired her form, but the cotton strips trailing from her arm rather ruined the effect.

"As you said, we are an ungodly household. We pray to Ba'al," Emily said earnestly. "Every evening. And to Apollo, god of the sun, at daybreak. We would like it very much if you joined us."

Jane had to clamp her lips together to keep from bursting into laughter.

"There are *so* few heathens in England, and you look like a big, strapping addition—"

Doctor Fallon turned bright red and grabbed the bills from Jane's hand. "You are right," he said coldly. "I cannot—I *must* not stay in this household."

Alice wordlessly handed him the wicker case she had packed, which now contained the implements of his trade.

"I take my leave of you," Doctor Fallon proclaimed. "I will not come back, no matter how you might beg, until you repent and accept—"

"What is going on here?"

Jane and Emily turned to the door as one. Oh, God. That was all this farce had needed. Uncle Titus had come into the room. He looked around in blinking confusion—at Doctor Fallon, waving a wicker case that smelled of acid, at the notes that fluttered between his fingers. He looked at Emily, smiling up at the man winsomely.

"Girls," Titus repeated, "what is going on here?"

"This house!" Doctor Fallon said. "This house—it is a place of heathen infamy. I have been lied to, seduced…" His eyes slid to the bills in his hand, and he clutched them to his chest. "I have been *bribed,"* he said hoarsely. "I wash my hands of the lot of you, may the devil take you all."

So saying, he snatched up his case and marched out. It was a good thing, Jane mused, because if he had stayed, he might have explained to Titus that he meant his last statement as the literal truth.

Their uncle watched him go in stunned silence. He waited until he heard the front door slam, before turning to Jane and Emily.

This, Jane thought, was going to be tricky. Very tricky.

"I was in my room," Jane said cautiously. "And I heard noise. It was the sound of…of ranting."

"It's true," Emily said. "I was sitting here, waiting for a fit to come on so he could test his methods, and suddenly he was pointing his finger at me and making all kinds of horrid accusations."

Emily was better at lying, and so Jane let her do it.

"I don't know what set him off," Emily said earnestly. "He just kept…he kept *looking* at me. Just looking at me and muttering to himself about how I was seducing him. But I *wasn't*. I was just sitting down. I wasn't doing anything."

It was a good story, Jane thought. Emily was uncommonly pretty, and even Titus understood what that meant. For a moment, Titus nodded his head, his brow wrinkling in sympathy.

"Oh," Titus said. "I…I…" But he didn't say that he understood. He frowned and wrinkled his nose. "Why was he holding those bank notes?"

"Who knows where he got that?" Emily said. "He had already started ranting about Ba'al. No doubt he intended to reject Mammon, too."

It was too much. As Emily spoke, Jane caught her eye. They exchanged a look—an unfortunate look that she never could have described to anyone else. It was a look that only a sister could understand, sly and happy and furious all at once. It let Jane know that she wasn't alone in the world.

It was too much. Involuntarily, they both broke into betraying laughter.

⌘   ⌘   ⌘

"JANE," HER UNCLE SAID, shaking his head. "Jane, Jane, Jane. Whatever am I supposed to do with you?"

In lieu of giving her opinion on the matter—she'd made enough trouble for herself already—Jane looked around Titus's office.

She wasn't sure why he called it an office. It wasn't as if he did real work in it. He had students, but they rarely met here. The only time he did work was when he grew enamored of some idea he heard at some lecture. For months when she had first come, he'd talked of nothing but some man's take on the *Odyssey;* another time, he'd become fascinated by a visiting lecturer's discussion of workers and capital. He'd read industriously, scribbling his own ideas on paper. But eventually, he always gave up, moving on to the next item that caught his attention. It didn't matter what subject he pored over. Her uncle never altered. He always took whatever it was that he was doing too seriously, and imagined that his involvement, puny though it was, was vital for the intellectual health of the community.

Their discussions had much the same pattern. She couldn't count the number of times they'd had this particular conversation.

"Jane," Titus said, "I am so disappointed with you."

She had been nothing but a disappointment to him ever since he'd found himself guardian to a handful of girls two years ago.

"This was an honest effort," he told her. "From a good man, one who was willing to take on a patient who offered so little reward as Emily."

"Did you even ask for his credentials?" Jane said. "Or speak to happy patients he had cured?"

But, no. He looked at her in bewilderment. "He was a good man," he repeated.

"I had not noticed that there was a paucity of doctors offering to experiment on my sister," Jane tried again, and then bit her lip. That was enough. She had no reason to antagonize him further. Best to hold her tongue. He'd shake his head at her and be disappointed. And then he'd forget and get wrapped up in the question of which map of the world he should purchase to grace the south wall of his office. They'd hear of nothing but various projections and cartographers for months, and finally he'd settle on just the right thing.

"Up until this point," Titus said, "I have forgiven your many, many foibles." He shook his head gravely. "You are argumentative and stubborn as befits the indelicacy of your birth. I have always hoped that my kind, patient attentions would prevail upon you to change your ways." He steepled his fingers and looked upward. "I begin to despair of my object."

Quibbling with the label *argumentative* had somehow never altered his opinion of her.

She donned an expression of contrition. "I'm sorry, uncle," she said, as meekly as she could manage. "I *am* trying."

The faster she expressed an apology, the sooner they could have this conversation over with. The one good thing about having a gullible uncle was that Jane could usually apologize her way out of anything.

But he didn't start in on the usual lecture, the one she almost had memorized. There was no temporizing over the immoral tendencies that she had so clearly inherited from her mother, the ones she needed to guard against. Instead he frowned.

"What worries me this time," he said, "is that you appear to have wrapped your sister up in one of your ploys."

Jane swallowed.

"I had thought that I would serve as a softening influence on you, but I fear that the reverse is happening. Your ways are instead extending to your sweet younger sister. In her innocence, I suppose she imagines that you feel affection for her."

"I do," Jane protested. "Do not doubt that, if you doubt anything."

He simply shook his head. "If you cared for her," he said, "you would not draw her down your dark path."

"What dark path?"

"The path of lies," Titus said gravely. "You have taught your sister how to lie."

Emily hadn't needed any teaching on that front.

"If this continues," Titus said, "I will have to send you away to my sister. Lily is not as kind as I am. She wouldn't allow you to gad about to party after party without making an attachment. She tells me on a regular basis how I have erred with you. She'd have you married off in no time."

Marriage—marriage to any man—would have been bad enough. As a married woman, she simply wouldn't have the excuse of living in her uncle's home. Her husband might take her away from Emily for months at a time. But marriage to a man her aunt favored…

Jane clutched her skirts under the table. "No," she said. "Please, Uncle. Don't send me away. You haven't erred. I *am* trying."

He didn't accept her apology. Instead, he shook his head as if Jane had run to the end of even his vast gullibility.

"Jane, you bribed the good doctor to tell lies," her uncle said patiently, holding up a finger. "You convinced your sister to tell him falsehoods about our prayer habits, when I have done my best to raise you both as good Christians." Another finger went into the air. "You interrupted him and drove him off before he had a chance to see the effect of his treatment on Emily. The treatment he described was sound."

"It was quackery," Jane said. "He exposed her to electric shock, Uncle, and he planned to do so repeatedly just to see what it would do."

She shouldn't have spoken, shouldn't have argued. But this time, he didn't lecture her on her recalcitrance. He simply shook his head sadly. "And that is not all. Even I, as insulated as I am from the madness of the social whirl, have heard tales of your behavior."

Only Titus would refer to the tepid occasional dinner engagements held in Cambridge as "the madness of the social whirl." Most Cambridge events were unsuitable for young women, seeing as how they involved young men who were pretending to be adults for the first time in their lives.

Titus had a healthy competence that paid a few thousand pounds a year. Because of that, he'd never needed any sort of profession, and consequently, he hadn't bothered to get one. He'd enjoyed his years at Cambridge so much that he was now something of a hanger-on. He styled himself a tutor. "A tutor for the right sort of boys," he often told others, jovially.

He had only one such boy this year, and she suspected he preferred matters that way. He attended lectures, halfheartedly looked for students who wanted his assistance in studying for the Law Tripos, and generally imagined himself a figure of greater importance than he was.

"Why is it," Titus said, "that nobody likes you?"

It stung, those words. Even though it was a reputation that she herself had assiduously cultivated. Jane flinched.

"My information does not say that your behavior is *improper,*" her uncle said, "and for that, I am grateful. But there is improper behavior, and there is behavior that is unacceptable, and by all accounts yours falls into the latter."

The unfairness of it stung her.

"A right-thinking lady," her uncle said, "never insults a gentleman. She never talks when her betters speak. She eats very little, and that with her mouth always closed. She always knows the correct fork to use. She never uses her hands, except when it's appropriate."

"Appropriate!" Jane said. "How am I supposed to know what is *appropriate?* Every other girl has had a governess since birth. Some of them attended finishing schools; the others were finished by aunts and mothers and sisters—anyone willing to spend the years necessary to make sure they knew all the rules. How to curtsy, and to whom. How to eat. How to speak to others."

She drew in a ragged breath, but it didn't assuage her hurt. It wasn't fair. It *wasn't.*

"My father," Jane said, "put his wife and daughters away for nineteen years. Mother passed away when I was ten. For nine years after that, I lived on an isolated manor, begging my father to do something with me. I had no governess. I learned no rules." Her voice was shaking. "And then you inherited me and decided I needed to be married off. What did you *imagine* would happen when you tossed me out in polite society with no training?"

"A true lady," Titus said primly, "would have known—"

"No, she wouldn't have. Or there would be no finishing schools. Babies aren't born knowing how to curtsy. They aren't born knowing what subjects of conversation are not allowed."

He looked mulishly stubborn.

"I didn't know," Jane said. "I didn't know anything. You threw me out to society with no preparation or instruction, and you have the temerity to criticize me because I didn't take?"

"Jane," her uncle said, "I don't want to hear this disrespectful claptrap again."

She opened her mouth to argue once again, before remembering that it would do no good. He had already made up his mind. And that—despite her angry words, despite how things had started—at this point, she bore a great deal of responsibility for her own reputation. She'd made that choice. *Mostly.*

"I think," Titus said, "that I will give you another chance. My every rational impulse counsels against such a thing. I will not let your sister follow in your footsteps. But…" He sighed.

"If you'd only let her out, sir. She is—"

He cast her a look. "Enough of that. She is too fragile to be allowed out. I'm giving you another chance, Jane. Don't use it up before you leave this room."

Shut up, Jane. Learn when to shut up. She closed her mouth and swallowed all her protests. They tasted bitter.

"Behave *properly,* Jane," he said quietly. "Stop arguing. Stop influencing your sister to do wrong. Do your best to attach a man. You may be overplump, but you have money and I suppose that will do. And if I hear tell that you've bribed another doctor…" He trailed off ominously.

"You won't," Jane promised. "You won't hear a thing. I promise."

He wouldn't hear a thing. Next time, she would bribe better.

Four hundred and seventy-one days of this. How was she to keep up this façade for a year and a half? She felt ragged and weary, impossibly tired.

"Yes, Uncle," she said. "I'll do everything you say."

Chapter Seven

THERE WAS AN ASSEMBLY THAT NIGHT, a glittering gathering of young men and delicately arrayed women. Oliver had come, and he still wasn't sure why. To see Miss Fairfield, he suspected, but his reasons for that...

He was not going to take Bradenton up on his offer. He'd find some other way to bring the man around. Bradenton could be reasonable, after all.

He's not asking for a reasonable thing.

Oliver shoved that voice away. He'd watched Miss Fairfield's face turn to wax as her maid informed her of the waiting doctor of galvanics. He'd been right. Whatever she was facing, it was awful. Bradenton would turn reasonable, and that was that.

But if he doesn't?

Oliver shook his head. He would be.

The assembly room was smaller than most London ballrooms. But then, there were far fewer people—no more than perhaps a dozen couples with only a few more on their way. Everyone had already mingled and made introductions. A few ladies had glanced Oliver's way shyly—ever since it had come out that he was a duke's son, there had been a little more interest. He talked to them halfheartedly. He might have enjoyed the conversations, had he not been waiting for Miss Fairfield.

It was not so much that he wanted to see her.

She was pleasant enough to look at—the parts of her that she didn't drape in hideous apparel, at least. Earlier in the bookshop, he'd enjoyed their conversation. He'd enjoyed it so much that he'd stopped noticing the head-splitting pattern of her day gown.

And now here he was, waiting for her to arrive. Waiting with an eagerness that seemed a little out of proportion to simple curiosity.

Just when he was on the verge of giving up hope of her, she walked into the room.

Oliver saw her immediately and was so stunned that he could not move. For the first few ticks of the clock, nobody took notice. Ladies talked; gentlemen offered their arms. Glasses were raised and drunk from.

Then one man glanced up, and another. Ladies' heads turned. There were no gasps—the dress she was wearing was beyond gasps. Oliver himself had to close his mouth. Silence rippled over the room—an active, electric silence, the stillness between the lightning strike and the rumble of thunder overhead.

The cut of her gown was completely unobjectionable. Rather modest, in terms of lace. It had no more pattern than a few delicate twining vines at the hem. But aside from those curling green tendrils, the gown was the bright pink of…of…of…

All comparisons failed Oliver. It wasn't the bright pink of *anything*. It was a furious shade of pink, one that nature had never intended. It was a pink that did violence to the notion of demure pastels. It didn't just shout for attention; it walked up and clubbed one over the head.

It hurt his head, that pink, and yet he couldn't look away.

The room was small enough that he could hear the first words of greeting. "Miss Fairfield," a woman said. "Your gown is…very pink. And pink is…such a lovely color, isn't it?" That last was said with a wistful quality in the speaker's voice, as if she were mourning the memory of true pink.

"Isn't it lovely?" Miss Fairfield spoke loudly enough to be heard by all. "I asked Miss Genevieve, and she said that pink is always appropriate for a debutante."

"Well," said that other woman, "there's…certainly a great deal of pink in that gown."

"Yes," Miss Fairfield responded happily. "I think so too!"

Everyone was looking at her. Literally everyone—there wasn't a single person who could do anything but gawk at that gown.

It would have been bearable if there were not so much of that fabric, but the seamstress had not stinted. It wasn't just the pink bodice and the pink skirts, but the excessively pink sash—all pink, no vines on that—which had been looped and wired to stand out from her gown. There were floridly pink flounces, which were trimmed with gouge-your-eyes-out pink lace.

So much vicious, pink fabric. And all of it was shiny.

She smiled brilliantly, as if she were proud of that confection and utterly unaware that she was the cause of all those titters.

Oliver had once watched a man eat a lemon. His own mouth had dried in vicarious response, and he'd looked away. He felt like that now, looking at her gown. She didn't hold back one bit. She wore her too-bright gown and spoke in her too-loud voice, and she didn't flinch while everyone gawked at her.

She was going to get burned, not caring. She went about the room greeting people. Behind her, a gentleman made a rude gesture at her backside—a flip of his hand that was too crass for a ballroom—and the laughter that erupted had an ugly tint to it.

Miss Fairfield smiled as if she'd done something brilliant.

No, it was not just that she was going to get burned.

She had already been burned. She was afire now. She smiled and laughed and she didn't care what they thought of her. It was as painful to watch as that fellow had been, casually peeling a lemon and then eating the slices one by one as if nothing were wrong. Oliver wanted to tell himself that he wouldn't hurt her, that he wasn't that kind of man. But right now, all he wanted to do was push her so far from him that he never had to see this, never had to hear that low, mocking laughter again.

He remembered being laughed at. He remembered it all too well, and he remembered its aftermath. They'd come find him later, taunting, a group of them when he'd been caught out alone...

No. He couldn't watch this. He turned away.

But it did little good. He could still hear her.

She greeted the hostess, cheerily. "Mrs. Gedwin," she said in a carrying voice, "I am *so* delighted to be in attendance. And what a lovely chandelier you have. I wager it would look almost new, if it had been dusted recently."

Oliver's fists clenched. *Stop playing with fire, you foolish girl, before you hurt yourself.*

"Good God," said a woman near him. "Even her *gloves* match."

Sebastian had said that nature chose its most brilliant colors as a warning: *Don't eat me. I'm poison.* If that were the case, Miss Fairfield had just announced that she was the most poisonous butterfly ever to grace the drawing rooms of Cambridge. She flitted about the room, leaving dazed looks and cruel titters behind her.

By the time she made her way to him, he had a headache. Hell, he didn't need Bradenton to offer him his vote. He might have pushed her away just so he wouldn't have to listen to everyone laugh.

"Mr. Marshall," she said.

He took her hand and inhaled. And that, perhaps, was what brought him back to himself. Amidst all that was unfamiliar, there was one thing he recognized—the smell of her soap, that mixed scent of lavender and mint. It spelled instant comfort, and it made his course of action quite clear.

He'd promised not to lie to her. That was all he had to do now—not lie.

"Miss Fairfield," he said in a voice pitched normally. "You look well today."

She dimpled at him.

He let his gaze drift down briefly, and then looked up at her. "Your gown, on the other hand..." He took in a deep breath. "It makes me want to commit an act of murder, and I do not consider myself a violent man. What are you wearing?"

"It's an evening gown." She spread her outrageously gloved hands over her hips.

"It is the most hideous shade of pink that I have ever seen in my life. Is it actually glowing?"

"Don't be ridiculous." But the smile on her face seemed more genuine.

"I fear it may be contagious," he continued. "It is setting all my preternatural urges on edge, whispering that the color must be catching. I feel an uncontrollable urge to run swiftly as far as I can in the other direction, lest my waistcoat fall prey next."

She actually laughed at that and brushed her shoulder. "This would make a lovely waistcoat, don't you think? But don't worry; the color isn't virulent. Yet."

"What does one call a color like that?"

She smiled at him. "Fuchsine."

"It even *sounds* like a filthy word," Oliver replied. "Tell me, what sort of devilry is fuchsine?"

She glanced around them, ascertained that nobody was near enough to hear. "It's a dye," she said, as if that were not obvious. "A new one, a synthetic one, made from some kind of coal tar, I believe. Some brilliant chemist with a talent for experimentation and no sense of propriety came up with this."

"It's…" There were still no words for it. "It's malevolent," he managed. "Truly."

She leaned in. "You're maligning the shade," she whispered. "Don't. I actually love it. And I wager that everyone else here would, too, if it had been someone *else* wearing it first."

He swallowed. "Maybe. That other person might have been wearing it in greater moderation."

"I had it made up specially. The gloves, the lace. I thought about having little brilliants sewn all over the bodice in sparkly patterns, but…" She shrugged expressively.

"You decided you didn't actually want to be responsible for blinding the entire gathering. Thank you."

"No. I decided that I would save that for the virulently *green* dress." She gave him a waggle of the eyebrow. "There must be some escalation, after all. What's the point in being an heiress, if you aren't allowed to make anyone cringe?"

Oliver simply shook his head. "Yes, but…"

"It's the most amazing thing. I don a gown like this, and you're the only one who tells me to my face how utterly hideous it is. Everyone else has been giving me the most contrived compliments. Here comes someone else, no doubt to compliment me on the extraordinary color."

He shook his head. "That must take some calculation, Miss Fairfield. Determining precisely the line you must walk to prevent yourself from being bodily hurled from the assembly."

She smiled. "No calculation at all. They put up with me for one reason, and one reason only. I call it the heiress effect."

The heiress effect. Maybe that was it—that was what stood between those ugly whispers and the prickle of hair on the back of his neck. He managed a halfhearted smile.

"Miss Fairfield, you frighten me. You and your wardrobe."

She tapped his wrist with the fan. "That," she said briskly, "is the point. This way, I can repel dozens of men in one fell swoop, all without even opening my mouth. And nobody can say it's not demure. I'm even wearing pearls."

He glanced down. If anyone asked, he was looking at her pearls. Definitely looking at her pearls, which were displayed to admirable effect by her bosom. That lovely swell of sweet flesh, so soft-looking. Her breasts made even the pernicious pink fabric that framed them appear touchably good.

"Miss Fairfield," he said, after a moment of silence that stretched a little too long. "I would ask you to dance, but I fear our last conversation was interrupted."

The smile slowly slid off her face, and her brow crinkled in little lines of worry. "There's a verandah," she finally said. "We could go out. It is a little cold, but… Other people are getting air. Not many of them, but we'll be in sight of the company. If anyone asks, you can claim that you were doing the assembly a favor. Ridding them of the horror of looking at me for a quarter hour."

She smiled as she said it. She sounded perfectly serious.

And Oliver… Oliver felt a twinge deep inside him. He wasn't that man. He wasn't going to humiliate her. He wasn't.

You will, his gut whispered back.

"You're not horrid," he said. "Your gown is."

⌘ ⌘ ⌘

"I CAN GUESS," MR. MARSHALL said a little later, as they made their way onto the verandah, away from the press of other people, "as to why you are doing this." His gesture encompassed her gown of fuchsine.

Jane had expected as much. He seemed a clever man; he wouldn't have missed the import of the conversation he'd overheard. But she looked away, concentrating on the gray Portland stone of the verandah, the stone balustrade ringed by naked trees, cast in flickering shadows.

"Is it your sister?"

"Emily."

"She's ill, then."

"*Ill* is not the right word. She has a convulsive condition. That is to say, she has convulsions. Seizures. F—" She was talking too much again, and she bit back the even longer explanation that popped into her mind.

"It's not epilepsy?"

"Some doctors call it epilepsy," she said cautiously. "But she has seen so many of them. The only thing they can agree on is that they don't know how to cure her fits."

He nodded thoughtfully. "What I overheard the other day, that's the nature of the typical experiment, then? The doctors want to send an electric shock through her?"

"Among so many other things." Too many treatments to list. Too many for Jane to think about without feeling sick to her stomach. "They've tried bloodletting and leeches and potions that make her vomit. Those are the easy ones to talk about. The rest..." If she closed her eyes, she could still smell the poker burning into her sister's arm. She could still hear her scream. "You don't want to hear about the rest."

"Her guardian, I take it, is in favor of experimentation. You are not."

"Emily is not," Jane said tightly. "Therefore, I am not."

She waited for him to argue with her. To tell her what Titus always said—that young girls had guardians so that someone could make them do the things they did not wish to do.

"I can scarcely imagine," Mr. Marshall finally said. "My sister-in-law, Minnie—she's the Duchess of Clermont—bother, never mind her title."

Jane blinked, but he went on, as if he called duchesses by their Christian names every day. Maybe he did.

"In any event," he said, steering her around a few dormant rose bushes, "Minnie's best friend is married to a physician. Doctor Grantham and I have had some frank discussions on the state of medicine. I don't think it is possible to speak with five doctors without hearing of some terrifying practice."

"Twenty-seven," Jane said softly. "She has seen twenty-seven doctors, and I'm not counting the ones who haven't the proper credentials. It's simple, really. If I marry, I'll leave her alone in the household. I have money, but she does not. As she is not yet of age, if I gave her money it would simply be held in trust by her guardian. Who, needless to say, would use it to find more doctors. So I must stay in the household, unmarried, so that I might bribe them to leave her in peace." There was so much more to it than that. She worried about her sister, left alone so much. Emily had so much vitality in her; restricting her movements left her restless. And Emily needed companionship, friends of her own age.

But he nodded. "That much I had gathered. But why is it that you make this particular attempt?" He gestured at the doors of the assembly. "Why not simply say that you don't plan to marry?"

She sighed. "It's my uncle. He is a very dutiful man. He allows my presence only because he believes he is doing me a favor—helping me find a husband who will curb my tendencies. But I'm not his ward any longer. If he wanted me out of his household, he could have me out."

"Your tendencies?"

"I am," she said swiftly, "stubborn, argumentative, and…and he fears, considering my birth, potentially licentious." She didn't look up at him to see how he would take this. She probably shouldn't have told him that. What he would think…

There was a pause. "Lovely. My favorite kind of woman."

"You're very droll."

"Was I joking?" He held up his hands. "I wasn't joking."

"No man wants a woman who argues with him," she said. "He especially doesn't want a…licentious woman."

He laughed. "You," he said, "have a very odd idea of what men like in a woman. Most men I know prefer a woman who favors a good, long night of…" He trailed off, leaning in.

"Of what?"

"Of argument," he replied.

"That's ridiculous." But she found her lips tugging upward in a smile. "I have proof positive you are wrong on this point. I argue with men all the time, and they absolutely despise me."

"Ah, see, you've got the idea now. Contradict me again, Miss Fairfield, and see how I like it."

"You don't."

"That, my dear, you cannot dispute. We can argue over the general preferences of my sex until the cows come home, but we cannot argue over what I like. I will always win."

"Why should that stop me?" Jane asked. "I have made an entire career out of losing."

The smile slipped off his face. He took a deep breath and regarded her. "Yes, as to that. We have established why you do not wish to marry. But there are a great many easier ways that a woman can stay unmarried. What made you choose this one?"

She'd not expected the question. Even her own sister had never asked her *why* she'd chosen this particular route. And that brought back memories—memories that still itched under her skin, if she let them.

"It suits me," she finally said.

"I don't think it does."

"You cannot argue over what I like," Jane retorted. "I will always win."

"Miss Fairfield." He did not seem to be saying her name as a prelude to anything, but simply to be speaking it for the pleasure of the syllables. He shook his head slowly as he did, and then put his hand over hers.

Jane looked around. Nobody was looking at them, and even if they did, they'd see two people standing by a stone wall. He'd touched her so casually that apparently even he hadn't noticed. But she had. Oh, she definitely had. She drew in a shocked breath.

"Miss Fairfield," he repeated, "tell me that you are perfectly happy with your choice. That you don't mind being laughed at every time your back is turned. Tell me that you are not starved for rational conversation. Convince me that this role that you are playing suits you, and I'll happily concede the point."

"I…" Yes, she could make an argument, she supposed. Something about how she was better off without the friendship of everyone who was cattish enough to mock her.

She could make that argument, but she couldn't even convince herself.

Instead she held perfectly still, absorbing the warmth of his hand, hoping he wouldn't notice what he'd done and draw away. "I can't claim that it makes me happy. But I *am* good at this. Mucking up conversations. Not knowing any of the rules. Doing things that I ought not do, saying things that I am not supposed to say."

He kept silent. And of course, she kept talking. That was what she always did when she was nervous.

"It started before I had any idea that I'd need to stay unmarried. I was nineteen when we first came to my uncle's house. He had not yet engaged a bevy of doctors to see my sister." She swallowed. "My uncle…for a number of reasons, he had a dim view of me from the start. He wanted me married off, and I was happy to comply. I wanted a family, my own house. I'd lived in an isolated manor all my life. I'd had no children to play with besides my sister. I wanted *friends.*"

She'd thought he was unaware that he'd touched her, but his hand tightened around her fingers. She looked down, but he didn't pull away. Instead, his fingers curled into hers.

"I'd never had a governess. I had never had an etiquette lesson. My uncle purchased a book for me." She laughed softly. "It was sixteen years out of date."

"I can see where this is going."

"I had nobody to instruct me on my gowns. All I knew was what I liked, and what I like is dreadful." She shut her eyes. "For instance, I love this gown. Yes, it's outrageous, but... I had awful tastes and the money to indulge them, and my manners were even worse. I was a complete disaster. You cannot imagine how much of a disaster I was."

"I can," he replied. "You should have seen me at Eton the first few months. I continually had bruises. It took until I was seventeen to get to the point where between my brother's threats and my learning how to behave, I wasn't accosted on a daily basis."

"I have never been good with names, but when I called Mr. Sanford 'Mr. Smith' on accident, you would think that I had robbed a carriage at gunpoint. I ate the wrong foods. I asked questions about trade in mixed company. I have always talked too much, and when I'm nervous, I have difficulty stopping. Is it any surprise that I did everything wrong? They started the whole 'Feather Heiress' thing the first month. That was all I heard—in front of me, behind my back. 'It's like being beaten to death by feathers.' They played a game where the boys would all come to talk with me in a group. And they'd say, 'What would you rather be doing now?' 'Oh, I'd rather be mauled to death by lions.' 'I would rather bathe in a vat of acid, how about you?' As if I were so stupid that I could not figure out that they were talking about how much they hated me."

"Jane." His thumb rubbed the side of her hand.

"Don't feel sorry for me." She raised her chin and banished that cold, dark feeling from her heart. "I do not. When I realized how much my sister needed me, I thanked God that I had so easy a method of avoiding marriage. They thought I was awful? Well, I would give them awful. They wanted to gawk at my ignorance? Well, I would give them something to gawk at. They'd exaggerated my flaws just to have someone to laugh at, and so I vowed to make them exaggerations no more. The more they mocked me, the harder it would be for them."

Her voice shook as she talked. And his thumb continued its gentle caress—up, down. Up, down.

"They are a pit of vipers," Jane said fiercely. "And I hate them. I *hate* them. I didn't choose this role, Mr. Marshall. But it chose me, and I have used it."

He didn't say anything, not for the longest time.

"I know what you are thinking," she finally said in a rush. "Because I treated you the same, when first I met you. You hadn't done anything to me, and I…"

He shook his head. "I wasn't thinking that."

"I know it's wrong," she said. "But at this moment, everything in my life is so wrong that the right, proper thing to do would be dreadfully out of place. I don't know when I stopped playing a role and when the role started playing me. Now, though, I don't see how I could stop. Everyone expects me to be someone else. They're assured of it. That is the rub; I *am* awful." She licked her lips. "And I don't see any way for me to become anything else."

God. She hadn't meant to tell that much. Even when she'd imagined telling him everything, she hadn't told him that.

Jane squeezed her eyes shut. "I'm sorry. I don't mean to complain to you. I've done nothing but talk and talk and talk. You scarcely know me. You have far more important things to do. It's just—you're so lovely."

She winced, hearing the words out loud, wondering what he must be thinking at the moment. Licentious, indeed. Licentious, forward…

"I mean, you're forthright and trustworthy, where everyone else has been…" Talking more wasn't making it better.

"Miss Fairfield," he said.

His voice was as deep as the night around them, and she turned to him.

But he didn't look disgusted by her admission. He didn't even look amused by her babbling. He looked… She wasn't sure what that expression was on his face. His eyes were clear, so clear that in the moonlight they looked almost colorless.

He took his hand from hers. "Never trust a man who claims that he is telling you ninety-five percent of the truth."

His words came over her like a cold wash of water. There was something grim in his face, something she couldn't quite understand. She peered up at him. "What do you mean?"

"What would you do," he said carefully, "if I were to tell everyone of this conversation? If you think matters are impossible now, when they think you merely ignorant, what do you suppose they would do if they knew you had done all this on purpose?"

She opened her mouth to answer and then shut it, ever so slowly. "But you wouldn't tell."

He shook his head. "Miss Fairfield," he said, "why do you think I was kind to you?"

"Because—you—that is to say…" She swallowed. "You mean to say, that's not just the way you are?"

"No. If I'd had my choice of matters, I would have simply avoided you after that first awful night. I talked to you because Bradenton asked me to do it."

She took a step back involuntarily. "Bradenton! What has he to do with any of this?"

"He thinks you need to know your place. He offered me a trade: his vote in Parliament, if I'd deliver a sharp lesson to you. I talked to you to figure out if I could do it."

Her head spun. She should have known. This wasn't real. That hand on hers, that look in his eye. None of it was real. He *had* been too nice, and she was—

She shook her head, dispelling those thoughts. "You wouldn't be telling me of this if you intended to take him up on the offer."

His lips compressed. Then he took her arm. "Walk with me," he said.

There wasn't much of anywhere to go—just a little circuit around the verandah. But when they got to the far edge, he stopped, gesturing for her to sit on a bench. He'd led her out of view of everyone else. He looked around and sat down next to her.

"There's something you should know." He wasn't looking at her now; he was staring off into the night sky. "I tell myself the exact same thing you just said—that I would never do it. But there was a time. I was fifteen years old at Eton." He leaned forward, setting his elbows on his knees. "I didn't fit in. My brother and my cousin did their best, but when they were not present, I had to take care of myself. I did it, too. There were a handful of us who weren't born to a grand position in society, and we made our way by banding together. Walking together. Working together. Offering such small encouragements to one another that would make the days bearable."

"Did none of the adults stop what the other boys were doing?"

He turned and gave her a level glance. "Boys will be boys, Miss Fairfield, and generally speaking, the punishment we were subjected to wasn't so awful. We were tripped, insulted, occasionally set upon. The sort of thing every boy experiences at school. We just had a larger dose. Enough so that we would know our places."

For some reason, his mouth set into a harder line at that, and he didn't speak for a minute.

"I had it a little easier than most. My father had been a pugilist, and the other boys learned to be wary of me. They wouldn't take me on unless there were two or three of them at a time."

She bit back a horrified gasp.

"It doesn't matter how good you are at fisticuffs, though. At some point, you get tired of bruises."

Jane reached out and took his hand. She'd been afraid he would push her away, but he didn't.

"There was another boy. Joseph Clemons. He was small for his age and timid. He hid behind me every chance he got." He sighed. "And you know what? I hated him. I tried not to. It wasn't his fault he was set on so much. It wasn't his fault that I'd stand up for him. It wasn't his fault his father was a shoemaker, nor was it his fault that he was a brilliant Latin scholar, the likes of which the school had not seen in dozens of years. Still, I resented him so for causing me such difficulties. I just protected him out of…"

He shrugged. His hand clenched around hers. Out of some innate sense of fair play, she suspected.

"Out of spite," he said. "One fight is nothing. Two fights are nothing. Three years of fighting makes you weary. One day, I came upon Clemons with two older boys. I was going to stop them, because that was what I did. But Bradenton was nearby. He said, 'Marshall, all they want is for you to stop challenging them. Walk away and leave them alone.'" He looked up. "I think he could have given me any reason to walk away at that point and I would have taken it. I did."

"I take it that Bradenton was wrong."

"Oh, no," Oliver said softly. "He was right. Those particular boys never came for me again. As for Clemons… I don't know what they did to him, but when he left the infirmary, he never came back."

She gasped.

"So, yes, Miss Fairfield." He looked over at her now. "You might think you know who I am. What I'm willing to do. I tell myself all the time that I'm not that man. That I wouldn't be so awful as to cause harm to someone else. But I know better."

She dropped her gaze from his. "You can't blame yourself for what the other boys did."

"It wasn't the only time." His voice was harsh. "Anyone in my position, anyone born without power, who aspires to more… Trust me, I didn't arrive here by standing on principle my entire life. I've learned to keep my mouth shut when it must be shut, to do what a man in power asks because he asks it. I count myself lucky that I've survived as unscathed as I have. Don't fool yourself, Miss Fairfield. I could hurt you. Badly."

She didn't say anything for a moment. But by the light in his eyes—that cold, serious gleam—he meant every word. His hand felt clammy in hers, but she squeezed it.

"And you are telling me this because…"

"Because I don't think what is happening to you is right, Miss Fairfield." His voice was tight. "Because no matter how many times I tell myself I would never do it, I cannot trust myself. The bait that is dangling before me is too tempting. I'm giving you a chance to run off before my ambition overwhelms my better judgment."

She opened her mouth to speak, and then closed it once more. It made no sense, what he said. It made no sense, not unless…

She turned to him. "Are you always this starkly honest?" she demanded. But she knew the answer to that already. She had seen him in the group with the others—smiling, talking, always seeming to know what to say so that nobody looked at him askance. He knew how to belong with them. He *couldn't* always be honest.

"You're special." His voice was low. "I resented Clemons. I rather like what I know of you."

She looked up, and he reached out with his free hand and, very gently, drew a finger down the side of her face.

"There are so few people in this world to whom I dare tell the whole truth. I hate to waste a one."

It wasn't a frisson she felt. A frisson went only skin deep, just a prickle of hairs on the back of her neck. This was a full-body experience. As if the past years had tightened her internal organs into a snarl of emotion, and he had just convinced them to relax. She found herself tilting toward him, ever so slightly. Wanting that moment, that point of contact, to last and last.

He drew away, letting go of her hand. Her fingers felt suddenly cold. "You see," he said, "even now, I'm doing it." His voice was low, almost like a caress. "I'm telling you everything, but I'm making it worse, too. You should not let me touch you, Miss Fairfield."

She didn't want him to stop. Jane swallowed. "Oh," she said. "Very well." She turned away, unsure what to think.

"Good. Now you're angry."

She shook her head. "I suppose I should be. But I'm not, really. It doesn't surprise me that you'd want to betray me. Everyone else already does." She laughed again, but her laughter rang a little high to her ears. Too much like nervous giggling, and not at all like the half nausea that she felt turning in her belly. "So there you have it. You might betray me, but you're my favorite betrayer thus far."

He made a noise. "You should be angry, Miss Fairfield. You should push me away."

"Mr. Marshall, haven't you figured it out? I'm too desperate to be angry."

It sounded bald and terrible in the night. But it *didn't* sound pitiful— almost as if giving voice to the truth made her less vulnerable.

"Maybe," she continued, "if I had a slew of true friends, I could afford to fly into a rage. But as it is, all you've confessed is that someone told you to do a cruel thing to me, and you have considered doing it. Most people don't need to be asked to be cruel to me, and they do it straight away."

"Damn it, Miss Fairfield. Listen to what I'm saying. I don't want to do this. I don't want the damned temptation hanging over my head. I don't want to be the man who hurts a woman for personal gain. Slap me right now and have done with it."

Jane shrugged. "Have your temptation, Mr. Marshall, and be welcome to it. I don't expect anything of you, but at least for the moment I can pretend that I have a friend. That there is one person in the world besides my sister who cares whether I wake up in the morning. If you've never been without, you can have no idea what it is like to not have it." She looked up at him, her eyes wide. "And to have him be a man like *you* on top of it all…"

Her cheeks flamed as she realized what she'd implied.

"Oh," she said. "Not that I expect—not that I would think—that is, you've already said that I'm the last woman you would marry. And I have no intention of marrying as it is…" She'd lost control of her mouth. She clapped her hands over it and refused to look up at him. "Oh, God," she said.

He didn't say anything for a moment, and she wondered if she'd succeeded in frightening him off after all.

"Oh, God," she repeated, squeezing her eyes shut. "Why do I always do this?"

"What do you always do?"

"I talk. I talk so *much*. I talk as if my life depended on nothing but words filling the space. I talk and talk and talk and I can't stop. Not even when I tell myself I must." She gave a little sobbing laugh. "I do it all the time—tell myself to shut up—but generally, I'm talking too much to listen to my own advice."

She glanced over at him. He was watching her with a hooded, unreadable look in his eyes.

"Just say it," she begged. "*Shut up, Jane.* See? It's not hard."

"Keep talking, Jane," he said softly.

"Stop. Stop humoring me."

"If you won't push me away, why should I return the favor? You're bright and incisive. And as I do not like to talk all of the time, I don't mind listening to you."

"What?"

"I think that you've been told to shut up so often that you've started saying it to yourself."

"Oh?" She swallowed. "You think…"

"You say things that make other people uncomfortable. Of course they want you to shut up."

"Don't I make you uncomfortable?"

He smiled. And then, he reached out and set his thumb on her lips. It was a casually intimate touch—as if her lips were his to caress. Jane's breath caught. She had the sudden, horrible urge to suck his digit into her mouth.

Instead, she exhaled.

"You make me uncomfortable," he murmured. "But not, I expect, the way that you mean."

"It's because you're an absolutely lovely man," she confessed. And then she heard what she'd said aloud and flushed warmly. "Oh, God. Not that I think you're attractive…"

That was worse. Far worse.

"I mean, of *course* I think you're…"

Worst of all.

She screwed her eyes shut. "Shut up, Jane," she whispered to herself.

"No." He drew his thumb along her bottom lip. "Keep talking, Jane."

"That's a terrible idea." Her own voice sounded husky. "There's no way to come out ahead. It doesn't matter whether I think you're attractive. You don't care what I think. Even I don't care what I think."

A finger joined his thumb on her lips. "I think you're very brave," he whispered. "You're a fire that should burn itself out in five seconds of brilliant combustion. I know what it's like to put forth that much energy, and yet you do it night after night. And nobody—not marquesses nor guardians nor physicians, not the whole weight of society's expectations—can make you stop."

She let out a sigh, a trembling sigh that had her lips brushing against his thumb. So much like a kiss.

"If people want you to stop talking, or to stop dressing the way you do, or to change who you are, it's because you hurt their eyes. We've all been trained not to stare into the sun."

Another finger joined his thumb against her lips. "I can't look, and I can't look away. But never fear, Miss Fairfield. I care what you think."

He tilted her chin up. He did it gently, as if he were asking a question. But if his fingers on her face asked a question, his eyes answered it. They were clear and blue and stronger than she'd imagined.

"So which one is it?" he asked softly. "Do you find me attractive, or…"

"There is no or," she told him.

He leaned close to her. So close that she could feel the heat of his breath against her lips. So close that she imagined that if she breathed in, she'd get a lungful of his essence. She felt an electric sense of expectation, as if she were putting together a jigsaw puzzle. As if she were about to set two pieces together, and she knew in her entire being that they would fit.

Instead, he straightened with a grimace and let his hand fall away.

"Is it something I said?" Jane asked. *And if so, which sentence?* There had been so many of them, after all.

"Impossible girl," he said softly.

It stung that he would call her that after all they'd exchanged. "It's only by choice," she snapped, but she knew it was more than that. Deep down, she knew that even if she had tried to get everything right, polite society would never have loved her. "I may be impossible, but at least I'm not—I'm not—"

"That's not what I meant." He reached out as if to touch her again, and Jane went still. Wishing those few inches between her cheek and his fingers would disappear. Her whole face tingled, and she sucked in her breath.

"Impossible girl," he repeated, but this time his tone was soft and low, making the words into something sensual. "I'm saying it for me as a reminder, not for you as an insult. Jane. Brave girl. Lovely girl." He did touch her cheek then, laying his fingers against it once more. And, oh, how good it felt, that tiny little touch. That point of connection.

"Girl I should not touch," he said. "Or kiss. Or have."

His smile was a little sad, and she could recall him saying that she was the last woman he would ever marry.

"But bright. So bright. It's a shame you're so impossible, Miss Fairfield, because otherwise, I think I would try for you."

She had preferred it when he'd called her Jane. She liked the way he said her name, not short and terse, a spare syllable to be gotten over with, but long and slow, a bite to be savored.

She reached up and laid her hand over his against her cheek. Warmth met warmth. He let out a noise, not quite a protest, but he didn't move away.

"Remember," he finally said, "what I am contemplating. I don't think I should be making you more vulnerable to me. Not at all."

"Too late for that," she told him.

He pulled his hand away as if it would make a difference. It didn't matter. He'd slipped past the layers of lace that she'd used to shroud her heart. She wasn't anything so foolish as in love with him; even she was not that brave. But...

"You're the most scaldingly honest betrayer I've had," she told him.

He grimaced. "Come, Miss Fairfield," he finally said. "It's getting cold and we ought to go in."

Chapter Eight

"MORE THAN TWO WEEKS IN CAMBRIDGE," the man Oliver had called father all his life said from his vantage point overlooking the stream. "And you're just now visiting?" He didn't look at Oliver as he spoke; he was examining the lure on the end of his line.

It was mid-afternoon—the worst time for fishing—and January to boot. But his father hadn't quibbled when Oliver suggested a trip to the stream.

Hugo Marshall was a good bit shorter than Oliver. His hair was an untidy brown, his features square, his nose broken. He looked nothing like Oliver, and with good reason: They were not actually related. Not by anything other than time and affection.

Oliver very carefully didn't look at his father. They had situated themselves next to their fishing pool—a wide, flat stretch of water where the stream went still. A large, gray rock on the bank made an excellent seat. "It took me far too long."

His parents' farm, just outside the tiny village of New Shaling, was a mere forty minutes' ride from Cambridge. When he'd been at university, he'd visited every weekend he could.

"Free thinks you're avoiding her," his father said.

She *would* think that. His youngest sister had always had a temper—and a tendency to think the world revolved around her. That it appeared to do so on a regular basis had done nothing to dissuade her.

"Of course I wasn't," Oliver replied. "I was avoiding you."

His father chuckled obligingly.

Oliver didn't laugh. Instead, he busied himself with his own rod and line.

"I see," his father said after a moment. "What horrible thing have I done now?"

Oliver cast his line with vicious intent into the pool, watching little ripples rise up in the otherwise still water. "Not you. Me."

His father didn't say anything.

"I'm struggling with a question of ethics."

"Ah." Hugo Marshall's gaze abstracted. "Is it a thorny question of ethics? Or is it the sort of ethical question where the right choice is easy, but the unethical answer is too tempting?"

Trust his father to see to the heart of his problem without having heard a word of it. Oliver fiddled with his rod and didn't look up. Normally, he'd have laid the whole thing before his father. But this time... This time, he wasn't sure if he wanted to tell the story. Too much of it had to do with Hugo Marshall himself.

His parents had scrimped and sacrificed and saved so that Oliver could have the chance he did. He'd only barely begun to understand what his parents had given up for him.

When Oliver's brother, the duke, had reached his majority, Oliver had visited Clermont House for the first time. Oliver had dimly known that his father had once worked for the Duke of Clermont in some capacity, but he'd never known details.

Not until he was twenty-one. Not until he'd arrived in London alongside his brother and was introduced to the staff. A good half-dozen servants remained from the time twenty-two years ago when Hugo Marshall had worked for the duke. They had been very curious about Oliver...and even more curious about what had become of Hugo Marshall.

"I knew him," the housekeeper had said. "I was only first maid, then, and we'd all fight over who had to take him tea. None of us wanted the task, he was that fearsome."

Fearsome. He'd seen his father angry a few times in his life, and Oliver supposed he was fearsome. But he'd understood that she had meant more than that. His father was fiercely intelligent and brooked no foolishness.

The housekeeper had sighed.

"He was the sort of man who I thought would be running all of London in twenty years. Sometimes you meet a man, and you just *know* about him. You know he's going to be something more." She'd sighed fretfully and readjusted her cap. "That's what we all said at the time. We just *knew*. It was a feeling you had, looking at him. And then it all came to nothing."

It all came to nothing.

Oliver glanced at his father. Hugo had cast his line in the deep pools at the edge of the river and sat without speaking, without expecting. Waiting to see if Oliver wanted to talk, assuming that anything that needed to be said would be.

It hadn't come to precisely nothing. All that energy had been devoted to this—into fishing trips with boys who were not really his sons, to money made and then immediately invested into his children.

Every bit of excess that the business had produced had gone to his family—helping Laura and her husband start a dry-goods store in town, paying for Oliver's university tuition, managing Patricia's shorthand lessons and then, when she had married Reuven, giving them enough to start their own business in Manchester.

It all came to nothing.

No. It wasn't going to be nothing. Oliver was going to make his father's sacrifice mean something. He was going to make it mean *everything*.

"Does it matter," Oliver asked, "if I want it very, very badly?"

"What is it you want?" his father asked.

I want you to be proud of me. I want to do everything you dreamed of and deliver it at your feet.

Oliver reached out and pulled a twig from the dirt, rolling it between his fingers. There were uglier wants, too, ones that made him feel almost uncomfortable.

I want them to pay.

Instead he shrugged. "Why did you do it? Give up everything to raise another man's son?"

His father did look up at that. "I didn't raise another man's son," he said sharply. "I raised my own."

"You know what I mean," Oliver said. "And that's precisely what I am talking about. Why claim me? Why treat me the way you have? It must have been an enormous struggle deciding what to do about me. I know you loved Mother, but—"

"You were as much my salvation as your mother was," his father interrupted brusquely. "You were never a burden that I had to grow accustomed to carrying. It was quite simple. If I could make you mine, in defiance of blood and biology, it would mean that I wasn't *his.*"

"Whose?" Oliver asked in confusion.

"My own father. If you were mine, I wasn't his."

Oliver leaned back and watched the ripples on the river. He knew—vaguely—that his father's father had not been a good man. His father had made a few curt remarks about it over the years, but he spoke little about it.

"Claiming you was like claiming myself," his father said. "It was that easy."

Oliver shut his eyes.

"So what is this thing you want so badly?"

"I want to be someone," Oliver breathed. "Someone…who matters. Who can make things happen. Someone with power." Someone who would never be shoved around again. Bradenton had it right; he had power, and Oliver had wants. That was a balance that begged for reversal.

His father didn't say anything for a while. Finally he spoke. "Of all my children, you and Free are the most like me. It's a gift, and like all gifts, it comes with a sting."

"Odd," Oliver said quietly, "that I should take after you more than the older girls."

His father made a noise of protest in the back of his throat, but didn't speak.

"I know," Oliver said. "I know. I don't mean to imply that you've been less than a father to me. It's just that… The son of Hugo Marshall shouldn't consider the offer I'm toying with. I might be the son of the Duke of Clermont. I have it in me."

"Hmm," his father said. "You have an odd view of me. I've done a great many things I'm not proud of."

"Me, too. There are times I've been quiet. There are times I've spoken when I shouldn't, just to keep myself from the effort of fighting."

"That doesn't make you into a man like your sire," his father said. "It just makes you into a man."

Oliver's line had floated too far. He shook himself and reeled it in before the lure could tangle in the brown weeds on the far side of the stream.

"Hypothetically speaking," Oliver said, "suppose that there was a man— a marquess—who promised me his vote on a very important issue. And all I would have to do in exchange…" He took a deep breath and looked away. "All I would have to do was humiliate a woman. Nothing physical, mind you. She wouldn't be ruined. Just…"

He glanced up into his father's eyes, and that was all he needed. There was no *just*. He knew Jane's situation. He knew how she felt, what it would do to her to have Oliver hurt her.

She wouldn't be ruined, but I could shred her spirit.

"We're speaking hypothetically?" His father snorted.

"If the issue in question was important enough, would you…"

"You're ten years a grown man," his father countered. "If I still need to tell you what to think of a proposition, I've done a poor job raising you, in which case my opinion shouldn't count for anything."

"But what if it is a *very* important issue? What if it would mean a very real difference for everyone, and it's just one woman who would suffer?" God. He couldn't even bring himself to spell out the personal consequences.

"No, Oliver. Keep your moral dilemmas to yourself and your university friends. You can't shunt that burden off to me. I refuse it."

"You're annoying. You always act as if everything is so easy. 'Well, Oliver, it seems to me that your choice is either to quit or continue,'" he mimicked, remembering his father's advice when he'd been on the verge of leaving school.

The other man only smiled. "I'm your father. It's my job to annoy you."

It was not the season for fishing, and unsurprisingly, they hadn't caught anything.

"When does it stop being one woman?" Oliver finally asked. "And when does it start being…a disgusting thing to ask in the first place?"

"Here's what I know," his father replied. "No fish will swim up and leap at your lure three feet off the ground. Cast."

Oliver flushed and did so. Once more, his lure and sinker hit the pool with a splash.

"What does it say about me that I'm still considering it?"

His father shrugged.

"You're useless," Oliver accused. "I thought you were going to tell me what to do."

"I'm not here to be used. I'm here to fish."

Oliver contemplated his fishing line for a moment longer. "You know," he said contemplatively, "I think you're a fraud. You act as if you're so wise, and what you mostly do is make idle comments about fishing and expect me to figure it out myself."

His father let out a guffaw. "That comes as a surprise? I taught you that trick years ago. When you keep quiet, people fill in their own most intelligent thoughts on your behalf."

After another forty minutes of silence, in which they'd managed to catch one four-inch trout, which was tossed back without comment, Oliver finally spoke.

"When I'm not here, do you fish alone?"

"Free usually comes with me."

"I didn't mean to displace her. Is she angry with me? She scarcely spoke last night before disappearing behind a book."

His father was eyeing the artificial fly tied at the end of his line, prodding it back into shape after the depredations of the fish. "You didn't displace her," he said evenly. "I asked her if she wanted to come along, and she declined."

"So she *is* angry at me. I wonder what I did."

"Ask her," his father said placidly. "I'm sure she'll tell you."

Oliver was sure she would, too. Free wasn't the sort to hold anything back.

"I worry about her," his father finally said. "I never realized how easy Laura and Patricia were. They wanted normal things. Security and marriage and a family. They wanted more than that, of course. But Free… I didn't realize your mother and I were going to pass on all our ambition concentrated in one child."

"What is it that Free wants?" Oliver asked, slightly puzzled.

His father smiled wryly. "What does she not? Ask her. I thought you were ambitious, Oliver. You've nothing on your youngest sister."

⌘ ⌘ ⌘

OLIVER FOUND HIS SISTER waiting for them on the way home. She was standing on top of the hill by the stream. Her arms were folded and she hadn't put her hair up. It blew behind her, a brilliant banner of orange the same color as his own close-cropped hair.

He paused a few feet away from her. "Free."

She didn't answer, but her chin squared. Yes, she was definitely angry with him.

She didn't have a temper, or at least not the temper that people generally thought of when they imagined a woman with hair somewhere on the brighter end of the spectrum. She was patient and kind. She could also be stubborn and immovable.

"Free," he said again. "How are you doing? Did you want to talk with me?"

She didn't look at him. "Why would I?" She didn't blink. "You haven't kept your promise, so why should I talk to you?"

"Promise?" He stared at her in confusion. "Did I promise something?"

Now she finally turned to him. "Of course you did," she said. "You promised to spend some time speaking Greek with me. Mama doesn't know Greek, so she can't, but you went to Eton."

"I promised?"

"More than a year ago, at Christmas," she said, with a firm nod of her head.

A vague recollection came back to him—of a late night sitting with his sister in front of the fire, passing pages of the newspaper back and forth.

"I can manage some of it from books," she was saying, "but I need to practice. I need you."

"As I recall," Oliver said, "I promised I would help as soon as I had time, and I haven't had any. In the intervening year, I've been…"

"You've spent months with the duke." She folded her arms accusingly.

"That was different. I was talking to men in London about reform. That's the whole reason I haven't had any time. When this is all finished, *then* I'll…"

Her chin rose. "When this is all finished? How long will that take, Oliver?"

"I'm really not sure."

Her lips pursed. "It took more than three decades for the issue to receive serious consideration in Parliament again, after the last Reform Act. Last year's bill was soundly defeated. It stands to reason that your goal might be years away."

"That's why I'm working so hard," he told her. "The harder I work now, the sooner it will happen. Learning always keeps. Greek will still be there once I'm done with this."

Her eyes flashed. "Oliver, if I start learning Greek two years from now, it will be too late."

"Too late for what? Too late because you'll be married?"

But she shook her head. "Too late for me to go to Cambridge."

He stopped dead and looked at her. He felt a little chill run down his spine; he wasn't sure where it had come from. He wanted to reach out and grab her, to fold her in his arms and keep her safe. From what, he wasn't certain. From herself, perhaps.

"They don't let women study at Cambridge," he finally said.

"Do you not pay attention to anything?" she demanded. "Not now, they don't. And there are no plans to open the University itself, of course. But there's a committee talking about a women's college in the village of Girton. I'm not old enough yet, Oliver, but by the time I am..."

God. She wanted to go to *Cambridge*. He pulled in a long breath and stared at her, but it didn't help. His head seemed to be ringing, echoing with a noise that repeated over and over.

Well, some practical side of himself whispered, *it could have been worse. She could want to go to Eton.*

He refused to think about Free at Eton.

Instead, he took a few steps forward and took hold of her hand. She was smaller than he was—not so large a difference that he thought of it much, but his earliest memories of her were of vulnerability. Watching out for her. Picking her up and sweeping her in his arms in a wide circle while she screamed in delight, making sure to hold on tightly so that she wouldn't fall.

"You think that all you'll have to do to go to Cambridge is learn a little Greek?"

She stared up at him, her eyes clear and defiant.

"Do you have any idea what you're taking on? When I went to Cambridge, I was barraged with an unceasing deluge of insult, both subtle and overt. I couldn't go a day without someone telling me that I didn't belong. You'll have every one of my disadvantages—except I had my brother and Sebastian. You'll be alone. And you're a woman, Free; everyone will be against you. They'll want you to fail twice as much as they wanted me to—first because you're a nobody, and second because you're a woman."

She shook her head. "Then I'll have to succeed three times as hard as they want me to fail. You, of all people, should understand that."

"I love you," he said. "That's all this is. I love you, and I don't want you to suffer. And…for me, Cambridge was the beginning. It was a handful of classes and exams and professors and papers, and afterward, the camaraderie of having attended school with a group of friends. And enemies." He looked over at her.

She raised her chin defiantly.

"It won't be like that for you. Going to Cambridge will not be a thing you do, followed by another thing and another thing. Going to Cambridge will define who you are forever after. For the rest of your life, you'll be The Girl Who Went to Cambridge."

"Someone will have to be The Girl Who Went," she said. "Why shouldn't it be me? And don't worry; I have no intention that getting a college degree will be the last of the dreadful things I do. I'd rather be the Girl Who Did instead of the Girl Who Didn't." She sniffed and looked away. "And I never thought you would talk me out of it, Oliver. Of all the people who I imagined would wish me to fail—"

"I don't wish you to fail," he said tersely. "If you *are* going to Cambridge, I wish you to succeed. I wish you to succeed against all odds. I only wish they didn't have to be arrayed against you."

"Then don't be one of my barriers." She spoke quietly. "You said you would help me learn Greek, Oliver. Everything else, I'm managing as best I can on my own. But Greek…"

"I'm not very good at Greek. I can manage the basics, but that's all. If you want to succeed against all odds, you'll need the best help you can get." He waited a moment longer. "Mama and Papa have their rules about taking the duke's money, but…it really is mine, you know. Shall I hire you a tutor?"

She swallowed. "Is that what you think I need? I'd be more comfortable with you."

"I'm not just saying that to get out of the duty," he said. "I don't think you understand how awful my Greek is. If you're going to do this, you're going to have to learn to be uncomfortable."

Slowly, she lowered herself down to sit on the ground. "What will Papa say?"

"I leave that to you to worry about." He sat beside her and hooked his arm over her shoulder. They sat there like that for a long moment, not speaking. Oliver wasn't sure what to say. He knew his sister too well to attempt to change her mind, but then…

He also knew what was waiting for her. That thing she yearned for right now with all her heart? The shine would come off it, he suspected, and the only way she'd make it through would be by gritting her teeth and bulling her way to the end. He wouldn't wish his Cambridge years on anyone. Least of all someone he loved.

"I worry about you," he finally said to Free. "I'm afraid that you're going to break your heart, going up against the world."

"No." The wind caught her hair and sent it swirling behind her. "I'm going to break the world."

She almost seemed not to have heard the words she'd said, so absently did she speak. As if it were a conclusion she had come to years ago, one she didn't even need to examine any longer.

He watched her breathe in. The sun fell on her skin—she was going to freckle dreadfully—but she wouldn't care. Her eyes were shut, and she turned to face the breeze as if the wind could take her to another place.

"Is that what happened to you?" she finally asked, without opening her eyes. "Cambridge broke your heart?"

He barely kept from startling. His eyes widened and he turned to her. But she hadn't moved, and she didn't say anything at all to him. She just sat there, her head thrown back, a little breeze catching a strand of her hair. Oliver wasn't sure why his heart was racing. Why his fists were clenched as he stared straight ahead.

"Don't be ridiculous," Oliver finally said. "It's just a school. That's it; it's just a school."

Chapter Nine

THE UNIVERSITY OF CAMBRIDGE had an extraordinary set of botanic gardens, carefully planted with exotic species brought back from around the world and arranged in order of Linnaean classification. No matter how strange the species were, however, they could not rival how oddly Jane felt.

She could feel the kiss that Mr. Marshall *hadn't* given her still lingering on her lips three days after he'd declined to give it. It tingled, a sharp, sweet secret, that undelivered kiss, and she felt as if it painted every word that came out of her mouth with the fullness of its ungranted promise.

"You seem quite taken with Mr. Marshall," Genevieve Johnson said to Jane as they walked together.

They were passing an evergreen from China, branches laden with green needles drooping low to the ground.

"He's amusing," Jane said.

The twins exchanged glances.

"That is to say," Jane tried again, "I am sure he is a dependable fellow."

"I'm sure he is," Geraldine agreed, taking Jane's arm with an expression that would have been a smirk on another girl.

Jane should make a remark about his station, something to depress their interest. She couldn't bring herself to do it.

"He's a duke's brother," she finally said. "Surely that elevates him to the status of at least a marquess."

The sisters exchanged a longer glance.

"No," Geraldine finally said. "You might think of a duke's brother, but I don't think you should consider a marquess."

There was something faintly off in their mannerisms, and the two of them were so rarely off. Genevieve's lips pressed together; Geraldine looked somber. It took Jane a minute to understand. Of course. They *knew* a marquess. Good heavens. Geraldine was engaged to the Earl of Hapford, but his uncle was unattached. Had Genevieve set her sights on Bradenton?

She wished her joy of him. The girls were of excellent family—cousins to an earl—and had good dowries. But she'd long suspected that Bradenton needed far more than a dowry that was merely *good* by country standards.

"Under no circumstances a marquess," Geraldine was saying. But her sister took her elbow and gave her a little tap—that, and the tilt of her head, no more, and Geraldine stopped talking and turned.

For there in the gardens, just beneath an awning covered with some creeping vine that had dropped most of its leaves for winter, stood the marquess himself.

Jane had never been particularly enamored of Bradenton, but she'd not thought he held any particular distaste for her. He was after all, too much enamored of himself to care about her. But Mr. Marshall had told her last night that the marquess wanted Jane humiliated and hurt.

Humiliated.

She felt a flush of fierce resentment at that. The marquess was watching her with cold, glittering eyes. She wanted to smack him, to let him know that he could not conquer her.

"Shall we greet him?" Geraldine said softly.

"No need," Jane whispered. "He looks busy. We wouldn't want to put him off with our forwardness."

"Indeed," Geraldine agreed, a little too swiftly. "Indeed, Miss Fairfield."

"After all," Genevieve said in too high a voice, "I should hate him to see me outside of my evening finery."

"And in direct sun, no less. Oh my, he'll see every flaw in my skin."

They spoke swiftly atop each other, nodding the whole while. "Good," Geraldine said, "it's settled. Oh, da—drat, he's seen us. He's coming this way."

"Jane," Genevieve said urgently, "is my powder smudged? Tell me quickly."

Jane peered into the other girl's face. As usual, it was flawless. She didn't even look as if she were wearing powder.

"Oh, nothing to worry about," Jane told her merrily. "It's only smudged a little here." She indicated her right cheek.

Genevieve whipped out a handkerchief, but it was too late.

"Miss Johnson. Miss Genevieve," Bradenton said. "How lovely to encounter you. And Miss Fairfield, too."

If Jane had been caught with a handkerchief in her hand, she would have done something dreadful with it—like drop it, or shove it into a pocket, leaving an unshapely lump in her skirts.

Genevieve simply smiled and treated the folded square of linen as if it were a bouquet, a perfectly natural thing for her to be holding. She used it to add a little flourish to the perfectly executed curtsy she made.

"My lord," she said in unison with her sister.

Jane came in a few moments later with a lopsided curtsy of her own. "Bradenton."

The marquess gave Jane an annoyed glance at that familiarity. "As it turns out, ladies," Bradenton said, "there's a new plant in one of the greenhouses. I had thought to show Miss Fairfield."

The two ladies looked at one another. "Of course," Geraldine said. "We should love to see it above all things."

"Ah, that's the thing." Bradenton shook his head sadly. "It's delicate. Very delicate. We could not all crowd about it without risking its demise."

What claptrap. What was the man getting at?

"I propose we all walk to the greenhouses," Bradenton said, "and I will conduct Miss Fairfield inside. You'll be able to see her through the glass— there will be no chance of impropriety—and I'll be done in a matter of minutes."

There was a pause—a longer, more reluctant pause. If Genevieve had set her sights on Bradenton, she was probably thinking murderously jealous thoughts at the moment. But if she aspired so high, she did not let it show. After a moment, the twins simply nodded.

"But of course, my lord," Genevieve said.

"Whatever you say, my lord," Geraldine told him.

The word *greenhouse* called to mind a single structure of glass. The greenhouses here were actually a complex of glassed-in buildings, jutting out like spikes from a central hallway. They were made of heavy brick mortared over in gray from the ground up to waist level. Above that point, windows made up the walls and ceilings. On some, the top windows were open a few inches. Jane could feel the warm air tickling her face as they passed. Bradenton walked along a side path before opening a door.

"We'll just be a moment, ladies," he said to the twins, before he ushered Jane inside.

She'd been in the greenhouses before. A main hallway stretched in front of her, with individual rooms connected off it, each with its separate temperature and humidity. The hallway itself was moist and heated; jungle vines flourished on the walls.

The specimens here were labeled in both Latin and English, and sometimes in letters and numbers that meant nothing to Jane. Some university botanist must be studying them, Jane supposed. Steel pipes made a quiet gurgling sound, hot water flowing through them, radiating warmth. Jane had dressed for the cold, and suddenly she was sweltering.

Geraldine probably wouldn't have done anything so uncouth as *sweat*.

Bradenton bowed her into a room of clay pots and sand with a smile. Jane didn't smile back. This was the man who wanted her hurt. Humiliated. Who was willing to trade a vote in Parliament to get that result.

"So, my lord," Jane asked, "where is this exceedingly rare plant?"

He contemplated her. "I cannot make you out."

"Whyever not?" Jane spun around, taking in the plants in the room. "You and I are so similar." It was dry and hot; a big, square planter to the left contained rocks and sand and a number of squiggly misshapen green things. They'd have been swallowed up by the underbrush if they'd dared to grow in the Cambridge woods.

"Similar?"

"But of course." Jane still refused to look at him. "We're simple people. The sort that nobody would care about if circumstances were different. I'm elevated by my fortune. You're elevated by your title."

He made a sound of disbelief. "That's why you spurned me? Because you think you're my *equal?*" There was an ugly tone in his voice.

Her heart beat faster. She put him off because that was what she *did*. But perhaps she'd made a special effort with him. Others had talked and laughed about her, but after those first few weeks, he'd encouraged them. And he'd tried to pretend he didn't.

"Spurn you?" she said with a laugh. "How could I have spurned you? You've never offered me anything to spurn."

He made a noise. "No matter."

"I can't imagine *why* you'd offer," Jane said. You're a marquess. You don't need…" She stopped, as if something had just occurred to her. "Oh."

His eyes burned into hers, but Jane wasn't going to let his glare stop her. She wanted him to feel a fraction of the pain he wished on her.

"You *do* need my money," Jane said. "Don't you?"

"Shut up."

"Of course." Jane kept her face a mask of solicitude. "I feel dreadfully for you. How embarrassing that must be. You write all the laws, you can't lose your lands even by mismanagement, and yet with all those advantages, you can't even fix the game to turn a profit on your own estates. Good heavens; that must take singular skill."

He took another step toward her. "Shut up," he said on a low growl.

"Oh, don't worry. I won't tell anyone. You know I am the very soul of discretion."

He made a strangled noise in his throat and took yet another step toward her.

She'd gone too far. Twitting him was one thing; taunting another. She froze and looked up at the menace that had taken over his features. For all that the Johnson sisters were watching, there was nothing they could—quite possibly nothing they *would*—do to save her if he wanted to hurt her. She was effectively alone with the man, and he wished her ill. He wanted her to shut up.

It had never been one of her skills.

She smiled blindly at him, clinging to her pretense of ignorance. "I feel for you, Bradenton. Did you hear of me and imagine a poor, impressionable child, one who would be overwhelmed by your wit and charm? You must have been so disappointed. You imagined my dowry was yours, and then I laughed at you the first time you gave me a grandiose compliment."

If anything, his eyes grew angrier. "You little bitch," he whispered. "You've been doing it on purpose."

"Doing what?" Jane held on to her smile as if it were the only thing shielding her from a dragon's flames. "I haven't been doing a thing except stating a few facts. Don't you like facts, my lord?"

No. He didn't. He took a final step toward her, and this time he raised his walking stick, clenched like a truncheon in his fist.

Her hands went cold. She really *had* gone too far.

She kept smiling. "You were going to show me a plant, my lord."

He stopped, shook his head, as if remembering that they were in a greenhouse. That the walls were glass. That no matter what words had been exchanged, she was a lady—and if it got out that he'd struck her, his reputation would suffer.

He took a breath, and then another, and then yet another, until his countenance presented as smooth a lie as Jane's.

"There." He inverted his walking stick so that the curved head pointed to a clay pot filled with sand. "That is it."

It was greenish-gray, an ugly mess of a plant. Fat snakes as thick as her thumb pointed up in a tangled knot, radiating sharp little needles.

"It reminds me of you, Miss Fairfield." A trace of venom still carried on his voice.

No wonder.

"I quite like it," Jane mused. "It seems a brave little thing in all that sand. Here, let's find a plant for you, my lord. I know just the thing. I saw some sort of weed when first we came in."

There had been a foul-smelling creeper of some kind back in the jungle-like hallway. She started to turn away.

She saw it out of the corner of her eye. He swung the head of his walking stick down hard. Little bits of that snaky, spiney cactus went flying.

Her stomach turned to ice. She had no way to bluff past that act of violence, no way to smile it off. She had only one choice—to pretend she didn't see it. She kept on turning to the door and marched away, even though her hands were shaking.

"It's here," she said. "In the hallway. Let's seek it out, shall we?"

He was breathing heavily. "No. Let's just get back to the others."

He hadn't meant it as a threat, she told herself. She'd irritated him, that was all, and once he'd passed the point of frustration, he'd snapped. The little cactus had been an unfortunate casualty of his anger.

They walked in silence—Bradenton unwilling to speak, and Jane unable to say anything more. They went back through the humid central hallway, opened the door onto the path. Genevieve and Geraldine were waiting for them, turned to each other, speaking in low, urgent tones.

"You saw it," Geraldine said. "You saw it, and—"

At the sound of the door, they stopped talking. They turned as one and broke into twin smiles.

"My lord," Genevieve said.

"My dear Miss Fairfield." Geraldine stepped forward, her hands outstretched for Jane. "So good to see you once more. Thank you for returning her to us."

"Here you are," Bradenton said. "Ladies, I give you back your friend."

Jane's head was still ringing. Her hands were shaking. She could scarcely pay attention as the twins murmured polite invitations to the marquess.

"I don't suppose you would like to join us on our further ramblings?"

She wasn't even sure who spoke. *No,* she was thinking. *No. Go away. Go away.*

"Sorry, ladies." He gave them a cool smile, one that didn't touch his lips. "I've already been out for far too long. It was a pleasure, to be sure. Miss Johnson. Miss Genevieve." He stared at Jane. "Miss Fairfield."

Jane's heart was still beating in hard, heavy thumps.

Genevieve pouted. "If you must," she said. The two of them stationed themselves between Jane and Bradenton, watching him retreat down the path away from the greenhouse. A few steps away, he stopped and turned—perhaps to look at Jane. The sisters stood shoulder to shoulder, though, and if Bradenton had any particular message he wanted to send—a frown or a scowl—his visage was blocked by the twins. Geraldine lifted her hand and gave him a little wave.

Never had Jane been so relieved by their incessant flirtation. Her breath was finally beginning to slow when the sisters turned back to her.

They weren't smiling. In fact, they were looking at her with something that she might have thought was concern, had it been on anyone else's face.

Geraldine took a step forward. "Miss Fairfield," she said, her voice delicate and musical—everything that a lady's should be. "Miss Fairfield, we were watching through the window. We couldn't help but notice…"

"What was it he said?" Genevieve asked.

Jane's throat closed up. She couldn't talk about it—not with these two, not with anyone. She couldn't care about their foolish, misplaced jealousies.

God. He'd killed her plant. He'd been on the verge of hurting her.

"Nothing," Jane said. "It was nothing." Pray that they couldn't see her hands shaking.

"Tell me, Miss Fairfield." Geraldine reached out and touched Jane's wrist. "When we decided to…befriend you, we agreed with one another that we would…take care of you."

"After a manner of speaking," Genevieve added.

Jane shook her head. "It was nothing. He showed me a plant. He said it made him think of me. Isn't that…" *Sweet.* She'd been going to say it was sweet, but even she could not get that word out of her mouth.

Geraldine's mouth tightened. She turned to her sister. "You're right," she said. "We have to tell her."

What new horror was this? She couldn't play games any longer.

"I have a headache," Jane demurred. But Geraldine tightened her grasp on her wrist.

Genevieve came to stand by her side. "Miss Fairfield," she said gently, "there is no good way to say this. Sometimes…" She looked over at her sister. "Sometimes, I think that you are…"

Geraldine gave a sharp nod. "Sometimes I think that you are not always good at understanding other people's intentions."

Jane stared at them, her mind reeling.

"And so maybe," Genevieve said, "maybe you didn't understand what it was that Bradenton was saying to you. And I don't think you saw when you turned away—that look on his face, and the thing that he did."

Jane had understood it. She had understood it perfectly well. That they had, too… She couldn't let them see, couldn't have this conversation. Hearing it from their mouths made his threats feel real in a way that she couldn't explain. He wanted her hurt. He wanted her humiliated.

"But we did," Genevieve said. "His intent was unmistakable, even through the window." She took a longer, deeper breath. "We haven't always been kind to you."

What were they saying? What were they *doing?* It took Jane a moment to look into Genevieve's eyes, to see that this wasn't going to turn into some jealous tirade. The two sisters exchanged glances, and then nodded at one another.

"In fact," Genevieve said, "since the first few weeks we knew you…we probably haven't been kind to you once. We've been making use of your particular skills. I know this may be hard to hear, that you might not understand what we're saying."

She couldn't speak, couldn't say anything at all.

"But," Genevieve continued, "please believe me when I say this—I do not think you should ever be alone with Lord Bradenton again. Not even for a walk in a garden with other people nearby. We haven't been very kind to you, but we *did* promise when we started that we'd keep you from the worst of it. I can't be sure of Bradenton's meaning, but I refuse to stand idly by while we find out."

"That was foul." Geraldine folded her arms. "Extremely foul. I don't care what nonsense you spout. That was outside the bounds of fair play. And given what Hapford told me of his conduct…" She made a disgusted sound. "No, Miss Fairfield. I should have spoken before now. You oughtn't be alone with him."

Jane didn't know what to say. She'd expected the worst for so long that she didn't know what to do when it didn't come. Her throat was closing up. She hadn't expected…this.

Genevieve touched Jane's elbow. "Maybe you don't understand this, either." Her hands were gentle. "But no matter what—no matter how we've treated you in the past—we aren't going to let anything happen to you. I promise."

Jane let out a slow, shaky breath, then another. Then another one. She looked from side to side. The sisters were half a foot shorter than she was, but they seemed to loom over her. She wasn't sure which of them saw the suggestion of tears in her eyes first, which of them moved closer, putting her arms around her.

"There, there," Geraldine said. "There, there. It's all right. It will be all right."

She hadn't known how much fear she had—how alone she'd felt—until they spoke. And now that they had—now that they'd broken through that barrier—there was no stopping the flood of emotions. Jane let out a gasp, and then another one. She had thought herself entirely alone, a wizened, puny, ugly thing of spikes deserted in a sea of sand. But when she staggered, Genevieve caught her.

"There, there," Geraldine was saying. "There, there."

"I've felt worse and worse with every passing month," Genevieve said. "Dirty. No better than Bradenton. We've been awful, truly awful."

"It was just so fortuitous," Geraldine continued for her sister. "You were the perfect excuse to drive Genevieve's suitors away."

Jane couldn't help herself. She'd been angry, frightened, and then taken utterly by surprise. At that, she began to laugh.

"I don't think she understands," she heard Geraldine say.

Jane straightened. She took a deep breath and looked around her, at a world that she no longer quite understood. Then she exhaled slowly.

"Geraldine," she heard herself say, "Genevieve, I have a confession to make. I haven't been very kind to you, either. Not from the first few weeks."

They stopped, their matching china-blue eyes widening.

"I…" She took a deep breath. "I'm this awful on purpose. I owe you both an apology."

"Oh, no," Geraldine breathed, stepping forward, a smile spreading across her face.

"Indeed." Genevieve laughed. "Skip the apology. I'd rather have an explanation. This has to be good."

⌘ ⌘ ⌘

THE WOMEN WALKED FOR HOURS, talking, scarcely looking at the plants around them.

"You see," Genevieve said solemnly as they finally came to the end of their time together, "I don't wish to marry. Every time I think of a man pawing over me, I just start to panic."

Geraldine patted her sister's arm. "Mama says she'll grow out of it. But Geraldine and I do everything together. We had our first menses on the same day. It's foolish to imagine that this will change when we've always differed on this score. So I am supporting her out of sisterly solidarity until she's of age."

"It's such a shame." Genevieve sighed. "I'd make such a marvelous wife, if I could marry the equivalent of her Hapford. I'd so love to spend my husband's money on charitable works. Instead, I shall be forced to *economize*. So she's going to have all the babies. And I shall spoil them and be the exciting, wicked aunt. I shall give them sweets until they're all riled up, and then hand them back to the nurse and be on my way."

"You were such a godsend," Geraldine said. "We've always done everything right until now. Genevieve was so afraid that she'd be lambasted into accepting some reasonably ordinary gentleman, and being miserable all her life. And then we met you. All we had to say was, 'Oh, no, we couldn't possibly attend without our bosom friend Miss Fairfield,' and suddenly our invitations dwindled. It was so fortuitous."

It had been fortuitous for them all. Now that they'd spoken about it, it had planted the roots of something warm and real in the remains of their previous cold, twisted friendship.

"Tonight, then?" Geraldine asked, almost two hours later as the ladies came back up to the entrance of the gardens.

Mrs. Blickstall was waiting for Jane, seated at a bench near the entrance. She glanced up, but if she found anything odd about the fact that the ladies were walking arm in arm and smiling at one another with genuine pleasure, she didn't say it.

Genevieve kissed Jane's cheek, and then Geraldine leaned in and did the same.

"Things will be better now," Geraldine whispered. "For all of us. You'll see." They waved goodbye.

Mrs. Blickstall stood to go.

But somehow, leaving seemed wrong. Jane wasn't sure why until she remembered what she'd left in the greenhouse. She'd pretended at the time that she hadn't seen what had happened, but some part of her still saw that shattered plant out of the corner of her eye.

"I need a little longer," she said.

One lovely thing about bribing her chaperone was that Jane always got her way. Mrs. Blickstall shrugged and subsided into her seat. Jane walked back into the gardens, down the path alongside the brook, back toward the greenhouses.

She was a blight. A poison. A pestilence. She was the enemy of all proper conversation. Grown men would rather be mauled to death by lions than converse with her.

She'd hated everyone for the jests they'd made at her expense.

So when had she started believing them? That she was a plague, that nobody could truly like her? That every word out of her mouth was a burden for others?

She came to the greenhouses and headed back to the desert room. She opened the door, hoping her memory exaggerated the damage. But no. That poor little plant was still in pieces. Bradenton had hit it so hard that it had split all the way to the root.

But it wasn't a blight or a pestilence. It was just a plant, and it didn't deserve to die.

Jane didn't know how to go forward, how to remake the person she had become. She was never going to be like Geraldine or Genevieve with smooth manners and perfect skin. She would always talk too much, say the wrong things, wear the wrong clothing. But maybe…

Maybe things really could change. A little.

And she knew the first thing she needed to do.

⌘ ⌘ ⌘

JANE HAD TO RAP on three doors before one opened at her knock.

Beyond the doorframe, Jane saw a glassed-in room and tiny plastic pots of little seedlings. A woman in a dark dress, covered by a navy smock, her hands in dirt-stained garden gloves, stood at the door. Her eyebrows were raised as she contemplated Jane. She took in Jane's gown—bright orange-and-cream, with fussy cherubs on her skirts—and those eyebrows went up even farther.

"Well?" the other woman asked. "What is it?"

"I'm so sorry to bother you," Jane said. "But I was walking in the greenhouses and…there is this cactus. Something happened to it."

The woman did not look impressed. "It is a cactus," she said. "They usually look like they're dying. That's normal." She started to close the door.

"No, wait," Jane said. "It's been broken to bits. It looks like a boy hit it."

The woman looked up and sighed. "Oh, very well. Maybe I should have a look." She turned away, rummaging among items on a metal shelf until she found a small pot, a set of shears, and another pair of gloves. "Let's go see this cactus."

Jane trotted down the hall. She'd expected to find an old, hoary gardener, or a young man with calloused hands and a broad accent. But this woman, by her cultured tones and the stiff, starched fabric under her gardening smock, seemed to be a well-bred lady.

"I'm surprised," Jane said. "I hadn't thought that the Botanic Gardens would hire a lady."

"Hire?" The woman huffed. "Don't be ridiculous. I volunteer."

The other woman hadn't spoken a sentence longer than a handful of words and did not give the air of being particularly talkative. "Of course," Jane said. "I'm sorry." She wasn't sure what she was apologizing for. "It's in here."

"I know," the woman replied. "There's only one greenhouse for the desert succulents." So saying, she swept into the room. With her smock, she reminded Jane of a nurse—aproned and gloved and ready to fix any ills. Her eyes lit on the plant that Bradenton had destroyed. The center had been smashed to bits, and the little spiky green tentacles lay about it, hewn off.

The lady stopped. "Oh," she crooned, in a far different voice than the steel-laden one she'd used to converse with Jane. "You poor, poor baby."

She gathered up the clay pot almost tenderly and gently poked through bits of broken cactus.

"Can you save it?" Jane asked.

"It's a cactus," the other woman replied absently. "They grow in deserts. They've evolved to withstand sun and slicing sandstorms." She sounded proud. "You can kill a cactus, but it takes a sustained effort—consistent overwatering and the like. This piece of vandalism?" She shrugged. "This is just an act of propagation."

So saying, she scooped up a little sand into the smaller pot she'd brought with her. She trimmed the damaged cactus, removing the broken tentacles, piling them on the ground as she worked.

"There," she finally said. "Now we get to the fun bit." She picked up the green tentacles and poked them back into the soil. "First there was one cactus, now there are seven, eight…" She took the last piece and stuck it into the pot that she'd filled. "Nine."

"What? That's it? No water, no special potions?"

"It'll take a few months for them to take root," the woman replied. "Water them only when the sand is dry. But yes, as I said. The cactus is a hard plant to kill." She handed the pot to Jane. "Here. For you."

"Oh my goodness," Jane said in surprise. "Can you do that? Just *give* me a cactus like that?" She frowned and looked at the woman. "Wait. You're only a volunteer. You can't."

"If you walk out the doors with it, you'll own it nonetheless," the woman replied. "I had not thought that the intrepid Miss Jane Fairfield would balk at a little thing like ownership."

"How did you know my name?"

"I'm Violet Waterfield. The Countess of Cambury." She looked expectant.

Jane blinked at her. "Pleased to meet you, my lady."

She seemed nonplussed. "You don't know who I am? Oliver always does forget the honorary members." She held up her left hand in her glove. "Brothers Sinister? Oliver, Sebastian, Robert?"

"Oliver. Do you mean—"

"Of course I mean Oliver Marshall," the woman said.

"How did you know—"

The countess smiled mysteriously. "I know everything. That's my duty in our little group."

"I see," Jane said puzzled. "What a lovely vocation."

"Vocation?" Another huff. "Of course not." There was a particularly self-satisfied smile on her face as she spoke. "I volunteer."

Chapter Ten

JANE'S MIND WAS STILL WHIRLING when she entered her sister's room late that night.

For years, Emily had been her only confidante, the one she told all her troubles. Now, over the course of the past few days, Jane had gathered a host of secrets she couldn't tell her sister.

There's this man. He was thinking about humiliating me, but never mind that—let me tell you about the Johnson twins.

Did you know that Bradenton has put a bounty on my head? Apparently, I'm worth an entire vote in Parliament. Or the destruction of a cactus. I'm not sure which one honors me more.

Do you think Mr. Marshall likes me? I have no notion what to think of him.

But that was a lie, too. She knew exactly what she thought of him.

While she was gathering her thoughts, her sister spoke instead. "Did you know that there are people who don't drink alcohol?"

Jane put her head to her side. "I'd heard." In Cambridge, surrounded by young men, she'd mostly heard those people mocked. "Is it the Quakers who don't believe in imbibing or the Methodists? I never can remember." She glanced over at her sister, who was watching her intently. "Why?"

"I read about it." There was a faint flush on Emily's cheeks, though, one that suggested that it was more than a matter for idle speculation. "There are…other sorts, aren't there, though?"

"Hmm. I hardly go around asking."

"Of course." Her sister looked down, fingering the fabric of her night rail.

Jane was trying to formulate what she might say to her sister. If she started telling the story, she could hardly withhold a piece. And now she had other people's secrets to keep. She couldn't tell her sister what Genevieve had said. That wasn't her secret to disclose. Jane had argued with Emily before, but she'd never had secrets from her.

"You're pensive," Emily said. "What on earth has happened to you?"

"Nothing," Jane lied.

Emily looked at her. She looked across the room at the new cactus plant on Jane's chest of drawers and raised an eyebrow. "Oh," she said. "I see. And here I thought *I* was the one that nothing happened to."

Jane winced. "I'm sorry, dear."

"Don't humor me," Emily snapped. There was nothing to say to that—nothing that wouldn't make it worse at any rate—so Jane held her tongue.

Emily finally spoke again. "Did you know there are people who don't eat meat?"

It was apparently a night for odd questions. "I knew a man who didn't like the taste of ham."

"Not just ham. All meat." For some reason, Emily wasn't looking her in the eye, and Jane had a sudden suspicion.

"Emily," she said softly, "do these people who don't eat meat or drink liquor have names, by any chance?"

Her sister shrugged insouciantly. "Of course not. Or at least they don't have names that *I* would know. How would I?"

If Jane hadn't known what an excellent liar her sister was, she would have thought nothing amiss. But Jane knew Emily far too well. And so she stopped and studied her, and realized that something was different.

Emily wasn't fidgeting. No little bounces on the edge of the bed. No jigglings of her leg. She only drew idly on the coverlet with her finger.

Before they'd come to Titus's, she could have mapped her sister's activities during the day by her fidgets at night. Had she run outside for two hours? She could sit calmly and orderly by bedtime. Had it rained, keeping her indoors? She'd not be able to sit still, jumping up and moving around.

Emily wasn't moving right now.

Suspicion gathered at the edge of Jane's mind. There *was* rather more color in her cheeks, and…

"Emily, have you—"

Her sister looked up sharply. "Nothing," she caroled sweetly. "I've been doing *nothing*. See how it feels?"

Jane shook her head. "Never mind. I don't actually want to know. If Titus finds out, I want to be able to claim ignorance, and I'll hardly be able to do that if you're telling me everything."

A wistful smile touched her sister's face and she looked away. Jane knew that smile.

"Just tell me that whatever it is you're doing"—Jane trailed off—"or not doing…"

Whatever it was her sister was doing, she had to be leaving the house. By herself; Blickstall had been with Jane today. There were risks there, and not just the foolish worries Titus held.

"Tell me," she said, "that you're staying safe."

"Even Titus could not object." Emily gave her a wicked smile. "I'm reading his law books, that's all." Her finger traced a curlicue on the coverlet.

"In the course of reading his books," Jane said softly, "perhaps you'll have noticed that people do each other harm from time to time. I'd hate for you to have to discover the criminal from personal experience."

"Oh, no." Emily sketched a curling tendril with the tip of her finger. "There's no chance of that."

"There's always a chance—"

"Hypothetically speaking," Emily said, "if someone is unwilling to eat an animal because he does not believe in doing it harm, it follows that he would think the same of humans."

"No," Jane said, "it does not follow. Please do not think it follows."

Emily paused in the midst of her tracery. She stopped still—something she did so rarely that Jane felt herself leaning in, wanting to shake her to make sure that she was still breathing.

"If a rock never moves," her sister finally said, "the water wears it away all the same. I *am* being hurt, Jane, and if I stay still, Titus will wear me away. Sometimes I wonder that there's anything left of me at all."

"Emily." Jane touched her sister's hand. "I won't let that happen."

"It's not up to you to *let* it. That's what Titus would say." Her sister raised her eyes. "Don't counsel me to stay home because I might get hurt."

"I won't. I promise."

Emily squeezed her hand. "Then you keep your nothing, and I'll keep mine."

⌘ ⌘ ⌘

IT WAS THE THIRD TIME that Emily had slipped out of her room to meet Mr. Bhattacharya.

If her uncle knew what was happening, he would have had a fit of his own. He would have delivered her lecture after lecture about her innocence and how she was too kind and good and young. How men were not to be trusted.

But Mr. Bhattacharya had proven far too trustworthy for Emily's tastes. He smiled at her. He took her arm when they found a path that was narrow, but he relinquished it when the footing was secure. He looked—oh, he definitely looked. But he hadn't done anything untrustworthy. Nothing at all.

Today, he was quieter than usual. He'd been perfectly polite in greeting her. And then they'd walked and walked along the brook, following the path until it met up with the road. He'd not said a word. After about a half an hour, he finally spoke.

"I'm sorry," he said. "I'm not the best of company. I'm preparing for the Tripos, and I'm trying to figure out some of the trickier points of common law. It makes my head hurt."

"Would you like to talk it over?"

She'd started reading Titus's law books again just to see what Mr. Bhattacharya was talking about. Her uncle had been a little confused, but had finally said that she might enjoy the stories in the cases so long as she skipped over the conclusions of law.

Mr. Bhattacharya didn't act as if she couldn't follow the reasoning, as if the things he learned were above her. He just talked to her.

Last time, he'd pulled one of his books from his satchel and they'd read through a passage together, their heads bent over it in tandem, so close that he could have reached out and set his hand over hers.

He hadn't.

Today, though, he didn't take out his book. He looked up at the sky instead. "There is a case," he finally said, "where the courts conclude that a bequest is invalid because an eighty-year-old woman could have had a child after the will was drafted." He made an annoyed noise.

Emily folded her hands, waiting, but he didn't say anything else. He simply glared at her as if the centuries-long foibles of Chancery could be foisted on her shoulders.

"Perhaps," Emily finally said, "if you could explain to me precisely where you are having difficulties, I might be able to be of more help."

"I—" He blinked at her. "How is it not obvious where I am having difficulties? Start with the fact that an eighty year old woman does not bear children."

"Sarah had children in the Bible," Emily said, "and she was at least eighty years old, so—"

"The Bible." He shook his head. "If we are allowed to argue from that authority, I still don't understand it. The rule in question says that it must become clear who a bequest is going to within twenty-one years of the death of a person who was living at the time the bequest was made. If we take the Bible as authority, we need only use Jesus Christ as a person living at the time of the bequest. Since he rose from the dead and lives forever, then—"

"No, no," Emily said, trying to stifle a laugh. "I know very little of law, but I'm certain that you can't use Jesus."

"Why not? Did Jesus live after he rose a second time or didn't he?"

"They'll call it sacrilege, that's why."

He shrugged, as if sacrilege were of no particular worry to him. "Very well. Let me see if I understand how this works. We can use Sarah from your holy scripture, but not Jesus. I assume that if I mentioned the *Bhagavad Gita*, the response would be hostile."

"What is that?" Emily asked curiously.

"You might call it some of our Hindu scripture."

She contemplated this. "I do not consider myself an expert on English law, but I believe you are safe in assuming that citing Hindu scripture in an English court may not be the best choice."

"English law is incomprehensible. Your scripture is the only valid argument that can be made, and even then, it is to be used only when it is convenient to support an argument, but not otherwise. How does that make any sense? There is no guiding principle."

"I think, Mr. Bhattacharya, that you understand well enough," Emily said. "Your problem is not one of understanding. It is one of acceptance."

"You have it backward," he said, calm and unruffled. "I *accept*. But how am I to apply illogic? And you claim that English law is the pinnacle of civilization."

"Me?" Emily took a step forward. "*I* haven't claimed anything about English law. English law says that I can't make my own decisions, that even though I'm old enough to marry and have children of my own, that I cannot choose who I live with and who touches my body. English law says that I must abide by my uncle's wishes, when he would have me confined to my room."

He was looking at her oddly. "Your uncle," he said slowly. "But I thought your uncle..." He glanced around the path. "What do you mean, he would confine you to your room?"

She swallowed. "He is, perhaps, not as permissive as I represented."

He took a step back. "I'm not sure you should be defying your uncle. He's family. That isn't just law; it's good sense. I thought..."

"I smoothed over the truth a little," she said testily. "My uncle is not..."

"*I* wouldn't defy my family like that."

"Of course you would," Emily responded. "If your family asked you to do something distasteful. Suppose, for instance, your father was a tyrant like Napoleon, and that he commanded you to—"

But he was shaking his head again. "Now I really don't understand you. What was so terrible about Napoleon?"

He was so even-tempered, so often smiling, that at first Emily thought he was joking. Then she found the furrow in his brow, the dark look he gave her.

She threw up her hands. "You're being ridiculous. He was bent on conquering the entire European continent, never mind the cost in…in…"

She swallowed, as her mind raced to a conclusion ahead of her.

"Oh," she said in mute horror.

He didn't even raise an eyebrow.

"Oh," she repeated, setting a hand over her belly. For a few moments he said nothing at all.

He spoke when she was feeling the height of her stupidity. "The East India Company laid claim to Calcutta more than two centuries ago. You cannot imagine what I have seen. Ten years ago, there was an uprising in the north. You probably have not heard of it."

He said that without blinking. And he was right. She hadn't. "Go on," she muttered.

"Several of the Indian battalions mutinied. Indian killed Indian." His hands made fists, but his eyes had shifted inward. "My brother was in the army. They called him to help."

Just those few words, but she could see the grim set of his jaw.

He shook his head and looked away. "I knew people," he finally said. He gave himself a shake, a firm, hard shake, and those dark eyes looked up at her.

"Which side did your brother fight on?" she asked slowly.

He made an annoyed noise. "I'm here. You have to ask?"

She shook her head.

"It started because the East India Company issued rifle cartridges to the sepoys that had been greased with animal fat. Pork fat, beef fat; whatever they had to hand. Since part of the training required the soldiers to put the cartridge in their mouth…" His hand clenched.

They had talked about this enough that Emily understood what that would mean. She swallowed.

"The English didn't understand that they were asking for a desecration. They didn't know why everyone became so furious when the news came out." He looked up at her. "They didn't understand why the fighting grew so bad, spreading from province to province. And when they counted the dead, they didn't include our counts. So no, Miss Fairfield. Napoleon is not so bad."

She held her breath. "I take it," Emily finally said, "that you are in favor of home rule for India, if not outright independence."

He looked so calm, not one muscle in his body twitching. And yet there was that sadness in his eyes. She wanted to wipe it away.

"No. Were you not listening to what I said before? I do not dare favor such a thing."

She swallowed.

"My family is well-to-do," he said. "It is complicated to explain if you don't know the system. My eldest brother was an officer in the Indian forces. My second brother is a magistrate. My father is in the civil service, a position of responsibility directly under the commissioner of railways. I am here precisely because my family accepts British rule. How could I talk of rebellion? What would happen to them?"

She shook her head wordlessly.

"Even if they were not, my brother told me about the Sepoy Mutiny. How it started. How it ended. Indian fighting Indian for the British. What do we have to gain?" There was a bitterness in his voice. "So no, I do not dream of home rule. I dream of the things I can achieve, not the ones that are outside my grasp."

"But—"

"If I dreamed of home rule, I could accomplish nothing." His breath came faster. "I'd be too radical to stomach, and in the end it would all come out to the same thing. Violence all over again, and to what point?"

She tried to imagine not being able to even dream of freedom.

He turned away from her. "So don't talk to me about Napoleon. You cannot possibly understand what he is like."

For all that Emily had only ventured a few miles from her uncle's house, she felt her horizons crumbling, as if she'd been pulled inside out. God, how blind she had been.

"This is not a subject for polite conversation." His tone had evened out. "You have my apologies."

That fierceness had left his eyes. He smiled evenly, as if nothing had happened. It was wrong, all wrong. A mask of pleasantry.

"No," she said passionately. "No. *Never* apologize for that. Never. I don't know what you dare to do anywhere else in the world, but with me…" She wasn't even sure why she was so upset. "This is my escape," she finally said. "The one thing I do that makes the rest of the day worthwhile. It should be yours, too."

For a long moment, he didn't say anything. He just looked at her, his emotions hidden behind a mask. "I should tell you that you shouldn't defy your uncle," he finally said.

"If there were no civil service, no danger of violence… Tell me, Mr. Bhattacharya, what flag would you hoist?"

He inhaled. "I don't think it's a good idea to think about that. I think you are trying to change the subject."

"*I* think," Emily said, "something quite different. Did you really believe me when I said my family was that unconventional? To allow us to wander about for days on end without so much as an introduction?"

"I…" His lips twitched. "Well…"

"You knew. You might not have wanted to know, but you *knew*. If you don't think I ought to be sneaking out, why are you here?"

For a long moment, he didn't say anything. Then, ever so slowly, he reached out and took her hand. Not to guide it to his arm or to steady her over rough footing. He took her hand and caressed it with his thumb, until her fingers unfurled in his. And then—still looking in her eyes—he bowed and kissed her palm.

And that was when Emily realized that without intending it, she'd swum into deep waters.

Chapter Eleven

TEMPTATION, OLIVER TOLD HIMSELF, was best conquered by avoidance. If one didn't want to indulge in too many sweets, it was best not to buy them. If one didn't want to partake of alcohol, one ought not visit a pub. And if one wanted to keep from humiliating a lady…

Well, Oliver figured it was best to keep his distance. He'd managed the trick for three days, and he hoped that tonight's dinner would prove no different.

Her gowns didn't improve. There had been the blue and gold affair, perfectly acceptable in coloration, but printed in a pattern that shimmered and pulsed, seeming to grow and shrink before his eyes until Oliver had to look away. There was the Red Gown of Hellfire—as Whitting had called it—moiré silk that did, in fact, call to mind flame.

And then there was the gown she wore tonight.

Miss Fairfield had a gift for taking a beautiful concept and then marring it beyond all recognition. Oliver had seen lovely gowns made of gauze over satin. White gauze and blue satin made for an ethereal combination. Red gauze and white satin glittered pinkly in lamplight. Even black satin—and the satin of her gown was a deep black—topped by gold would have been lovely. If only she had stopped with the gold gauze. Of course she hadn't. Blue, red, white, green, purple—all those layers made up her flaring skirt of gauzes, running together in garish, impossible colors.

Impossible was the right word. Because she'd attracted the same gawking derision that she always drew. Like everyone else, Oliver could not look away. But unlike everyone else, he suspected he had an entirely different reason.

He liked her. More than liked her, if he were honest. If he let himself, his mind would stray idly to the pins in her hair, little enameled flowers in every garish color of the rainbow dangling from gold chains. He'd find himself thinking idly about taking them out, of sliding his hands through the soft silk of her hair, of stealing that kiss he'd almost taken.

Temptation, he reminded himself, was best conquered by avoidance.

She raised her head and caught him looking. And then—before he could turn away from her—she smiled and gave him a wink. He felt it all the way down his spine. His groin contracted in answer.

He should have known that wouldn't be the end of it.

She found him a few hours later. "Mr. Cromwell," she said, a glint of humor in her eyes.

"Miss Fairchild," he heard himself reply, but even that hint of playfulness was too much. She smiled. He'd joked once that he feared her gown might be contagious, but it was her smile that was catching.

It caught him now. He felt hooked by it, no desire to do anything except smile back at her.

"Miss Fairfield," he said in a low voice, "I had thought us in agreement. We aren't doing this. It's impossible."

"Agreement?" she whispered back. "*You* said. I held my tongue. That is not agreement."

He hadn't stopped smiling.

"Then I shall remedy that immediately. Jane, we mustn't do this. We mustn't be…friends."

Friends. That hadn't been *friendship* that had made him touch her cheek the last time they'd been alone together. Worse than that. He was a little susceptible to her, to be sure, but he knew the way she looked at him. The way she smiled when she saw him. She was vulnerable, and he could remember her saying, *I am too desperate to be angry.*

"Something has changed." She lifted her chin and looked him in the eyes. "Everything has changed." She moved her head as she spoke, and the lamplight sparkled off the multihued flowers in her hair.

"Oh?" he heard himself say.

She smiled, a fierce, hot smile. One that seemed to set something burning deep inside him in response. She leaned in. "If you think that I'm going to let Bradenton win, you're vastly mistaken."

"I have no intention of letting him *win*," Oliver said stiffly. "But—"

"Do you think you're squabbling with him over me?" She smiled more brightly. "Oh, no, Mr. Marshall. You're wrong. *I'm* squabbling with *him* over *you.*"

He swallowed.

"You think me dry tinder," Jane said, "vulnerable to the slightest spark. You're afraid to send me up in flames because you think that once I am burnt out, there will be nothing left but desolation."

She looked up at him as if daring him to contradict her. He couldn't. He'd thought something very much like that just a moment ago. But the look on her face was brighter than any he'd ever seen, and he felt something coil in him in anticipation.

"I have something to tell you," she whispered, and he leaned in to hear her secret. "I am not a blight. I am not a pestilence. And I refuse to be a piece sacrificed for the greater glory of your game."

She wasn't touching him. So why did it seem as if she was? He could almost feel the phantom pressure of her hand against his chest, the heat of her breath on his lips. He could almost taste the scent of her, that light twist of lavender. He felt as if she'd shoved him off-center, and he couldn't quite find his balance.

"You are not any of those things," he said. "What are you, then?"

"I am ablaze," she told him. And then she smiled and gave him a curtsy. She swirled on her heel, leaving him staring after her.

Her words shouldn't have made any sense, but as she turned, the many-colored gauzes of her overskirts fluttered behind her in the lamplight. It put him in mind of a prism, grabbing hold of the light and splitting it into all the colors of the rainbow. She was…ablaze.

He watched her go, and all his worries and second thoughts about temptation went up in flame. With that, he wasn't just giving into temptation; he was inviting it over for tea.

Yes, some deep part of him thought. *That's done it.*

What it was that had been done, he didn't know. He could make no sense of it, so he watched her for the rest of the evening, trying to figure out what had just transpired. Or maybe… Maybe he just watched her.

He watched her laugh in the corner with the Johnson twins. He watched her talking to the other men, who seemed not to have noticed her transformation to phoenix. He even watched her talking to Bradenton, smiling while the man ground his teeth.

The marquess looked up from her and saw Oliver from across the room. The expression in his eyes spoke with a cold, whispering intent.

Oliver gave him no response.

Bradenton found him a few moments later. "In nine days," he said. "I'm having guests over. Canterly, Ellisford, Carleton—you recognize the names, I take it. My friends in Parliament will be here. I'll be introducing Hapford to them."

Bradenton looked across the room to the place where Jane stood. Oliver could hear her laugh all the way over here.

"Maybe once I wanted you to prove something about yourself." His gaze hardened. "Maybe I still do. But mostly, I just want to see her pulled down." He shook his head, turning back to Oliver. "Do it, Marshall. If you do it before everyone leaves, I'll bring them around."

Oliver's future. This vote. Everything he'd ever dreamed off, offered up to him so easily, yet at such a price.

Weighed against that was the image of Jane. Of her bright, brilliant smile. God, he felt sick.

I am ablaze.

Fire washed away sickness. Oliver didn't smile. He didn't look Bradenton in the eye. He simply shrugged. "Nine days, then. If that's what I have."

⌘ ⌘ ⌘

THE NEXT MORNING CAME on a wash of gray clouds. Oliver awoke with the memory of the previous night in his head—like a dream, gauzy and insubstantial, the sort of thing that could not really have happened.

He sat up. He was in a spare room in his cousin's house. He waited for his head to clear. And instead of dissipating into impossible nothingness, as dreams were wont to do, his recollection solidified, memory after memory coming atop each other. Jane's smile. Her gown. The look on her face as she'd smiled and said, *I am ablaze.*

God. What was he going to do?

A knock sounded on his door. "Are you ready?"

It was his cousin. Yesterday, he'd foolishly agreed to accompany Sebastian on his morning ramble. Oliver rubbed his eyes, looked out the window. It was early yet, dawn still combing gray fingers of mist through the fields. From the back window, he could see fog stretching over the River Cam and the fields beyond.

"Hurry up, Oliver," Sebastian called.

"It's not fair," Oliver responded. "Why is my cousin the only rake I know who *likes* getting up in the morning?"

The only sound that came in response was Sebastian's laughter.

It took half an hour to get dressed and leave. The mist was beginning to burn off in the early sunlight, and a bird called somewhere. But for the first few minutes of the walk, it was too cold to do anything but tread briskly, rubbing gloved hands together, until the exercise brought its own warmth. They crossed the Cam, went up the backs of the colleges, and wandered out into the fields before Sebastian spoke.

"Are you going to finally tell me what you're up to?"

"Here? I told you already. Bradenton—"

"Hang Bradenton," Sebastian said. "I never liked him anyway. That's not what I mean."

Oliver quirked up his mouth, perplexed. "I don't know what you're talking about."

"I don't mean your Miss Fairfield, either." Sebastian sighed. "I'm talking about something far more important. *The* most important thing, if you will, the center of the universe, Copernicus be damned." He smiled broadly. "I'm talking about me."

Oliver glanced at Sebastian. His parents had told him about his sire when he was young. They'd described his half-brother, living in a grand house with a less-than useful father. Oliver had known all about Robert.

He hadn't known about his cousin Sebastian until he was twelve years old.

The Duke of Clermont's elder sister had married an industrialist in a desperate—and as far as Oliver could tell, futile—attempt to fill the Clermont family coffers. Sebastian Malheur was the result of that marriage. He was dark-haired and handsome, and he smiled at everyone. He had always been up to mischief when they'd been in school together. And somehow, that had never changed.

This sort of charming boast was precisely the sort of thing that Sebastian did best. Oliver was never sure what his cousin believed because he was so rarely serious.

Sebastian was smiling. "You keep asking me open-ended questions such as, 'How are you?' and 'Are you really delighted to hear…' All this stuff about my *feelings*. I thought I would give you the opportunity to be direct. You act like I'm going to die. Why are you doing that?"

Some things never changed, but…

Oliver sighed. "It's your letters. Since I was heading down here anyway, Robert asked me to see how you were doing."

"My letters." Sebastian looked around as if expecting some Greek chorus to pop up and serenade him in explanation. "What have I been doing wrong in my letters?"

"I don't know." Oliver shrugged. "But Robert says there is something wrong with them. That you're not yourself. And you know how he is. He's always right about those things. He'll never figure out what's wrong on his own, or how to fix it—but he knows when something is off. And he says that you don't sound happy."

Sebastian beamed beatifically. It seemed like a ridiculous charge to make with the early morning sun touching his cousin's face.

"Not happy?" Sebastian said. "Why *wouldn't* I be happy? I've achieved the sort of success that most men only dream of. I have set all of England—indeed, the entire world—on its ear. I've wrought mischief of the highest order, and the lovely thing is that I am demonstrably, provably right. So tell me, Oliver, under those circumstances, why wouldn't I be happy?"

Oliver glanced at his cousin and then shrugged. "I don't know," he said. "But in all that lovely, long speech just now, the one thing you never said was that you were happy."

Sebastian looked at him, and then gave a wry shake of his head. "Minnie," he said, as if that were an explanation. "Robert married her, and now the two of you are parsing language for all the meaning you can shake out of it. It's a good thing she's not here, because if she were, she'd see what *wasn't* happening. You're an amateur."

"What isn't happening?" Oliver asked.

Sebastian ignored him. "Let us suppose for the sake of argument that you are correct. I am deeply wounded and unhappy to my toes, but I don't want to explain why." He smiled as he spoke, as if to show how ridiculous the notion was. "Wouldn't we all be better off assuming that I had reasons for that choice and respecting them?"

"Maybe," said Oliver slowly. "But... I feel as if you aren't really yourself lately. There's something different about you."

"Again, assuming that you are right," Sebastian said, "you won't make me feel any better by telling me how miserable I appear to be."

"Very well, then," Oliver said. "Have it your way. This is just like old times." They walked on down the path, past a yard where a farmer's daughter was feeding geese, past a man carrying water in yokes about his neck.

"What did you mean back then," Oliver said finally, "about what wasn't happening?"

"So many things aren't happening," Sebastian said airily. "I'm not flying. You aren't turning to gold when I touch you. I have yet to strike a deal with the devil."

"If you want to tell me something, you should come out and say it."

"Here's the thing." Sebastian looked serious. "If I *had* signed a Faustian contract in blood, so to speak, it probably would have a clause that enjoined me from speaking. So let me just say this. Being me...is not as amusing as it once was."

Oliver could believe that. Fame had come quickly to Sebastian. It was not so long in the past he'd been just another indulgently wealthy man, born of good family with no reason to exert himself. He'd done what indulgently wealthy men of good family so often did—he'd sampled the ladies of town and developed a bit of a name for himself as a hedonist.

Yes, he was clever. And he had always been riotously funny. But if someone had asked Oliver a decade ago what Sebastian would do with his life, he would never—not in a million years—have guessed that his friend would achieve fame in the natural sciences.

And then quite out of the blue, Sebastian had published a paper on snapdragons, of all things. It had been well received; he'd put out another paper six months later on peas, and then another a few months later regarding lettuce.

A mere three months after the bit on lettuce, Sebastian had announced that what he had discovered was not a few oddities to be noted about the breeding of flowers and vegetables but a system—a system demonstrating that traits were passed down from progenitor to child in a systematic fashion, one that could be predicted mathematically.

This, Sebastian had said, served as a measuring stick. One could use it to determine what random chance would unleash on offspring—and one could therefore see how nature deviated from random chance. If it differed significantly, Sebastian had argued, in response to changing conditions, it would prove Mr. Darwin right.

He could not have published a more inflammatory piece. That paper had contained four examples demonstrating how nature had deviated from random chance. And that was the moment when Sebastian Malheur had stopped being seen as a mildly eccentric scientist with hedonistic tendencies. He'd become a heretic and a heathen.

"I worry about you," Oliver finally said. "I worry about you a great deal, Sebastian."

"Well, worry more productively." Sebastian spoke decisively. "I don't need any of your pity. In fact—"

"Ah, indeed!" called a voice behind them. "Mr. Malheur? Is that you, Mr. Malheur? Hallooo!"

Sebastian turned and saw a man shuffling toward them at something half between a walk and a jog. He waved an arm at Sebastian in greeting.

"Who is that?" Sebastian squinted and swore under his breath. "Whoever he is, I don't want to speak to him. Hide me, Oliver."

Oliver looked around. There was nothing but the path they walked on, marking its way alongside the river and ankle-high grasses. The landscape was punctuated by a few scrubby bushes, but was empty of anything that could serve as cover. "He's already seen you. You can't hide."

"Pretend I've turned into a tree?" Sebastian shrugged. "I would do a very good job pretending. I promise."

The other man was practically on top of them. He tripped down the last section of the path, breathing hard.

"Mr. Malheur!" he said. "I've been looking for you ever since last we spoke. I've sent you messages—did you not receive them?"

"I receive a great many messages." Sebastian frowned at the man. "Who are you again?"

"Fairfield," the man said. "Mr. Titus Fairfield."

Oliver blinked and examined the man once again. Fairfield. It was a common enough name. It could have been a coincidence. On the other hand…

Mr. Fairfield reached up to wipe his handkerchief across his sweating brow. "Of course I don't expect you to remember me. Of course not. I am a gentleman who resides here in Cambridge." He smiled—a weak smile that looked as if it were out of practice. "A gentleman, yes. No need to work, although from time to time I take on a promising student as tutor." He nodded at them both.

A private tutor taking on only one student, instead of a team? He couldn't have been much good.

Sebastian must have thought so, too, because he gave a little half-sigh.

"I make it a point to keep my time open, so that I might live the life of the mind. Like you." Mr. Fairfield drew himself up a little uncertainly. "A little like you."

Sebastian caught Oliver's eye, and twitched his lip.

"Your work," Mr. Fairfield said after an awkward silence, "your work— it has absolutely confused me and left me in wonder. I have thought of nothing else, since last I saw your talk. The implications, Mr. Malheur, the implications! For politics, for government, for economy."

Sebastian simply looked at Mr. Fairfield. "I didn't realize that my work on snapdragons had an implication for politics and economy."

"I have not quite grasped it," he said. "You are my superior in knowledge here. But doesn't it follow that if there is some inherited basis for evolution we might as a species triumph? Ought you not put your mind to that?"

Sebastian's answering smile was sharp as a knife. "What, with a managed breeding program amongst humans?"

Fairfield blinked.

"That's what I would have to do. Breeding humans is far more difficult than propagating snapdragons. As a general rule, humans prefer to breed themselves without outside direction. I myself have that preference. I'd hate to impose it on others."

Fairfield frowned. "You could pay…"

"*You're* the tutor in law. Is it now legal to pay people for intercourse?"

"Ah. A good point. I see. That does make things difficult." Fairfield frowned. "This needs more thought, more thought indeed. Perhaps we might meet to discuss it?"

"No," Sebastian said with a brilliant smile. "We won't. That sounds hideous and disgusting."

"But—"

"No *buts,*" Sebastian said. "Now if you'll excuse me, my cousin and I must turn off the path here."

There was no path leading absolutely anywhere. Sebastian pointed vaguely across the fields.

"Good day," Sebastian said, waving. "I'd love to stay and chat, but I must abscond instead."

"Wait," Oliver started. But his cousin took hold of his wrist and plunged into the grass. The field was still dew-soaked. In a matter of seconds, Oliver's stockings were damp. Sebastian smiled the whole time, a brilliant, awful smile. But he pressed on at a punishing pace, not letting go of Oliver's wrist until they'd gone half a mile.

"There you have it," Sebastian said. "One of my supporters. Now tell me, Oliver, why shouldn't I be happy?"

Chapter Twelve

IT WAS AN UNSEASONABLY BRIGHT, warm day, a few days after Jane had so brazenly informed Mr. Marshall that she was battling with Bradenton over him. In those intervening days, she'd wondered what she had been thinking. How she'd dared to say anything so audacious.

But when she saw Mr. Marshall again, she didn't wonder.

It was high noon. She'd been walking on Jesus Green with the Johnson sisters, pretending to watch a cricket game that was being lost very, very badly, enjoying the warmth of real friendship. She saw him first, walking slowly along the other side of the green, gesturing as he talked. He was talking to a boy in a black gown.

She had never seen Marshall walk before. Oh, she'd watched him amble about a room. But out on a lawn, he had a long stride and an easy grace to him. The wind caught a hint of his hair under his hat, ruffling his fringe.

And Jane knew why she'd said what she had to him. Because she wasn't ceding this man, this man who'd told her to keep talking, who'd told her she was brave, to anyone.

It was a shockingly fierce, possessive thought. It came anyway.

Mine.

He'd touched her, and she'd liked it.

Mine.

"Jane?"

She whirled around, startled, to see Genevieve and Geraldine smiling at her.

"Tell me," Geraldine said, "what *were* you thinking of just there?"

Jane shook her head. "Nothing."

"Even Geraldine isn't that bad," Genevieve sang out, "and that's her fiancé over there. Does *nothing* have auburn hair and spectacles?"

Jane flushed. She hadn't even realized it was Hapford with Mr. Marshall.

Geraldine leaned in. "Is *nothing* walking next to Hapford?"

"No," Genevieve put in. "I think that *nothing* is approaching. Come on, Jane. Wave at him."

Jane held up one gloved hand. Even separated by fifty yards of close-clipped lawn, with half a cricket-match between them, she felt a hot flush.

He raised his hand as well. And then he walked toward her.

I am ablaze, she thought, but she was truly on fire, burning hotter with every step he took in her direction.

"Mr. Marshall," she said, as soon as he was near enough. "My lord."

"Miss Fairfield. Miss Johnson. Miss Genevieve." His words were proper enough, but his gaze lingered on Jane alone.

Beside her, Hapford made a similar greeting. Geraldine came forward to take his arm, and Genevieve went with her. That left Jane with Mr. Marshall. They weren't alone, but they had a little privacy.

"Do you like my walking gown?"

His gaze swept up to her bosom, then down to her toes, as palpable as a caress.

"Tell the truth," she said, gesturing ahead of her. "They can't hear." Indeed, the Johnsons had obligingly taken Hapford five or six paces ahead.

"It's an improvement on *screeching horror,*" he told her. "It ranks almost as high as *sick fascination.*" He gave a mock shiver. "But really. Are those vermilion bananas printed on the fabric?"

"Yes. I love it. Look." Jane held out her pendant, a green enameled monkey with fierce topaz eyes. "See? Isn't that wonderful?"

He stepped forward and looked obligingly.

Maybe not so obligingly. She was close enough to see his eyes behind his spectacles, dropping not to her pendant but...

Technically, her gown climbed halfway up to her neck. Also technically, the upper fabric of her bodice was dark lace. And lace had holes.

Nothing showed that wouldn't have shown in a ball gown, but it still *showed.* If someone stood close, pretending to look at a necklace...

He lifted his gaze to her face and gave her an unapologetic smile.

"You're right. That quite makes the outfit." He crooked his finger. "Let me see it again."

Jane flushed, and in front of her, Geraldine coughed.

"Oh, Geraldine," Genevieve said loudly, "I hope you're not coming down with something."

"Nonsense," said Hapford. "That didn't—"

But Geraldine interrupted him. "I'm afraid I might be. We'd better go. Hapford, you'll walk me?"

"But..."

She linked her arm with her fiancé's. "Come along," she said.

"But... Oh."

"Unless," Geraldine said, "you wish us to stay, Miss Fairfield?"

"Um." Jane flushed hotter. "No. That would be unnecessary."

Genevieve waved at her, and the three of them walked away. Jane watched them go, the entire time feeling Mr. Marshall's eyes on her…necklace. She turned back to him and he raised his eyes to her face.

"You have a smudge on your spectacles."

"I do?"

"Yes." She lifted her hand and placed it deliberately against the glass. "A fingerprint right there."

He gave her a look of mock annoyance and took off his glasses to clean them with a handkerchief.

"That's what you get for ogling my monkey. Now imagine what I'll do if you take Bradenton up on his offer."

That smile that had curled the corners of his lips faltered. His breath sucked in. "Jane."

"What vote is it?" she asked. "The one that's so important."

But he didn't answer right away. Instead, he held out his elbow to her. "Walk with me." They passed by the cricket game.

"You know," he finally said, "that I'm a duke's byblow."

"Yes."

"Legally, I am not any kind of bastard. My mother was married when I was born and I was acknowledged by her husband. Up until a few years ago, I wasn't even publicly recognized as the duke's progeny. Some people knew, of course, but it was at best whispered about, never spoken aloud."

Legally, Jane wasn't a bastard, either. But she still was treated like one.

"Sometimes," he said, "I forget that people think I'm Clermont's son. They don't believe that Hugo Marshall is my father. It's odd, because he's never been anything else to me. Just…father. He never acted as if my sisters who were his flesh and blood were more important than I was. I didn't realize how extraordinary this was for most of my childhood. It just was."

Oh, she felt a twinge of jealousy at that, one that twined around her heart at the thought of having a real family.

"What was it like?" she asked, her voice low.

"He taught me how to fish, how to set a snare for a rabbit, how to fight politely at fisticuffs, and how to win a fight very impolitely using dirty tricks. If necessary." Mr. Marshall took a deep breath. "He taught me how to balance books and how to fold a piece of paper into a box. He showed me how to whistle on a blade of grass. My father taught me everything. And so I call him father because that's what he was. In every sense of the word except that one tiny thing."

"So you were a part of the family, then?"

"Oh, yes. I grew up with them. They ran a small farm. And that's what brings me to all of this. My parents have never been wealthy. They have always had enough. My mother and father are both clever. Twice a year, they lease out factories for a week, just long enough to distill oils and make soaps. Not great big bars of soaps, produced for the masses, but scented, molded soaps. My mother packages them for ladies and charges twenty times their worth." He smiled and glanced at her. "You use it, I think. *Lady Serena's Secret.*"

She did. The boxes appealed to her in their colorful range of pastels. The bars of soap had come wrapped in tissue, accompanied by a slip of paper explaining the scent. There were different scents for every month of the year, altering with the seasons. She paid five times more for those small, sweet-smelling bars than she might otherwise have laid out, but unwrapping them gave her pleasure so she'd accounted it money well spent.

"My parents do well for themselves," Mr. Marshall continued. "But I have three sisters. Two of them have recently married, and they've laid out funds to establish them in their new lives. There was my own schooling at Cambridge. And while the current Duke of Clermont—my brother—settled money on me when I came of age, they've refused to take anything from him on principle."

"Are you telling me your family is poor?" she said.

"No, not at all." He swallowed and looked away. "Although…yes, I suppose you would think so. I am telling you that my father is a tenant at will in a county constituency. He pays an annual rent of forty pounds a year."

She shook her head, not seeing the relevance.

"I worshipped my father. I used to think he could do anything," he told her. "That's the way of it, when a man teaches you everything. And then, when I was sixteen, I learned otherwise."

She squeezed his arm. "Everyone is fallible. Even the best of men."

"No. I didn't mean that I discovered he had flaws. I meant what I said. There is one thing my father is not allowed to do."

She waited for his answer.

"He cannot vote."

She looked up in surprise, her eyes widening. "That's…that's…"

"Imagine," he said, his voice tight, "that there was someone who owed you nothing and gave you everything. A family. A place in the world. Love. Imagine that the entire world around you said that he was worth nothing. What would you do for him?"

"For her," Jane whispered involuntarily. She took her hand off his sleeve and hugged her arms around herself. "When you have almost nobody… For her, I'd do anything." She was silent for a moment longer. "That's what Bradenton promised you? A vote on the Reform Bill?"

He nodded. "More than that. Not just the vote, but the credit for changing his mind. He's the leader of a group nine strong. He's grooming Hapford to join them. If I can bring the entire group in, it will prove my worth. It will be the first step forward." He looked away. "Miss Fairfield, I won't apologize to you for the choice I must make. Bradenton and his set will all be in town in a matter of days—all nine of them. I don't know." He made a frustrated sound. "That is—I think I would be better off leaving. Now." He spread his hands. "Parliament will sit in a few weeks anyway. It is time to get on."

Mine.

Maybe it was rash on her part. Maybe it was injudicious. But then, Bradenton had broken her cactus and she wanted him to pay.

"Tell me, Mr. Marshall," she said. "How would you get on with your first step forward if you brought back eight votes instead of nine?"

"I've been trying precisely that. You just saw me talking to Hapford." He stopped and looked at her. "But the rest of them...the bonds of friendship count for much, and if Bradenton speaks ill of me..." He shrugged.

"That's the thing," Jane said. "I've never met them, but Bradenton doesn't even have a solid hold on Hapford. He cannot truly control the other men. And if you could do something to put a little pressure on those bonds of friendship..."

He just looked at her.

"They're going to be here," she said. "It's the perfect opportunity. You only need a little something. Enough to get them to listen to *you* rather than him. You'll have the votes you want, minus one. You'll get the credit." Her voice dropped. "And Bradenton, well... I think that would really annoy him."

He blinked. "My God." A slow smile spread across his face. "But how would it be done?"

"Oh, Mr. Marshall," Jane said, long and slow. "I have been thinking of nothing else."

⌘ ⌘ ⌘

AFTER HER LAST CONVERSATION with Mr. Bhattacharya, Emily had felt unsettled. She'd watched Titus more carefully, trying to be...well, not *obedient,* but at least more respectful.

It had made absolutely no difference to his behavior, but she'd found that the less she raged at her uncle, the more she could bear.

Now, standing on the side of the brook and waiting for Mr. Bhattacharya to arrive, she felt nervous all over again. What if he decided that he didn't want to see her? What if he decided that her uncle's approval was paramount? Her heart raced with every little noise, imagining it to be his footfalls. The palms of her hands tingled, as if her skin remembered his.

And then she saw him and she felt herself burst into a smile as he drew near. He was always an excellent dresser. Far too many Cambridge students were quite slovenly—that was what came of wearing robes over their clothing, she supposed; they stopped caring about what they believed few others could see. Mr. Bhattacharya was always neat and clean, his clothing evenly pressed, his hat situated firmly on his head.

"Mr. Bhattacharya," she said, as he came nearer.

He came to a halt a few feet away and regarded her quizzically with his dark eyes. "Is that the way you're planning to greet me?"

She flushed at that. "Did you have something else in mind?"

He was surely talking about a kiss. Not on the lips—the idea of that made her whole body flutter with nervous anticipation. Lovely, sweet, anticipation, a yearning that filled her with sudden force.

"You don't remember my given name, do you?" He spoke a little ruefully.

Oh. He was talking about *that* kind of greeting. Emily blinked, dispelling the force of her want.

"Of course I do. It's Anjan."

He broke into a smile to match hers.

The meeting *after* you held a gentleman's hand was, Emily decided, more awkward than the one before. Was she supposed to snatch his hand straight off, like some prize already won, or did she need to work up to it?

He took another step forward.

"Pretty Emily," he said. "Clever Emily. Sweet Emily." He reached out, then, but he didn't take her hand. He brushed one of her curls, fingering her hair ever so softly.

"I think," Emily said shakily, "that you are the best dream I have ever had."

He raised an eyebrow in question.

"My guardian thinks I'm taking a nap," she explained. "I know. I shouldn't have lied to you. I'm…trying to do better."

He didn't let go of her hair, but she could see his face tensing, his jaw shifting ever so slightly, his nostrils flaring.

"I see," he said.

"You probably don't. Pretty Emily. Clever Emily. Lying Emily. Almost my entire life is a falsehood."

He looked into her eyes. "Mine is, too. I'm Indian. I'm the good-natured one, the one who doesn't hear half of what is said in front of him. The one who doesn't complain no matter what. I suppose I should not be surprised that you're lying to your guardian after all. There are very few parents in England who would allow me to court their daughter, no matter what my prospects might be."

Emily swallowed. "Court?" she said. Court was a word with hard edges, a word she didn't quite understand. *Flirt* she might have understood. *Bedazzle.* She would have said that he was enjoying her company. But... He was going out this year. And her guardian didn't even know what was happening.

"Aren't you going back to India after you receive your degree?" she asked.

He contemplated her. "No."

"You'll...surely be marrying an Indian woman. I had..."

"It's not likely," he said again. "I have a friend here by the name of Lirington. His father has offered me a position when I graduate. I'm staying."

"Here," she said blankly. "Here with the boiled spinach and bread. Here with all of us Napoleons. You're staying *here?* I know how much you miss your family. Why?"

He didn't say anything for a very long time. Finally, he let out a long breath and turned away. "My eldest brother," he said. "We were quite close even though I was ten years younger. I worshipped him, followed him everywhere. He told me all about his plans. He had always intended to go to England, he said. In India, they never saw him as anything other than another soldier, another fellow with brown skin. 'There are so many of us here,' he said, 'they never see us as people.' He told me that if things were going to change, he would have to go to the English in their home country. He'd planned to move here when he was twenty-five, to set up a business. To live here the rest of his life. To know them, and have them know him."

He'd started speaking quietly; by the time he reached the end of his sentence, he had returned to normal volume.

He swallowed and looked away.

"Without that," he said softly, "he feared that more lives would be lost by idiocy. The Sepoy Mutiny... That was started by criminal thoughtlessness. I don't think it was ill intentioned, but it was foolish. If the English had listened, they would have understood what it meant. To them, it was just grease. Pig lard and beef fat are just parts of an animal. They didn't understand that they were asking the Indian soldiers to go against their holy beliefs. That was the sort of thing Sonjit would tell me—that he could save

lives and stop this stupidity, if only he could make the English understand."
Anjan swallowed. "As I said, I worshipped him."

Emily only watched.

"During the Sepoy Mutiny, he took a knife to the gut. It wasn't even
during a battle; someone just ran up to him on the street, yelling. By the time
he was brought home, it was too late to do anything except watch him die.
When I saw him, he said, 'Well, it looks as if I won't be going to England.'"
Anjan's voice was tight. "So I promised him I would do it."

She reached out and touched his hand. "I'm so sorry for your loss."

He shook his head as if throwing off old memories. "I told my parents
what he had said, told them I wanted to go in his memory. We...talked. I'd
had a marriage arranged, but the girl died young, and they hadn't arranged
another yet. I told them they shouldn't. That I'd be more accepted if I..."

He paused.

"If you what?"

"If I was unmarried," he said, without blinking. "Or if I found a wife in
England instead of bringing one with me. It was not a happy conversation.
My parents argued over it for years, but they eventually gave in. Even so, I
suspect my mother still hopes to surprise me with a nice Bengali girl."

Emily stared at him. "You had a marriage arranged before you were
ten?"

"It's not what you think. My parents love me. They wouldn't want me to
be unhappy. They would have picked someone I would grow to love,
someone with a temperament like mine. They did quite well for my
brothers."

He looked away again, and then slowly took off his hat. He turned it in
his hands.

"The post is slow between here and India," he finally said. "But I wrote
and asked for their approval."

Emily swallowed. She couldn't imagine the enormity of what he was
talking about. She'd been enjoying his company. Enjoying it very much, as it
was. But this...

"Our children would have to spend time in Calcutta," he told his hat.
"She would insist on having a chance to spoil them. My mother, I mean."

"Anjan," Emily heard herself say. "Are you asking me to marry you?
Because..."

"No, of course not," he replied. "It's too soon for that. We haven't
known one another very long, which I hear is important for you English.
And I have not heard from my parents, which is important to me. I'm just
telling you a story, that's all."

A *story*. A story. She swallowed, trying to envision the story that would follow. It wouldn't be an easy life, that much she knew. He rarely talked about how he was treated, but she hadn't received the impression that many people were kind. Quite the reverse. And that would be what she entered into? That would be what her children would experience? She felt too young for children, let alone for a decision of this magnitude. She wrapped her arms around her waist.

"Here's another story," she said quietly. "I'm not of age. My uncle hasn't even let me come out because of my fits. He would never let me marry." *Least of all you,* she thought, but she didn't want to have those ugly words said. "No matter what happened, I would have to wait until I turned twenty-one. And that's a year and a half away."

"Would you?" he asked. "Would you consider the wait, if we were in a story?"

But as much as she'd pretended this was an escape, this wasn't a story.

"Every day we meet, I tell myself I shouldn't come," Emily said. "I'm afraid my uncle will find out, that he'll start thinking of me as he thinks of Jane—well, never mind that." She shut her eyes. "How can I consider the rest of my life when I can scarcely contemplate tomorrow?"

He drew back. "I'm sorry."

"Don't be sorry. It was a story. A story and a rhetorical question." She looked at him and felt a wash of sadness. "The strange thing is, I think that if our parents had arranged our marriage, I would be happy with the prospect. Isn't that daft? It's only because I have a choice that I'm fretting."

He took a step toward her. "You'd have a choice," he said softly. "Your mother would love you. After we met, she'd come to you alone. 'How did I do?' she'd ask. 'Do you like him?' A parent offering her beloved child a precious gift and hoping that it finds favor."

Emily thought of her father—the one who hadn't even visited every year. She thought of the mother she didn't even remember, one who had brushed off her inconvenient children, seeing them only as an audience to listen to her complaints about the country life her husband had forced on her. She thought about Titus's sad little pout when she and Jane had driven off that horrid Doctor Fallon with his foul-smelling jars.

"No," she said, trying not to choke on the words. "That isn't what would happen. He'd say, 'nineteen-year-old girls are given guardians because they cannot choose for themselves.'"

Anjan didn't speak for a moment. Then he lifted his hand and slowly, ever so slowly, touched her cheek.

"This part isn't a story," he said. "This part is just the truth. If he won't hold you precious, then I will."

It was just his hand. It was just her cheek. Her eyes stung. She didn't move away, didn't try to hold back the liquid that burned her vision. She couldn't say anything in response, and so she just stayed with him—long enough that a cloud slid lazily across the sky, casting them in shade, and then passed on, putting them in sunlight once more.

"I'll consider your story," Emily finally said huskily. "For all the difficulty I see in it, it would have its rewards."

Chapter Thirteen

THE EVENING OF BRADENTON'S GATHERING came all too quickly. After a few feverish days of planning, Oliver found himself in Bradenton's home once again. This time, though, the house was packed with the marquess's allies in Parliament, and so the rooms were rather too warm. There were more than twenty here tonight—a smattering of lords, Members of Parliament, and accompanying wives.

"Marshall." Bradenton made his way to Oliver through the gathered group, looked about, and leaned in. "I have to say I'm disappointed. Disappointed and surprised." His voice was low, scarcely audible in the din of conversation. "Everyone is here, and yet Miss Fairfield's reign of ridiculousness continues unabated. I had expected better of you."

Too bad Oliver's own expectations had intervened. He smiled faintly. "Oh ye of little faith," he intoned. "You said tonight, and tonight I plan to deliver."

The marquess, who had been shaking his head, paused. "Really?"

They'd gone through the plan inch by painstaking inch. Across the room, Hapford caught Oliver's eye. His fists clenched, and he looked away.

"Let's just say," Oliver said, "she is primed. By the end of the night, Miss Fairfield will know exactly where she belongs."

"How delightful." Bradenton smiled. "I knew you would come around. And yes, here she is." He shrugged. "Knowing what I do, I can even be gracious." He walked forward, a smile on his face. "Miss Fairfield. How lovely to have you here."

Miss Fairfield's response was lost in the noise, but Bradenton bowed and walked away.

Oliver approached her a few minutes later. "Miss Fairfield," he said. "How are you this evening?" He already knew the answer. Her fingers twined together in nervous anticipation; her eyes were alight with possibility. He felt it, too—the thing they might achieve here tonight.

He felt a twinge of something stronger than anticipation looking at her. At the lips he hadn't kissed, the veins in her wrist that he'd not examined with his fingertips. Of the smooth swell of her breasts, no longer occluded even by black lace.

Don't touch.

And so he didn't. He inclined his head to her as if she were a trifling little acquaintance, and then let her go talk to the others. She wasn't his, after all. They were just...

Friends.

Yes, he thought. That. How had they come to be just that?

For once, her heavy gown was almost unobjectionable. Yes, her wrists blazed with sparkling stones, and the brocade at her hem was a little too colorful. But the great excesses had been slightly muted, changing her from utterly impossible to merely overly exuberant.

Bradenton returned to her side with a lemonade. She took it—and then, when he offered his arm—took that too. Oliver watched as the man introduced his set—Canterly, Ellisford, Rockway—one after the other, running through the names so swiftly that nobody would have been able to recall them. Jane, of course, had been coached. She greeted everyone politely by name. She smiled. And—oh, yes—she wasn't perfect. She flubbed Lord James Ward's title—he was Lord James, as his father was a duke, not Lord Ward—but one of the Johnson twins, who flanked her, whispered in her ear and she flushed and apologized prettily.

He could almost see her as one of them. Almost, if he ignored the over-long stares the other women gave her. If he refused to admit that her voice carried over everyone else's.

They sat down to dinner.

She didn't interrupt anyone's conversation or insult anyone's clothing. The twins spoke almost as much as she did.

In the end, it was Lord James who brought up politics.

"So," he said, "I had a visit from the Countess of Branford. She said the women have been talking about the Contagious Diseases Act, of all things."

"Ah, ah," Bradenton said, wagging a finger. "Look about." He inclined his head an inch to the left, indicating the Johnson twins.

The discussion of politics wasn't always allowed in polite company, but in a group like this—men who thought of nothing else for much of the year—it was inevitable. More than half the women present were political wives or sisters and were used to such discussions at the table.

Lord James blinked in surprise. "I'm sorry, my lord," he finally said. "I had thought Miss Johnson—but never mind."

"Oh," Miss Fairfield interrupted, two feet down the table from him, "please don't stop on our account. I do so wish to hear everyone's opinion. Starting with yours, Lord Bradenton."

Bradenton looked up. Oliver could almost see him weighing the matter. He stroked his chin once, then twice.

"Humor Miss Fairfield," Oliver said, with a pointed raise of his eyebrow at Bradenton.

Bradenton smiled broadly after a half-second's hesitation. "Of course," he said. "We all know how I feel—that the Act must go on, however harsh the consequences—and I gather we are in general agreement. But why don't you tell us your opinion on the Contagious Diseases Act, Miss Fairfield? I'm sure you have a great deal to say."

"Why, yes," Miss Fairfield told him. "I do. I believe we should expand the scope of the Contagious Diseases Act. Radically."

Bradenton blinked and glanced at her. The entire table was shocked into silence.

"How radical do you mean?" Lord James asked."

Canterly nodded. "You'd extend it to more cities? Or would you, ah, hold suspects longer? Or—" He stopped, glancing at Jane, at the two sisters who were seated up the table from her.

Bradenton smiled more broadly, perhaps as if he thought he knew Oliver's plan. Lure her into talking about sexual matters. Start a rumor, perhaps. The gossip would run amuck from there. Young virgins simply did not engage in frank conversations about the government's policy of locking up prostitutes. The disgruntled mutters about Miss Fairfield would turn into outrage.

"It's simple," Jane insisted. "I know just how to do it. Instead of just locking up the women who are suspected of being ill, we should lock up *all* the women. That way, the ones who are well can never get sick."

At the foot of the table, Whitting scratched his head. "But…how would men use their services?"

"What do men have to do with it?" Jane asked.

"Um." Lord James looked down. "I take your point, Bradenton. This is…perhaps not the best conversation to be having at the moment."

"After all," Jane continued, "if men were capable of infecting women, our government in its infinite wisdom would never choose to lock up only the women. That would be pointless, since without any constraint on men, the spread of contagion would never stop. It would also be unjust to confine women for the sin of being infected by men." She smiled triumphantly. "And since our very good Marquess of Bradenton supports the Act, that could never be the case. He would never sign on to such manifest injustice."

There was a longer pause at that.

Bradenton had listened to this speech in stony silence, his lips pressing more and more closely together. He glanced over at Oliver, a warning in his glittering eyes.

"Yes, well," he said tersely.

"She has you there." Canterly smothered a smile.

"Do I?" Jane asked innocently. "Because if that's so, then I win this round of our game, Bradenton."

That was met with an even more prickly silence. Bradenton squinted at Jane, leaning forward, as if trying to make her out from a distance.

"Our game?" he repeated.

"Yes," Jane said. "Our game. You know, the one where I play at ignorance and you play at insults."

Bradenton inhaled. "*Play?*"

"It is play, of course," Jane said. "The alternative is that you've been carrying a grudge against me all these months, simply because your fortunes were in a decline and I had suggested that you needed to find another heiress."

Bradenton stood up. "Why, you poxy little—"

Next to him, another man put his hand on Bradenton's sleeve. "Come now, Bradenton." Bradenton looked down and then—very slowly—he sat.

"Good heavens," Jane said, "you're not upset about the *game,* are you? And here I thought it was all in good fun, after all."

"I don't understand," Canterly said.

"There's only one part I regret," Jane said. "Mr. Whitting, a few weeks ago, I implied that you were deficient in understanding. That wasn't well done of me. In my defense, you've said worse of me, but..." She shrugged. "I still ought not have done it."

"A game," Bradenton said, choking on the words. "A *game.* You think this is a game."

"You seem so surprised. Here I thought you *all* gamesters." Jane looked around the table. "After all, Bradenton did offer to sway your votes to the newly proposed Reform Act if only Mr. Marshall would humiliate me. Are you telling me the rest of the table knew nothing of this?"

Silence met this—a long, deep, uncomfortable silence. One that Oliver reveled in.

Across the table from Jane, Mr. Ellisford set down his spoon. "Bradenton," he said seriously, "you know I'm your friend. I've known you far too long. You'd never prevail on our friendship for such petty reasons. I know you wouldn't." But despite the certainty of his words, there was a question in his voice.

"Of course I wouldn't," Bradenton said heartily. "You have only her word for it. She's hardly reliable. Ask anyone here." He looked up at Oliver. "Except Marshall. He's a bastard, and he'd tell any lie to get ahead."

"No," Oliver said quietly.

"No, you're not a bastard? You can't deny your parentage."

"No," Oliver said. "I'm not the only one who will speak on her behalf."

"I saw you threaten her," Genevieve Johnson put in. "Geraldine and I both did. We feared for her safety."

A murmur swelled around the table.

Bradenton's eyes narrowed. "You misunderstood."

Across the table from her, Hapford shut his eyes. "I'm sorry, uncle." He spoke softly.

"What?" Bradenton said.

"I'm sorry," Hapford repeated more loudly. His hands had worked his serviette into a ball. "But I don't think my father would want... I do not think he would want..." He trailed off. "Miss Fairfield is telling the truth. I was there when the marquess made his offer to Mr. Marshall. You offered him precisely what she said—your vote, your help swaying the men here, if only he would show Miss Fairfield her place." He swallowed. "I didn't like it then, and it has not sat well with me since."

The silence grew again, threatening like thunder.

Hapford blew out his breath. "When my father recommended a relationship with you men to me on his deathbed, I did not think he intended to attach me to a group of small-minded power-mongers, intent on hurting women. He recommended you as a group honestly interested in the best interests of England."

"Yes," Ellisford finally said, pointedly turning away from Bradenton. "You have the right of it. That's what I thought we were, too."

"Then maybe we can listen to Mr. Marshall without having him pay so high a price."

⌘ ⌘ ⌘

"YOU'VE CONVINCED ME," Ellisford said to Oliver several hours later. "I'm rather glad we had this talk. I'd never imagined..."

His eyes darted to the left. The gentlemen in the library sat with cigars and glasses of port. Bradenton was the only one who kept his silence. He'd stewed the entire evening: through dinner, through the conversations after the men separated from the ladies. Just as well he'd kept quiet; nobody else seemed inclined to talk to him, even though he was the host.

"I feel the same," Oliver said. "And we'll talk again in London."

"Of course."

Bradenton's silence shouted sullenly, but nobody was paying him any mind.

Oliver had won. Not Bradenton's vote—he'd never get that now—but all the things he'd wanted. The votes of Bradenton's little set. His own integrity. He could afford to be magnanimous—and in this case, magnanimity meant letting the man stew in peace.

"Well," Oliver said, "shall we rejoin the ladies?"

Everyone agreed. But when Oliver stood, Bradenton finally spoke. "Not you, Marshall," he growled. "You and I have business."

"Of course," Oliver said, as congenially as he could. Everyone else trooped out with only a few scant glances behind. Strange; the fire seemed to dim as they left and the shadows of the furniture seemed to grow, now that there was no warm conversation to fill the empty spaces.

"You think you're so clever," Bradenton snarled as soon as they were alone.

"I? I hardly said anything at all."

"You know what I mean. But you can't win." Bradenton stood and paced to the fireplace. "You can't win," he repeated.

Oliver forbore from pointing out that he had just done so.

"You can't win," Bradenton said a third time, turning to Oliver, his cheeks ruddy with anger. "You might achieve a few trifling little victories here and there, but that's what it means to be you—that you can never stop trying. That every inch you win, you must fight to keep. As for me?" He threw his arms wide. "I am a marquess. No matter what you managed today, you spent weeks considering doing my bidding."

"That much is true."

"Men like me? I'm rare. I was born a victor. What I have cannot be given or taken away. What are you? You're one of a thousand similar men. One of ten thousand. Faceless. Voiceless. It's men like me that run the country."

Bradenton nodded, as if he had just convinced himself, and Oliver let him rage in peace.

"It will give me great pleasure to vote against the Reform Act," he said. "Great pleasure indeed."

"I would never begrudge you your amusement," Oliver said. "Especially not when you must savor it alone."

The two men stared at each other until Bradenton's lip curled away from his teeth in a snarl. "I do believe we are done with each other, Marshall. I won't forget this."

Oliver shrugged. "I told you Miss Fairfield would discover her place tonight, Bradenton. She did."

Chapter Fourteen

THERE WAS ONLY ONE WOMAN OLIVER WANTED TO SEE when he joined the company. Jane was sparkling. Not just the diamond bracelets that ringed her wrists. It was her laugh, too loud, and yet just right. Her smile, too broad, and yet exactly as friendly as it needed to be. The look in her eyes when she turned and saw Oliver.

She was magnificent.

He greeted her politely and then leaned in to whisper. "Can you meet me afterward? I want to…"

There were too many ways to finish that sentence. He wanted to kiss her. Congratulate her. He wanted to slip that gown off her shoulders and have her legs around his waist. Her eyes slipped to her chaperone, sitting against the wall. "Northwest corner of the park," she replied sotto voce. "After I leave."

His pulse leapt at the thought. His imagination came alive. But he nodded to her politely, as if he'd not just arranged for an illicit rendezvous with her.

She arrived half an hour after him.

"You would not believe who I had to bribe," she said by way of breathless greeting. "I have half an hour until Alice returns with her beau."

She was beautiful, glowing with the victory she'd obtained.

"I would believe anything of you."

Only a hint of light spilled into the park from a distant street lamp; moldering leaves crunched underfoot as he walked to her.

"You can't imagine how I feel. I don't have to pretend any longer. I'll need a new way to not get married." She laughed. "I'll think of something. Maybe this time I'll just say no."

"I've heard that works wonders." He couldn't stop smiling at her. But his smile felt so false, for all that he couldn't contain it.

"Maybe you'll meet someone," he said softly. "And maybe…"

She lifted her head and took a step toward him. "Oliver."

He didn't want her to meet anyone. He didn't want anyone to have her but himself. But… He hadn't asked her here to dally with her, no matter how dazzled he felt at the moment.

"I'm leaving," he heard himself say. "Parliament is sitting in less than two weeks, and there's a great deal left to do. I must get back to London."

Her eyes grew wide. "I see."

There was nobody else about, and so he did what he'd wanted to do for an age. He turned to her, and then ever so slowly, reached out and set his hands on her sides and drew her to him.

"I see," she repeated, her voice trembling. "I wish I didn't see at all."

With his hands at her waist, their bodies touching ever so slightly, he could feel her breath. Her chest rose, brushing his; a few moments later, her shoulders fell, and that point of contact diminished. A puff of warm air against his collar marked her exhalation.

"I haven't been counting," she said quietly.

It seemed an intimate confession, whispered in that low tone of voice. He didn't say anything in response. He leaned down until his lips brushed her forehead. It wasn't a kiss he gave her. Not a kiss, but something close.

"I don't know when I ceased counting days," she said. "When I did not, at the time when night came, look up at the ceiling and say, 'there's another one down; tomorrow will be four hundred and whatever it is. I'll have to count once again.'"

Another inhalation; another brush of their bodies. And this time, that gap between them didn't disappear when she exhaled. It took Oliver a moment to realize it was because he'd pulled her closer.

"It was sometime after you arrived," she continued. "That was when I stopped dreading each coming day."

"Jane." He made little circles with his thumb against her waist, leaning in to her.

She smelled of lavender. Of comfort. Of *home,* truth be told, and he didn't dare find his home in her.

"I need to stay with my sister for a little over a year." She set her own hand on his arm, and then gradually, ever so slowly, slid her hand down his sleeve. "After that…maybe we might see one another again."

It was not quite a question. He felt every one of her breaths, rising and falling against his chest. So he could also tell that she had *stopped* breathing. That the warm breeze of her exhalation had ceased, that her body tensed against his chest.

Seeing her again? That was a euphemism. His own want reached out, red and demanding. He didn't just want to see her. He wanted her in his bed. She wouldn't hold back, not an inch. She was clever and curious and passionate, and he suspected that if he ever had her under him… God, he couldn't think of that. Not now, not with her so close.

He wanted more than that, though. He wanted to argue with her about politics, to hash through every bill, every proposed amendment with her. He wanted to sit with her of an evening, when they were both tired of talking. He wanted her, everything about her.

Everything except… Her.

Because no matter what she might mean to him when they were alone, he'd seen the other women tonight—quiet wives who held back, silently goggling at Jane as if she were some strange sort of beetle crawling across the table. She was Jane of the too-bright gowns. Jane of the dubious reputation. Jane, too blunt, too outspoken. Too much a bastard, just like him.

She was the exact opposite of what he needed in a wife. So why couldn't he let go?

"Impossible girl," he breathed.

"Don't call me that. Tonight, everything is possible."

"That's what I meant. You're a doer of impossible things. I need a wife who will stick to the possible."

Still her eyes were bright. "In a year…"

"Jane," he said, "in a year I might be married."

He'd been waiting for her to take a breath, but the one she drew in nearly killed him. She made a choked sound in the back of her throat—more of a gasp than an inhalation.

"If the reform bill passes," he said baldly, "they'll elect another Parliament. That will be my chance. My chance to run, my chance to obtain a seat. They'll expect me to marry if I do."

"I see." She didn't say anything for a while, and Oliver went back to counting her breaths—too fast, too harsh, growing more ragged as time slipped on.

"You saw what they were like tonight," he said. "The women who marry politicians. Part of me wants to ask you to become one of them, but how could I? Ask you to mute the best of you? To make yourself into a drab little wren, when you've become a phoenix?" He dropped his voice. "I could never forgive myself if I asked you to extinguish your fire."

"I see," she repeated. This time, she sounded hoarse. She pulled her hands from his coat and stepped away. He couldn't see her face in the dim light, but he could see her wiping at her eyes.

He fished in his pockets and came out with a handkerchief.

"Don't tell me to be reasonable," she said, taking it from him. There was a hint of anger in her voice. "Don't tell me not to cry."

"I would never do that."

"I know I'm being foolish. I scarcely know you. What is it that we have—three weeks' acquaintance? It's not possible to fall in love in so short a space of time. I don't even *want* to marry you." She scrubbed at her cheeks and then wadded up his handkerchief. "I *don't*. I just want something to look forward to at the end of this ordeal."

It couldn't be him.

"But you're right," she said. "I know you're right. I can't imagine myself as one of them, either. I've only just found myself. To take on another pretense so soon… No. I wouldn't want to, either." She looked up into his eyes. "So this is the end, then."

No.

Oliver hadn't let go of her. "These next months won't be easy for you."

"No, likely not. But I've survived thus far, and I imagine I'll continue to do so."

"If you ever really need me, let me know. I'll come."

She blinked, looking up at him, her brow wrinkling in puzzlement. "Why?"

"I should say it is because I owe you. One day, you'll realize how great a favor you did for me today." He shook his head. "I would say that I owe you a debt of gratitude. But that's not why I offered to come. The truth, Jane, is that if you need me, it will give me joy to be at your side."

"You'll be married."

He didn't want to think about that.

"I won't be unfaithful to her, Jane—but marriage can't erase friendship. And no matter what else we might have been, we *are* friends."

The silence seemed soft as velvet and yet darkly dangerous. "What might we have been?"

They both knew the answer to that. But if he spoke it aloud, he'd give it life. He'd make it real. He'd change it from an insubstantial wish into a solid possibility.

Instead, he set his finger against the divot at the base of her neck. Her breath caught as if snagged by his touch. Then he dragged his fingertips up, up, up the smooth expanse of her throat. He felt her swallow.

By the time his thumb reached her lips, he ached all over. That possible future he refused to acknowledge aloud filled him. It pushed against his skin, clamoring to be let out.

"This," he whispered, and leaned in. "This, impossible girl."

She made an inarticulate sound in her throat as their lips touched.

He couldn't change her past. He refused to let go of his future. That left only the present: the warmth of her kiss, that sweet taste of something that might have been…and the bitterness of a love that would not be.

She kissed him back, lips to lips, and then tongue to tongue. She kissed him until he wasn't sure who was kissing and who was kissing back. The kiss took on a life of its own, roaring through his blood. As if somehow, if he kissed her hard enough, he could avoid the past and the future altogether. He might stay in the present forever.

He pulled back before that impossible future became all too probable.

Jane looked up at him with wide eyes. "I hate your future wife," she said simply.

"At the moment, I'm not much in charity with her myself."

She set her hands on his shoulders and kissed him again. This time, though, the kiss didn't overwhelm. It reminded. This was the last time he'd feel her lips, the last time he'd taste her breath. It was the last time he'd trade his body for hers, nibble by nibble. This was the end, and they both knew it.

He finally drew away.

"If you ever need me, Jane…" Those words came out a little hoarse.

She let out a short, sharp breath. "Thank you. But I won't. I'm stronger than that."

"I know. But…" He swallowed and looked away. "Nobody should feel alone. Even if you don't need me and won't ask for me, you should know that I'll come. That no matter how difficult things are or what you must bear, you're not alone. I can't change anything else." He reached out and drew a finger down her cheek. "But that much," he said, "I can give you. The sure knowledge that if you need me, you need only send word."

"Care of the Tower in London, Mr. Cromwell?"

She was trying to make a joke of it, but her voice shook.

"Care of my brother in London. The Duke of Clermont." He leaned his head against hers. "I can't give you anything else, Jane, but I can give you that. You're not alone."

Chapter Fifteen

A LAMP SHONE IN THE ENTRY OF THE HOUSE, and a glimmer of light echoed from down the hall, marking her uncle's study. Other than those feeble hints at illumination, though, the house seemed cold and empty. Colder and emptier now than it had been a month ago. Oliver had transformed everything, and now he was gone.

She'd done the count in the carriage on the way home. Four hundred and fifty-three days remained.

But she was stronger now. She was *more*. She had the memory of a kiss to sustain her through the hardest times.

Jane handed her wraps to a yawning footman, rang for a maid to help her undress, and then started up the stairs. She'd made it halfway up before she heard footsteps in the hall below.

"Jane?" a voice called.

She bit her lip and looked upward in entreaty. The last thing she wanted to do tonight was to talk to Titus.

It wasn't as if she had a choice. She waited, trying to disguise her impatience, hoping that he wouldn't be able to tell that she'd wept earlier.

He plodded forward into the dim circle cast by the lamp. "I must speak with you." He scrubbed his hand over his head. "Come to my office."

She would much rather be in her room. She wanted to be in her bed, surrounded by a fortress of blankets, hidden safely under covers. She could block out the world until she forgot all about Oliver Marshall. Following her uncle to his office for a late-night chat sounded like an absolutely horrid thing to do.

"Of course," she said dutifully.

But his eyes glimmered, and he frowned at her. "None of your sass."

Maybe she hadn't spoken as dutifully as she'd intended. She bit her tongue and followed him anyway.

He pulled out a chair for her, and then settled himself ponderously into the leather-backed seat on the other side of the wooden desk. He didn't look at her, not for a long while. Instead, he beat his fingers against the tabletop as if he were trying to imitate the sound of raindrops.

Finally, he heaved a sigh.

"This is very important," Uncle Titus said. "How long have you known that your sister was leaving the house during the day?"

He'd caught her off guard, or she would have done a better job of lying. But Jane was tired. She was victorious. She was heartsick. She was glorious. This night, she'd won and then she'd lost. All her energy had been devoted to maintaining her calm in front of her uncle. And so instead of the confusion she might have mustered at any other moment, there was a moment when the truth shone guiltily on her face.

She *had* known, and she hadn't said anything.

Titus probably would have believed her responsible no matter what the truth was. But his eyes narrowed at the guilty expression on her face. He shook his head sadly. "As I thought."

A denial popped into her head—something like, *but I did tell her to be careful.* She managed not to say it out loud. She had no idea what Titus knew and had no intention of incriminating her sister.

"Did something happen to her?" she asked. "Is she well? Has she been hurt?"

Titus waved a hand. "Her body is as well as it ever can be, poor child. But she was unrepentant when I found her. She attempted to reason with me, to…" He sighed. "To convince me."

"She's right. There would be no problem, if only you—"

"If *I?*" He slammed his hands against the desk and leaned forward. "So you'll lay this at my feet, too? You encouraged her to defy me. You likely showed her how to leave, and told her—"

"She's not a simpleton," Jane snapped back, "nor is she led on strings. She's a nineteen-year-old woman. She's old enough to marry, to make her own decisions. Nobody needs to *show* her how to do things. She does them on her own."

If Titus heard this, he didn't show it.

"I can no longer avoid contemplating the ill effects of your influence," he said piously.

Jane took a deep breath. "She's a normal girl. She has high spirits, that's all."

Titus shook his head. "It is your telling her such things that causes these problems. A normal girl? She is no such thing. She is *afflicted,* Jane, and you let your sister wander about the countryside unchaperoned. What if she had met a man?"

"What if a burglar broke into her window?" Jane countered. "She's not Rapunzel, to be locked away for good."

Titus stared into her eyes. She wasn't sure what she was looking at—anger, surely, but something more. Something halfway between anger and triumph. "That," he finally said, "was a test. I know that she met a man. She told me so herself. I had given you that one last chance for honesty, you see. Your refusal to tell me the entire truth..." He shook his head, sad once more. "You disappoint me, Jane. You disappoint me deeply."

It wasn't fair. She wasn't going to apologize for refusing to betray her sister. Especially since she would have received the blame no matter how Titus found out. He'd failed Emily and Jane both, thrust them into this untenable position where the choice was either to lie or to accept a future where Emily was isolated from company and tortured by physicians.

"You will leave tomorrow," Titus said. "Your aunt, my sister Lily, will take you in." His lip twitched distastefully. "She will find you a husband in short order. Emily will not write. You may not visit. It will be as if she has no sister. I have hopes that I may yet undo the damage you have caused."

"No." Jane choked on the word. "No. You can't take her away from me."

"I can." He folded his arms in satisfaction. "I will. I already have, Jane. Your things are packed. You'll be escorted to the train station tomorrow. Mrs. Blickstall will accompany you to Nottingham."

Jane stared straight ahead of her, too dazed to cry. Her lungs burned. She couldn't think of anything at all. If she were not here, what would Emily do? Her sister wouldn't have books to read or companions near her age. And that was to say nothing about what would happen if Titus decided to bring in yet another charlatan to cure Emily's condition.

She took a deep breath. "I'll go, but if I do, there will be no doctors. No attempts to experiment on her."

"Jane," Titus said in a tired voice, "you cannot dictate terms. You are not your sister's guardian. I am. *I* am responsible for her, and I will determine what is best for her welfare."

If you need me, Oliver had said.

That thought filled her with a terrible, wistful hope. Surely this counted as need. Surely *this* was a situation where his promise would require him to return, and if he did...

He was not a full hour gone from her life, and she was already contemplating bleating for him like a little lost lamb. As if she'd been a foolish child when she'd told him that she was strong enough. Her lip curled, and she contemplated her uncle.

In the orangish light of the lamp, he looked old and tired. The lines on his forehead seemed gouged into his skin, deep dark ruts marking a lifetime of fretting.

Jane raised her chin. She'd beaten Bradenton, by God, and he was stronger than Titus.

She could still feel Oliver's kiss on her lips. She imagined a box made of carbonized steel—steel as strong as the girders of a steamship, steel as thick as an engine boiler, able to withstand the heat and pressure of a thousand infernos. She could lock all Titus's ineffectual rage away forever inside such strength.

She put the feeling of Oliver's kiss inside the box and closed it tightly so that nothing could happen to it. While she could remember what it felt like, she was not alone. He'd said so, and she believed it.

She lifted her head and stared into her uncle's eyes. Her greatest fear had come true, but…this was freedom, not disaster. She had no need to pretend any longer. Not with anyone. She held Oliver's kiss close, until she drove the tremor from her hands. Until she was calm enough to speak without croaking.

"No," she said softly. "That is not what is going to happen."

He blinked at her in confusion. "You can say no all you wish, but you have no legal power."

"No," Jane repeated. "You are wrong. You're Emily's guardian, but you aren't mine. You have no way to control what I do."

He gave her a haughty look. "Speak sense for once, because I do not take your meaning."

He couldn't win. Why had she never seen it before? She'd been so busy hiding in the shadows that she'd ceded all her best weapons.

"I don't *have* to go to our aunt's house," Jane said. "I have money. I can do anything I wish. You haven't noticed because all I've wished for is my sister's happiness and wellbeing. You're so set on believing me disobedient. You've not realized that I have been trying to obey your edicts. Think what I could do, if I chose to be difficult."

He shook his head. "I don't understand."

"If I wished, I could purchase a house next to this one. I could live there with a string of lovers. I could purchase an advertisement in the newspaper announcing that you suffered from a malady of the brain."

As she spoke, he turned white. "You wouldn't."

She leaned forward. "I could tell everyone I met about your sordid medical practices. I'd let them know how unfit a guardian you were. I could make your life impossible. That's who I am, if you haven't noticed. I'm an impossible girl, and you cannot rid yourself of me. Not with threats. Not with words. Those are my terms."

He stared at her in mute, baffled confusion, as if she had suddenly transformed into a bear and he didn't know whether to scream and run or fetch a rifle. "I will not have you in my household."

"Then it'll be the newspaper," she said with a shrug. "And—"

"But you may visit," he squeaked. "Once a month?"

She stopped and looked at him, and he managed a weak smile.

"I can't keep you out of Cambridge," he said, looking down at the desk, "but I *can* dictate who Emily sees."

If Jane bought a house in Cambridge, that would mean the end of any freedom at all for Emily. Their uncle would be guarding her too closely, trying to keep them apart. And—Jane realized—she couldn't really carry out her threats. If she did, she'd have no leverage on him. Even Titus might prove dangerous if he had nothing to lose.

At least this way he was negotiating.

"You'll go to my sister," Titus said. "You'll do as she says. You won't make a scene or a fuss. You see Jane, I do care for your welfare even if you do not. I want you to safeguard your reputation, not throw it away in some desperate attempt to lead your sister down your path."

"My path." Her cheeks burned. "For all you talk of it, you don't know anything about my path. You've never tried to really help. You've just given me orders."

He waved a hand. "Spare me the histrionics."

She caught hold of herself. She brought the shrouds of her dignity about her and glared at him.

"The truth is, Jane," he said, "that if you hadn't had me to look out for you, I do not know what you would be doing. Go to my sister. Find a husband." He sighed wearily. "God, you girls tire me so."

She would never convince him. "I'll see Emily every other week," Jane said. "And she'll write as often as she wishes."

"I will monitor the correspondence."

She'd expected nothing less. She shrugged at this. "You'll stop torturing her with those dreadful physicians," she said.

"No. If I hear of someone who can do her good—"

"Then you may speak to me. I'll want proof—testimonials from former patients who have a malady similar to Emily's, patients that the physician has helped. The lot of them are far too quick to experiment, and heedless of the pain they cause. And you'll ask Emily if she wishes to proceed."

He snorted. "Your sister does not know what is good for her because you coddle her. This is why nineteen-year-old girls have guardians, Jane—to make them do the things they would not choose on their own. Frankly, you've just proven that you're not any better."

She glared at him. "This is not negotiable, Titus. It is either that, or I will embarrass you. Badly."

His nostrils flared and he pressed his fingers to the bridge of his nose. "Very well. Before I embark on a course of treatment, I will…consult." He made a face as he talked, his lips lifting away from his teeth as if he were a snarling dog. "God. When will this ever end?"

He could claim weariness as loudly as he wished so long as he left Emily alone.

Jane nodded.

"Then we are in agreement," she said.

"You'll leave tomorrow."

⌘　⌘　⌘

BY THE TIME SHE CRAWLED INTO BED, Jane had lost the ability to make sense of the world.

She had let everyone know that she was not as stupid as she'd pretended. Oliver was gone. On the morning, she was leaving Emily behind and going to live with her aunt in Nottingham. She'd held Titus to a bargain, wresting concessions from him with threats.

She wasn't sure who she was any longer. She seemed both bigger and colder than the person she had been even a few nights ago.

There was only one certainty in her life.

Even though Jane was tired, she waited, fighting the waves of weariness that threatened to drag her down into sleep. It took almost fifteen minutes before her door swung open.

"Jane?" Emily's voice was small in the darkness.

Jane turned to the sound.

"Can I—"

Jane didn't even wait for her sister to finish her sentence. She pulled back the covers, and Emily ducked under them and joined her. Her sister made a mass of warmth under the blankets.

It had been a long time since Emily had climbed into bed with Jane. Not since she was eleven and afraid of thunderstorms. Back then, she would have made her sister a little cocoon out of coverlets to try and keep her safe.

She wasn't going to be able to keep her safe any longer. She'd done her best, but she knew what Titus was.

"I'm sorry," Emily said. "I'm so sorry. I didn't mean to get you sent away. I just wanted to—needed to—get away. And I kept going. Twice a week, and then three times... I'm so stupid."

"Don't apologize."

"How can I not? It's my fault that this is happening. I knew what Titus was, what he would do, and I still—"

Jane tried to put her finger over her sister's mouth. In the darkness, she missed and jabbed her cheek instead.

"Ow."

"Oh, dear." She converted the motion into a shoulder pat instead. "It's *not* your fault, Emily. It's Titus's fault."

"But—"

"He's an adult. All his mental faculties are in functional order, no matter how flawed they might be. He doesn't have to be unreasonable; he just chooses it. You didn't force him to act irrationally. It's ridiculous to say that you are at fault when he's the one making demands."

Emily let out a long breath. "I'll try to be good," she finally said. "To reach him with reasonableness." She laughed. "I'm not sure it's possible."

"I'll visit," Jane said. "I've worked it out with him. I'll still see you. I'll be able to slip you money, so that if you ever need it—if you have to bribe physicians yourself—you'll have it. You have a little more than a year until he's no longer your guardian. Once you turn twenty-one, there is nothing he can do to hold you here."

"I know," Emily said. "I love you, Jane, but..." She swallowed. "Don't worry for me. I shall manage on my own."

Jane smoothed her sister's hair. "Who knows? Maybe Titus will get better."

Emily laughed. "Maybe. And maybe he... But no. I won't make fun of him."

"There's a plant on my desk," Jane said. "A cactus. I want you to keep it while I'm gone. So you'll have something of me."

"Oh, God, Jane. I always forget to water plants. I'm going to kill it."

"Forget to water this one." Jane smiled. "You're supposed to."

Her sister nodded and curled up against her.

"Was it worth it?" Jane asked. "This man you were slipping out to meet... Was he worth it?"

Emily paused. "He's going to be a barrister. He asked me to marry him. I've not given him my answer yet. I was waiting for some kind of a sign. And now this thing has happened with Titus."

"Titus is never a sign of anything but Titus," Jane said. "Does your barrister love you?"

Emily waited even longer before answering. "I don't know," she finally said. "It's hard for me to read him. He says that I'm pretty."

"Anyone would say that, silly. You are. But he was meeting you in secret. I can't like that. Is he a rake?"

"He's the farthest thing from a rake. I told you, he's gentle. Except when he's not. When he's angry, he speaks his mind quite clearly."

"Does this not-rakish gentleman have a name?"

She could feel her sister stiffen beside her with some inexplicable tenseness. "He does."

Was it someone Jane knew? Someone she had mentioned? *Not the Marquess of Bradenton,* she prayed. *Let it not be him.* But she didn't ask. She didn't push. She simply waited. And after about half a minute, Emily continued.

"It's Anjan," Emily said. "Anjan Bhattacharya."

Jane's eyes widened in surprise. There were a thousand responses she could give. She mulled them all over and finally settled on one.

"Tell me," she said sleepily. "Tell me all about him. Does he say your name the way you say his?"

Her sister pondered this. "He told me once that my guardian should hold me precious. But Mama didn't. Papa didn't. Titus, oddly enough, has come closest, and he, well...." She sighed and turned in the bed. "That leaves only you, Jane. You're the only one who has ever thought me a treasure."

Jane gathered her sister in her arms, holding her close. "Of course, Emily. Of course I do."

"So who did you have?"

Jane's throat tightened. Emily had never asked that before. She'd always been the younger sister, never thinking that *Jane* might need someone, too. Jane shook her head numbly.

"And now you're going away." Emily's own voice was hoarse. "Promise me that you'll take as good care of yourself as you did of me. Promise that, and I'll manage to take care of myself."

"Emily."

But her little sister kissed her fingertips and set them against Jane's forehead. "Promise. Promise that you'll do it."

Jane folded Emily's hand in her own. "I promise," she whispered.

Chapter Sixteen

ANJAN BHATTACHARYA HADN'T KNOWN how much he cared until Emily stopped coming. The first day she'd not appeared at their agreed-upon meeting, he wandered up the banks of the brook where they normally walked. He strolled down the other side, where there was no path, only unbroken fields boot-high in winter grasses.

Maybe she'd not been able to get away.

He walked and he waited. After an hour and a half passed, he left.

He waited the second day at the usual time. He waited and he waited and he waited until his feet were sore from standing. He waited until the sun slid from the sky and kissed the horizon, until even his vast well of hope had begun to run dry.

On the third day, a servant was there for him. She frowned at Anjan. "Are you...uh...Mr....uh..."

"Yes," he replied, because he answered to Mr. Uh almost as often as he did to his own name.

"This is for you," she said, holding out a square of paper. He broke the seal and unfolded the letter.

Dear Anjan, Emily had written. *My uncle has discovered everything. I've tried twice, and I can't get away to see you. I might be able to make it one day, but I can't ask you to wait for weeks on end on such hopes.*

The world, he decided, was vastly unfair.

I have been considering everything you said the last time we spoke. I enjoyed the story you told me, but I'm not sure what to do about it yet.

Emily

He folded the paper carefully. She was considering. He could guess what that meant. The Law Tripos would be administered in a few months, and after that, he'd be gone. He needed proximity, not consideration.

If he were another man, he would march up to her uncle's house and demand to see her.

He suspected that if he tried, he'd be shot. Or thrown in gaol and accused of some horrendous crime. Nobody would believe him when he said he just wanted to talk to her.

She'd been a bright spot in his day. And now…

He started back toward town.

He was beginning to get angry. Not at her, at a fate that taunted him with something so lovely, and then just as it seemed to be within his reach, snatched it away. Fate was cruel.

He passed through the gates of his college in a black study.

By now, most of his classmates were used to him. If they were the sort to make remarks, they rarely did it around him. He made his way across the green, scowling at the ground.

"Ho, Batty!" a man called.

Anjan almost didn't stop. He took three strides.

"Batty, where are you going?"

Ah, yes. *Batty* was him. He halted. Before he looked around, he found his smile. Even now, he could put it on his face with so little effort. It wouldn't do to scowl at a man just for being friendly. And George Lirington was one of the good ones—one of the people who talked to Anjan, who had first invited him to play cricket. He had even talked his father into finding Anjan a position.

"Batty," Lirington said, "where were you today? We needed a bowler. We were desperate without you."

"Lirington," Anjan spoke as pleasantly as he could. "You look as if you've just come from the cricket field. Did they have you bowling, then?"

"Yes, which is why we lost."

His friend smiled, and began to describe the game in detail, acting out the most important points. Anjan was *Batty* because Bhattacharya had too many syllables. He'd told one man his first name; the fellow had blinked, and then had immediately dubbed him John. That's who they thought he was: John Batty. These well-meaning English boys had taken his name as easily, and with as much jovial friendship, as their fathers had taken his country.

And Emily had called him Bhattacharya. He'd fallen a little bit in love with her the moment she'd said his name as if it had value.

His fist clenched, but he kept on smiling.

⌘ ⌘ ⌘

OLIVER DIDN'T THINK OF JANE MUCH. In the last week of January, he managed to keep his thoughts of her to a minimum—a few wistful imaginings at night, wondering what might have happened between them if matters had been different. If she'd had no need to drive suitors away. If she'd been a legitimate daughter of a well-respected family. If he'd been able to court her.

Court. Ha. He didn't think about anything so sedate as *courting* her. His thoughts ran darker and deeper, starting from their kiss and ending against stone walls and thick trees. His thoughts ran far ahead of his sensibilities, until he had to take the problem in hand to solve it. But after, when sanity returned...

He still couldn't imagine Jane in plain white and demure pearls. So he made himself give up that fantasy.

In February, he scarcely thought of Jane at all. He didn't have time to think of her. Parliament was sitting once more. The queen herself addressed the nation's lawmakers and urged them to extend the franchise. The work began in earnest. Oliver hashed out his plan with Minnie, his brother's wife, who had a head for strategy; between them, they planned a series of dinners. Working men from all over the country were brought in by train. Oliver gave short two-day courses on etiquette and the workings of politics. The men then ate with dukes and duchesses, barons and baronesses. Members of Parliament sat down for an hour with bakers.

The message was clear: These are reasonable, rational men. Why should they not vote?

He very assiduously did *not* think of Jane in those moments. He didn't want to contrast her with the pallid, smiling wives he encountered, women who never made a single faux pas, who would blush if they heard the word "fuchsine," and would certainly never don a glove of that color, let alone a gown.

He smiled instead. And when those women mentioned their unmarried sisters or cousins or nieces, he smiled again, this time a little more distantly, and tried not to call to mind brilliant colors.

By the time March rolled around, Oliver had stopped telling himself he wasn't thinking of Jane. It didn't matter whether he was thinking of her or not; she wasn't here, she was still impossible, and he was unlikely to ever see her again. If he found himself still a little enamored of her memory, it was hardly worth moping about. Not when there was so much to do. Dinners gave way to arguments. Bills were drafted; bills were rejected. He wrote a series of articles for a London paper, on the subject of the representation of the people, that was well-received; he wondered, idly, if Jane had read them and what she had thought of them.

At the end of April, the men Oliver was working with took him aside and asked him when he was planning on running for Parliament. *When,* not *if.* He had their support, they assured him. He nodded calmly and spoke very little. He let them tell him the things he had always known—that he was levelheaded, intelligent, articulate, that he had ties to the nobility and ties to the working class. He let them tell him that he was exactly the sort of man who should be joining them. He let them tell him that he would succeed, while inside he was dancing a jig.

The future he'd envisioned so long ago was opening wide.

Then they told him that all he needed to complete the picture was domestic felicity. That, he passed over somewhat.

Oliver went home that night and shared a bottle of port with his brother, trading jokes back and forth until he got a little tipsy. They drank until Minnie, his sister-in-law, came downstairs. She smiled and shook her head at them, and then escorted her husband to bed.

She left Oliver behind to contemplate the fruition of all his dreams.

Once the port and his brother had deserted him, the euphoria drifted away.

All he needed was domestic felicity. A pleasant girl, someone who would smooth his way. There were hundreds of women who would do. Surely, one of them would eclipse Jane. He just had to meet her.

He wasn't in love with Jane, after all. He just admired her spirit. That was it. He poured himself another half glass of port, all by himself in the darkness.

Well, perhaps it was more than her spirit. He admired her intelligence. The way that she'd walk into a room and immediately determine who was in charge and how best to alienate him. He wanted a wife just like that—except, of course, she'd have to do the opposite of alienation. Someone just like Jane, he mused. That's who he wanted. Just like Jane, but completely opposite. He finished off the port in his glass.

It was more than her spirit and intelligence he admired. Because there was her body. There was definitely her body.

At this point, he was too steeped in liquor to rouse any real physical ardor, no matter how heated his thoughts. That was a good thing, because once he'd started to think of her body—of the generous swell of her breasts, the soft curves of her hips—it was rather difficult to stop thinking of what he'd like to do with her.

He hadn't touched her enough. Not nearly enough. His thoughts turned wild, then, and even though the port had rendered him unable to do anything about it, he thought of it all—of the slide of his hard member into soft, willing female flesh, at the noise she would make when he did it. He wanted until he was half mad with drunken lust.

Yes, he whispered to himself as he stumbled up the stairs to his room. Jane was exactly the sort of woman he wanted. Someone exactly like Jane, but totally opposite. It was a good thing he wasn't in love with her or it might be difficult to find that other woman.

He had a terrible headache the day afterward, and he couldn't quite decide if it was caused by the liquor or the dissonant irrationality he'd indulged in.

In any event, he had no time to consider the question. Parliament still had come to no agreement, and the Reform League promised to hold a demonstration in Hyde Park. Not just a few hundred men, either; they were talking about having everyone available show up. The government, fearing the inevitable unrest and violence that would be associated with such a gathering, had promised to arrest anyone who attended. Neither group would back down. Plans were made in London to initiate special constables just to handle the rabble.

May arrived, and people began to come for the demonstration. Not one or two or even five thousand of them, but tens of thousands.

Members of Parliament who had refused to consider some type of reform now grew uneasy with the threat of that crowd hanging over their heads. The papers contained reports from the police, detailing the number of guards that would be needed to stop such a gathering. Someone pointed out that there weren't that many constables to be found in all of England, that deadly force would be necessary to stop the crowd.

Oliver refused to be distracted by thoughts of a distant woman when so much else was at stake.

The evening before the planned rally, he sat with Minnie and Robert and read report after report—reports of meetings, of inns full to bursting, of courts convened for the sole purpose of commissioning special constables.

Matters were going to be ugly on the morrow.

He slept fitfully and was awoken at dawn by a knock on his door. When he answered it blearily, though, it was not his brother with news of violence already started.

It was a footman with an urgent telegram.

Oliver was still half asleep, and his dreaming mind ran away with him. A strange certainty leapt up in him. It was from Jane. She needed him. He'd go to her. He'd have to marry her after all, to save her from some horrible, unknown fate.

Never mind London. Never mind impossibility. Never mind the wreckage that would make of his life.

He rubbed his eyes, found his spectacles, and focused on the message.

It wasn't from Jane—of course it wasn't from Jane. He refused to be disappointed that his life wasn't in shambles. It was from his mother.

FREE GONE

PLANS TO ATTEND DEMONSTRATION PROTESTING FAILURE TO INCLUDE WOMEN IN VOTING REFORM

FIND HER

His sleepy, half-sexual imaginings vanished, and he reread the telegram once again, this time with dawning horror. Then he called for schedules and cursed. The mail train would have arrived at Euston Station a few hours ago.

Free was already here, alone in London. She was going to an illegal demonstration alongside several hundred thousand angry men, men who would be pitted against half-trained constables who were crazed with fear at the thought of the mob. And—knowing Free—she was going to tell all those men that she wanted the right to vote, and they'd better give it to her.

"Holy mother of God," Oliver swore.

His sister was going to get herself killed.

Chapter Seventeen

ON TODAY OF ALL DAYS, Oliver had expected to see constables on patrol, monitoring every street corner. But when he stepped out onto the street, there was no sign of the special constables that had been so much discussed over the past days. In fact, there was no sign of police presence whatsoever.

Instead, there were hundreds milling about the streets. The crowds grew thicker as he came closer to Hyde Park. It was there that he saw the first constables of the day: A lethargic pair had stationed themselves at the park gates. They made no attempt to stop the throngs from streaming into the park; in fact, one of them was congratulating people as they entered. They appeared to be making a half-hearted effort to stop costermongers from profiting off the event—and even then, as Oliver watched, a pie-seller slipped by, handing over a pasty as silent payment.

How they would have filtered out the elements intent on demonstration, Oliver didn't know. A group of ladies had come up on horses to watch the festivities; they were seated with gentlemen nearby, with servants pouring wine and passing out little cakes. He'd heard someone say the other night that if there was going to be a clash between the Reform League and the police, they intended to have a front row seat. He'd assumed it had been a joke, but apparently, it had been honestly meant stupidity.

Hyde Park looked more like the scene of a carnival than a pitched battle. There were already thousands of people present. How was he to find Free in this throng?

He wandered around the park in confusion, hoping that nobody would take it amiss if he stared, and then realized that he was one of thousands of gawkers. Nobody cared about him.

He'd feared that matters would get ugly. He knew only too well that a throng this large could turn vicious all too quickly. But thus far, the complete absence of blue-uniformed officers had made the event festive. The promised clash between the event organizers and the government looked unlikely to materialize, and the relief left everyone giddy.

When the members of the Reform League began to appear, they were cheered as if they were heroes returning from battle. They came in groups, waved at the crowds, and led people in chants. As soon as Oliver had a chance, he started asking questions. "Pardon me," he said. "Have you seen a woman talking about universal suffrage?"

This got him an odd look. "Of course I have," one man said. "I see one regularly. I'm married to her."

The next man made a face at the notion of universal suffrage and shook his head, refusing to answer.

By the time he'd talked to the third fellow, he'd perfected his technique. "Is there by chance a group of women advocating universal suffrage here?"

"You'll want to go over to where Higgins is speaking," a man said, indicating a distant quadrant of the park.

He made his way over to the indicated place. It was on the other side of the Serpentine, hidden by a cluster of trees, and it took him three-quarters of an hour to make his way through the crowds. Thankfully, he hadn't been misled. There were shouts here agitating for the vote for all, not just for working men.

When he broke through the crowd, he saw a large group of women. They were clustered thickly together, arms joined. There, right in the middle of them—

For the first time since he'd awoken that morning, Oliver felt a deep sense of relief. He strode forward. "Free!"

Before he could reach her, a wall of women intervened, arms linked. They glared at him. A dark-haired lady of forty narrowed eyes at him and wagged her finger in his direction.

"None of that," she said sharply. "There's no men beyond this point."

"I was just—" He gestured. "I just wanted to talk to her. To Frederica Marshall."

"Well, you can't."

"Free!" Oliver called.

"Stop it, now." The two women nearest him took a step forward, eyes glinting in menace.

"Free!" he said again, waving more desperately.

"Off with you," one of them said. "Or must we ask someone to remove you?"

"No, wait, I just—"

It was at that moment that Free turned.

"Wait!" Free called. She dropped the arms of the women next to her and came over. "Don't send him off," she said. "He's my brother."

"So?" The dark-haired woman looked unimpressed. "You wouldn't want to know what *my* brother's been willing to do."

"He won't harm me," she said. "He's just being ridiculous and protective. Give me a few moments and I'll make him stand down."

Oliver snorted, but when the women in front of him looked at him with narrowed eyes, he raised his hands. "She's right," he said. "I only want her to be safe."

The women exchanged glances—but then with a shrug of their shoulders, they unlinked their arms. Free stepped between them and linked her arms with theirs.

"Oliver," she said, in a tone of disgust. "What are you doing here? It's not safe."

He stared at her in disbelief. She always did this to him—made him feel that his world was upside down and backward. "What am *I* doing here?" He looked around. "It's not *safe?* I'm not a girl of sixteen, Free. I didn't sneak out of my home in the middle of the night, all alone, to make my way to London."

"Yes," Free said. "I want to know what *you* are doing here. You likely left your home in the middle of the morning, and I don't see *you* with a chaperone."

"This isn't about me." He looked her in the eye. "It's about your coming to the most dangerous place in all of England, one where violence is threatened."

She cocked her head and looked around. "Oh," she said slowly. "*Violence.* I see." She raised her eyebrow at a street-seller hawking his wares directly behind them. "What's he going to do, hurl pies at me?"

"Besides," Oliver said, ignoring this inconvenient aspect of reality, "you're sixteen. I can't believe you took the train alone."

"You keep using the word *alone,*" Free said. "But you told me once that I should seek answers before arriving at conclusions. Mary Hartwell drove me in her father's cart to the station. We took the train together. And because we'd communicated our intention to participate to the women's chapter of the Reform League, we were met at the station. I've never been *alone,* not once." She jiggled her arms. "Do I *look* alone?"

"Yes, well, but still…" He glanced to her side, at the dark-haired woman who was pretending not to listen to their conversation, and then to the other side where the blonde was openly grinning.

"From four in the morning until six, I've been with this group," Free explained. "We discussed the practicalities of the rally. Women may not be as strong as men, but we can be formidable in number."

"I have to admit that your friends make an effective barrier. Still, there was some risk—"

"We had procedures," Free said. "We discussed them this morning. Every one has two women watching out for her, and watches out for two other women in turn. That way, we know everyone's safe at all times. We don't wander off. We don't let anyone into the perimeter." She cast Oliver a hard glance. "If one of us is arrested, we've all committed to being taken to the station."

"Free." He rubbed his eyes.

"Anna Marie Higgins—she's the lady over there in the sailor hat—she's been taken to the station thirteen times already." Oliver glanced to his right.

Miss Higgins didn't look like a hardened suffragette. She was dressed in a lovely, fashionable sky-blue dress. She'd topped this off with a sailor's hat, one that she'd adorned with bright blue ribbons that waved in the breeze.

A passing man raised his fist in the air. "Votes for all!" he said.

Miss Higgins blew him a kiss.

Oliver shook his head and turned away. "I'm not sure that you should admire a woman whose main recommendation is that she's managed to garner a baker's dozen of arrests."

"Who else am I supposed to admire?" Free asked. "You? You're here lecturing me on how my behavior was unsafe, but I took greater pains to secure my safety than you did. You're a duke's son in the midst of a potentially hostile mob. For God's sake, they're playing the Marseillaise over there. Who knows what could happen to you?"

"That's ridiculous!" Oliver said hotly. "I only came to find *you*. Don't turn this around to be about me. I don't care what safeguards you took; it's still dangerous. This is risky. Even if it turns out that nothing goes amiss, this could have been a violent mob."

Free refused to be ruffled. "You appear to believe it's acceptable to risk that danger to come and, uh…*rescue* me." She rolled her eyes. "I believe it's acceptable to risk that danger to come and say that women deserve the vote. Why is your risk gallant and mine foolish?"

"Damn it, Free. This isn't the time to chop logic. We need to get you out of here."

Free only smiled. "Oh, that's so lovely. When I induce you to swear, it's because I've argued you to a standstill. Cut line, Oliver. You know I'm right even if you refuse to admit it. And stop being ridiculous; I'm not leaving. If the crowd turns to violence, I'm safer surrounded by a hundred women who have discussed the finer points of safety than I would be all alone with you. What would you do if we were attacked by a mob?"

"I would—" He paused.

"You would be ripped limb from limb." She gave him a beatific smile, completely at odds with her words. "Don't worry, big brother. I'll keep you safe."

"Damn it, Free," he repeated.

She laughed and looked back to her friends. "This is my brother," she said. "His name is Mr. Oliver Marshall. He likely won't leave until everything is over. Where should he stay and glower?"

"You can't cross the perimeter," one of the women said to him. "Only women inside the circle, and I hope you can understand the reason for that. But my brother is standing against that tree there, watching out for us in case anything goes wrong. If you'd like to go join him, you'd be welcome."

Oliver shook his head at his sister, and she grinned at him. "Enjoy yourself, Oliver. The Reform League has promised Miss Higgins the chance to speak, and I'm sure you'll love what she has to say."

⌘ ⌘ ⌘

THERE WASN'T MUCH to say after the rally. The constables intervened only so far as to suggest that people vacate the park before dusk fell, and by then, nobody seemed to object to this suggestion.

The mood was jubilant. The government had promised to quash the demonstration with all its might; the people had promised to quash the government's quashing of their demonstration.

The people, it was generally agreed, had won. Decisively.

Free's friends relinquished her to Oliver's care with reluctance. The cabs were overrun; the streets crowded with foot traffic. There was no chance of taking a carriage.

Instead, they walked. For the first fifteen minutes, Free was cheerful, burbling about the crowd, the mood, how much fun she'd had and how she couldn't wait to do it again. All her energy made him feel old and weary.

"Where are you taking me?" Free finally asked after they'd traipsed through a handful of dingy streets. "It looks like we're going to Freddy's."

Oliver blinked and turned to his sister. "I thought you liked Aunt Freddy. You write to her every week. You're her namesake."

Free rolled her eyes. "For the last four years, Oliver, I have only been writing her *angry* letters, and she has been answering them with just as much vituperation. You never pay attention to anything. We are arguing."

Had it been four years since he'd last spent any significant time at home? Oliver totted up the time…and then swallowed.

"You argue with everyone," he finally said. "I didn't pay that any mind."

"She's going to lecture me. Do you know what Freddy will say when you tell her what I was doing?" Free's eyes narrowed. "Is that why you're bringing me to her? Because you want her to say—"

"Honestly, Free." Oliver looked skyward. "I was bringing you to Freddy's because I thought you would like to see her. I can take you back to Clermont House, if you'd prefer, but the last time you were there you complained that you didn't know anyone and there was nothing to do. I hadn't thought about Freddy's lectures, and if I had, I wouldn't have brought you. I don't know what it is about Aunt Freddy, but the instant she tells me *not* to do something, I find myself most wishing to do it."

Free's lips twitched up reluctantly.

"And she never used to lecture *you,* in any event. Not like she did the rest of us."

Free sighed. "That's changed. I told you, we are arguing. We've spent the last Christmases pointedly talking about each other, loudly, to other people so that we can be overheard. How did you not notice?"

Aunt Freddy was so prickly that it was difficult to tell when she was actually upset and when she was just making noise about something or other to try to make some ridiculous point. She'd been making dire predictions of gloom as long as Oliver had known her. None of them had ever come true.

"What did you argue about?" Oliver said. "Or do I want to know?"

"She needs to go outside."

Oliver took a deep breath. "Oh."

If Freddy knew what they were doing now—walking on regular city streets—she would have complained of palpitations of the heart. If she'd known they were doing it with crowds about, she would have fainted.

When he was younger, he'd accepted as fact that his Aunt Freddy refused to leave the tiny flat that she inhabited. His mother said that she had once gone out—briefly—to the market, but even that had ended once she'd found someone to deliver the necessities of life. It had just been the way of things, an immutable characteristic inherent to Freddy.

"She didn't like my manner of telling her to go outside," Free said, "and she told me to apologize. So I told her that I was very sorry for my hasty words, and what I had meant to say was that she should be going outside *every day.*"

"Oh," Oliver repeated, shaking his head. "You know, our aunt is the one person who is too stubborn to be bullied by you."

Free shrugged. "She told me I was an impertinent little baggage, and so I told her that if she could lecture *us* on how we should be living our lives, I would lecture *her* on what she was doing. That if she could sniff and say, 'it's only for your own good,' I could do the same."

Oliver let out a sigh. "Free," he said quietly, "I don't really understand what is wrong with Aunt Freddy. But I really don't think she *can* go outside. If she could, she would have done it years ago. Spending three decades cloistered in one tiny room is not something someone chooses to do in a fit of pique."

Free looked even more rebellious. "Maybe she can and maybe she can't, but she *should*. And even if you're right, why can she not just tell me that? Instead, she refuses to talk about it—always by pointing out my flaws. It's not fair that she can tell me how I need to use lemon juice to get rid of my freckles, and I can't even tell her to get some fresh air."

Oliver shook his head as they came to the building where his aunt lived. "You're right," he said. "It's not fair. I suspect it's even less fair that Freddy can't go outside. Have a little compassion for your aunt, Free. Since we're here, maybe this is a good time to apologize to her."

"Why would I apologize? I'm not wrong."

Oliver sighed again. "Then you can come up and say absolutely nothing. That will be fun for you both."

Oliver passed a few pennies to a flower girl on the corner in exchange for a bouquet, and they marched up the stairs of the building. There was a bit of rubbish nestled in the corner of one landing—weeks-old rubbish, by the looks of it. Oliver made a note to talk to the owner once again. If his aunt was going to spend all her time here, it should be as nice as possible.

He knocked on the door and waited.

"Who's there?" Freddy's voice sounded a little more quavering than Oliver remembered. .

"It's Oliver."

The door opened a crack, and he caught a glimpse of his aunt peering at him. "Are you alone?" she said. "Has the city erupted in flame? Are there riots?"

"No," Oliver said. "The gathering was orderly."

She opened the door wider. "Then come along in. It's so good to see you, love." She began to motion him inside. But as she did, her eyes landed on Free, standing a foot behind Oliver.

For a second, Freddy's face transformed. Her eyebrows lifted; her eyes lit. She swallowed, and her hand twitched out to Free. But then she seemed to catch herself back, and that transmutation happened in reverse—happiness turned into obstinate denial.

Argued, indeed. They were two of the most stubborn women that he knew—possibly why they cared for each other so much, and certainly why they'd been "arguing" for four years when they clearly loved each other. Oliver shook his head. "Can we come in, Aunt Freddy?"

"Everyone *respectful* can come in," Freddy said, her eyes darting to her niece.

"Well, then," Free said. "That settles it. I suppose I'll just wait here in the hall while you finish up with her."

"You can't—" Freddy's mouth pinched, and in that moment Oliver realized that his aunt looked awful.

Her skin was sallow and sagging. There was a slight tremor to her hand. And there was something else about her, something that made her seem thin and fragile. She was only a few years older than his mother, and yet anyone seeing them together would have imagined Freddy to be the elder by decades.

Freddy took a deep breath. "Oliver, tell your sister that she can't wait in the hall. Laborers live above me now, and heaven knows what they would do if they found her here. They're likely all excited from whatever it was they've done today." She said the word *laborer* in a low voice, as if it were somehow filthy, and then frowned. "You weren't at that…thing, were you?" She glanced at Free as she spoke. "Even *you* would not be so foolhardy."

Free tossed back her head. "If you hear me screaming, Oliver, I hope you can come to my aid. I know Freddy won't, as I'll be out in the hall, and that's two feet too far for her to bestir herself."

Freddy's eyes flashed.

"Maybe," Free tossed off, "I'll go outside. There's a park two streets away. I might sit on a bench. It's not that dark."

"Free," Oliver said, "can you manage to be civil for a few moments?"

Her nose twitched.

"You might as well have her come in," Freddy muttered. "I can't have her death on my hands. She'd make the most uncivil shade ever, and I refuse to have her haunting my hallway."

Free actually smiled at that—as if the thought of being an extremely rude ghost pleased her—and she came in. Freddy closed the door behind them and locked it carefully. Then she did up a second lock. Oliver and Free took seats at her tiny table.

"Oliver," she said. "It's good to see you. Would you like some tea?"

"No, thank you."

"I don't want to hear 'no' for an answer. You're a—" She paused. "You're not a growing boy, are you? But other people here might still be growing, and there's nothing like tea with milk for retaining one's health." She glanced over at Free. "Even if *some people* here don't care for their own health. And *clearly have not been* wearing their bonnets, no matter how often they are told of the danger."

"Oh, yes. In my future, a man will control all my possessions if I marry him, I shan't be allowed to vote, and I won't be given the opportunity to earn a living by any means except on my back—but by all means, the most dire threat I face is freckles. Maybe I should just spend all my time locked in a room. That way, I won't freckle at all. It will be *lovely* for my health."

Freddy's lips tightened. "Tell your sister I take my exercise," she snapped. "I do twenty circuits of my room every day. I'm fitter than she is."

Free looked Freddy up and down. She probably hadn't seen her since Christmas, and the changes were even more dramatic, Oliver supposed, spaced out over that many months. Free was no doubt cataloging the stoop in their aunt's shoulders, the shallowness of her breath, the thin bones of her wrist.

Her eyes glistened, and she sniffed. "Tell *my aunt* that I'm so glad that she's in such formidable health." Free's voice shook. "That I see that her choices are excellent."

"Tell your sister that it's none of her business if I die early."

Free jumped to her feet. Her eyes glittered. "It's none of my business if you die early? How hard is it for you to accept that we love you, that you're killing yourself like this?"

Freddy folded her arms and looked away. "Remind *your sister*," she repeated, "that I'm not speaking to her until she talks to me civilly. Until she apologizes for every harsh word she's spoken."

"What, like telling you that I hate seeing you like this? You want me to apologize for saying that you need to bestir yourself? You want me to apologize for caring about you? Never. I am *never* going to apologize. You are wrong, wrong, wrong, and I hate you for it!"

"Tell your sister," Freddy said, even more cuttingly, "that if she cannot speak to me civilly—as I required when I opened the door—that she's no longer welcome here."

"Very well! Don't stop me." Free strode to the door. Her grand exit from the room was only partially foiled by the intricate locks—she fumbled with them—but she still slammed the door behind her once she'd worked them open.

Oliver stood.

"You'd better go after her," Freddy said. Her eyes darted to the locks, now hanging uselessly. She didn't say a word, but her breathing accelerated. "You don't know—what's out there." She swallowed. "It's dark. She really shouldn't be alone."

"She'll be all right for a few moments." Oliver went to the door and redid the locks. "She won't go outside. She really does have more sense than that."

All the ire went out of Freddy, but none of the unease. She slumped in a seat. That, in and of itself, tugged at Oliver. He sat down again, reached across the table, and took her hand. "Freddy," he said, "if it's making you so miserable, why do you keep fighting with her? I know she loves you. All you would have to say was that you miss her, that you love her, and you could end all of this."

Freddy stared straight ahead. "I know," she whispered.

"Why do you persist?"

"Because she's right."

Oliver jumped. In all his life, he'd never heard Freddy utter those words about anyone other than herself—or, on rare occasion, people who agreed with her.

"She's right," Freddy whispered. "She's right. I'm trapped in here." Her eyes glittered. "I'm too terrified to go out, and yet here I'm stuck. Without anyone at all, with nothing to do. I don't even know who I am some days."

"Oh, Freddy."

"I opened the door yesterday," Freddy said. "I put one toe out before I had such palpitations of the heart that I had to stop."

Oliver put an arm around his aunt. "I'm so sorry. Why can't you tell her that, though? She'd understand, if you'd just tell her that you're *trying.*"

"What, and admit that she's right?" Freddy snapped. "Not likely. I know exactly how I'm going to end this. One day, I'm going to open my door. I'm going to walk down the stairs, just like I've always been doing it. I'm going to open the front door…" Her voice paused; her hands were shaking. "And I'm going for a walk in the park." She gave a nod. "And *then* I'm going to write to her and tell her that she's *wrong.* That I can go outside, that I *did,* and that I'll take no more of her impertinence."

"Freddy."

She sighed. "Very well. *You* tell her I'm trying," Freddy said, and then before Oliver could promise that he would, a mulish look crossed her face. "No," she said. "Don't tell her. I want it to be a surprise. I want it *all* to be a surprise. I'll show her. I'll show her *everything.*"

He patted her hand. "I'm sure you will. Would it help if I came over to assist you?"

"You're a sweet boy, Oliver. Don't have much of your mother in you at all."

Oliver stilled. "You think so?"

"Of course I think so," Freddy replied. Her gaze abstracted. "Some people, when they're hurt…they remember the challenge. They grab hold of the fire once, and when they're burned, they make plans, trying to figure out how to hold live coals. That's your mother. But some of us remember the pain." She reached out and patted Oliver's hand. "You're like that. You remember the pain, and you flinch. When you were young, I thought you were like your mother—a regular coal-grabber. But no. Now I see more clearly." She smiled sadly. "You're like me."

He let out his breath and looked at his aunt. She probably intended that as a compliment. But the flesh under her eyes had darkened. Her skin hung loosely on a too-thin frame. He'd never known what she feared, what had made her this way. His mother said that Freddy had never offered an explanation. Maybe, at this point, she didn't even remember it.

"I can come over more often," he repeated.

"No." She shook her head. "Our monthly visits will do, dear. Other people just make me nervous. Even you." Her chin went up. "But don't worry about me. In another week…or so…I'll be in that park. Just you wait."

He looked at her. Her jaw was set in place, firm and yet quivering. Her eyes flashed with defiance.

"One day," she said, "one day, I will walk out that door and march around that park. One day soon."

"I love you, Freddy," Oliver said, and then, because he knew it was true, he added, "Free loves you, too. You know she does."

"I know." Freddy paused, bit her lip. "And she's out there all by herself." Her hands shook. "You'd better go after her, Oliver."

Chapter Eighteen

Some hundred miles to the north of London in Nottingham.

"SHE WASN'T HERE."

The little grove Jane was in shielded her from view. At the sound of that too-familiar voice, she rested her head against the trunk of the tree. Better that than banging her head against the rough bark in frustration. Not that she cared about the damage to her forehead, but the noise might draw attention, and that was the last thing she needed.

That last few months had been…difficult. Annabel Lewis had warned her of this—that her aunt and Lord Dorling had seemed a little too friendly when Jane wasn't about. She hadn't wanted to believe it, but…

Jane looked up. The leaves on the trees were no longer young; they waved in the morning breeze, rustling. And her aunt, Mrs. Lily Shefton, harrumphed in the clearing behind her.

It was still early—an odd time to be out, in fact, but her aunt had insisted that this morning would do nicely for a walk in this woodsy park on the outskirts of Nottingham. They had come here, and her aunt had promptly absconded, leaving Jane alone.

She had been trying to throw Jane together with Dorling. Jane rolled her eyes. Whatever did she imagine would happen?

"You'd think," her aunt was saying from the clearing, "that a little thing like a woman's affection would be a simple thing to capture. I've given you every opportunity, Dorling, and you haven't yet managed to pull the thing off. What is wrong with you?"

"It's not me. It's your blee—your recalcitrant niece."

Jane couldn't see Dorling's expression, but she could imagine it. The Honorable George Dorling thought a great deal of himself. He'd importuned Annabel before Jane had arrived and had presented a wealthier target. He had the usual rumors attached to him—a baron's second son, sent down from London for raking and gambling.

"Well, hurry it up," her aunt advised. "This whole thing makes me feel dirty as it is. I told my brother I'd see her married, and so I shall. If you can't help, I'll find someone who can."

"Yes, yes," Dorling said lazily. "Do have a little patience. It's a delicate matter courting your niece. Is it any surprise that she thinks I'm after her money? She has so much of it to recommend her, and so little of anything else."

Jane's mouth curled in a reluctant smile.

Dorling wanted her money. Her aunt wanted her gone. It was hardly a surprise that they'd formed an alliance. It wouldn't do any good, of course—Jane had no intention of marrying anyone—but at least it gave her aunt a purpose. She was thankful for small favors.

"This is unacceptable," her aunt said, cutting through Jane's amusement. "My brother has everything in readiness. He can't act until you take care of the girl."

Jane's breath caught. Whatever could she mean, her uncle had everything in readiness? That Jane needed to be *taken care of*?

"I will," Dorling said, "just as soon—"

"There is no time," her aunt scolded. "He's more and more worried about her sister. She's been acting oddly."

Unhappy was the word Jane would have used. Emily wasn't allowed out, and her uncle exercised more care now in making sure she did not slip away. It was small wonder that her sister wasn't her normal self.

But Aunt Lily wasn't finished. "If the doctors corroborate his fears, he'll have her sent to the Northampton Lunatic Asylum by June. It'll be the best thing for her, poor girl. You *need* to act now."

Jane couldn't help herself. She gasped aloud—and then, when she realized what she'd done, she clapped her hands over her mouth. Sent to an *asylum?* Emily was angry, not mad.

And yet the last time Jane had visited, Emily had mentioned doctors who had come only to ask her questions. Odd questions. They'd shrugged it off, thinking nothing of it. But if Titus were thinking of lunacy, those physicians had been examining her mind, not her body.

It was a warm, sunny day, but Jane suddenly felt cold all over. If Titus had Emily declared mentally unfit… It would be awful.

She'd made a mistake. She'd simply accepted the legalities of the situation. She should have absconded with her sister months ago, and never mind the fact that it would have been a crime.

The chill that traveled through her had nothing to do with the weather.

"Don't worry," Dorling said. "Once she's mine, she won't have any way to kick up a fuss."

The cold that had worked its way into Jane's fingers seemed numbing. She had thought that her aunt only wanted her married off. But the truth was far worse than that. Now she could see the plan. If Jane married, she would no longer control her fortune. All those threats she'd made to Titus were worth nothing if she could not act. They meant to make her helpless, to strip her of all support. She would be alone.

"We could end this tonight," Dorling said, "after the assembly, if you'd just let me into her room like we talked about before."

Jane had been cold before. She was ice now. She couldn't move. She didn't want to believe her ears.

"And I told you," her aunt snapped with some asperity, "I refuse to feel dirtier about this than I must. It's a filthy business as it is. I won't countenance rape, not for any purpose." There was a pause. "Besides, I doubt she cares for her reputation that much."

Jane clutched the trunk of the tree and silently thanked her aunt. She was rude and awful, yes, and she was conspiring against her. But for that, Jane could have kissed her.

"I won't need that," Dorling said. "I can be very persuasive. Trust me on this."

No. Don't trust him with anything. But Jane didn't get a vote.

"I...well..." There was a long silence.

No, Jane wanted to scream. Don't hesitate, not on that front either.

"I'd need your promise," her aunt said slowly. "Your promise that you'll persuade only."

Jane couldn't bear to listen to the details. She didn't want to know what they would plan. Slowly, as quietly as she could, she backed away from the clearing.

Every snap of a twig, every rustle of leaves, made her imagine enemies coming for her. By the time she reached the city streets, her hands were shaking.

She had to get out of this place, had to go find her sister. Damn Titus's guardianship—she should never have respected it. He couldn't put Emily away if Jane made off with her first.

They could be on a ship by...

No. If she disappeared without explanation, her uncle would have a telegram on his desk before Jane could arrive in Cambridge. He would never let Emily out of his sight.

Sometimes, it felt impossible to get ahead. She'd come to know Oliver Marshall and he'd left. She'd made friends with Genevieve and Geraldine, but she'd been sent away and they'd gone on to London. Now she was just beginning to make friends with a few ladies here, but she was being ripped away from them… And Emily, the one person she'd believed she could count on, was in danger.

Companionship was an illusion, one that could be snatched away at any moment. She'd been fooling herself. She stopped in the street, her hands shaking.

She was alone, all alone.

No. The thought came to her on a whisper of warmth. *You aren't.*

That thought brought back a rush of memory—of Oliver's hands, his eyes. Of the heat of his mouth. She'd tried—and failed—not to think of him in the months that had passed. It wouldn't do any good, she'd told herself. She would never see him again. Thinking of him was a weakness.

So why, now, did thoughts of him make her feel strong?

For one glorious moment, her heart skipped a beat. The cold extremities of her fingers tingled with new life. *You're not alone.*

It wasn't rational thought that brought her down the street to her bank. It was a warm well of certainty. She wasn't alone. She didn't have to be. She smiled at the clerk, who knew her well. When she wrote out the amount she wanted withdrawn, his eyes widened. But he didn't argue. He simply counted the bills.

Maybe it was foolish. She surely didn't need him. Still, her next stop was the telegraph office. It was not far from the bank. It shared space with a confectioner, in fact, since neither were terribly busy, and the same round, jovial woman ran them both.

She didn't need him. But she wanted, oh, she desperately wanted, to believe she wasn't alone.

Jane was filling out the form, dreaming foolish, ridiculous dreams of Oliver Marshall thundering in on a white horse—what the horse had to do with anything, she didn't know—and sweeping her away.

The store bell rang; the door opened. And Dorling walked in.

Her dreams vanished like popped soap bubbles. Her palms went cold. The little pencil she'd been holding fell to the floor, her nerveless fingers no longer able to grasp it. He looked about with purpose; when his eyes lit on her, he smiled quizzically as if surprised to see her.

Of course he had come here. He'd come to send the telegram she had feared—the one to her uncle, the one letting him know that Jane had fled and that he needed to keep watch on Emily.

"Miss Fairfield," he said, coming to stand beside her. "Whatever are you doing here?"

Jane set her hand over the paper she had been filling out and nudged the pencil under the display with her foot.

He rubbed at his sideburns. "I, uh, I encountered your aunt this morning. She said you had gone missing."

Jane looked George Dorling in the eyes. She imagined that he was Oliver Marshall. That was the only way she managed to manufacture a smile for him.

"I had need of a few things," she said airily. She turned back to the woman in front of her. "Two shillings of peppermint, please."

So saying, she shoved the scarcely filled-out paper and a heavy coin at the woman.

She turned back to Dorling. Behind her, she heard the mechanical gears of the register whir and click, the rustle of a bag as the woman started filling it with candy.

Pretending was so easy.

"My aunt," Jane said, "is the most tiresome woman. She was driving me mad with her complaints this morning. 'No, Jane, don't wear those gloves.' 'No, Jane, stop talking so much. Nobody wants to hear about coal aniline dyes again.'" Jane heaved a put-upon sigh and looked down. She'd tasted something sour when she'd said those words, *driving me mad.*

"How untoward of her," Dorling said softly. "Putting off a woman as sweet as you? She must be unbearable."

Across the counter, the woman slid a bag of peppermints to Jane and a handful of small coins.

Would she even send the telegram, incomplete as it was? Would it even matter?

It didn't, actually. The paper had done its job. Whether he got it, whether he came... Jane didn't feel as if she were alone any longer. That left her with a renewed sense of purpose. She wasn't going to let anyone steal her sister away.

She looked over at Dorling, who smiled warmly. Even though her skin crawled, even though she wanted to go home and scrub herself all over to rid herself of the thought of his *persuading* her, she gave him a saucy wink.

"My aunt," she repeated, "is driving me mad. I can't spend another night in the same house as her."

"Can't you?" He smiled back. It wasn't affection in his grin or even pleasure. It was, she imagined, the smirk of a cat facing a mouse in a corner.

"I can't," Jane confirmed.

Luckily for her, she wasn't a mouse. She was an heiress, and good mousers could be bought for a few shillings.

"You," Jane said, "are just the man I was looking for. You are going to help me."

Chapter Nineteen

OLIVER HAD LOST SOMETHING in the time between his mother's telegram and the time when he escorted his sister home. He felt as if he were constantly checking his pockets; when they turned up the usual contents, he'd glance at his watch.

But it wasn't a forgotten appointment or a mislaid coin purse that plagued him during the days that followed. It was something deeper and more fundamental.

After a few morning meetings on one bright day in May, he went back to Clermont House and retreated to his chambers.

It was the same room that he'd been assigned when he was twenty-one—when his brother had come of age and had first invited him to London. Robert had said that Oliver should treat Clermont House as his own.

"You understand," the young duke had said when Oliver had demurred, "that I don't intend that to be an analogy. I do not want you to treat this house *as if it were* yours. It *is* yours. If matters had been different, you would have grown up here. You are my brother, and I won't hear any argument to the contrary."

After the first few months, Oliver had stopped feeling like an interloper and started believing that he belonged. He'd stopped apologizing when he rang the bell. He'd started acting as if he had a place in this world.

But now... Now he saw his surroundings through doubled vision.

He wandered to his window. It overlooked a square below, a well-trimmed affair equipped with a few trees, a bit of a shrubbery, and a bench on either side.

His mother had sat on that bench when Oliver had been nothing but a bulge in her belly. She'd been denied entry to Clermont House, had gone unacknowledged by the old duke. Hugo Marshall—Oliver's *real* father, the man who had raised him—had worked here, but he'd come and gone by the servants' entrance.

It was all well and good for Robert to say that Oliver had a place here, but nothing that either of them said or wanted could alter the history that was woven into this home.

He felt like a pretender.

His sisters had no place in this massive edifice. Oh, when Free had stayed the night, she'd been welcomed politely. She and the duchess got on famously, in fact. But Free had been a guest, and this was not her home.

She had laughed when Oliver had rung for food. "Can't you get it yourself?" she'd asked. "Does being a lord make you lazy?"

"I'm not a lord," he'd informed her.

She'd raised an eyebrow at him. "Not legally, I suppose. But you're rescuing young maidens" —a roll of her eye had shown what she thought of that—"and hobnobbing about in Parliament. There's little enough difference that I can see."

"They see the difference," Oliver had said shortly, thinking of Bradenton.

But she'd shrugged. "You're turning into one of them."

Was he?

"Why couldn't you have needed a proper rescuing anyway?" he'd teased her. "I'm your elder brother. You have to make me feel useful."

"No, I don't," she'd contradicted. "You're a grown man. Find a use for yourself." But she'd smiled as she'd said it, snuggling into his side as she had when she was young.

Decades had passed since his mother had sat in that square, insisting on recognition.

Still, the sight of her bench shouted out to him. *Your place isn't here.*

Oliver sighed, looked upward, and then left his room and its unsettling view.

His brother's suite of rooms was in the other wing of the house, separated from his by a wide staircase. He made his way there, held his breath and contemplated the door to Robert's chambers.

Behind the thick wooden planks, he could hear Minnie laughing. "No," she was saying, her voice an indistinct murmur, "not like that. I—"

There was nothing for it. He would be interrupting no matter what he did. He knocked.

All of Minnie's bright laughter disappeared. There was a pause, then, "Come."

Oliver opened the door.

His brother and his wife were sitting on a sofa together, looking as if they'd put inches between them just a few seconds before. Minnie's hand was curled in Robert's, and her cheeks were flushed. Oliver was clearly interrupting.

Oliver had grown up knowing he had a brother, but the discovery of Robert Blaisdell, the Duke of Clermont, in the flesh had been something of a revelation. Robert had been like a baby bird that left its nest too early. Nobody had ever taught him anything important. He didn't know how to make a fist or duck a blow, how to tie a lure or where to cast his line so that the fish might choose to nibble.

He hadn't known how to write a proper letter, either. He was technically three months older than Oliver, but Oliver had always felt like the elder.

Look, Robert, this is how you do it. This is how you behave like a proper human being.

In turn, Oliver knew how important he was to Robert. Oliver had sisters and a father and a mother. Robert had…well, he had Oliver and Minnie.

Oliver was an ass for thinking that he should lay something as foolish as his inchoate feelings before his brother. Robert had other things to worry about.

"Oliver," Robert said. He paused and tilted his head. "What is it?"

Robert had an uncanny ability to figure out when someone was upset. He was terrible at guessing *why* someone was upset, as a general rule—but he could tell when something was wrong. It was an extremely annoying skill.

"Robert, I…"

He didn't know how to have this conversation. He only knew that he had to say something. He paced across the room and then turned to face the couple.

"I don't feel like I belong here," Oliver finally said.

If his brother was excellent at knowing when others were upset, it was almost impossible to tell when he was hurt. Oliver had learned to look for those tiny signs—the slight tensing of his muscles, the way Robert drew himself back. The way his wife's hand curled around his.

"I don't want you to feel that way," Robert finally said. "What can I do?"

Oliver shook his head. "It's not anything that you're doing or not doing. I don't know why things have changed. I just… I need to be…" If he knew how to complete that sentence, he wouldn't even be here. He wanted to go back to a time when he'd belonged. Back to the time when he still had Jane ahead of him. "I don't feel like I belong anywhere."

Robert nodded and took a deep breath. "How long have you been feeling this way? Maybe we can determine the cause of it."

Since January, he wanted to say. But then he remembered Jane. That late, fateful night, when he'd convinced her to trust him by spilling out his own wants and ambitions. He'd tasted bitterness, knowing what he didn't have, and had recognized in her a kindred spirit.

Oliver looked away. "I think I have always felt this way."

This time, he didn't have to try to see his brother's flinch. He knew, damn it, he *knew* what Robert was like. So hesitant, so careful, always afraid that someone was going to walk away from him.

"It's not you," Oliver told him. "You've always made me feel welcome. Whatever you think, don't doubt that. You're my brother and you always will be. I just… I just don't know. And I hate not knowing."

"Is there something that precipitated this?" Minnie looked at him. "You've seemed…distant since you returned from Cambridge."

Cambridge. That word tightened around him like a fist clenching, gripping him with a bitter nostalgia. *Cambridge.* There was a word that whispered of walks along a green in the day and in a park at night. Of a woman who didn't flinch at anyone's proclamations.

Jane was the most fearless woman Oliver had ever met. Sometimes, Oliver thought that society was like an infant trying to shove a square, colored block through a round hole. When it didn't go, the child pounded harder. Oliver had been shoved through round holes so often that he'd scarcely even noticed that his edges had become rounded. But Jane…Jane persisted in being angular and square. The harder she was pushed, the more square—and the more colorful—she became.

It was a good thing Oliver wasn't in love with her. If he had been so foolish as to admire her that much, he wasn't sure how he could ever find his way out.

"Did something happen with Sebastian?" Robert asked.

"Yes," he said. "But…not what you think." He sat down on a chair across from them. "I don't know what it is," he finally said. "You always know who you are and what you want. And right now, I'm a total muddle."

Robert stood up and crossed to him. "Muddles," he said, "I understand." He put his hand on Oliver's shoulder. "If you're feeling muddled, I don't know what I can say. Except…don't question whether you have a place here."

Oliver shook his head.

"You're my brother." Robert hesitated, and then, just a little more quietly, said, "I love you. I will always love you. You have a place here. You just don't have to use it."

Oliver looked up.

"Stop moping," Robert said, punching his shoulder. "Maybe it's simply that with the Reform Act creeping its way through Parliament, you're needing a new project. You've worked on this for how long now? It can be a surprising letdown to see something you've worked for come to fruition. It leaves an emptiness in your life."

"That's precisely what it is." Oliver shut his eyes. "An emptiness in my life. I'm just not sure what would fill it."

There was a tap behind them. Oliver turned to see a servant standing in the doorway.

"Sir," he said, bowing to Oliver. "A telegram has come for you."

"Oh, lovely," Oliver said aloud. "I wonder what Free has done now?"

The servant didn't answer and Oliver took the envelope in bemusement. The flimsy paper inside contained three lines

NOBODY ELSE I CAN TURN TO
AM IN NOTTINGHAM
TOMORROW I WILL

That was it. That was the entirety of the message. It seemed curiously abbreviated, and the last line—he hesitated to call it a *sentence* when even in the truncated language of telegrams it lacked necessary parts of speech—made no sense. Tomorrow I will...who was this I?

Oliver had no idea.

Eat, drink, and be merry, some amused part of him whispered, *for tomorrow I will...*

He looked the paper over. He didn't know anyone in Nottingham. And the only person who would send him a message asking for help, aside from his family, was...

He stared at the paper and reread it.

Jane Fairfield.

He licked his lips.

"Robert," he said, "tell me if I am wrong, but this would be a most inconvenient time to leave town, would it not?"

There were ongoing debates in Parliament. Details were being settled on a regular basis. But the thought of staying—of going to yet another dinner with yet more people who made him feel strange inside his skin—seemed impossibly wrong.

Free hadn't needed him. She hadn't even asked for him. But Jane...

"Oliver," Robert said, "is everything well? It's not your sister again, is it?"

"No," Oliver said, almost dazedly. "It's not my sister."

He could go to Jane. If it was Jane who had sent this message.

A stupid idea. He tried to dispel it with logic.

The world didn't turn on Jane, he lectured himself, and everything *would* alter if the voting reforms were watered down. What were one woman's problems when compared with the entire world? He wasn't even in love with her. This might not even have come from her.

But for one second, he imagined seeing her again. He imagined spending a few days with a colorful, square block—a few blissful days without a single round hole in sight.

"I'm going to Nottingham," he said.

And for the first time in four months, he felt right—as if he'd turned toward home after a long journey in a foreign land.

Robert blinked.

Oliver laughed, feeling almost giddy with relief. "I don't know what I'm doing there," he said. "Or why I need to go, or how long it will take. But I'm going."

"You're going now?"

Now seemed like a good time. An excellent time. After all, the sooner he went, the sooner he could come back. And maybe, just maybe, when he saw her, he could figure out how she managed to keep from being worn down. Maybe he needed a little dose of the impossible.

That was it. He wasn't in love with her, but... God, he ached to see her.

"I'm going," Oliver said, "as soon as I can put together a few things."

✻ ✻ ✻

He repeated that mantra on the train, chanted it in time with the rushing clack-clack-clack of the wheels.

He wasn't in love with her; he was just fulfilling a promise.

He wasn't in love with her; he was merely going to visit an old friend.

He wasn't in love with her; he was simply going to set right a wrong.

The train steamed on through the afternoon, and Oliver let himself believe every word.

He wasn't in love with her. He just *wasn't*.

✻ ✻ ✻

WHEN HE ASKED CASUALLY at the inn upon arrival, he was told there would be an assembly that night—starting in a mere fifteen minutes—and that all the eligible young ladies would attend. "Including," the maid said, "an heiress." She blinked at him. "I hear she has the most outrageous gowns. I do wish I could see them."

So did Oliver. It *had* been her telegram, then. She needed him. He was going to see her, and the thought of it filled him with an electric anticipation.

He wasn't in love with her. He was just smiling because he knew she'd appreciate being called outrageous.

He wasn't in love with her; he was just going to the assembly without taking the time to unpack his valise. Nothing wrong with that, was there?

He made excuse after excuse as he dressed, as he made sure his coat pockets contained all the necessary things one would need if a woman ended up in danger—money and a pistol pretty much covered it.

He wasn't in love with her; he was just being careful.

He told himself those same lies when he joined the throng in the assembly. He was just looking for her—a perfectly normal thing to do, wasn't it? To look for a woman you'd traveled a hundred miles to see. It was normal that his breath seemed heavy in his lungs, that the seconds without her seemed to weigh on his shoulders.

And then he saw her. The assembly doors opened, and she entered the room. She was dressed in a gown that clung to the curves of her breasts and flared at the waist. It was green—the kind of green that a monk might have used in an illuminated manuscript of old to sketch out a venomous snake whispering temptation from an apple tree.

Someone else might have found that gold fringe at her ankles gaudy. They might have winced at the color of her dress or the sparkling beads that adorned it. They might have blinked at her garish headpiece.

But this was Jane. It had been four months since Oliver had last seen her. She was utterly gorgeous, from the bejeweled slippers that peeked out under the edge of her gown all the way up to the poison-green feathers plaited into her hair. Jane. His Jane. His breath caught, and for the first time in what seemed like forever, he felt as if he had landed precisely where he belonged. Here, in this assembly that he'd never attended, amongst a crowd of strangers.

He'd been lying to himself all these months.

He *was* in love with her. And he had no idea what to do about it.

Chapter Twenty

"THAT GOWN IS HIDEOUS," Jane's aunt said for what seemed the fifteenth time. "Do you want everyone to think you a…" She paused, but as there was no particular social message that was sent by wearing a viper-green dress, she had no way to continue. "Are you trying to be a ninnyhammer?"

"A ninnyhammer," Jane said, "sounds like a magic hammer. One that I can use to smite ninnies. I have a great need for one of those."

Her aunt was struck dumb by this. She stared and sniffed, and finally shook her head. "How will you ever bring Dorling up to scratch dressed like that?"

Jane didn't dignify that with an answer. She refused to talk about the man with her aunt. Instead, she stared blankly at the carriage wall. Dorling was the author of half of her current misery, and she cared approximately nothing for him. It was when she thought of Emily—of what her uncle might do, what he might already have done—that she began to worry.

The telegram might not have gone through. Even if it had, what she'd remembered writing on the card in a tearing hurry was utter gibberish. She hadn't given him an inkling of what she needed, when she needed it, where they should meet, or any other pertinent information—such as, for instance, her own name. Oliver had an entire life to live, people that he cared for, things to do. He wasn't going to rush off because he received a telegram that might or might not have come from a woman he might or might not have forgotten.

He was likely married by now. He had almost certainly put aside his foolish promise. Besides, there wasn't any time. The telegram had gone out just before noon. Scarcely seven hours had elapsed, and her plan was already in motion.

God. It was all going to happen tonight, whether she was ready or not. She had nobody to rely on but herself, no weapons except two rolls of bills. One was strapped to her thigh; the other was lodged rather uncomfortably between her breasts.

The assembly room was up a flight of stairs. The exercise made her too warm. With every step, those bills between her breasts chafed. On the plus side, there was no way that the money would slide out on accident, wedged in there as they were. On the other hand, she feared they would leave a permanent, bill-shaped imprint against the sides of her breasts. It was a good thing she didn't need a pistol. *That* would hurt, stuffed down there.

So Jane smiled at her aunt, squared her shoulders, and marched into the assembly room.

It was blazing hot in that crush of bodies, so hot that Jane felt almost overwhelmed by the blast of warmth. She had less than half an hour to find Dorling, to explain to him what she needed.

But it was not Dorling her eyes lit on as she perused the crowd. It was another man entirely.

"Oh," she said aloud. She had to be imagining him—those eyes, alight with some inner humor, pale blue and sparkling. That bright shock of hair. Those spectacles.

He was dressed in dark clothing with long tails on his coats. The cuffs of his shirt gleamed whitely at his sleeves. His hair shone in the lamp light like a bright beacon. He looked about, adjusted his spectacles on his nose, and saw her.

It had been months since she'd seen him last, and the sight of him felt like a blow—a welcome blow, one that nearly knocked her over with the weight of relief. Everyone else in the room vanished. There was only him—him and her—and the distance and time that lay between them seemed to dwindle away.

It took every ounce of self-control that Jane had—every last scrap of restraint—to keep herself from dashing across the room into his waiting arms.

But…her aunt was watching.

And so she waited demurely, trying to ignore the unsightly trickle of sweat that slid down her back, trying not to scratch at her breasts. She waited, talking to others with her mind in a daze.

How had he come so quickly?

Oh, it was *possible,* of course, that he might have done so. But he would have had to get on a train almost immediately after he'd received her telegram.

She was still dazed when Mrs. Laurence came up with Oliver in tow. Jane barely heard the words of introduction; she had no idea what story he had told. She only nodded in dumbfounded agreement when he asked if he might walk her around the room.

"Miss Fairfield," he said with a smile.

"Mr…" She looked up at him. She couldn't even remember if he'd used his real name in introduction. She hadn't been listening. "Mr. Cromwell," she finally said.

An amused light came into his eyes.

"You came." She wanted to clutch his arm.

"Of course I did. I told you I would." He glanced down at her gown. "What ungodly color are you wearing?"

"Green," she said. "Serpent-belly green. Or perhaps it's the green of a cloud of poisonous chlorine gas."

"And yet nobody is shrieking and averting their eyes." He gave her a smile. "Nice trick. How do you manage it?"

She gave him a brilliant smile. "Simple," she said, adjusting the diamonds at her neck. "I already told you. It's the heiress effect." She smiled at him again. "You came, Oliver. I can't believe you came. And so quickly, too."

"Didn't I tell you?" he smiled at her. "You're not alone."

"But it's been months." She looked over at him. "We only knew each other a few weeks. I assumed that you would be…" But maybe he *was*. She looked up at him in horror.

"I'm not married," he said simply. "Nor engaged. Nor even courting."

She wasn't going to let herself feel glad about that. She refused to do so.

But her refusal didn't seem to be working. A lightness pervaded her.

He gave her dress a pointed stare. "Although if I had realized that you were trying to blind the entire assembly, I would have brought blinkers. As for a horse." He held up his hands to either side of his head, demonstrating. "They would keep me from getting skittish."

They were smiling at each other, and for the first moment since that morning, Jane felt as if everything would turn out. Somehow.

"Now," he said, stepping closer. "Is this a place where we can talk about what you need, or shall we arrange for a better time?"

"Time." She laughed. "In fifteen minutes, I am supposed to meet the Honorable George Dorling." She gulped. "For purposes of eloping with him."

Something shifted in his expression—something that washed that humor out of his visage. He took a step toward her. "I'll be *damned* if you do."

He wasn't married. She had sent him a nonsensical telegram, listing only the name of the city, and he had come in a matter of hours. Jane wasn't particularly good at figuring people out, but even she could add two and two and come up with a number larger than three. She felt herself smiling despite everything.

He, on the other hand, took a deep breath and shook his head. He looked upward, and then…

"Terribly sorry." His voice was a little rough. "That was overdone on my part." His hand curled into a fist. "Is that what you want?"

"It's not like that," Jane said. "It's a false elopement."

He frowned.

"Or it will be. There's no time to explain. I have to go bribe my pretend-bridegroom. You see, if he is pretending to elope with me, my aunt will think I've gone to Gretna Green. If she thinks I have merely run off on my own, she'll let my uncle know I'm on my way. Then I'll never be able to steal my sister in time."

Any other man might have been taken aback at that. Oliver simply nodded.

"That makes almost no sense," he said. "But I gather we're on a tight schedule. I suppose you have an elopement to fake, and then…"

"Then we must make our way to Cambridge. As swiftly as possible."

"That part I can manage. I'll find transportation." Oliver frowned. "If we're going to Cambridge, and we don't want your aunt to know…there are no trains any longer tonight. She'll hear if we stay at a hotel in town."

"I had my friend bring a valise for me to the Stag and Hounds over in Burton Joyce. I planned to overnight there and then catch the early train."

He nodded. "I'll have my things sent over and a separate room arranged." He paused. "God, Jane…" His hand twitched toward her, but he brought it back swiftly. All he said was, "It's good to see you. Go bribe your swain."

She laughed.

He started to leave and then turned back. "I wasn't expecting this."

She shook her head in mock solemnity. "Nobody expects a false elopement."

He reached out and touched her hand. Jane had to bite her lip to keep from grabbing hold of him and refusing to ever let go.

"That's not what I meant," he said, his voice low. "I never forgot about you at all. So why is it that now that I'm here, I feel as if I'm recalling things I've never known?" He looked into her eyes. "I missed you, Jane."

Oh, God. She looked back at him, wishing the entire world away. All those dreams she hadn't wanted to let herself remember… They all came rushing back on a wave of heat. But all she said was, "I missed you, too."

⌘ ⌘ ⌘

Dorling was already waiting for Jane in the side room where they'd
agreed to meet. She paused at the doorway and contemplated the man. She
would have felt badly about using him except that he was using her as badly,
and had planned far worse.

"Dorling," Jane said.

He turned, dropping a fob watch back into his pocket as he did so. It
would be wrong to say that he smiled. That expression didn't look like any
smile Jane had ever seen. It was far too practiced, too sly.

"You've taken care of everything?" Jane asked.

When she'd talked to him earlier, she'd told him the bare basics. That
she needed to leave. With him. That night—details to be determined later.

She'd never actually said she would elope with him, but she had strongly
implied it.

He smiled at her. "I did," he said. "Did you bring the money?"

Jane could feel that roll between her breasts. "Yes. We need to talk."

"Plenty of time for that on the way to Scotland."

"Yes, well. That's what we need to talk about. You're under a
misapprehension. I'm not eloping with you."

He blinked at her, his smile dying on his face. "But I've already told
your—that is, I sent your aunt a letter. Think of your reputation."

She snorted. Her reputation? For a year, she'd cultivated the reputation
of an abrasive, foolish, awful woman. She'd done it on purpose. Her
reputation wasn't black, but it was definitely stained. Another blot wouldn't
hurt.

"There's no time to explain," Jane said.

"But—"

"I'm *not* going to elope with you. I will give you money to pretend to do
so. This isn't hard. You can have nothing, or you can have a vast sum. Your
choice."

"Money?" He looked struck by this. "How much money?"

"Five hundred pounds. All you have to do is leave town tonight and not
return for another three days. Five hundred pounds for that, Dorling."

"But—"

"No negotiations. Just cash."

He huffed. "That wasn't the choice I wanted. Ah, well. Let's see the
money then."

She turned her back to him. She had to take off one of her poisonous
green gloves to worm her fingers between her breasts. But it was lovely to
get that roll of bills out of their hiding spot, to not have them digging into
her skin. She rubbed surreptitiously at her bosom, and then realized belatedly

that rubbing her breasts with Dorling around, no matter how innocent her intentions, was probably not a good idea. She turned back to him.

As soon as she did, her breath caught in her lungs. She was looking into the shiny metal barrel of a gun. Her whole body went cold, the world narrowing to a barrel-sized pinpoint. Her hands seemed nerveless. She barely managed to keep hold of her glove.

"Hate to do this, sweetling," Dorling said. "But I can perform basic mathematics. You're offering five hundred pounds to let you walk away, but I'll have a hundred thousand if we marry. There's really no comparison." As he spoke, he reached out and plucked the roll of bills from her fingers.

"You can't marry me at gunpoint," Jane said.

"No." He sounded ridiculously unhappy about that. "But I can make you leave with me. I know this looks bad, kitten, but I do mean to be a reasonable husband. You'll forgive me eventually."

"You mean that you'll let me use my money to embarrass my uncle if he mistreats my sister?"

He smiled. "Ah, you must have overheard that this morning. Now it all makes sense. Sorry, darling. I gave my word to him on that point. If you couldn't trust my word, why would you marry me at all?"

A curious question. He seemed unaware that he had just robbed her of five hundred pounds at gunpoint, that he was proposing to take her freedom by a similar method.

"How nice," Jane said, "that you are a man of honor."

Luckily, he didn't hear the sarcasm in her tone. Jane glanced surreptitiously over her shoulder, but there was no sign of Oliver.

And what would he have done? She *needed* Dorling. He needed to disappear so that her aunt would think that Jane had eloped.

All Jane had to do was be smarter than him, and hope the opportunity presented itself quickly. Because there was only a narrow window of time they had, that time when her aunt would believe Jane was eloping rather than haring off on her own to rescue her sister.

"You leave me no choice," Jane said.

Dorling smiled. "Good," he said. "Then there's no need for me to use the ether. Let's get to the carriage."

Ether. Jane tried not to twitch. "Of course," she said. He took her arm—she managed not to flinch from his touch—and guided her down the hall.

She didn't dare look back.

"Where are we going?" she asked bravely. "And what route are we taking?" The more she knew, the better she could plan.

Chapter Twenty-One

ABDUCTION, JANE REFLECTED SEVERAL HOURS LATER, was deathly boring. Dorling sat across the carriage from her still holding his pistol. The carriage they were in was closed, the glassed windows on the door showing nothing in the night but the dark blur of woods. They'd been traveling for a good long while northward, and all Jane wanted to do was yawn.

"Is there an inn nearby?" she asked. "Are we stopping for the night?"

"Eventually," Dorling snapped.

She yawned again and peered out the window. Silhouettes of big, knotty oaks flew past. She tried counting trees. At forty-seven, the carriage stopped—which surprised her, as there was no evidence of civilization nearby.

"What are we doing?" Jane asked.

But Dorling looked just as confused as she felt. He shook his head and gestured her back.

A few moments later, the carriage door opened. The driver was a dark, cloaked silhouette in the doorway.

"Is there a problem?" Dorling asked.

"Aye," he responded. "One of the horses has gone lame." The man had a broad farm accent. Jane wondered, idly, if he was bribable. There *was* still that roll of bills strapped to her thigh.

"God damn it." Dorling's nostrils flared. "Of all the times… What is wrong with you, man, that your horses go lame? This shouldn't be happening. Now what are we going to do?"

The driver shrugged. "Come take a look."

Dorling glanced over at Jane. "I'm not sure."

The driver shrugged again. "Give it to me, then. I'll watch her. You go see." Dorling handed over the pistol and stepped out of the carriage. But the driver didn't follow him immediately. He turned in the doorway, and then, very carefully, raised a finger to his lips.

Jane let out a breath. "Oliver," she whispered.

"Shh. A moment longer."

"God damn it," Dorling's voice came again. "One of the beasts has a stone in its hoof. I don't think it can walk at the moment. *Now* what are we going to do? Do you have any idea how bloody inconvenient this is?"

Oliver turned to the man. "Yes," he said in his normal voice, "I do. Because I hadn't planned on riding double back to town."

There was a long pause. "What?' Dorling asked.

"Riding double," Oliver said. "You would not believe how fortuitous your appearance was. I was looking for transportation, and there, just outside the hall, was a man who had transportation—transportation that I knew he wouldn't be needing. Imagine my delight." He shook his head. "It was a good thing I managed to make another arrangement with the driver."

"I don't understand," Dorling said. "Who are you?"

"I had planned to jettison you a little farther from civilization, but this will have to do. Stay with the cart, and the driver will come pick you up mid-afternoon tomorrow. You'll be back in Nottingham by night, which I presume will give us enough time." Oliver walked to the back and began to rummage in the boot. "There are blankets and wine and some spare food back here, so you won't be too uncomfortable."

"You can't make me! I have a—" He started to brandish his empty hand and then stared at it.

"Yes." Oliver's voice came from behind the carriage. "A little advice: Next time you try an abduction, don't give your weapon to someone you don't know."

Jane smirked.

"This is outrageous!" Dorling said. "Who are you, and what have you done with my cart driver?"

Oliver came back from the boot carrying a saddle. "Jane, I'm sorry to say that we're going to have to ride double. Are you game?"

Jane found herself smiling. "How did you know? How did you do this?"

"Simple," he said. "I told you you weren't alone. Did you really think I would leave you?"

She didn't know what to say. She just shook her head and watched him saddle the horse. It was the first time she'd ever seen him do anything physical, and he did it so swiftly and so smoothly that she was reminded that he'd grown up on a farm. He could argue politics and rescue impossible girls and saddle a horse with equal ease.

She'd spent months thinking about him. Thinking about what she might have said to him if only she'd been brave enough.

She wouldn't let it go unsaid much longer.

"We don't have much time," he said, "but it will be enough." He mounted the horse, and then held out his hand to Jane. "Come on," he said. "Let's go."

"Wait," she said. "The weapon, if you please."

He held it out to her without asking. Jane turned, and Dorling's face went white. "Please," he said. "Don't… You don't need to…"

Jane rolled her eyes. "Oh, stop blubbering. I want my five hundred pounds back."

"But it means nothing to you! To me, it would be…"

"Yes," Jane said. "I know what it would mean to you." She pointed the pistol directly at his forehead. "That's why I want it back."

⌘   ⌘   ⌘

TWO PEOPLE, BOTH IN EVENING DRESS, could not ride comfortably on one horse. Oliver cinched his arm around Jane for the fifteenth time in four minutes and shifted in the saddle behind her.

Jane's skirts flapped voluminously in the breeze. Something sharp and protuberant in her skirts jabbed his thigh. And the beads sewn into her gown were itchy and uncomfortable.

Still, it wasn't wholly awful. After all, Jane was warm and soft, and it was all too easy to breath in the scent of her. She smelled of familiar soap.

Twenty-four hours ago, he'd been reading in a comfortable chair at Clermont house, thinking about how to exert influence on the Members of Parliament that he knew.

Now he was on a horse, God knew how far from civilization, with an heiress of dubious reputation, plotting to kidnap a nineteen-year-old girl from her guardian. It was as if he had exited reality and found himself plopped into the middle of some kind of medieval tale of chivalry, one where he needed his wits and his sword to survive.

He'd planned out the course of his life years ago—quiet service, eventual recognition, a slow rise to power. There was no room in that story for the ridiculously impulsive actions he'd taken today: leaving London on a bare half hour's notice, finding Jane, foiling abduction plots against impossible odds.

There would be plenty of time to come to his senses. He tightened his arms briefly around Jane, thinking of that dazzling moment when he'd first seen her on the stairs.

He had all the right emotions. He'd expected to fall in love one day. Just not like this. Not with her. He was in the wrong story with the wrong lady. Someone had made a mistake…and he very much feared it was him.

But Jane leaned back against him, and even though he could have written a list about all the ways that she was a mistake, she didn't feel like one.

"It's not fair," Jane said, echoing his feelings so closely that he sucked in a breath. "This is supposed to be romantic. What woman does not want to have a man rush to her aid and sweep her away on his fiery stallion?"

Yes, they had definitely found themselves in the wrong story. "I would refer to this particular steed more as a 'placid gelding' than a 'fiery stallion,'" Oliver said. "That's the first problem."

"In the books," Jane said, "the man always clasps the woman lovingly to him, and she melts in his embrace."

"My embrace isn't loving enough for you?"

His arm was around her. But no matter his intentions and his emotions—and God, what a morass those were—he couldn't call his clasp *loving*. It was more like a desperate attempt to keep her from sliding off the seat.

"I can't speak for your embrace," she replied. "But I don't think my body is *melting* into yours. I feel more like a ship being tossed against the rocks."

Oliver smiled again. "Friction is the very devil," he replied. "Also, women who want loving embraces ought not to wear an arsenal of beads. Then there's that thing that's poking into my thigh."

"Hmm?"

"Hard to think of romance with something that uncomfortable so close to my delicate parts," Oliver said. "In fact, I have to exert some substantial effort just to make sure that my voice doesn't go up an octave. That sharp pokey thing in your skirts is threatening to unman me."

"What do you mean?" She reached behind her and groped his thigh—an action he wished he was in a better position to appreciate. "Oh. That's just five hundred pounds in a roll. Stop whining, Oliver; it's better than having it stuffed down a corset." She sighed. "The stories never mention that saddles built for one rather than two make your backside go numb. Also" —she turned in the saddle, just enough that he had to hold her more tightly to keep from slipping—"did you know that your thighs are extremely hard? And I thought the squabs of the carriage were uncomfortable."

"You'd like it even less if I had pillowy thighs," Oliver replied.

She leaned back against him. "Mmm. Pillowy thighs. Those would be lovely right now. Thighs that I could shut my eyes and sink into. Your thighs are like oak logs. Very unrestful."

"Yes, but here's the problem. If I had pillowy thighs, I would have reached down to swing you atop my fiery gelding, and when I tried to heft you in the air, I would have dropped you. 'Damn it!' I'd proclaim. 'I just threw out my back!'"

She laughed softly.

"All the stories are wrong," he told her.

He meant it just how he said it—they were filled with falsehoods and euphemisms. But he also meant it how he didn't say it: that they were wrong to be here.

"Impossible girl." But his lips were so close to her neck that even that whispered label felt like an endearment, rather than a reminder.

There was a long pause. And then...

"Thank you. I didn't say that before, did I? I was too flabbergasted that you arrived, and then everything seemed to get away from me. Including myself. I'm afraid I've been horribly rude, and for once I didn't intend it."

She'd turned to him again—or at least, had turned her head toward him as best as she could manage on a moving horse. Despite the discomfort of it all, he was enjoying holding her. She felt lovely in his arms, a bundle of complex scents. Lavender and rose and a clean, citrus smell that reminded him of home.

She sighed. "And here I am, talking again. I don't know what it is about you. How is it that every time you're near, I can't seem to keep quiet?"

His arms were already around her. He could have set his chin on her shoulder if he'd leaned down a few inches. All the stories were wrong, but one thing seemed absolutely right.

"It's because you're thinking about this," he said, and kissed her.

There was no good way to kiss a woman who was sharing his saddle. His neck crooked awkwardly, and he had to hold tight to keep her from slipping off. But it didn't matter. All those months disappeared—those long, dark months without her there, when he could have been doing *this*. Holding her. Kissing her. Exploring her mouth, inch by luscious inch.

The horse, sensing Oliver's inattention, slowed to an amble. Even that damned sharp thing in her skirts stopped being so noticeable. There was nothing but her and the night around them. Crickets chirped somewhere; a bird that hadn't yet noticed that night had fallen called out. His hands were full of her. If he let go, she might slip bonelessly off the horse.

If he stopped kissing her, he might have to think about the future. He didn't want to contemplate a world away from this road, away from her kiss. So he didn't stop. He simply held her close and tasted her.

"Oh," she said, when he finally raised his head, subtly stretching out the kink in his neck.

But she didn't ask any questions. Instead, she leaned back against him. Her hair was beginning to fall out of its heavy coiffure. If this were a story, little curls would be coming undone, little tendrils of hair escaping down her back. Instead, the mass of her hair leaned to one side, canting like a half-uprooted tree. Occasionally, she'd reach up and do her best to adjust it back to straight, but inevitably, it would start falling once more. When he wasn't careful, her hairpins jabbed him.

"I suppose," she finally said, "that makes up for your horrible, hard thighs."

He smiled. "I would say that you've made up for your money, but that would be a lie. You've a long way to go."

She met his eyes over her shoulder. "How long a way?"

"Miles," he told her. "Miles and miles of kisses, taken at an amble like this. Maybe once we've made it to the Stag and Hounds, I'll be ready to stop."

Maybe they'd never make it there. Maybe the rest of the world could be held at bay, and they might spend forever uninterrupted in this darkness with nothing to do but kiss. Maybe that was all this story would be—a nightlong kiss, one where dawn never came.

"Then we must get started immediately." She tilted her head to his once more.

This time, the horse came to a complete stop. He held her in place with one firm hand at her waist, and let the other skitter down her shoulder, stroking her lightly, playing with the lace at her neckline, the fabric under it. Her skin underneath was warm and soft. When he skimmed the tops of her breasts, she let out a little gasp.

God, he hadn't wanted to know that she was that responsive. He hadn't wanted to know it, but now that he did, he couldn't stop himself from exploring. He wanted to hear her breathing arrest as he explored the soft curve of her breast. Holding her this close, he could feel that almost-inaudible moan she made. It was a vibration deep in her rib cage, one he sensed in the palms of his hands. He slid his fingers farther under her neckline, under her corset, until he found the place where her skin changed from the softness of her breast to the hard nub of her nipple.

She gave out a soft cry.

"There's only so much I can do on a horse," he murmured in her ear. "And perhaps it's just as well, because if I had you in a bed tonight, I don't think I could keep my mouth from taking the place of my hands."

He slid his finger in another circle around her breast.

She swept her hand down his shoulder. Not skimming the fabric. Not even dipping tentatively below the lapels of his coat. Her palm conformed to his chest, seeking out the shape of his muscles, as if the fabric were not even there.

It didn't matter where they were. What they were doing. That she wore a ball gown, that there were layers of silk and wool separating their skin. He burned for her, burned to kiss every last inch of her. He burned to touch the places he couldn't reach at this moment.

"God, Jane. God. Tell me not to pull you off this horse."

She did no such thing. She simply tangled her hand in his coat and pulled him closer.

He was not going to have her in the underbrush at the side of the road. He *wasn't*. But God, he wanted it. He wanted her, and he couldn't even remember why it was a bad idea any longer.

"Oliver." She said his name on a gasp, and it drove him wild.

"God, I love when you say my name like that."

She shifted, and her bottom rubbed against his groin as she did. He rolled her nipple between his fingers.

"Oliver," she moaned, and he kissed her harder. "Oliver. I'm not trying to say your name."

He pulled back, breathing hard.

"It's just, that's the third raindrop I've felt."

"Oh, damnation." He didn't want to be interrupted, not for rain, not for thunder, not for a flood sweeping down on them. He didn't want this to end. Once it did, he wasn't sure when it would ever start again.

But she was right. It had begun to rain. A cold, wet droplet fell on his nose, followed by another.

He had known their time together was going to end. It was probably just as well that it had. Nothing had changed. She was still...impossible. Utterly impossible. A few heated kisses couldn't hold the truth at bay, and more would just render this whole thing unsavory.

He wanted more. God, how he wanted more. He wanted it with the strength of four months' of desperate longing. He forced himself to concentrate on those cold, wet drops. He imagined each one washing away his ardor. Driving away thoughts of her breast under his palm, her legs wrapped around his waist.

The rain really wasn't helping.

The storm came on faster than their horse would go. One minute, there were a mild drizzle; the next, it felt as if they'd been enveloped in a sheet of water. It poured over them in a cold wave.

So why was he not chilled? Why was he still holding her, caressing her, kissing away the water drops that collected on her ear? Why were his hands exploring her curves?

Light sizzled across the sky in a jagged arc.

It highlighted the silhouettes of buildings, not so far away now. This interlude was already coming to an end. He couldn't let go of her, though. Couldn't stop his lips from tasting her neck again and again. Couldn't take his hands from her thighs—especially not now, with her gown plastered to her skin.

He took her to the inn.

There were a thousand ways that a man and a woman arriving at an inn, drenched, in the middle of the night, might finagle a room together. If he were a different man...

He handed her down. "Go in," he said. "Tell whoever's in charge some story about how you..." He really couldn't think of a story right now. He couldn't think of anything but her. "Make up something. Whatever you like. I'll wait half an hour and come in with a different tale. We sent our luggage over by different paths, requested different rooms. There's no need for her to associate the two of us."

"Oliver."

He didn't look at her. If he saw her eyes, if he looked at her gown, clinging to her wet skin, he'd never let her go.

He swallowed. The next words were harder to say than he had imagined, but he managed to choke them out.

"Sleep well. I'll see you tomorrow at the train station at seven."

Chapter Twenty-Two

JANE COULD NOT WAIT CALMLY. Time passed, and she watched the door, waiting to see the results of her subterfuge. It took forty-five minutes before Oliver strode in, still wet, but possessed of one of the towels that Jane had asked to be left for him.

"Jane." His voice was rough.

He ran his hands through his hair, ruffling it into wet, auburn spikes.

She lifted her chin and met his eyes. There was no lamp in the room, just a fire. The dim flicker of flame made his eyes seem dark and dangerous.

"What do you think you're doing?" he growled.

"You told me to tell the innkeeper a story," she said, managing to keep her voice calm even when her heart was beating at twice its normal rate. "I did."

"A story about how you came to be alone and wet and bedraggled to an inn! That's what I meant. Not a story about—about—"

"About how my lover, a duke's son, would be coming along shortly?" Jane raised an eyebrow. "About how we would be sharing a chamber?"

He tossed his towel over a chair and advanced on her.

"Yes," he said, "I want you. Yes, I've thought of having you over and over these last few months. Yes, I lost my head out there, Jane. But I didn't expect you to pay for my help with your body."

She stood. She'd changed from her sodden gown into a warm chemise with an embroidered robe over it. She could hear the beat of blood in her ears.

"Is that what you think? That I'm offering myself to you in payment for services rendered? Don't be daft, Oliver." She took a step toward him. "Do you think you're the only one who has been wanting these last months? The only one who lies awake, watching the ceiling, wishing for more? Look at me. I'm not a sacrifice."

Her heart slammed, but she reached up and undid the tie of her robe. He watched that piece of silk slide to the floor, his eyes hungry.

"Look at me," Jane repeated. She slid the robe off of her shoulders—she could scarcely breathe—and let it flutter down. Her skin prickled in the sudden coolness, but it wasn't cold she felt. "I'm not a gift," she said. "Or a prize that you've won. I'm a woman, and I want you because it will give me joy."

He was looking her up and down. She knew how sheer her shift was—translucent enough that he'd be able to see the form of her body silhouetted with the fire behind it.

He licked his lips. "I had every intention of being a gentleman. Of sleeping on the floor, or...or something."

"Is that what a gentleman would do?" Jane asked.

"Probably."

"Then gentlemen are idiots."

He laughed. "Jane. God. You are the bravest woman I have ever known."

She took a step closer. "I scarcely have the wherewithal to be brave about this." Another step, until she was close enough to set her hands on his chest.

"Do you know what to expect?"

"Only in the vaguest terms. The specifics..." She reached out and gently, very gently, took hold of his cravat. "The specifics," she repeated, "I'm looking forward to discovering."

"Then discover."

She undid his cravat, winding the fabric from around his neck.

"See?" She looked up. "I didn't know that—the look of your throat." She leaned forward and placed a kiss in the hollow there. The points of his shirt brushed wetly against her cheeks.

"Jane. You're killing me."

She hadn't understood what to do until she heard his voice—that hard rasp, so clearly indicating he was on the edge of his control. This, *this* was what she wanted. To kill him with every brush of her fingers, and to have him love it.

She pushed back the collar of his still sodden coat; he shrugged his shoulders, relinquishing it to her.

She'd seen men in their shirtsleeves before, but never like this. Not with the fabric practically translucent from rain, outlining the smooth curve of bicep and tricep. She undid the buttons of his waistcoat, slowly reveling in the glimpses she caught through the fabric—the slim tapering of his waist, the hard feel of his abdomen when she brushed her hand against the fabric of his shirt.

He hadn't moved, except to assist her in removing items. She was glad of it. He stood still, as if he understood that she needed to uncover him, little by little. To get used to the idea of what would happen. To let her touch before he touched her back.

The shirt proved more complicated. He had little silver studs at the cuff, and it took her some time to untangle the wet mass from his person, even though he gave her a little help. But when she had it off him…

Just the hint of his flesh through the shirt had made her mouth dry. The reality of him—of all that taut muscle, of the arrow of hair tracing down from his navel, the darker nubs of his nipples…

She reached out and set her hand on his skin.

"Oh my God," she said. "You're still wet. Of course you're still wet. And cold." She took the towel he'd abandoned and dabbed at his shoulders. His arms. Feeling it all as she went, that hard, smooth body of his, dangerously curved and yet waiting motionless. Allowing her to explore her fill of him. She dried off his back and addressed herself to his front.

He hissed as she rubbed his abdomen.

"Did that hurt?"

"On the contrary. It felt rather good." He looked her in the eyes. "Touch me there again."

He hadn't moved, not one inch, but he wasn't letting go of control. His skin was warming under her caresses, the color changing from chalk to a faint blush. She touched him, traced that line of hair vanishing into his trousers, felt the firm muscle tense under her fingers.

"Am I doing it right?"

"You're doing… Yes, Jane. Keep doing that. Please."

She ran her hand up his waist. Across his chest. When her fingers brushed his nipple, he hissed again, and she took a moment for further exploration. He responded to her touch, his flesh tightening, hardening. His breath shivered as she rolled the hard nub between her fingers, touching it the way he'd touched her earlier.

Oh, if only she'd paid better attention, cataloguing what he'd done.

What was it he'd said? That if he had her in a bed, he would…

She leaned forward and licked him.

"Oh, Jane." His hands closed around her shoulders.

"Was that…should I…" She pulled away. "Should I stop?"

"Lick me anywhere you like."

"Am I doing well enough?"

He took her hand in his and laid it across the damp placket of his trousers, splaying her fingers under him so she could feel the hard ridge beneath. "That's how well you're doing," he told her hoarsely. "So well that the danger is that I'll spill in my first few thrusts."

The thought of that caught hold of her, setting her lungs on fire. "Oh?" she heard herself ask. "How do I make you do that?"

His eyes met hers, fierce and intense, and her whole body seemed to melt. "You let me have a turn."

That sent a shot through her, a bolt of pure anticipation. He'd scarcely touched her since he'd come in the room; now his hands slid down her sides, over her hips.

He set his hands on her thighs. "Back a little," he said, giving her the barest guiding pressure. She took two steps in reverse and felt her legs hit the bed behind her. And then he stood, lifting her chemise as he did so. It slid over her skin, over her head. He disentangled it from her arms, and let it fall on the ground. She was completely naked.

She should have felt exposed. Off-kilter. But his eyes devoured her with such heat that she felt only…powerful. Wanted. *Ready.*

"There," he said, his voice hoarse. "Now that… That is a good idea." Her whole body tingled. She didn't know what he would do—whether he would push her to the bed and sink inside her, or touch her all over, the way she'd touched him.

Instead, he tilted her head back and kissed her. It was a long, sweet kiss, a kiss that drugged her senses. A kiss that made her aware of every inch of her skin—of the fact that as they kissed, he gathered her up in his arms, pressing against her. His chest. That hard ridge beneath his trousers. His legs, still damp. He kissed her until every part of her demanded more.

Just when she was ready to scream with a frustration she didn't understand, his hands swept up her body, cupping her breasts. She had one brief moment to react—to feel the rough brush of his thumb across her sensitive flesh—before he bent and kissed her on her breast.

"Oliver." Her hands closed around him. Her knees buckled. "Oliver. God. If what I did to you felt anything like that…"

"Then you'll spend in a few strokes," he murmured. "That's rather the goal."

He gathered her in his arms and bore her down onto the bed. But he didn't clamber on top of her as she'd expected.

"Don't you have to remove your trousers?"

"Not yet."

"But—"

His hands on her thighs silenced her. It was a warm, insistent pressure, fingers opening up her most intimate places. He knelt between her legs. "Not for this," he said, and set his mouth to her.

It was utterly electrifying. To have his lips there. As if all the things she'd yearned for he had heard through the tension in her muscle. As if her desire was spelled out with his tongue.

She let out a moan.

He took that as encouragement and spread her legs wider, and then, as she relaxed against him, he slid a finger inside her. His other thumb—his tongue—did something extraordinary, something that made her whole body light up with an unexplainable incandescence. Another finger, stretching her out, then another one. It was too much.

There was no way to understand all that glorious sensation rushing through her. It was as if their bodies held a conversation that whispered along every nerve ending. All thought vanished. What remained was pure light, engulfing her.

She bit back a scream.

When she could breathe again, he'd stood up. He was kicking off his shoes, taking off his trousers, coming back to her. The bed creaked under his weight.

"We can stop here," he said, his voice hoarse.

She reached out to him. "Don't you dare."

She hadn't seen this part of him before. His thighs were hard—not soft and pillowy, thank God, but tense with muscle. His erection was full. His breath shattered as she reached out, exploring it—that long shaft, hard and yet with that hint of softness to it.

She pulled forward and licked him.

"God, Jane." He moaned. "Another time, or it really will be three thrusts."

And then he was bearing her down, spreading her wide again. Rubbing the head of his cock against her slit, sending shivers down her.

"Tell me if it's too much." He pushed inside her. There was a pinch of red pain, so shocking in the midst of her floating arousal. Her hands closed around his shoulders.

Another time, he'd said. But that was too much reality to encompass now. There might not be another time. Just this one. This one time to feel the stretch of her body around his, to feel that pain dissipate, swallowed up by the growing rightness of him. He slid into her, further, then further, and the last hint of discomfort disappeared.

And then there was just him—his weight, his breath, his body bearing her down, joining with her so intimately. His hands, turning her face up to his, and his kiss, warm and sweet on her lips. There was no other time at all.

Just now.

Each stroke sent another little wave of pleasure through her. She felt overly sensitized to every thrust, every pulse of him. To the growing heat that rose between them, the low growl he made in his throat when she ran her hands down his naked back.

"God, Jane." He was reduced to incoherence. "Jane. Oh, God. Jane."

They were not just his thrusts, but hers. Theirs. She laid claim to them as much as he took her. Their bodies joined, came apart. She felt a tension building inside her. Different than the last time. Deeper. Called out by him. It came over her again, taking over her vision.

He stroked inside her harder as she came. Harder, harder, until his thrusts were almost brutal. At the last moment, he pulled out of her, spilling against her belly.

For a few seconds, he was poised above her. They looked into each others' eyes as best they could in the growing darkness. All hint of cold from the rain had been washed away. He was close, so close. Closer than anyone had ever been.

And then he pulled away from her. Only briefly. He found a towel, poured some water in the basin, and turned back to her. He didn't say a word. But gently, gently, he cleaned her off.

"Well?" he finally asked softly. "What did you think?"

Jane shook her head, unable to find words. It had been wonderful. Lovely, amazing, powerful, pleasurable. She couldn't even begin to describe it. It had been everything she'd imagined—except in one respect.

She'd thought that making love to Oliver would be a transcendent experience. A memory she could hold on to and cherish for the rest of her life.

But it wasn't. It hadn't been enough.

Chapter Twenty-Three

OLIVER WOKE TOO EARLY the next morning. The rain had stopped, and it was only five in the morning, if the church tower bells were to be believed. Oliver didn't think he'd had more than a few hours of sleep. Jane lay next to him, naked still, warm and soft.

He set a hand on her hip and tried not to think.

If he had at all been rational last night, he would never have done it. There were too many things wrong with the situation. He would list them, except…

He wanted to do it again this morning. Immediately.

He didn't think she would expect anything of him. And he'd been careful. Yet part of him—some horrible, treacherous part—wished that he had taken less care. That he'd done everything he could to get her with child. That he'd have her forced upon him so that he could take the thing he wanted so badly without having to decide to do it.

I love you, Jane. He ran his fingers down her body. *But you're still my impossible girl.*

It was a sad thought, singularly unsuited for a May morning.

She turned over. Her eyes opened and she smiled sleepily at him.

"Good morning," she said.

He hadn't wanted to know what that would sound like—her happy, sleepy greeting, as she turned to him in the bed.

"Good morning," he returned gravely.

She squeezed her eyes shut and then shook her head. When she opened them, she sat up. "I suppose we have to do this now."

"Jane…"

She set her fingers over his mouth. "Let me speak first. I have spent the last months thinking of my many mistakes. I wanted you so badly, and I almost never had you." She looked away and shook her head. "I have had months of thinking about you, Oliver. About that moment in the park when I simply accepted that because you could not marry me, I would have nothing. I've thought it through and through." She raised her chin. "You mustn't think of this as ruination. Only girls with no money can be truly ruined. And my reputation has never been one of my assets."

"Jane." He didn't know why he said her name except to say it. To hear it sing on his tongue. The entire world thought the word Jane was one syllable, but he knew better. When he said her name properly—when he whispered it slowly in the early morning, with the owner a few feet from him—it came out to almost a syllable and a half. *Ja-ane*.

He was so damned aware of her—of her breath, of the slight warmth in the air to his right where she lay. Of what they'd done together last night. Of what they couldn't do together any longer.

He touched her shoulder ever so gently.

"I am the last woman in the world you want to marry," she whispered. It was not quite a question.

He shut his eyes. "Yes. You're the last woman in the world I should want to marry. So why are you the only one I've been able to think of for months?"

Her eyes flashed.

"Jane." He reached for her. "I'm sorry. I never wanted to—"

"Stop apologizing for speaking the truth," she snapped out. "It is what it is, and there's no use my crying over it."

"But I—"

"I told you, I've had a long time to think it over. And you're right. Marriage between us would be a disaster. I know what I can do and what I can't. I can pretend to be a great many things, but even if I could act the proper hostess, the sort you'd need, I wouldn't want to do it. I'm done taking on the role of pretender."

It made so much sense when she spoke it aloud. It was only the other half of his own objections. If this was rationality, some part of him recognized it and agreed with it. The other part...

Well, she was near and she was naked. That curtailed most of his thoughts beyond the obvious.

"I have been thinking," Jane said to him. "In fact, I have been thinking for months now. Of what I would do when this was all over. Once Emily was safe and no longer dependent on my uncle."

He turned to her.

"It's unlikely I will ever marry. Not that I couldn't find a husband, but I don't need one, and I don't want the ones I can get." Her lips pressed together. "Any man who was honorable enough for me to fall in love with... Well, I think my birth and reputation will put him off. Even if he could look past it for himself, I would be nothing but a liability to him."

There was a hard note to her voice, something barren and desolate.

"Jane. That's not true."

"If I could find a man exactly like you, but without ambition…" She laughed. "A sun that was warm but not bright, a fish that lived in air."

He recognized the sentiment precisely, recognized it like the cruel edge of a knife blade that it was. "You want someone exactly like me, but completely opposite." How appropriate. How utterly appropriate.

This wasn't the way he was supposed to fall in love. He was supposed to meet someone, to discover that her wants and wishes coincided with his, that their dreams overlapped. He didn't want to meet a woman, to discover that the breath he drew seemed to come from her lungs, and then to realize that they couldn't both breathe at the same time.

"So that is that." She smiled sadly. "An impossible girl. I decided long ago that you and I should have been lovers, when we had the chance. Last night confirmed my belief."

He didn't answer. Oh, his body did; he'd gone from *interested* to *ready* at her words.

"We're here," she said. "We're together until we find Emily. Why not make the most of it?"

Because he didn't want to agree with her. He couldn't say *yes, Jane, you're right—we should be lovers*. It would remove what had happened last night from a land of fairy-tale pretense, one where he could imagine that the obstacles between them could be swept away without so much as a second glance. It would make what happened next real and therefore impermanent. This would be an affair. Nothing but an affair.

Her voice dropped. "I'm glad I started with you."

She leaned toward him.

He set his hand on her lips, blocking her kiss. "Jane." *Started* implied that Oliver was a beginning, that there would be another after him, and another after that. That Jane would be kissed by men who were not Oliver. If he acquiesced in this, he'd be admitting to the end when they had barely even started.

But the alternative… The alternative was just as impossible.

"Jane," he said helplessly.

"Oliver."

He surrendered and found her mouth.

If last night was a mistake, this was a deadly error. He could taste the end on her lips—a hint of bitter, and beneath that, the ravenous heat of her mouth, the sweetness of Jane.

"God, Jane," he whispered. "I almost lost you."

Her hands came up to touch his wrists, a tentative flutter at first. "I almost lost me, too."

And she kissed him back.

There were some things a man could not say in response to a confession like the one he'd heard.

I love you, but…

I want you, but…

He had nothing to give her except conditions and disavowals. Even the kiss he gave her was too aware—too much of his lips on hers, caressing her, kissing her, but…

There was always a but.

So Oliver didn't speak. And when Jane touched him, there was no hesitation in his response. She came on top of him, her breasts brushing his chest, her hair tickling his shoulders. He could do this forever, lose himself in moments like this.

He kissed her mouth and welcomed the weight of her against him.

"Oliver." Her hips flexed.

He could lose himself in her. More frightening, he could *find* himself in her. He was doing it right now, discovering how much it meant to hold her and touch her and show her how much he cared.

"Possible girl," he whispered. "Too possible."

She smiled at him.

They were entangled. It was already too late to avoid getting hurt. There was nothing to do now but hold out until the end. And so he let it happen. He kissed her neck, her breasts. He held onto his own arousal, letting it peak, stroking her until she was as ready as he was. Until she was wet and desperate, until he could bear it no longer. Then he guided her down onto his shaft. She was good, so good around him.

He'd needed just this all these months. He held her hands as she discovered the pace she needed, the pressure she wanted. And when she was close, he touched her just where it mattered and brought her to pieces. When she was still shuddering, he turned her over and drove into her until all his thoughts shattered and fled. Until there was nothing but the two of them.

Until, at least for that one final moment, there was no *but* after the silent *I love you* that he gave her.

❆ ❆ ❆

OLIVER STOOD BEHIND THE HOUSE where Jane's uncle liveed. The morning had been taken up with their journey to Cambridge by rail; it was mid-afternoon by the time they'd arrived. In the early summer heat, the residents had retreated inside to the cool. By his count, Dorling would just be meeting his cart driver. In a few hours, all would be over, but for now…

Oliver had taken off his shoes and his coat. A bit of ivy climbed the walls—a few pale, unhealthy strands, nothing he'd care to trust his weight to.

The past few days were beginning to catch up with him. It felt almost as if he had been woken briefly in the middle of the night and was being sucked back into the dream. Yes, he cared for Jane. More than he wanted to think.

And he'd volunteered to climb into her sister's room in the middle of broad daylight.

"Why am I the one doing this again?" he asked.

"Because," Jane whispered next to him, "I'm wearing skirts."

He was going to get shot. Or captured. Or…

Or maybe he wasn't. He hadn't felt like this in…oh, years. His pulse beat with excitement. The house was silent.

"Don't worry," Jane said. "The kitchen garden hardly produces because my uncle doesn't like setting snares for rabbits. If he discovers you, the worst he'd probably do is demand an explanation. A lengthy one."

"And I'll say, 'don't mind me, I'm just here to steal your niece. There's nothing to worry about; I've made away with one of them already, so two will hardly slow me down."

"Precisely." She smiled at him, and suddenly, the climb to her sister's window didn't seem quite so long, nor the possibility of discovery so painful. He clambered up onto the window ledge on the ground floor, used it as a stepping stone, and then swung up to the top of the window frame.

The drainpipe buckled; he readjusted his weight, shifting onto the slick stones. He made his way up the wall carefully, until he could hook his hands over the window ledge that Jane had promised belonged to her sister.

He tapped quietly on the window and waited.

Nothing. He didn't even hear anyone stirring in the room.

"Emily?" He didn't dare speak much above a whisper, but his breath scarcely fogged the window. He tapped again, this time more firmly. "Miss Emily."

"She's not a heavy sleeper," Jane whispered loudly, just below him. "And she never sleeps during her afternoon naps."

"Well, I don't see anyone inside." He rapped his knuckles against the windowpane. "Emily," he tried a little louder.

Nothing.

Nobody. He could see the bed from here, and while the shadows somewhat obscured his view, it didn't even look as if there were a telltale lump.

"Jane," he said softly, "when was your uncle going to have your sister taken away?"

He could hear her breath suck in. "Not so soon," she said slowly as if trying to convince herself. "Surely not so soon. He would want to make certain I was out of the way before he moved. I'm...I'm almost positive of it." But her voice wavered on the *almost,* and he suspected she wasn't as sure as she felt.

He would have guessed it would take longer. But then, he'd been wrong before.

"Might she have gone out for the afternoon?" he asked.

"No, of course not. Titus never lets her, and if she had slipped out herself, she would have left the window ajar." Oliver tried the edge of the window; it was closed all the way, but it hadn't been fastened on the inside. It was difficult work, getting the leverage he needed to hoist it up a few inches; the window squeaked in the casement. But he finally managed to raise it.

"She really isn't in here," he reported. He'd already completed the *breaking* portion of breaking and entering. No point stopping now. He climbed through the window.

"Look in the clothespress," Jane called from the ground. "See if her valise is there."

He crossed the floor, treading as softly as he could in hopes that the floor would not squeak. It didn't, but the clothespress door made a soft noise of protest when he opened it.

There were a few items of clothing inside, scattered about in a mess, but no valise. Oliver returned to the window. "Is your sister generally a tidy person?"

"Yes."

"Because someone has tossed her things around. Much of it, I gather, is gone. There is no valise, and what clothing remains is strewn about. It looks like someone packed in a hurry."

"Oh, God." On the ground, he could hear the fear in Jane's voice. "On the desk—look on her desk. Is there a small green cactus?"

"No."

"She's really gone. Oliver. What are we going to do?"

He'd never met her sister, but he'd have panicked if any of his sisters had been in similar straits.

"In an hour or so," Jane was saying, "Dorling will arrive back in Nottingham. It's only a matter of time until Titus gets a telegram. He'll know that I've disappeared."

Oliver shook his head. "I am going to climb down. And then we are going to talk. Rationally. For one, if he's already removed your sister, it doesn't matter what he knows of you. The strategy changes."

"Right." She nodded. "Right."

He started making his way down.

He could see her pacing on the ground out of the corner of his vision.

"This morning... What was I thinking?"

"Wouldn't have made any difference," he said, shifting so that he could brace himself against the side of the house.

"But if we had—"

"We couldn't have made the trains run any faster, and we were on the first one out. Don't blame yourself whatever has happened." Coming down was trickier; he couldn't see his footholds, and it made for slower going. But when he was within a few feet of the ground, he pushed off the wall, jumping the last little bit.

He landed and turned to Jane. It was wrong, what was going through his head. He should have been in full sympathy with her, for whatever it was that had happened to her sister.

But he didn't feel sorry. He was selfish, so damned selfish. He didn't care about her sister at all.

All he could think was that she'd said this would last until they found Emily. *It's not over. It's not over yet.* He'd have more of Jane.

"But if I—"

He took her hand. *It's not over yet. It's not over yet.* He shouldn't be smiling. And yet he couldn't keep a hint of triumph from his voice.

"Maybe the worst has happened," he said, "and maybe she's been put away. But what has been done can be undone. All we need to do is find out where he's sent your sister, and from there..."

"Titus will never tell me," Jane said. "And even if he did, how would we proceed?"

"There are ways of finding out," Oliver said. "But in this case, I think the direct route might work best. We'll just have someone ask him. Someone who could get the whole story on the matter."

Jane frowned up at him. "But there is no such person."

It isn't over. It isn't over.

Oliver smiled. "Actually, there is."

⌘　⌘　⌘

"...SO YOU SEE," OLIVER TOLD SEBASTIAN, "what we really need is to find Titus Fairfield, to trap him into a situation where he feels he cannot just walk away. Ask him where Jane's sister is being held. And..."

Sebastian was examining his nails as Oliver spoke, but he had a small smile on his face. He didn't look well. He hadn't shaved yet, although it was three in the afternoon, and there was a bloodshot quality to his eyes.

But if he had been up late the night before, it didn't show on anything other than his features.

"And trick him into telling you where she's being kept?" Sebastian shrugged. "I can do it. I'm giving a lecture this evening. I'll invite him, and then we'll see."

"Thank you," Jane told him. They were the first words she'd spoken since the initial greeting, but she said them fervently. "Thank you so much, Mr. Malheur."

But he simply shook his head at her. "No, Miss Fairfield," he said. "Don't thank me yet. Hasn't Oliver told you that my help always comes at a cost?"

She shook her head. "Whatever it is, I'll pay—"

"Not that kind of cost. When you ask me for help, you get help." His smile widened. "You get help *my* way."

Chapter Twenty-Four

THE LECTURE SEEMED INTERMINABLY LONG. Perhaps it was because Oliver knew what the stakes were. He'd caught a glimpse of Titus Fairfield in the back rows of the hall.

Perhaps it was because at the moment, Oliver could not dredge up the least interest in what Sebastian was saying about peas and snapdragons and the color of cats.

Perhaps it was because Jane wasn't here, but she was close. In a room nearby. So close that the yards between them seemed to whisper of all the things they hadn't done, the kisses they hadn't exchanged, the months they hadn't spent in bed.

No. Not the time to think of that. He peered at Sebastian and tried to pretend interest. Sebastian had always been in his element talking to a crowd. He gestured as he talked. But today, it seemed different. His gestures were too wide, almost wild. As if he'd lost his balance and was trying to regain it.

Next to Oliver, Violet Waterfield, the Countess of Cambury, leaned forward, and Oliver glanced at her.

He'd never known Violet the way Robert and Sebastian had. She'd been Sebastian's neighbor, and Oliver had never been invited to Sebastian's home during the summer. He'd heard of her, but he hadn't met her until he was almost nineteen. By that time, she'd been a countess already, cool and intimidating.

She didn't look intimidating tonight. Her usual calm demeanor had evaporated. She was watching Sebastian with rapt attention, her eyes opened wide, her lips spread in a welcoming smile. Oliver had never seen her look at anyone that way. Watching her was almost intimate—as if he were discovering a secret she had. As if she were in love, and in the moment, unable to hide it.

That was an unsettling thought. Sebastian had always insisted that he and Violet were friends and only friends—nothing more. Sebastian looked at anyone and everyone in the audience, making eye contact with even the men seated in the back who glowered at him with folded arms. He looked at everyone *except* Violet, and that was when Oliver began to realize that something was deeply wrong.

That sense lasted through the lecture. During the questions, Violet sat on the edge of her seat, leaning forward, her whole body focused on Sebastian, nodding to herself at his answers, as if he held the key to the universe. It lasted through the moment when Sebastian gave a final bow, and Oliver made his way up to him to put the second part of their plan into action.

"Good sense, Malheur," a man was saying, clapping Sebastian across the shoulder. "Always learn something new from you."

"Thank you," Sebastian said. "That means so much to me." His voice was warm, and he looked in the right places, but there was something mechanical about his delivery, as if he were scarcely paying attention.

Another audience member grabbed his sleeve. "Malheur, you slime." This man's eyes narrowed; he made a fist at his side, as if he were contemplating punching Sebastian in the face. "You are going to hell for all you've done, and I hope you'll burn for eternity."

"Thank you," Sebastian said warmly, making eye contact with him. "That means so much to me." He gave the fellow a pat on the shoulder—a friendly little pat, as if they'd just exchanged pleasantries—and moved on.

"I hope someone slits your puny little throat," a gruff, whiskered fellow muttered at Sebastian.

"Thank you very much," Sebastian replied. "That means so much to me."

It was as if he'd sent an automaton in his place.

Oliver made his way to his friend, almost afraid to remind him of what they had planned. He wasn't sure what he would do if he spoke to his friend and got that same warm, generic reply.

And maybe it was just as well. Because for every man that complimented him on his work, there were three who muttered imprecations in his direction. Threats. Complaints. A woman laid a hand on him and gave him a shove.

Sebastian treated them all alike. He gave them a smile, one that looked increasingly out of place on his waxen face, a nod, and warm, effusive thanks that seemed ridiculously genuine.

Oliver almost gasped with relief when Violet caught up with them. She knew Sebastian. They'd been friends for ages. And if she cared for him...

Violet had to reach out and physically take hold of Sebastian's sleeve before he turned to her. She smiled up at him, her face alight with a mere echo of the brilliance she'd directed at him during his talk.

"Sebastian," Violet said.

Sebastian had been smiling at all those people, smiling with such fervor that Oliver had wondered if he was ill. He looked down at Violet, and that humor disappeared from his face, the friendliness wiping away like chalk markings on slate.

"What?" he demanded curtly.

"You were brilliant, Sebastian," she said. "Utterly bril—"

He took a staggering step backward. "Fuck you, Violet," he said savagely. "Fuck. You."

He'd spoken into a momentary lull in conversation, so that everyone near could hear his words.

Violet winced.

Oliver came up beside his friend. "Sebastian," he said quietly. He steeled himself for a similar outburst.

But when Sebastian turned to him, he merely looked tired, not savage.

"Ah, Oliver. Perhaps you can explain—"

"Excuse me," Oliver said to the crowd around them, "he's drunk."

"I'm not—"

"You might as well be," Oliver whispered, and jerked on his arm. "What the hell are you doing? You *know* what's at stake here. What we have to do."

Sebastian opened his mouth to answer, and that's when Oliver heard it—that strangely diffident voice, the one he remembered from the walk he'd taken with Sebastian so long ago.

"Mr. Malheur? Mr. Malheur?" The voice spoke from behind them. "You wished to speak with me? That is, I had a message from you regarding a little tidbit you had to share?"

Sebastian and Oliver turned as one. Titus Fairfield stood before them, rubbing his hands together. He shifted uneasily from foot to foot.

"Is this not a good time?" he asked.

God, the man was inept. Anyone with a brain would know this was a terrible time—the worst time.

But Sebastian's face didn't change at all from his impassive mask.

"Mr. Fairfield," he said in a forbidding tone, completely at odds with his words. "You are just the person I want to see."

"I am?" Even Fairfield sounded dubious.

"You are. Unfortunately, at the moment, I am a little tipsy."

Oliver inhaled. That had not been the plan that he'd worked out with Sebastian. He took a step forward, reached out—but his cousin was already forging on.

"Luckily, my friend Violet here will explain everything. I trust her implicitly, so…"

"What are you doing?" Oliver whispered. "That was not the plan."

"Yes," Sebastian said, "I imagine that Violet could say anything I could. And turnabout is always fair play."

Oliver glanced over at Violet. He would have expected her to look hurt by Sebastian's savage outburst. At the very least, he had thought she would be confused. Instead she simply shrugged her shoulders.

"Come on, Oliver," Sebastian said, hooking his arm through Oliver's. "Let's leave Violet to it."

⌘ ⌘ ⌘

"THAT WASN'T THE PLAN," Oliver said to Sebastian, as Sebastian headed out onto the street. "That's not what we were going to do. We were going to—"

"Come on, Oliver," Sebastian said. "If we look back now, Fairfield will think he can talk to me. And right now, I can't bear him."

"This isn't about you," Oliver fumed. It's about—"

His cousin stopped on the street and looked about them. It was dark by now, and a little foggy; the lamps on the street had been lit, and they did their best to drive away the darkness with warmth. It wasn't quite enough.

"It's been a good long while since it's been about me," Sebastian finally said. "I think it's my turn."

And in that moment, Oliver looked at his friend. Sebastian looked...*wrecked* was the closest word that Oliver might have chosen.

"Violet will handle it," Sebastian said. "She likes Miss Fairfield, and she's the most frighteningly competent woman I have met. If you would pay attention, my dear cousin, you might have noticed that more than half the population of England wants me dead. I think I am allowed to crack under the strain. Once. I'm allowed."

It seemed impossible. Sebastian always seemed so indifferent to what others thought of him. He treated his infamy like a lark. He was...

Oliver had accused Sebastian of hiding unhappiness when last he was in Cambridge. But he'd suspected a mild melancholy, not...this. Sebastian had always joked, had always laughed. How much of that had ever been real?

They walked in silence for a few blocks. "You know, Sebastian," Oliver said quietly, "I don't pretend to understand what is going on—but you owe Violet an apology."

Sebastian snorted.

"I mean it. In front of an entire crowd, you—"

"You don't know what she did." Sebastian's voice was shaking. "What she's doing to me."

"I don't care what she's doing. How could it justify what you just said? In front of everyone?"

Sebastian shrugged and looked away. He didn't add anything else, which seemed uncharacteristically like him.

"Very well," Oliver said. "What is she doing?"

"Nothing," Sebastian said with a maddening shake of his head. "She's not doing anything." But his voice was a few notes higher than normal.

"Sebastian, you can't put me off—"

"Everyone hates me." Sebastian turned to him. "Everyone. At first it was just a few people. Now, everywhere I go, there are death threats, people wishing me ill. The papers are filled with vitriol. *Everyone* hates me, Oliver. Everyone."

"Surely not everyone."

"Enough as to make no difference," Sebastian retorted. "Does it matter if the entirety of England wants me dismembered, or merely a half of it? Either way, it's a bloody great lot of people howling for my blood."

Oliver swallowed. "I thought you liked that sort of thing—tweaking people, getting under their skin."

Sebastian threw his hands up in the air. "In all the time you have known me, Oliver," he said, his voice shaking, "in all that time—when have I ever made a joke at anyone else's expense?"

"Uh…"

"When have I ever done anything except make a fool of myself, expose myself to ridicule to get others to laugh?"

"Well…"

"Yes, I love tweaking noses." His friend paced away and then turned back. "But I like to be *liked,* Oliver."

How had Oliver never seen that before? Prankster Sebastian. Smiling Sebastian. But he was right; all of Sebastian's clever tricks and pranks had been aimed at making everyone else laugh. He mocked himself with greater alacrity than anyone else, and when they'd been in school together, everyone had loved him for it.

Oliver swallowed hard. "I'm sorry," he finally said. "I…I know that the response you're receiving must have taken you by surprise. Still… What you said to Violet just now? That was unconscionable."

Sebastian stiffened. "I am not talking about Violet with you."

"Well, then, I'll be the only one talking, because I won't let this go unsaid. Sebastian, I think Violet is in love with you."

He'd expected Sebastian to protest, to frown. To *think,* perhaps, and reconsider.

Instead, Sebastian burst into laughter. "No," he said, when he'd recovered himself. "No, she is not."

"Give it some thought. The way she looked at you when you were talking… It was like—I don't know, I can't describe it—"

"I know how she looked at me," Sebastian said, with a funny little smile on his face. "Trust me; I am quite sure Violet is not in love with me."

"You can't be sure. You didn't see—"

"I can," Sebastian said. He looked upward. "Just leave it, Oliver." He smiled. "I'll have to find my own way out of this morass. But never fear." His voice gained strength. Or maybe, he was just finding his ability to lie again. "Our intrepid hero, beleaguered on all sides, may have had a moment of weakness." His voice was deep and booming. "But so it always is. The darkest hour, indeed, is the one that comes before—"

Oliver shoved him. "Come on, Sebastian. Stop pretending. You don't have to make *me* laugh."

But Sebastian just raised an eyebrow. "I don't have to," he said. "But watch me do it."

⌘ ⌘ ⌘

JANE WAITED IN THE LITTLE ROOM to the side of the lecture hall for over an hour, each minute seeming longer than the last. The sounds of the crowd—never more than a dull murmur—were her only company. The rising volume of that murmur was the only indication that the event had ended and—she hoped—that her uncle would be coming soon. She waited long minutes after that, until she heard footsteps in the outside hall.

"…Not sure," she heard her uncle say, in his sad, rumbling voice. "It seems a little improper, in fact. Are you sure that Mr. Malheur—"

"I am positive," said a female voice. "There's an important point to be made, namely—"

The door opened. Behind it stood a woman dressed in dark brown—the woman who had given Jane her cactus at the Botanic Gardens. For a moment, Jane blinked. She couldn't recall the woman's name. And then she remembered. She was a countess—the Countess of Cambury.

She was the sort of woman who would have been called "commanding" rather than pretty—and she was almost old enough to fit that look on her face. She seemed perfectly coiffed, not a hair out of place, not a wrinkle on her gown, even though she must have been sitting on the uncomfortable chairs above. It was as if even gravity didn't dare to defy her.

She looked formidable, and Jane wanted to know how she did it.

"Well, Fairfield," the woman said in a tone that made it clear that she had not dropped the *Mr.* from his name for reasons of familiarity. "What have you to say for yourself?"

"Your pardon?" Titus gave her a toad-eating little bow. "I—well—I rather thought that Mr. Malheur had something to say to me." He bowed again; he hadn't even looked around the room to see Jane. "Of course I understand that he is busy. Naturally so. But—"

With a sigh, the Countess of Cambury shut the door.

"This is becoming most improper." Titus shook his head and rubbed his hands together in consternation. "In a room, alone—I could hardly think— that is to say—" A thought seemed to penetrate his head—a horrific one, by the pallor that crept over him, and the way he put his hand to his throat. "Oh, dear," he whispered. "Mr. Malheur surely has been thinking about a breeding program, the one we had talked of earlier... He does not think to start it with *me?*"

Jane felt like laughing aloud. Nobody—not even somebody so depraved as to start a human breeding program—would look at her fussy, stuffy uncle and think, "There, there's a fellow who ought to be included."

The Countess of Cambury simply blinked at this nonsense and then shook her head. "Fairfield," she said in cutting tones, "if you had been a hunter on the plains of old, the lions would have killed you while you were wandering around the savannah saying, 'Where is everyone, and what have they done with my spears?'"

Jane did snort aloud at that.

"Your pardon?" Titus shook his head.

The countess gestured at Jane. "We are not alone."

"We aren't?" Titus frowned, and then slowly, he turned to see what the woman was indicating. His eyes fell on Jane.

She'd imagined that he would look embarrassed or fearful at the sight of her. She'd been blackmailing him, after all.

Instead, he turned bright red. "You!"

He pointed, took a step forward. His hands made fists at his side. "You!" he repeated. "What have you done with your sister?"

Chapter Twenty-Five

IT TOOK JANE A MOMENT TO REALIZE what Titus had said. Her uncle advanced on her, his face blooming a brilliant crimson. "What have you done with her?" he demanded. "I'll have the constable on you, I will. You can't just rush in and grab her up, simply because you wish."

It came to her in a flash: Titus hadn't sent Emily away. And if she was gone nonetheless…

Jane couldn't help herself. She'd been caught up with worry for the past two days. She had faked her own elopement, had been abducted, and then rescued. She had traversed half of England believing that her sister's fate hung in the balance. She'd been as big a fool as Titus. She burst into laughter.

"Stop that," Titus said. "And surrender your sister, or I'll—I'll—" Failing to come up with an adequate threat, he narrowed his eyes at her. "Or I'll be very displeased."

"I don't have Emily," Jane said. "I'm only here because I thought *you* had her put in an asylum."

He blushed fiercely. "Why—uh—why would you think that? I certainly—well, I—which is to say, I was having her *examined* by physicians, to see if such a thing was possible. She was acting so…so differently. Less exuberantly. I was afraid that she was succumbing to melancholy, and was considering my choices."

"Listen to you. She yells at you, and you think she's disobedient; she stops yelling, you think she has melancholy. Can she win? No."

He flushed. "I just wanted to make sure she didn't go untreated. Yes, I talked to a few physicians, and yes, one of them said that he'd be willing to certify her, if I paid—" He cleared his throat loudly. "But the other two said she seemed quite in her own mind." Perhaps Titus realized that he was telling her details of his plan that didn't reflect highly on him. He shook his head swiftly. "Which is to say, it was all your fault. Your influence. You did it. And you have her. You can't bluff me!"

"Emily has herself," Jane said. "She always did. That's what is so funny—that I came all this way to rescue her, and…"

Titus waved a hand at Jane. "You're claiming that your sister just *ran off?* On her own two feet without any encouragement from you at all?" He looked dubious.

"Why not?" Jane asked. "I ran off myself, and she's almost my age."

"But you…"

"Yes, I have money. But last I'd heard, you hadn't found the hundred pounds I gave her. I imagine that when she ran off, she hired a coach. Or took the train."

He flushed. "I wasn't going to mention funds. I was referring to the fact that you are whole."

Jane felt her temper snap. She crossed the room to him. She was taller than him; how had she never noticed that? Probably because she had never stood this close, quivering with years of resentment. She slammed her hands into his chest.

"Emily," she said through gritted teeth, "is *whole.* She has *fits,* that's all. Joan of Arc had fits, and look what she managed to accomplish. The only person who is broken here is you, for being unable to see it."

"I don't know what you're talking about."

"When we find Emily, you'll discover that she's safe. That she had a plan. That she acted intelligently and rationally in the face of *your* stupidity." Jane shook her head. "Good God, you were trying to have her declared mentally incompetent by bribing doctors. Of all the low, dirty tricks—"

She remembered a moment too late that perhaps she could not claim the moral high ground on the bribing-of-doctors front, and so she glared at him instead.

"Rational." Titus sighed. "She can't be rational. I had only a note from her saying that she was going to meet her barrister. Her *barrister.* She doesn't have a barrister. I would know if she had one."

Jane felt her heart give a sudden thump, and she wanted to laugh aloud again. Trust Emily to send Jane a message out in the open, one that their uncle would never decode.

"Well," Jane said, "then she is probably going to get one. If you were planning on having her declared mad…" She trailed off.

"It's not rational," Titus said. "She'd need a solicitor first, not a barrister, and he would then go and get…" He shook his head. "I suppose that's where I should start looking, then. I'll begin to ask around London. See if anyone has seen a young girl asking barristers for help." He frowned glumly. "If you should happen to find her, tell her… Tell her I'm willing to reconsider." He swallowed. "I'll sign a paper if she wants. I just…I want her to be safe. That's all I want. That's all I've ever wanted."

The sad thing was, Jane believed him. He'd wanted her safe, and safe he'd kept her. He'd kept Emily so safe that he'd shielded her from everything else, too. When she'd screamed about it, he'd accused her; when she'd stopped screaming, he'd wondering why she was so altered.

But then, Titus had only given her the things he wanted for himself. He'd stayed in Cambridge long after his university days had ended, wanting to think the same things over and over. She almost felt sorry for him.

Almost. Then she remembered Emily's scars.

"If I find her," Jane promised, "I'll tell her what you said. But where to start searching?" She glanced away as she said that so that he wouldn't see the knowledge in her eyes.

"Where indeed." Titus nodded glumly. And then, he reached and very lightly tapped Jane's shoulder. "I can see it now," he said. "You do worry for your sister. Even though you do it all wrong—I can see you care for her, in your own deeply troubled manner."

It was almost as if they were having a moment of sympathy. Jane nodded; he pulled his hand back from her shoulder and then quietly left the room.

"I suppose you know which barrister she's visiting?" the Countess of Cambury asked. "I would have said more to force the issue. But it hardly seemed necessary." She shrugged, and then smiled at Jane. "You handled yourself very well."

Jane smiled back. "Of course I know where she is," Jane said. "At least, I know his name. Or, rather, I know the sound of it—and I don't think he'll be that difficult to find."

⌘ ⌘ ⌘

Earlier that day in London…

ANJAN DIDN'T THINK HE WAS EVER going to get used to the noise of London. He'd grown up in a more populated city. One might have thought, he supposed, that London was nothing. But the noises here were a totally different thing. Nothing he could pinpoint aside from a collective *wrongness*.

It bothered him, that difference, even at the desk he had in Lirington and Sons.

Anjan had a position. A position with a battered desk in the copyists' room, true, and never mind his graduation with honors or his recent admission to the bar. But it was a start, and for a start, he'd smile and sit with the copyists. Once he made himself invaluable, matters would begin to change.

As if in answer to that, George Lirington opened the door to the room. He looked over the bent heads of the scriveners before his eyes lit on Anjan.

"Ho, Batty," he said. "You're wanted."

Anjan stood. Lirington and Sons specialized in maritime issues. They'd hired Anjan for a number of reasons—not least of which was the fact that he spoke both Hindi and Bengali. Being able to understand the lascars aboard ships had its benefits.

Anjan reached for his notebook and stood. "Is it the Westfeld accounts again?"

Lirington shook his head. "No. It's a lady. She's alone and she wants to hire us." He glanced at Anjan curiously. "She asked for you by your full last name."

"Tell me it's not my mother." She'd arrived in London a few weeks past, and even though he'd let her know, very nicely, that she couldn't visit him at work... Well, she *was* his mother.

"No, I said already. She's a lady." He looked at Anjan again. "I didn't know you knew any ladies, Batty. You've been holding out on me."

Anjan hadn't realized he knew anyone who might visit. He simply shrugged, gathered up his notebook, and followed his friend. They traversed the file room, and then turned into the front chambers. The room nearest the entry was used for discussions with clients. The door was ajar a few inches; Lirington stepped inside and nodded to someone there, just as Anjan came in behind him.

He stopped dead in the doorframe.

Emily—Miss Emily Fairfield—was standing at the window.

She had always looked marvelous, but she stunned him now. Her hair shone in the daylight that streamed from the windows. She wore a blue muslin gown, so different from the walking dresses he'd seen her in. Those had sported gathered sleeves and loose waists. This, though—this fit her figure to the waist as if it had been poured over her body. He and Lirington paused in the doorway together and issued a joint sigh of appreciation.

Anjan didn't know what to think. She was here after all these months. What could it mean?

Lirington—perhaps, Anjan thought, because he did not know Emily—recovered first.

"Miss Fairfield," he said. "I've brought Mr. Batty, as you requested." He walked to a chair and gently pulled it out for her. "Please sit," he said, "and tell us how we might be of service to you."

She glided over to the table, slid her hands over her skirts, and then—Anjan swallowed hard—folded herself gracefully into the chair.

"Batty," Lirington said over his shoulder, "fetch some tea, would you please?"

She frowned at that, a slight hint of darkness flitting across her features.

When Anjan returned with a tray, she was seated properly, looking as comfortable in the chair as if she took tea in the office every day.

"You know, Miss Fairfield," Lirington was saying, "I do hope we can find a way to be of service to you, but I suspect we will not. You'll have to find a solicitor, of course, although I have some excellent suggestions there. And our specialty is maritime matters. So if you would tell us what it is that is bothering you…?"

"If you can't help me," Emily said calmly, "I'm sure you can refer me to someone who can. I had hoped you would listen to my story."

"Of course," Lirington said smoothly.

She had gazed at Anjan briefly when he'd returned to the room—a cool, questioning look. But she folded her hands and contemplated them now without sparing him a second glance.

"My uncle is my guardian," she finally said. "I have a medical condition, one that Doctor Russell here in London says is a convulsive condition." Her fingers played with a button on her cuff. "There is no cure for it, not one that has been discovered, at least." She shrugged. "It is an annoyance, of course, but it leaves me in no danger."

Anjan nodded, remembering the fit he had seen.

"My uncle," she continued, "nonetheless wishes to seek a cure. He believes that no man will wish to marry me until the matter is resolved."

So saying, she set her hands to her cuff at her wrist and very deliberately undid it.

"I say," Lirington said. But he didn't speak beyond that. He stared at the pale skin of her wrist, utterly riveted at the sight, leaning forward. Anjan wanted to smack his friend or turn him away from the sight of her skin.

"He has had me shocked with galvanic current," she said, undoing a second button. "He had a man hold my head underwater. There was the man with a contraption. It utilized leverage to apply bruising force to my leg when a convulsion started." She undid more buttons as she spoke. "We stopped use of the machine after it broke my femur."

His eyes rose to hers, and he felt a moment of sick comprehension. When she'd talked of their walks being an *escape*, he'd imagined her as simply rebellious. But this? This was awful.

She spoke so matter-of-factly that Lirington simply nodded in tune to her recital, as if these things that she were listing were normal activities. If he hadn't been looking for it, Anjan would have missed the way her fingers shook as she undid the next button and rolled up her sleeve, revealing a white, perfectly round scar.

"A doctor had me burned with a red-hot poker," she said. "He thought it would disrupt my convulsions. It did not."

Anjan gripped the arms of his chair. Barbaric, that's what it was. It was barbaric. And how had he not known this? All those weeks they had walked together, and she had said not a word. He'd lectured her about family. About doing as her uncle told her.

He felt a fury rising in him.

"Gentlemen," she said, still calm, "I hope you will understand when I refrain from showing you the burns on my thigh."

"Miss Fairfield," Lirington said in confusion, "this is all well and good, but I am at a loss as to how we are to help you. It is your guardian's duty to provide medical care, after all."

"It is not well," Anjan heard himself growl. "Neither is it good."

She heard him and smiled. "Well, one possibility is to petition for a change of guardian. I had hoped…"

"We handle maritime affairs," Lirington said. "This is a matter for Chancery." He shook his head. "As grievously as you no doubt have suffered, I do not see how we could be of service. My secretary, Mr. Walton, can provide you a list, but—I am desolate to admit—we ourselves can do nothing. Now, if you'll excuse us…" He stood. "Batty, as you're here, I think we should discuss the Westfeld accounts after all. My father is in his office, and—"

He turned as Emily stood. For the first time in her visit, she looked perturbed. "But I don't know them," she said. "I don't know those other people. And the situation is more urgent than can be solved by a motion in Chancery. I've objected to the treatment. In return, my uncle is—that is, I found correspondence with…" She swallowed and met Anjan's eyes. "He wants to declare me incompetent. He'll put me away. I'll never be able to make my own decisions."

Anjan swallowed away a sick feeling. People made jokes about Bedlam, but the things he'd heard… An asylum was no place for anyone, let alone Emily.

"Already he refuses to allow me out of the house. When he discovered I was sneaking out…" She turned her head to Anjan, and nodded. "…he had a servant start sleeping in my room. I didn't even have a chance to say good-bye."

Lirington shook his head. "I'm sorry." It was a dismissal, not an apology.

Anjan didn't move. He was rooted in place, everything he knew about her falling into order.

Her breath was coming faster now. "My sister will help. She's of age, and she has enough money to pay whatever it is you need."

"I do wish you the best," Lirington said, "but—"

"Be quiet, Lirington," Anjan heard himself grate out. "She never asked for *your* opinion. She came to me."

"That's ridiculous." Lirington frowned, though, and then his lips quirked, as if he were just remembering that in fact, she *had* asked for Anjan. By name. "I don't understand," he finally said. "Why would she do that?"

Anjan didn't answer.

"Because I knew," Emily said. "I knew if I came here, I would get a fair hearing. I knew, at the very least, that you would listen. That you would care."

"Is that what you think?" Anjan said, almost curious to hear her answer. "I haven't seen you in months; you disappear with scarcely a word to me. And you think that you can just arrive and tell me that I care?"

Emily tossed her head back. "Don't be daft," she said. "I know you do."

Anjan felt a smile spread across his face—a slow, real smile. "Good."

"I told you once that if our marriage had been arranged, I would not complain," Emily said. "Since then…"

Anjan leaned forward, ignoring the surprised noise Lirington made.

"In the worst months of my uncle's excesses, when my sister was away and I had no outlet for my frustration, I imagined that it was so. That I *knew* I would marry you. That I had that to look forward to, no matter what happened in the meantime."

Anjan swallowed.

"And then I discovered that my uncle had been corresponding with an asylum." She shut her eyes. "I couldn't stay and risk that. And that was strangely freeing. I could go anywhere, could choose anything. Nothing was arranged, not a single thing in my future except the things that I could arrange for myself."

Anjan couldn't look away from her. She smiled at him, and he felt himself smiling in response.

"So I came here," she said. "To you."

Lirington looked at Emily—really looked at her—and then turned his head to look at Anjan. "Batty," he said slowly, "I do believe you've been holding out on me."

Across the table, Emily grimaced again and slapped her hand against the table.

"The name," she said primly, "is *Bhattacharya*. And since it's going to be mine, you had best learn to pronounce it properly."

Chapter Twenty-Six

"My sister left on her own," Jane said when Oliver returned to the hotel late that evening. "I know where she's gone, and I think she's safe."

Jane was smiling at him in open, friendly welcome. They'd obtained rooms on opposite sides of the hotel, for propriety's sake. But shortly after he'd come back from his walk with Sebastian, she'd slipped through the hallways and knocked on his door.

She now sat on his bed, shoeless, her hair down, and he didn't want her anywhere else. He wanted time to freeze. He wanted her in his room. He never wanted her to leave. And she knew where her sister was.

Perhaps it was the very shortness of the love affair that made every moment seem so dear.

"I'm so happy," she said. "We have only to find her."

It was easy for Oliver to put his arms around her, to draw her in close and inhale the scent of her. To think her not only possible, but likely—the only likelihood that he could comprehend.

He refused to think of the end.

He nuzzled her neck instead. "I'm glad everything is turning out for the better," he said. "You'll need me then, just a little longer. Just to be sure." He held his breath.

"Yes. If you don't mind."

He kissed her ear, pulling her close. He didn't want to let go of her. His hands played along her hair, tangling in it, and he inhaled her scent.

"You're affectionate," she said.

"No. Just besotted." Besotted and beset by that worry in his gut. Once she was reunited with her sister, once the threat of her uncle's guardianship dissipated, he would no longer have an excuse. He could sense the end now, so close he could smell it, and he didn't want to let her go.

"Where is she?"

"London," Jane replied. "I'm almost certain of it."

"How…useful," Oliver said. "I have to go to London, too."

But he'd been hoping they would have to go somewhere else. Oliver had duties waiting for him there. He shut his eyes and imagined those duties—the neglected appointments, the newspaper column that he might write about the latest proposed amendments—and then pushed them aside. "But we're not there yet," he said. "We're here. And now."

"I had noticed," Jane whispered. "What should we do about it?"

He pulled her close. "This," he said. And he turned her face to his and kissed her.

⌘ ⌘ ⌘

"I DO NOT KNOW, ANJAN."

The woman who sat on the other side of the table from Emily wore a purple and gold silk sari draped about her. She had Anjan's eyes, dark, ringed with impossibly long eyelashes. Mrs. Bhattacharya's face was unwrinkled except for the frown that she leveled at Emily. Her arms were folded, and Emily tried not to twitch under her perusal.

Anjan's mother sniffed and looked at her son. "Is something wrong with her? She looks sickly."

"She has not been outside much." Anjan seemed entirely calm.

A feeling Emily did not share. Her stomach danced, and it took all her effort to keep herself still.

Mrs. Bhattacharya simply shook her head. "And what will your father say when I tell him that your bride-to-be has fits? We only want the best for you." She frowned at Emily. "Could you not find some other girl? A nice girl from home, maybe…"

"I suppose that is possible," Anjan said politely. "But Miss Emily's father is a barrister, and her uncle is a tutor in law. She can introduce me to people besides just Lirington's parents. It's an advantageous match in that regard."

Mrs. Bhattacharya narrowed her eyes at her son. "Of course you try to convince me that way. You are just being *sensible.*" There was a hint of amusement in her voice as she spoke. "You do not care that she is pretty. You did not write to me that you could talk to her of everything. It has nothing to do with any of that, does it?"

Anjan's lips twitched into a real smile. "Of course," he said dryly. "What could be more pragmatic?"

She gave him a look. "I am not stupid, Anjan."

"You know me too well. But I've already told you I'm in love with her. If I want to someday have influence on the English, I need someone who understands them. Someone who does that, and yet doesn't wish me to forget who *I* am, too."

"Forget?"

"Practically everyone in England eats meat and drinks alcohol," Emily said. "Imagine your son going to a gathering and being served a roast. Who would you talk to beforehand to make sure that didn't happen? Who would make sure there was lemonade in his glass instead of white wine? Taking care of such arrangements is a wife's work." She glanced over at Anjan. "I do not think you son would ever forget, of course, but I could help smooth the way."

Mrs. Bhattacharya frowned, considering this.

"And of course we're hiring an Indian cook."

"Hmph." Anjan's mother looked somewhat mollified. But when she realized that her expression had softened, she glared at Emily with renewed intent. "Meals are meals. And India? You want him to forget about India? To never come home, never have his children know where they are from?"

"No," Emily replied. "Of course not. We'll visit as often as we can."

"I see. Who is this girl, Anjan, who wants everything you want? I am not sure I believe her."

"But I don't want everything Anjan wants," Emily said. "He explained to me how it works. I want everything *you* want."

Silence met this at first. Then Mrs. Bhattacharya tilted her head and looked at Emily. "You do?"

"Of course I do. I know nothing about being married to Indians, raising Indian children. Who else would I ask for advice?"

Mrs. Bhattacharya raised one eyebrow and turned to her son. "You told her to say that."

Anjan coughed into his hand. "I promise, Ma, I didn't. I *did* tell her that you were in charge, but she figured the rest of it out herself."

Mrs. Bhattacharya shook her head, but her lip twitched, too—an expression of suppressed humor that reminded Emily of her son. "Well, at least she knows how to go on."

Anjan smiled at Emily, and she found herself smiling back. Getting lost in his expression…

His mother rapped the table smartly. "Did I say you could smile at each other like that? I promised my husband I would not go easy on you. There are still seventeen items on my list. We are by no means finished."

The list ranged from questions of how Emily felt about hosting family members who came to sit for the civil service examination, children, religion, children again, Emily's fits and her family's history, children…

"Do you love him?" Mrs. Bhattacharya finally asked.

"Yes," Emily said. "In fact—"

"No need to convince me," the other woman interrupted. "Of course you do. Who couldn't?"

Emily smiled.

Mrs. Bhattacharya's expression scarcely changed. "We'll have to talk with your family about the most auspicious time to have the wedding."

Emily's smile spread. Anjan had told her not to worry, that if they were both respectful, they could bring her around. But maybe she hadn't really believed it.

But then Mrs. Bhattacharya continued. "You don't have a mother. Who is responsible for you?"

"I have a sister." Emily grimaced. "And an uncle. But it might be better if…if…" She trailed off.

"What is she saying now?" Mrs. Bhattacharya asked, an expression of disbelief on her face.

Anjan came over and sat next to Emily. "Ma," he said, "there may be a little difficulty with her uncle."

"Difficulty? What kind of difficulty?"

"I'm not of age," Emily said. "I need his permission."

Anjan spread his hands.

"Oh." Mrs. Bhattacharya's jaw set. "That difficulty." It was such a familiar expression on her face—hauntingly familiar, in fact. After a long pause, she shrugged. "I will talk to him. When your father was having those kind of difficulties with Colonel Wainworth, I handled it."

But Anjan shook his head. "No," he said softly. "I appreciate the offer, Ma, but this time, I think I must do it."

⌘ ⌘ ⌘

JANE STOOD AT THE WINDOW, peering down into the street below. The hotel Oliver had brought them to was on a quiet street, far from the pressing crowds they'd encountered at the train station. He'd given a false name when they had signed in. He'd come up to the room, but he had paced back and forth for ten minutes before finally dashing off a handful of notes and ringing for someone to deliver them.

"My brother," he'd said by way of explanation. "And an acquaintance, who will inquire of the bar as to the whereabouts of your sister's…barrister."

She didn't ask him why he had needed to think so long before deciding to let his brother know he was in town. Or why he'd given the hotel a false name. Or why they had come here, to this quiet hotel more than a mile from the center of town. She already knew.

It wasn't that he was ashamed of her. He just…didn't want anyone to know of their affair. That was all.

So why did it rankle?

A few minutes back, the boy he'd sent to deliver the messages had returned, this time laden with a bag. It had been filled with paper: newspapers, copies of parliamentary minutes, notes, invitations. He'd made his excuses and retired to a desk, leaving Jane to look out the window and think her own thoughts.

If there was one thing she had learned in the months since she had met Oliver, it was that problems were best met with bold action. Every time she'd cowered and hid or made herself smaller, her problems had grown in size. This—this growing affection between them, this love affair that was impossible—was a problem.

She wanted a bold solution.

But what she was getting instead…

Watching him work through the papers was like watching him work himself away from her. With every letter he opened, every new amendment he read, he seemed more distant. More aware that the card he'd received invited him to a supper where Jane would never fit in.

Wrens, he had said, not phoenixes. She had told him once that she was ablaze, but the women who married men like Oliver wouldn't even have dared to strike a match and light a fire.

She could do it. She could simply throw money at the problem—hire etiquette instructors who would browbeat Jane night and day until she stopped making mistakes. Hire a woman who would be wholly responsible for Jane's uninteresting, drab, perfect little wardrobe. She had enough money to cut all her feathers and bleach them beige. With work, she could make herself fit.

But when she thought of an existence composed of lies, she shivered. Once was enough.

She shook her head and turned back to the window, back to the question of how to find a bold solution to a very quiet problem.

Chapter Twenty-Seven

"Who are you?"

Anjan had been let into the dim study at the back of the house. It took him a moment to focus on the man who must have been Titus Fairfield. He was rounding and bald, and he watched Anjan with a grave expression on his face.

Anjan had seen him before. Years before, another Indian student—one who had taken his degree the year Anjan had arrived—had pointed him out as a private tutor. Not one that could be used; one who was unlikely to take on an Indian pupil. If he had known that man was Emily's uncle...

He probably wouldn't have asked her to walk in the first place. Just as well he hadn't known.

He'd dressed in sober colors, had made sure that he looked perfectly respectable. His collar was starched so stiffly he could feel the points against his cheek when he turned his head. He handed over a card.

"I'm Mr. Anjan Bhattacharya," he said, "and I'm here on a matter of some importance.

Fairfield set Anjan's card on the desk without glancing at it. "Well," he said in a jolly voice, "I'm not taking any pupils this year." He had a crafty look in his eye, as if somehow Anjan wouldn't recognize that he was being put off.

"Just as well. I have no interest in a tutor. I took the Law Tripos in March," he informed the man. "But I did know your last pupil—John Plateford. You did good work with him."

Mr. Fairfield had not expected flattery. He blinked and was unable to summon up the rudeness necessary to ring the bell and have Anjan thrown away. So Anjan sat on the other side of his desk. For a moment, Fairfield simply stared at him, unsure of the etiquette of the situation. His natural pride, such as it was, won out after a few moments.

"Yes, Plateford," he said happily. "He received first-class honors."

"A credit to you," Anjan replied politely. "So did I."

Fairfield blinked once more at that and then shook his head, as if to dispel the idea that *Anjan* might have ranked alongside his pupil.

"I'm a barrister in London now," Anjan continued. He waited one moment to see if Fairfield would connect his profession with the note that Emily had left.

But he didn't. Fairfield sat there frowning owlishly at Anjan.

"A few days ago," Anjan continued after too long a pause, "Miss Emily Fairfield came to me."

Her uncle sucked in a breath. "You?" he said in shock. "Why would she go to you?"

"Because I'd asked her to marry me," Anjan said. "And because she wanted to tell me yes."

"Ridiculous!" Fairfield shook his head, pushing against the desk as if he could thus reject the words Anjan was saying. "Insanity! It's not possible."

Anjan might have listed all the ways it was possible—starting with the good-luck kiss she'd given him the prior evening. He might have mentioned the long talk they'd had last night, discussing their future. Instead, he decided to misunderstand the man.

"I assure you," Anjan said, "there is no prohibition."

"That isn't what I meant." Fairfield grimaced. "*You* know. I meant that you can't marry her."

"You mean that I can't marry her on account of the fact that you object."

Fairfield looked relieved to have the matter stated so plainly. "Yes. Yes. That's it. I object."

"I don't blame you," Anjan said. "I am here to relieve you of your objections. I know you must be feeling a little worried about how your niece will be treated."

"Indeed." Fairfield puffed out his chest. "I am worried about her treatment."

"I can understand that," Anjan said. "My father is highly placed in the civil service. My uncle is the native aide-de-camp for the Governor-General. I know you must be worried that I will think your niece beneath me."

Fairfield blinked rapidly. "Uh. Well."

"Never fear," Anjan said. "I don't. I'll care for her as well as any lesser man might. We may be better off than your humble circumstances, but I am just another one of her Majesty's loyal servants." The words hardly tasted badly in his mouth as he spoke them.

Mr. Fairfield seemed nonplussed. He skimmed his hand over his head, grimacing oddly. "That was not…"

"Ah. It's her fits, then? You fear she wasn't truthful with me about them. Mr. Fairfield, I applaud your desire to make sure that there has been adequate and proper disclosure between all parties before entering into a permanent relationship. But I assure you that I've known of them from the start. They're scarcely worth thinking about."

"You don't understand." Fairfield was beginning to look pale.

"Ah," Anjan slowly stood, setting his hands on the desk. "It's because I'm Indian."

There was a long, pregnant pause.

"I am not sure that Emily is well enough to marry," her uncle finally said. "But if she were, then, yes, I'd refuse you. Because you're—you're—"

"From India," Anjan supplied helpfully. "It's the name of a place, not a loathsome disease. You'll have to learn to say it; we're going to be family."

"No, no, of course we're not," Fairfield said mulishly. "I don't have to say anything. I won't give permission. I won't."

"Perhaps you can explain."

"Because I know your race," Fairfield growled. "You're weak and you'll take ten wives and if you die, you'll force my niece to burn herself on your funeral pyre."

"Yes," Anjan snapped back. "Because it would be so much better to let her have no husband at all, to burn her with pokers while she's still alive, and to subject her to electric shock. You've no call to lecture me on that front, Mr. Fairfield. *I*, at least, have never hurt her."

Fairfield swallowed. "That's different. She was—is—ill. And...and..."

"And you made it worse. Did you know that I have only seen your niece cry once? It was when I told her that her guardian should treat her as a precious treasure."

"But—"

"While we are discussing the matter, I suppose a few points of clarification are in order. Hindus believe in monogamy; I do not know a Hindu who has more than one wife. When my brother passed away, his wife mourned him, but she is still alive." Anjan felt his hands shake with anger. "I don't claim that my race, as you call it, is perfect, but I *try.*" He glared at the man. "I've seen Emily's scars, and that's more than you can say."

Fairfield shrunk away from the anger in Anjan's voice. "I meant well," he whispered.

Anjan leaned forward across the desk until he was an inch away from the other man. "Mean better."

Fairfield slouched in his seat. "I..." He looked around. "You...you've seen her scars?"

Anjan nodded.

"But they're…"

Anjan nodded.

"She would have had to…remove a bit of clothing to show you them." He looked perturbed, and Anjan decided not to mention that he hadn't seen *all* of Emily's scars. "You say that when Emily ran away, she went to you?"

"She did."

"Then she's…ruined. She has to marry." He licked his lips.

There was no point clarifying the exact state of Emily's ruination.

Mr. Fairfield didn't say anything for a long while. His lips moved, as if he was arguing with himself…but at least he appeared to be arguing back. Finally, he straightened. "You're Indian," he finally said. "Doesn't that mean that you have…special healing abilities? I think I remember hearing about them. Special…" He made a gesture. "Things. With stuff."

Anjan had his degree in law from Cambridge—the exact same degree that Mr. Fairfield had earned. He wanted to laugh. He ought to have corrected the man.

"Yes," he finally said. "I do things with stuff. How ever did you know?"

"Maybe this is for the best," Fairfield said. "You might know of a whole range of cures that I have not been able to access. This might be the best thing for her after all."

Anjan didn't nod. He didn't smile. "I'd be happy to try anything that seems like a good idea," he said, and Fairfield looked pleased with himself.

"Good, good. But—just to make sure—we're putting it in the settlements. No burning her alive."

"Well," Anjan said generously, "you do have to look out for your niece."

⌘ ⌘ ⌘

THE END CAME UPON HER so swiftly that Jane didn't even realize she was looking at it until the moment had already passed.

The end came first in happiness—when Oliver's inquiries were swiftly answered in the affirmative. There was a barrister named Anjan Bhattacharya. Addresses were discovered; messages exchanged via swift courier, and two hours later, Jane found herself at her sister's hotel, flying into Emily's arms.

Emily was nearly incoherent. She had just received a scrap of paper—a telegram—from Titus of all people.

"I can't believe it," Emily said. "I have no idea what Anjan said to him, but he *agreed*. I'm getting married! He won't be my guardian anymore. It's over."

It was over. Jane laughed with her sister—and agreed to be her maid of honor—and hugged her and listened to her describe the difficulties of needing two marriage ceremonies.

She heard more about Anjan, too.

"You'll have to meet him when he returns. You'll like him, I promise. Oh, Jane, I'm so happy."

There were details to be hashed through after that—details of settlements for Emily, her trousseau… These were happy details. Jane floated back to the hotel room she shared with Oliver.

He now had a second pile of paper in front of him. He kissed her, though, long and slow. "I'm glad that's all settled," he said, when she explained everything.

But he didn't sound glad. And he didn't meet her eyes when he said he had to get back to his work. It *was* all settled…and he'd only talked about this affair lasting until Emily was found and made safe.

Jane retreated to the dressing room to change her gown for dinner. The hotel maid had undone the laces of Jane's gown when the knock came.

She heard the door open.

"Mr. Cromwell?"

Jane recognized the voice of one of the hotel staff, and hid a smile at the assumed name.

"Yes."

"There's a woman here to see you."

"A woman?" Oliver asked. "I'm not expecting a…" He trailed off.

Jane was stripped to her corset. Even if she had been dressed, she could not have walked out into that room. To announce her presence in his room at a time like this… She might not care much for her reputation on her behalf, but *his* reputation still had some value.

There was a pause, the sound of footsteps. And then…

"Mother?" he said. There was another pause. When he spoke again, his voice had altered from swift and business-like to anguished. "Oh my God, Mother. What's wrong?"

Jane motioned to the servant and sent her away through the smaller servants' door. No maid needed to overhear this. Jane shouldn't either, but she had no place to retreat to.

"I'm just glad I found you in time," the woman—Oliver's *mother*—said. "The duke said—well, never mind. I can't really think—Oliver, listen to me, I can't get a straight sentence out of my mouth. It's just…"

"Take a deep breath. Take your time. Tell me."

The other woman's voice broke. "It's Freddy."

"What happened to her? We can take care of her, find her the best doctors, give her—"

"They found her in her bed a day and a half after she passed away."

"No." But Oliver didn't sound as if he were denying it, just reflexively pushing away the words. "That can't be. I saw her not so long ago. She looked a little ill, but…"

"It was an apoplexy. They say she didn't suffer."

"Oh, Mother." Oliver's voice was muffled. "I should have said something to you when I saw her, should have let you know she wasn't doing well. I should have had you come out and—"

"Enough. I told her I loved her the last time I saw her. We've had our differences, but we've also had our good times." The other woman's voice quavered. "Don't lay blame. There's more than enough sorrow without it."

There were no words for a while after that, just a few sniffles. The sounds of family giving—and receiving—comfort.

Oliver had mentioned his aunt Freddy in the bookshop all those months ago. It was one of the first things that had drawn Jane to him—that he'd talked about a woman who obviously had her own peculiarities with such respect and affection.

It was as if someone had whispered to Jane that if he could love an ornery, stubborn, strange old woman, he might like *her.*

And he had.

"It's tomorrow," his mother said. "The funeral. Everyone is down—Laura and Geoffrey, Patricia and Reuven. Free and your father. We're having dinner tonight."

"Of course I'll be there."

There was a long pause.

"And Oliver, the woman who is staying with you…"

Jane froze.

"What woman?"

"Don't be ridiculous. You're here under an assumed name. You've never used my soap, and yet someone here has washed with my May blend. I smelled it the instant I walked in. I only wanted you to know… There won't be many of us present, just family and a few others. If she's important to you, if she would bring you comfort, you should bring her."

"*Mama.*"

"I won't pinch your cheek in front of her, and if you're worried about the example you'll set for your sister…"

"Mama, please."

"…don't. Free will probably lecture you better than I could."

There was a long pause. Oliver had to know that Jane was listening. He had to be wondering what she was thinking, what she would make of all this. Jane wrapped her arms around herself and wanted. Even if this didn't last. Even if they never saw each other again after their days together, even if he married his perfect little wren next month.

Right now, she wanted to be the one who comforted him.

"I'll..."

"Think about it, Oliver."

Jane bit her lip and looked away, trying not to feel the sting of it. They had agreed, after all. And he was upset. She really didn't have a place in his life, and it was the work of a moment—one soul-squeezing moment—to forgive him the small pain he caused her.

"I'll see," he said.

Chapter Twenty-eight

OLIVER KNEW WHAT WAS COMING the instant he closed the door after his mother. He didn't even want to turn around. Didn't want to have to look at Jane and see what he had done.

But he did. He went and found her where she was still seated on a bench in the dressing room. She was wearing petticoats and a corset and was gazing off into space. She looked up as he came in.

"Good," she said. "You're here. I suppose we need to…" She trailed off and looked at her hands in her lap.

"Jane." He felt a lump in his throat as he faced her.

"I need someone to help me put on my dress." She pointed to a blue silk with red ribbons. "That one."

"Jane…"

"I'm not going to have this discussion with you when I'm half-dressed," she said, and so he helped her put it on. It was agonizing, to brush her soft skin. To want to kiss her shoulder, as he smoothed fabric over it. He wanted so much with her…but he suspected that this was the end, the donning of this dress, and not a beginning.

When he had finished to the best of his ability, she turned back to him.

"I can…" No. He couldn't exonerate himself.

"Explain?" she asked. "You don't need to explain. You already have. I am the last woman in the world you want to marry. You're upset because of your aunt. Why would you introduce me to your family? You haven't said anything I don't already know."

He took a step forward. "It's not that."

"Oh?" There was just enough of a dubious quality in her voice.

"It is that," he said, "But it's so much more. I love you, Jane."

She tilted her head. "*What?*"

"I love you. And if I let you share in this—if I bring you in at this moment—I don't know how I could ever let you go. You'd be a part of me. A part of my family."

She already was. There was some part of him that felt as if he were still on a dark forest road with her. With nobody else around—just the two of them against the rest of the world.

She had not said anything yet.

"I want that," he said. "It hurts how much I want that. Come with me, Jane. Not as my lover, but as my fiancée."

She didn't say anything.

"I know there will be difficulties, but we can work them out. Minnie can sponsor you; she could get the Dowager Duchess of Clermont to train you. And—"

"Train me?" Jane said. "What am I, a horse?"

Oliver winced. "No. Of course not. But a few lessons…"

"A few lessons on what?" Jane's chin came up, but her lips trembled. "On how to act, how to behave, how to dress. Is that what you mean?"

He couldn't say anything.

"Tell me, Oliver, how long do you think it will take me to learn to hold my tongue? To talk quietly? To dress as everyone else does?"

"I—Jane…"

"If you want a wren, marry one. Don't ask me."

He shut his eyes. "I know. I know. It's such a horrid thing to ask. But…" He paused, trying to regroup. Trying to explain. "I've made a career of keeping quiet. Someone from my background has to be particularly careful. My brother can advocate whatever he wishes; I have to be cautious. To make sure that when people think of me, they think of a reasonable man. Someone who is just like them. Someone who…"

"Someone who doesn't have an awful wife," Jane said. Her voice was thick.

"Yes," he whispered. And then seeing that flash in her eyes, he shook his head. "No. That's not what I meant. It's just what everyone else would think."

She stood up. "It's just as well, because I…" She stopped, biting her lip, and then shook her head. "No, never mind. You've just been told that your aunt has passed away. I don't need to add to your burdens."

"Just say it," he snapped, "and spare me your pity."

Her chin rose. "It's just as well you don't want an *awful* wife," she told him, "because I had hoped for a husband with a little courage."

Oh, that hurt. He wasn't choosing between acceptance and Jane, between a ballroom filled with happy friendship and that dark road alone with Jane. He was choosing between a dark, lonely road with her, and one without her.

"You didn't go to Eton," he said to her. "You didn't go to Cambridge. You didn't spend *years* slowly fashioning yourself into the kind of person who could fit in and thus make a difference. Don't tell me this doesn't take courage. Don't tell me that." His voice rose with every word. "Don't tell me it wasn't courage that brought me back again and again, after every attempt to toss me out. Being like me takes courage, damn it."

She looked at him. It felt as if she looked *through* him. "Really, Oliver?" One hand went to her hip. "It took courage to walk away from Clemons and let the other boys do what they did? It took courage to consider Bradenton's offer to humiliate me? My. Courage isn't what it used to be."

Those words felt like spears in his stomach. The worst part was, though, he could see her hands, shaking. Her eyes, wide and full of hurt. As badly as she'd struck out at him, he'd hurt her that much, too. And he couldn't even say that he hadn't meant it.

"I thought so," she said, turning away from him. "I'll send someone over for the rest of my things." She swept past him.

He wanted to reach for her—to tell her not to leave. To take hold of her arm as she walked past. To do anything at all.

He didn't. She walked out and he didn't stop her. He let that moment slip by—the last moment he had to apologize and save it all—and he wasn't sure if it was courage or cowardice.

⌘ ⌘ ⌘

FREDDY'S FUNERAL WAS A QUIET AFFAIR. There weren't many people who had known Oliver's aunt—just the boy who delivered her groceries, a few ladies who had visited her, and her family.

Oliver's sisters had come down—Laura with her husband and Oliver's smallest niece, an infant who whimpered through the ceremony, and Patricia with her husband and their twins. Free had come, too. She stood for a long time at their aunt's coffin, looking in, not saying a word. She ran her hand along the edge and wept silently.

It felt wrong to have his aunt laid out in a church. She would have hated lying exposed in a strange place. She would have hated having everyone's eyes on her—even if it was only the eyes of those few who knew her. Freddy may have been the only person who would have sighed in relief at the thought of being buried six feet below the ground in a tiny coffin. When the grave had been filled in, Oliver laid his flowers on it.

"There you are," he whispered. "Nobody will get to you now."

After the burial, they retired with her solicitor to her small apartment.

Oliver had spent every Christmas that he remembered here. It had been a tradition born out of necessity. His mother hadn't wanted Freddy to be alone at Christmas, and Freddy had refused to leave her rooms to come to New Shaling. Therefore, their entire family had come here—even when the rooms had become too small to fit the family.

They made a multitude now, so many that there weren't chairs enough for everyone. Oliver and his sisters, his niece and nephews, his parents... His father stood next to a wall; Reuven sat with his boys on the floor.

It was somewhat of a surprise that Freddy *had* a solicitor. For that matter, he hadn't supposed she would write a will. It wasn't as if Freddy had much to give away, and hearing her few belongings dispensed with summary dispatch seemed cruel.

"This will," the solicitor said, "dates from late last week." He drew out several sheets of paper—far longer than Oliver would have imagined would be needed under the circumstances.

But then, this was Freddy. The preamble—lengthy and argumentative— had them all exchanging glances, uncertain if it was acceptable to smile so soon after her passing. It sounded so much like her that it almost felt as if she were here. She went on for a page about what she expected from each of them—the legacy that they would be upholding, the expectations she had.

And then the solicitor cleared his throat and started on the bequests.

His aunt left a few family heirlooms and a miniature of their mother to Serena Marshall, her sister.

"To Oliver, my nephew—I would leave you a portion of my worldly goods, but I don't think you have need of them. I leave you instead the few quilts I have sewn over the years that I have kept for myself. They're a good sight better than anything that can be purchased in the stores these days, and not a machine-stitch on them. Make sure you keep warm. As you grow older, you'll find yourself more susceptible to chills."

He felt a lump in his throat. Freddy had poured so much of her time and energy into her quilts that this was like getting a piece of her as a memory.

"To Laura and Patricia, I leave the remainder of the money I inherited as a child, to be divided equally among the two of them. I also give all my remaining household goods to be divided between them as they agree. I particularly commend the following: my paring knife, which has rarely needed sharpening; the wardrobe I have used for these last few decades, and my good china."

Laura looked at Patricia over their husband's arms.

"That can't be right," Laura finally said. "I can't imagine that the contents of Freddy's accounts are worth much, but this disposes of all her possessions without..."

They both glanced at Free, who sat in her chair looking down. Oliver ached for her. For Freddy. For the argument they'd had and never made up, the one that had led Freddy to cut her favorite niece from her will entirely.

"We did argue," Free said softly. "And I don't want—it's not about that."

No. It wasn't about the possessions. It was about knowing that she hadn't been forgiven.

"No," Patricia said, "it's simple. We'll just divide things evenly between the three of us. I'm sure Aunt Freddy would want that. That she's wishing that she had done just such a thing at this moment."

The solicitor adjusted his spectacles and looked over at the two of them. "But there is a bequest for Miss Frederica Marshall."

Everyone looked up at that. Laura gave a shrug to her sister, as if to say, *I have no idea what else it could be.*

"Lastly, I come to Frederica Marshall, my goddaughter, niece, namesake and scourge of my existence. Several years ago, as I am sure you are all aware, she was presumptuous enough to insist that I leave this apartment—that I go out in the world and have an adventure, even if it was so trivial a one as to buy an apple. After she left, I attempted to do so."

Free let out a broken breath, so close to a sob.

"I discovered myself incapable of leaving," the solicitor read. "For some reason, I could not fit through the door. But I did my best to make do, and so for that reason, I leave the proceeds of my grand adventure and the contents of my trunk to Miss Frederica Marshall. I suspect that she will make better use of them than I did."

Free looked up. "Proceeds?" she said quietly. "What proceeds would she be talking about?"

"The proceeds of Miss Barton's estate," the solicitor said. "Those would be the royalties on twenty-five volumes published to date, not counting the four that are in the process of publication."

Frederica blinked. "*Twenty-five* volumes?" she repeated.

Oliver felt a sudden, staggering pain. He knew which authoress had penned twenty-five volumes, one after the other, in quick succession. It had been only twenty-three last January, but... His sister walked over to his aunt's trunk, flipped open the lid. She reached inside.

There were sheaves of paper written all over in his aunt's crabbed writing. She picked up one and set it on the table.

Oliver knew—he absolutely *knew*—what he would see on the pages.

"*Mrs. Larriger and the Welsh Brigade,*" Free read. She took out another sheaf. "*Mrs. Larriger and the French Comtesse. Mrs. Larriger Goes to Ireland.*" Her voice caught. "Who is Mrs. Larriger?"

But Oliver knew. If his sister sifted through the papers long enough, Mrs. Larriger would find her way to China, to India, across all the seas of the world. He remembered mocking these books with Jane, laughing that the author had clearly gone no farther than Portsmouth.

He'd been wrong. The author had not even come that far. She had lived the majority of her life in scarcely more than a hundred square feet. And she'd had so much adventure hidden in her that it had poured out of her once she'd let it loose. It was almost impossible to take in the enormity of Aunt Freddy's secret. Mrs. Larriger had roamed the world—smoking peace pipes with Indians, befriending a flock of penguins, getting captured by whalers and winning her way free.

While Freddy sat in a small room watching the door, hoping that tomorrow she would be able to leave.

Maybe she had.

⌘ ⌘ ⌘

IT WAS A SHORT LIST.

Jane had brought up an entire sheaf of paper—beautiful, creamy paper—and had made sure that her inkwell was full.

She'd intended to fill pages with her plans. In the end, though, the list she had managed to come up with was tiny.

What I will do next, she had labeled it.

One thing wasn't on the list: Jane had no intention of submitting to another painful round of the social whirl. Of setting herself up to be judged and found wanting. Balls and soirees and parties might sound lovely in theory, but in reality they were exhausting and heartbreaking. Instead, her wants were simple.

Do good things.

Make more friends.

Keep the friends I have.

After a long moment's thought, she added one last item.

Prove Oliver wrong.

It belonged on her list. Fourth, she decided—he deserved no more importance in her future life than that—but it belonged. For now...

It still hurt. She ached from it hurting. She'd spent the afternoon with her sister, planning details of the wedding. She'd smiled so much she felt as if her mouth would crack from the effort.

It *hurt.*

But even beneath that ache, she felt a cool clarity: She was glad she had known him, glad that she'd broken away from the person she once had been.

From the façade that had played her more than she had played it. She wouldn't take on another role, least of all because a man who claimed to love her asked her to do it.

He'd hurt her, but she'd make it like all the other hurts she'd received: nothing more than an act of propagation.

Jane was poised on the verge of something even better. And she knew exactly how it started: with friendship.

Jane set her list to one side and pulled another sheet of paper to her.

Dear Genevieve and Geraldine, she wrote. *The last time we corresponded, you were in London and I was in Nottingham. Circumstances have changed, and I am now in town. I had hoped we might be able to renew our friendship...*

Chapter Twenty-nine

OLIVER WAS STILL IN A DAZE by the time he returned to Clermont House. He shrugged off his brother's condolences and retreated to his chambers.

Many months ago, Oliver had purchased a book. He'd intended to look through it at the time, but then events had intervened. It had been shunted to the bottom of this trunk; when he'd come back from Cambridge, it had been shuffled to a low shelf. He hunted through the books, checking dusty spines, until he found the one he was looking for.

Mrs. Larriger Leaves Home.

The pages were still crisp, the leather binding not yet cracked. He felt a lump in his throat as he opened the book to the front page. These were Freddy's words, Freddy's thoughts. He'd purchased it, and he hadn't known. He had scarcely known her at all. He smoothed back the pages and found Chapter One.

For the first fifty-eight years of her life, Mrs. Laura Larriger lived in Portsmouth in sight of the harbor. She never wondered where the ships went, and cared about their return only when one of them happened to bring her husband home from one of his trading voyages. There was never any reason to care.

Oliver swallowed, wondering what his aunt had seen from her window. What she had dreamed about, what she had wanted.

That day, Mrs. Larriger sat in her parlor. But the walls seemed thicker. The air felt closer. For almost sixty years, she had never felt the slightest curiosity about the world outside her door. Now, the air beyond her walls seemed to call out to her. Leave, it whispered. Leave.

That was something Freddy would have understood. No wonder that passage had seemed so true to life.

She took a deep breath. She packed a satchel. And then, with a great effort, with the effort of a woman uprooting everything she had known, Mrs. Larriger put one foot outside her door into the warm May sunshine.

Oliver shut his eyes and thought of his aunt. He thought of her putting a toe out of her door and having palpitations of the heart. He remembered her saying that she was trying, that she'd get it right one day. That she would go to the park and have a nice walk...

He hoped that she had managed to make it out before she passed away. But it was no longer so simple. What Freddy had been unable to do in one way, she'd managed in another. Somehow the most disapproving, dour, lecturing spinster of his acquaintance...

Somehow, she'd managed to make thousands of people dream of adventure. She'd done more than anyone would have guessed. The woman who had lectured Oliver about taking chills in her last will and testament had been braver than anyone had known.

He could remember the last time he'd seen her. *Your mother was a regular coal-grabber,* she'd said. *But you, you're like me.* At the time, he'd laughed it off. His aunt never left the house; Oliver had a busy, varied career. Freddy constantly warned him about any alteration in his schedules, however minor; Oliver did new things. He wasn't like Freddy.

You remember the pain, and you flinch.

He didn't flinch. Did he?

Not from the outdoors, no. But...

Oliver shut his eyes and drew in a breath. He'd flinched from a great many other things.

Like Jane. When he'd first met her, he'd scarcely been able to watch her. She violated the precepts of polite society without thinking, and he'd flinched at first when he'd seen her. Jane was a coal-grabber, all right.

But Freddy was right. There *had* been a time when Oliver had held on to coals himself. When he'd first gone to Eton, for instance. Those first years, he'd insisted on his due. He'd proclaimed loudly that he was as good as any other boy, and he'd been willing to fight to keep it that way. What had changed, and when had it all gone awry?

The walls seemed thicker. The air felt closer. He could almost feel the walls he'd built of his life closing around him. He'd not realized they were there, so quietly had he made them. And yet when he reached out, there they were. Freddy had insisted to Free that she needed to stay inside, to wear her bonnets. And Oliver had been saying the same thing. He had looked at his sister, at her face shining as she was surrounded by a hundred women in Hyde Park, and instead of feeling proud of her accomplishment or happy for what had happened, he had felt tired. He'd tried to warn her off Cambridge.

It was an old tiredness he felt, the weariness of an aging dog lying in the summer sun, watching puppies at play. As if exuberance belonged to the young. He could remember, faintly, an echo of that feeling. Days when he'd insisted—over and over—that he was as good as anyone else, that he wasn't going to bend to their ways, that he'd make them bend to his.

He turned the next page in *Mrs. Larriger Leaves Home,* but the words blurred before him.

He was asking himself the wrong question. Once, he'd been like Free, unwilling to back down or take "no" for an answer. The question wasn't when things had changed. It was this: When had he decided to simply accept society's rules, to play the game precisely as it had been laid out by those who already had power?

It had happened years ago at Eton.

When he'd finally learned to keep his mouth shut. When he'd discovered that he could accomplish more by holding his tongue and biding his time than by lashing out with fists and shouts.

He'd made a career of quiet, he'd told Jane. But at some point, quiet no longer carried the day. If he never learned to speak, what would be the point of achieving power? Simply to carry on carrying on?

With a great effort, with the effort of a woman uprooting everything she had known, Mrs. Larriger put one foot outside her door into the warm May sunshine.

It took Oliver a moment to remember his old self—the person he had thought was born of immaturity, the boy that he had put aside as he came into adulthood. He would never have thought himself *ashamed* of his background before now. And yet…

How was it that he'd taken the rules that he'd hated and adopted them for himself? He'd chafed when people told him he was a bastard. He'd raged when they'd said he would never amount to anything, that his father was nothing. How was it that *he* was telling the woman that he loved that she was nothing? That she was awful?

He'd started caring more about becoming the kind of person who could make a change than he cared about the change itself. He'd walked away from Jane, and by doing so, he'd told her all the things about herself that everyone else had thrown in her face: that she was wrong, broken, awful.

It was not the little lust of unmet physical needs that he felt for her. He loved her. He loved everything about her, from the fierceness of her devotion to her sister to the shrug of her shoulders when she found herself on horseback with him. He loved the way she smiled. He loved the way that she simply refused to feel shame simply because someone else didn't approve of her behavior.

He loved Jane. He was always going to love her.

He loved the person she'd made of him—a man who could foil abductions and break into houses when circumstances required. A man who could take on Bradenton and see a foe to vanquish, not a powerful lord to be appeased.

And he'd wanted to make her into nothing because that's what he'd done to himself.

He'd thought he needed a wren—some proper, upstanding woman who needed his money as much as he needed her breeding.

He could suddenly see his life with that unchosen woman. His ever-so-proper wife would never tell him outright that his father was uncouth and improper. She would simply intimate it with a sniff. Perhaps she might suggest that next year they might want to consider having the elder Mr. Marshall stay at home during the season, as he'd be so much more comfortable amongst his own kind.

She would bear his children—and she'd raise them to be quiet, well-behaved folk just like herself, faintly ashamed of their father's origins.

"Yes," he could imagine one of them saying, "perhaps there was that little defect of his mother, but at least our grandfather was a duke. That has to count for something."

They'd never speak of their Aunt Free—too bold, too forward, altogether too *everything*. Even Patricia, married to a Jew, or Laura, running a dry-goods store, would be suspect. Eventually, his cipher of a wife would suggest that perhaps they'd all be happiest if they just pretended that Oliver's family didn't exist.

Jane had it right: He'd traded his bravery for his ambition.

And if he didn't make this right—if he didn't learn to suppress that memory of pain and reach in and grab hold of the coals in front of him, he'd be locked up for life in the chains of his own silence. He'd let too much go already: Jane, his sister, even that time with Bradenton. He'd let Jane do most of the talking. He hadn't even told Bradenton to his face how disgusting he was.

With that, at least one thing came clear. Oliver stood. He didn't know how to make things right with Jane yet, but Bradenton…

Bradenton owed him a vote, and Oliver was going to collect.

He set the book down, retrieved his coat. He went down the staircase and out into the main entry.

And with a great effort—with the effort of a man uprooting everything he had made of himself—Oliver put one foot outside into the warm May sunshine.

⌘ ⌘ ⌘

IT WAS HALF AN HOUR later when Oliver was shown into the Marquess of Bradenton's study. The man looked extremely annoyed. He shook his head as he sat at his desk, tapping Oliver's card against the wood.

"I had three-quarters of a mind not to see you," he said.

"Of course you did." Oliver said. "But your curiosity got the better of you."

"But then," Bradenton said, "I recalled that Parliament would be voting, and I wanted to work on a speech. One about farmers and governesses. I figured I needed to study my source material."

Was that supposed to be offensive?

"Save your insinuations," Oliver said. "And your sly jabs. You'll need your breath to cast your vote to extend the franchise."

Bradenton laughed. "You can't be serious. With what you did to me, you think to win my vote?"

"Of course not," Oliver said. "How could I win your vote? You're a marquess, and I'm just one man out of a hundred. One man out of a thousand." He let his smile spread as he tapped his fingers on the table. "One man out of, say, a hundred thousand."

Bradenton frowned. "One hundred thousand?"

"More than that, actually. Did you go to Hyde Park a few weeks ago? I did. There was an infectious joy, an exuberance in the air. The people gathered. The people won. I read the estimates of the crowds in the paper later, and yes, that was the lowest number I saw bruited about. One hundred thousand."

Bradenton shifted uneasily in his chair.

"It's precisely as you've pointed out before," Oliver said. "There's one of you, and one hundred thousand of me. *You* seem to find that comforting. I can't figure out why." Oliver leaned forward and smiled. "They're terrible odds, after all."

"I'm entirely unmoved by the protestations of rabble." But Bradenton spoke swiftly, refusing to look Oliver in the eyes. "I have my seat in the House of Lords by birth. I don't *have* to bow to what the common people desire."

"Then you won't mind when the headlines proclaim that the Reform Bill was blocked once again, and this time by a margin that included the Marquess of Bradenton."

Bradenton's eyes widened and he sucked in a breath. But a moment later, he shook his head with vehemence. "I wouldn't be the only one."

"No. But think how good your name would sound in a headline. Bradenton Blocks Bill. It's alliterative."

Bradenton clenched his fists. "Stop it, Marshall. This isn't funny!"

"Of course it isn't. You're unmoved by the protestations of the rabble. When they gather outside your house, massed in numbers larger than you can count, you'll laugh in their faces."

"Shut up, Marshall," Bradenton growled. "Shut up."

"Yes, that's a good one. Tell them that while they're chanting. 'Shut up.' That might work. Maybe they'll listen. Or maybe they'll stop talking and start throwing rocks. Did you know they played the Marseillaise near the end of the demonstration?"

"*Shut up!* The constables—they'll throw the lot of them in prison."

"Oh, I saw constables on the day of the Reform League's gathering," Oliver said. "All two of them. They would make a lovely barricade, those two solitary blue uniforms arrayed in front of your house, their truncheons gleaming as they faced a crowd of ten thousand. They might stop a charge for ones of seconds."

"Shut up!"

"No," Oliver mused, "you're right. They wouldn't last that long. Because more than half the constables can't vote, either."

He let the silence stretch. Bradenton sat back in his chair, his breathing heavy.

"So you see, Bradenton, you *are* going to vote to extend the franchise. Because there are thousands of me and one of you, and we are not quiet any longer."

"Shut up," Bradenton said again. But his hands shook and his voice was weak.

"No," Oliver said. "That's the whole point. You have had all this time to shut me up. To make me follow your rules. I am done with shutting up. It's your turn."

Chapter Thirty

"I WANT SOMETHING BIG." Jane was seated on the sofa in the front parlor of the rooms she'd leased in London with Genevieve Johnson seated next to her. "Something utterly *huge*. Something as loud and as impossible to ignore as my gowns are. But this time, I want it to have purpose."

"Do you have something in mind?" Genevieve asked. "And what has this to do with me?"

Jane swallowed. "You told me once you wished you had a husband only for the reason that you would take great pleasure in spending your husband's money on charitable works. How do you feel about taking mine?"

Genevieve blinked. "Oh, my goodness," she said, leaning forward. "Tell me more."

"I'm offering you a position," Jane said. "A paid position on the Board of Advisers for the Fairfield Charitable Trusts."

Genevieve's eyes grew round.

"It doesn't exist yet," Jane told her, "but it will. I don't want to economize. I want to *act*. To do things."

"What kind of things?"

Jane shrugged. "I've always wanted a hospital. Or a school. Or maybe a hospital and a school in one, one that sets standards for the rest of the country. So we can stop charlatans from conducting medical experiments on the unsuspecting, for one."

Genevieve's eyes were shining. "A charity hospital," she said, "one with a reputation for major advancements. One that people will fight to sponsor, to be a part of. Oh, I'm going to have to take notes."

"I'll call for paper." But as soon as Jane picked up the bell—it had scarcely even made a noise—the door opened.

"Miss Fairfield," the footman said, "you have a visitor."

"Who is it?" she asked.

But suddenly she knew. Behind the footman, she saw a form. Her heart stopped and then started once more, beating with a ponderous weight that seemed to tear her equanimity to pieces. Jane stood, clutching her hands together, as Oliver came out of the shadowed hall. His spectacles gleamed in the late afternoon sun. His hair seemed to be made of fire. But it wasn't his face that riveted her attention, nor even the direct, demanding look in his eyes.

He walked in and suddenly—suddenly—she couldn't breathe.

"Oliver." She managed that word, and that word alone.

"Jane."

"What…" She swallowed, smoothing out her skirts, and shook her head. "Oliver," she finally choked out, "What in God's name is the color of your waistcoat?"

He smiled. No, it was too little to say that he *smiled*. The expression on his face was like sunlight after a dark cave—utterly blinding.

"Would you know," he said, "that on my way here, I was stopped by three men of my acquaintance, all of whom asked me the same question?"

She shook her head helplessly. "What did you tell them?"

"What do you think?" He gave her a smile. "I told them it was fuchsine."

"And? What did they say?" Her voice was low, her heart beating rapidly.

"And I found it strangely liberating," he said. "As if I'd just made a declaration." He was looking into her eyes, focused entirely on her.

"Precisely how liberated were you?" She could scarcely recognize her own voice.

"Jane, you are not a blight. You are not a disease. You are not a pestilence or a poison. You're a beautiful, brilliant, bold woman, the best I have ever met. I should never have implied that you were lacking. The fault was in me. I didn't think I was strong enough to stand at your side."

She was not going to cry. She wasn't going to hold him or allow him back in her life without question simply because he realized he had missed her. He'd hurt her too badly for that.

He took another step forward, and then bent to one knee. "Jane," he said, "would you do me the honor of being my wife?"

She didn't know what to think. Everything was all muddled. She shook her head, reached for the one thing she understood.

"Your career," she said. "What about your career?"

"I want a career." He swallowed. "But not that one. Not the career where I hold my tongue as other men berate women for wearing too much lace. Not one where I keep quiet while my youngest sister appears before a magistrate for the crime of speaking too loudly. Not one where the price of my power is silence about the things I most hold dear." He bowed his head. "I don't want you to compromise yourself. To be any less than you are. I won't ask you to change for me because I've realized that I need you precisely as you are."

Jane brought her hand to her mouth.

"I don't need that quiet wife. I need you. Someone bold. Someone who won't let me stand back from myself, and who will tell me in no uncertain terms when I've erred."

She didn't know what to say.

"I've needed you to shock me out of the biggest mistake of my life. To make me recognize my fears and to reach into the fire and grab hold of the coals."

His voice was rough.

"I need you, Jane. And I love you more dearly than I can say."

Behind her, Genevieve made a noise. "I think I should absent myself," she said.

Oliver blinked. "Oh, good God. Miss Johnson. I didn't even see you there."

Genevieve smiled. "It's Miss Genevieve. And I had noticed." She waved at Jane. "I'll be back later. With paper and ideas." So saying, she slipped out.

Oliver looked at Jane. He shifted uncomfortably on his knee and then sat on the floor. "There's something else I have to tell you."

She nodded.

"You were right about my courage. I know precisely where I mislaid it." He let out a deep breath. "I was seventeen years of age. My brother was a year ahead of me; he had gone on to Cambridge, and I'd been left alone at Eton for one final year. It didn't matter, I thought. I was wrong."

He shut his eyes.

"There was an instructor. He taught Greek, and he took it upon himself to teach me a little more than that. Every time he heard that I'd spoken up, he would take me to task in class. He would call on me to translate in front of everyone—texts that none of us had seen before. And when I stumbled he'd tell everyone how dull I was. How stupid. How dreadfully wrong."

He wrapped his arms around himself. "I could fight other boys, but an instructor, acting within his power? There was nothing to do. As the term went on, it grew worse. My punishments stopped being simple embarrassment. I was hardly the only boy to experience corporal punishment at Eton, and he never went beyond the line. But when it was happening every day, every time I spoke…"

Jane came to stand by him, and then slowly lowered herself to the floor next to him.

"Anything is bearable if you can fight it, but if you must sit back and take it… That breaks you in a way I can't explain." He took a deep breath. "I made excuse after excuse for myself as I grew more quiet. I was being pushed. Forced into it. It was temporary; I'd stop once I got out of there. But deep down, I've always known the truth: I wasn't brave enough to keep talking. I learned to shut up so loudly that I never managed to unlearn it afterward."

"God. Oliver."

"It doesn't sound like much. But it trains you, an experience like that. To feel sick when you open your mouth. To hold back."

She put her arm on his shoulder and he turned to her.

"I don't want you to feel sorry for me," he said. "I want you to know how much I love and admire you. Because they tried to do it to you, too, and it didn't take."

She smiled. "They didn't get to me until I was nineteen. I had a little longer to become set in my ways."

"Last time I asked you to marry you, I asked you to change." He took a deep breath. "This time, I can do better. Let me be the one who supports you. Who believes that you must not be any less. Who adds to your magnificence instead of asking you to make yourself less."

Jane ran her hand down his back. "I think you owe me a better apology."

He looked over at her. "I'm sorry. I was an ass. I—"

She set her fingers over his mouth. "I didn't mean that you should use words, Oliver."

It took him a moment to understand. A long, slow smile spread over his face. He put his arm around her and then slowly, ever so slowly, he reached out and touched her cheek.

"Jane," he said softly. "I love you." He tilted her chin up. "I love you." He leaned down, his lips so close to hers that if he spoke again, their mouths would touch. "And I am never going to fail you again."

That whisper brought their lips together. And then he did it again. And again. And again, a sweet kiss that she never wanted to end.

"Very well," she whispered.

"What's well?"

"This," Jane said, sliding closer to him. "Forgiving you. Loving you." She leaned into him and tilted her head up for another kiss. "Marrying you."

He wrapped his arms around her. "Good."

Epilogue

Six years later.

OLIVER STOOD AGAINST A WALL, watching the room around him. There was quite a crowd in his main salon tonight; he'd given up the count at several hundreds.

Sometimes, it seemed odd to remember that he *had* a main salon. He and Jane had purchased the house on the event of their marriage, and sometimes, even now, it felt strange to have a room large enough to fit the home where he'd grown up. This one was beautifully appointed: large plate windows at the front looked out over a park. The twinkle of lamplight in other windows was dimly visible across the square.

The window, indeed, was the most beautiful part of the room. Jane stood framed in it, after all, the center of attention.

This gown was an extraordinary one. Purple-and-green striped silk. Gold brocade, perhaps overdone by fashionable tastes. Heavy rubies at her throat.

Everyone had gone beyond wincing at her. They were used to her now; her garb was nothing more than an idle curiosity. She was too important to cut.

After all, at this event, a charity musicale for the Youth Hospital, *he* was the gracious, smiling spouse.

Over by the window, Jane was talking with animation to a baron, introducing him to the bearded man at her side—one of her sober young protégés, a fellow who—if Oliver recalled—she had sponsored through medical school. He was writing on medical ethics.

"Marshall," a voice said.

Oliver turned. It was the Right Honorable Bertie Pages, one of Oliver's colleagues in Parliament.

"Pages," Oliver said, with a nod of his head.

"Good speech today," the man said.

Oliver smiled.

"A bit forceful for my tastes, but effective."

"You always seem to say that," Oliver said. "If it's intended as a gentle rebuke, it has long since ceased to work."

"No… No." The other man turned and swept his arm out. "When you announced that you were marrying her, I thought you'd made a mistake. A grave mistake. She was…"

"She *is,*" Oliver corrected.

"Too loud," Pages said. "Too bright. That gown she's wearing—it's got no subtlety at all. There's never been anything of subtlety to her. And yet…"

"That's precisely why I married her. You'd best get to the *and yet* swiftly, because she *is* my wife."

"And yet her hospital has already attracted some of the brightest minds in the nation. The symposium she sponsored on medical ethics has had an extraordinary effect on the world. People pay attention to her."

Oliver smiled.

"And you have only gained respect as her husband."

In the end, it had been easy to get attention for his parliamentary campaign. Jane had already captured everyone's interest with her plans. The gowns she'd worn had simply fit in with her personality. She'd fascinated everyone—and once she began to accomplish things, she'd won their grudging respect.

"How did you know?" the man asked.

Oliver shrugged. "I had seen her in action. I knew what she could do. But come. Enough of that. There's a man I'd like to introduce you to."

Introductions were made; hands were shaken. Oliver chalked that one up to a job well done, and set his glass on a nearby table. Then he crossed the room. Nobody could tell—nobody but Oliver—but underneath her gown of striped silk, Jane's belly was growing. In a few months, it would be obvious that she was increasing with their second child. For now…

He stalked toward her. God, she was lovely. Her back was to him, leaving a view of the nape of her neck, adorned tonight by gold and diamonds. The curve of her waist begged for his touch. She was talking with great animation to the people next to her.

"There need to be some repercussions to all this fine theory," Jane was saying. "It's all well and good to say that doctors should act in the best interests of their patients, but what if they do not? Who determines what happens next? This is what I need you to consider. Then, we'll talk to Parliament."

"Speak of the devil," the doctor next to her said.

Jane turned. "Oh. It's you." But she glowed at him—the smile of a woman completely in her element—and she took his hand, entwining it in hers. "Did you bring Bertie Pages? I wanted to introduce him to Anjan." She leaned in. "Emily says that Anjan is considering joining you in Parliament."

"I know. I talked to him earlier. It's already done." Oliver gestured across the room, where his colleague was talking to his brother-in-law. Emily stood next to her husband, smiling.

"You are efficient," she said.

"Sometimes." He smiled.

Jane was framed in the window. Everyone else might think the décor in the salon a bit odd. There was, after all, a small collection of plants on the table by the window: six of them so far. One cactus for every anniversary they'd celebrated together, plus the one Jane had brought to their marriage. For their tenth anniversary, Oliver was going to try to get her a saguaro—but that was going to take some doing. For now...

"I came to see if you were tired," Oliver said. "After all this work, I'm sure that when you finish up, you'll need a rest."

For the first few months of the pregnancy, she had been exhausted. She'd needed naps and back rubs, and he'd been happy to oblige.

"I haven't been tired in a while," she told him. "But yes, after we're done, I'll be..." She trailed off slowly.

She met his eyes, saw his smile. Her hand, tangled with his, went still for a moment. Very deliberately, Oliver drew his thumb over her fingers.

She answered his smile with one of her own.

"Now that you mention it," she said, "I *will* be particularly tired after this. I might need a little help getting upstairs."

Her forefinger traced an answering line down the side of his hand.

"Yes," Oliver said. "I can manage that." He leaned in and brushed a kiss against her forehead. "Until then."

Thank you!

Thanks for reading *The Heiress Effect*. I hope you enjoyed it!

• Would you like to know when my next book is available? You can sign up for my new release e-mail list at www.courtneymilan.com, follow me on twitter at @courtneymilan, or like my Facebook page at http://facebook.com/courtneymilanauthor.

• Reviews help other readers find books. I appreciate all reviews, whether positive or negative.

•You've just read the second full-length book in the Brothers Sinister series. The books in the series are *The Governess Affair*, a prequel novella about Oliver's parents, *The Duchess War*, *A Kiss for Midwinter*, *The Heiress Effect*, *The Countess Conspiracy* (out December 2013), and *The Mistress Rebellion* (out sometime in 2014). I hope you enjoy them all!

You probably don't want to know what was going on with Sebastian in this book. You probably don't care what secret he has been hiding. If that's the case, you definitely don't want to read one of the first scenes from *The Countess Conspiracy*, the next book in this series. Whatever you do, don't turn the page. And if you do, don't say I didn't warn you.

The Countess Conspiracy: Excerpt

The Countess Conspiracy
coming in December of 2013

This is a short, unedited excerpt from somewhere in Chapter One.

THE MORNING SUN BEAT DOWN VICIOUSLY, slicing into Sebastian's eyes as he looked out over the garden. The rose arbor caught the early sunlight, and the beds of flowers glistened with dew. It was damnably pretty, and he might even have enjoyed it, were it not for the persistent throb of his head. If he hadn't known better, he'd have imagined he was suffering from the ill effects of drink. Except he hadn't had anything stronger than tea in the last forty-eight hours. No; something else plagued him, and unlike a few bottles of wine, it could not be cured by an efficacious potion.

It would take a far greater dose than any apothecary could deliver to change how he felt.

He'd known where he was heading from the beginning. Violet was in the greenhouse; when he rounded the shrubbery, he saw her sitting on a stool, peering at an array of little pots of soil. She'd hooked her boots around the legs of the stool. Even from here, he could hear her whistling happily to herself. Sebastian felt sick to his stomach.

She didn't look up when he opened the door. She didn't look up when he crossed over to her. She was concentrating so fiercely on those little clay pots in front of her, a magnifying glass in one hand, that she hadn't even heard him come in.

God. She looked so cheerful sitting there, and he was going to ruin it all. He'd agreed to this charade when he hadn't understood what it would mean. When it had just meant signing his name and listening to Violet talk, two things that had seemed like no effort at all.

"Violet," he said softly.

He could see her coming back into an awareness of herself—blinking rapidly, slowly setting down the glass she was holding before turning to him.

"Sebastian!" she said. There was a pleased note in her voice. She'd forgiven him for last night, then. But the smile she gave him slowly died as she saw the look on his face. "Sebastian? Is everything all right?"

"I should apologize," he blurted out. "God knows I should apologize for last night. I should never have spoken to you that way, and especially not in public."

She waved this off. "I understand the strain you're under. Really, Sebastian, after everything we've done for each other, a few harsh words hardly signifies. Now, there was something I needed to tell you." She frowned and tapped her lips. "Let's see…"

"Violet. Don't get distracted. Listen to me."

She turned back to him.

Nobody else thought Violet pretty. He had never understood that. Yes, her nose was too big. Her mouth was too wide. Her eyes were set a little too far apart for beauty. He could see those things, but somehow they'd never signified to him. Of all the people in the world, Violet was the closest to him, and that made her dear in ways he didn't want to comprehend. She was his dearest friend, and he was about to rip her apart.

He held up his hands in surrender to the entire world. "Violet, I can't do this anymore. I'm done living a fraud."

Her face went utterly blank. Her hand reached out, falling on her magnifying glass, clutching it to her chest.

Sebastian felt heartsick. "Violet."

There was nobody he knew better, nobody in the world he cared for more. Her skin had turned to ash. She sat looking at him, totally devoid of expression. He'd seen her like that once before. He'd never imagined he would be the one who did that to her again.

"Violet, you know I would do anything for you."

She made a curious sound in her throat, half sob, half choke. "Don't do this. Sebastian, we can figure out—"

"We've tried," he said sadly. "I'm sorry, Violet," he whispered, "but this is the end."

He was breaking her, but then, the last thing that was good in him had already broken, and he had nothing left to give her. He smiled sadly and looked around her greenhouse. At the shelves and shelves, filled with tiny little pots, each one labeled. At the bookshelf in the corner, twenty leather-bound volumes strong. At all the evidence that he kept waiting for everyone else to discover. Finally, he looked at Violet—at a woman he had known all his life, and loved for half of it.

" I will be your friend. Your confidante. I'll be a helping hand when you need one. I will do anything for you, but there is one thing I will never do again." He drew a deep breath. "I will never again present your work as my own."

Her magnifying glass slipped from her fingers, and landed on the paving stones beneath her chair. But it was strong—like Violet—and it hadn't shattered.

He reached down and picked it up. "Here," he said, handing it back to her. "You'll need this."

Want to know when The Countess Conspiracy *comes out? Sign up for my new release e-mail list on my website today.*

If you haven't read The Duchess War, *the first full-length book in the series, the first chapter follows.*

The Duchess War: Excerpt

The Duchess War
available now

Miss Minerva Lane is a quiet, bespectacled wallflower, and she wants to keep it that way. After all, the last time she was the center of attention, it ended badly—so badly that she changed her name to escape her scandalous past. Wallflowers may not be the prettiest of blooms, but at least they don't get trampled. So when a handsome duke comes to town, the last thing she wants is his attention.

But that is precisely what she gets…

The Duchess War: Chapter One

ROBERT BLAISDELL, THE NINTH DUKE OF CLERMONT, was not hiding.

True, he'd retreated to the upstairs library of the old Guildhall, far enough from the crowd below that the noise of the ensemble had faded to a distant rumble. True, nobody else was about. Also true: He stood behind thick curtains of blue-gray velvet, which shielded him from view. And he'd had to move the heavy davenport of brown-buttoned leather to get there.

But he'd done all that not to hide himself, but because—and this was a key point in his rather specious train of logic—in this centuries-old structure of plaster and timberwork, only one of the panes in the windows opened, and that happened to be the one secreted behind the sofa.

So here he stood, cigarillo in hand, the smoke trailing out into the chilly autumn air. He wasn't hiding; it was simply a matter of preserving the aging books from fumes.

He might even have believed himself, if only he smoked.

Still, through the wavy panes of aging glass, he could make out the darkened stone of the church directly across the way. Lamplight cast unmoving shadows on the pavement below. A pile of handbills had once been stacked against the doors, but an autumn breeze had picked them up and scattered them down the street, driving them into puddles.

He was making a mess. A goddamned glorious mess. He smiled and tapped the end of his untouched cigarillo against the window opening, sending ashes twirling to the paving stones below.

The quiet creak of a door opening startled him. He turned from the window at the corresponding scritch of floorboards. Someone had come up the stairs and entered the adjoining room. The footsteps were light—a woman's, perhaps, or a child's. They were also curiously hesitant. Most people who made their way to the library in the midst of a musicale had a reason to do so. A clandestine meeting, perhaps, or a search for a missing family member.

From his vantage point behind the curtains, Robert could only see a small slice of the library. Whoever it was drew closer, walking hesitantly. She was out of sight—somehow he was sure that she was a woman—but he could hear the soft, prowling fall of her feet, pausing every so often as if to examine the surroundings.

She didn't call out a name or make a determined search. It didn't sound as if she were looking for a hidden lover. Instead, her footsteps circled the perimeter of the room.

It took Robert half a minute to realize that he'd waited too long to announce himself. "Aha!" he could imagine himself proclaiming, springing out from behind the curtains. "I was admiring the plaster. Very evenly laid back there, did you know?"

She would think he was mad. And so far, nobody yet had come to that conclusion. So instead of speaking, he dropped his cigarillo out the window. It tumbled end over end, orange tip glowing, until it landed in a puddle and extinguished itself.

All he could see of the room was a half-shelf of books, the back of the sofa, and a table next to it on which a chess set had been laid out. The game was in progress; from what little he remembered of the rules, black was winning. Whoever it was drew nearer, and Robert shrank back against the window.

She crossed into his field of vision.

She wasn't one of the young ladies he'd met in the crowded hall earlier. Those had all been beauties, hoping to catch his eye. And she—whoever she was—was not a beauty. Her dark hair was swept into a no-nonsense knot at the back of her neck. Her lips were thin and her nose was sharp and a bit on the long side. She was dressed in a dark blue gown trimmed in ivory—no lace, no ribbons, just simple fabric. Even the cut of her gown bordered on the severe side: waist pulled in so tightly he wondered how she could breathe, sleeves marching from her shoulders to her wrists without an inch of excess fabric to soften the picture.

She didn't see Robert standing behind the curtain. She had set her head to one side and was eyeing the chess set the way a member of the Temperance League might look at a cask of brandy: as if it were an evil to be stamped out with prayer and song—and failing that, with martial law.

She took one halting step forward, then another. Then, she reached into the silk bag that hung around her wrist and retrieved a pair of spectacles.

Glasses should have made her look more severe. But as soon as she put them on, her gaze softened.

He'd read her wrongly. Her eyes hadn't been narrowed in scorn; she'd been squinting. It hadn't been severity he saw in her gaze but something else entirely—something he couldn't quite make out. She reached out and picked up a black knight, turning it around, over and over. He could see nothing about the pieces that would merit such careful attention. They were solid wood, carved with indifferent skill. Still, she studied it, her eyes wide and luminous.

Then, inexplicably, she raised it to her lips and kissed it.

Robert watched in frozen silence. It almost felt as if he were interrupting a tryst between a woman and her lover. This was a lady who had secrets, and she didn't want to share them.

The door in the far room creaked as it opened once more.

The woman's eyes grew wide and wild. She looked about frantically and dove over the davenport in her haste to hide, landing in an ignominious heap two feet away from him. She didn't see Robert even then; she curled into a ball, yanking her skirts behind the leather barrier of the sofa, breathing in shallow little gulps.

Good thing he'd moved the davenport back half a foot earlier. She never would have fit the great mass of her skirts behind it otherwise.

Her fist was still clenched around the chess piece; she shoved the knight violently under the sofa.

This time, a heavier pair of footfalls entered the room.

"Minnie?" said a man's voice. "Miss Pursling? Are you here?"

Her nose scrunched and she pushed back against the wall. She made no answer.

"Gad, man." Another voice that Robert didn't recognize—young and slightly slurred with drink. "I don't envy you that one."

"Don't speak ill of my almost-betrothed," the first voice said. "You know she's perfect for me."

"That timid little rodent?"

"She'll keep a good home. She'll see to my comfort. She'll manage the children, and she won't complain about my mistresses." There was a creak of hinges—the unmistakable sound of someone opening one of the glass doors that protected the bookshelves.

"What are you doing, Gardley?" the drunk man asked. "Looking for her among the German volumes? I don't think she'd fit." That came with an ugly laugh.

Gardley. That couldn't be the elder Mr. Gardley, owner of a distillery—not by the youth in that voice. This must be Mr. Gardley the younger. Robert had seen him from afar—an unremarkable fellow of medium height, medium-brown hair, and features that reminded him faintly of five other people.

"On the contrary," young Gardley said. "I think she'll fit quite well. As wives go, Miss Pursling will be just like these books. When I wish to take her down and read her, she'll be there. When I don't, she'll wait patiently, precisely where she was left. She'll make me a comfortable wife, Ames. Besides, my mother likes her."

Robert didn't believe he'd met an Ames. He shrugged and glanced down at—he was guessing—Miss Pursling to see how she took this revelation.

She didn't look surprised or shocked at her almost-fiancé's unromantic utterance. Instead, she looked resigned.

"You'll have to take her to bed, you know," Ames said.

"True. But not, thank God, very often."

"She's a rodent. Like all rodents, I imagine she'll squeal when she's poked."

There was a mild thump.

"What?" yelped Ames.

"That," said Gardley, "is my future wife you are talking about."

Maybe the fellow wasn't so bad after all.

Then Gardley continued. "I'm the only one who gets to think about poking *that* rodent."

Miss Pursling pressed her lips together and looked up, as if imploring the heavens. But inside the library, there were no heavens to implore. And when she looked up, through the gap in the curtains…

Her gaze met Robert's. Her eyes grew big and round. She didn't scream; she didn't gasp. She didn't twitch so much as an inch. She simply fixed him with a look that bristled with silent, venomous accusation. Her nostrils flared.

There was nothing Robert could do but lift his hand and give her a little wave.

She took off her spectacles and turned away in a gesture so regally dismissive that he had to look twice to remind himself that she was, in fact, sitting in a heap of skirts at his feet. That from this awkward angle above her, he could see straight down the neckline of her gown—right at the one part of her figure that didn't strike him as severe, but soft—

Save that for later, he admonished himself, and adjusted his gaze up a few inches. Because she'd turned away, he saw for the first time a faint scar on her left cheek, a tangled white spider web of crisscrossed lines.

"Wherever your mouse has wandered off to, it's not here," Ames was saying. "Likely she's in the lady's retiring room. I say we go back to the fun. You can always tell your mother you had words with her in the library."

"True enough," Gardley said. "And I don't need to mention that she wasn't present for them—it's not as if she would have said anything in response, even if she had been here."

Footsteps receded; the door creaked once more, and the men walked out.

Miss Pursling didn't look at Robert once they'd left, not even to acknowledge his existence with a glare. Instead, she pushed herself to her knees, made a fist, and slammed it into the hard back of the sofa—once, then twice, hitting it so hard that it moved forward with the force of her blow—all one hundred pounds of it.

He caught her wrist before she landed a third strike. "There now," he said. "You don't want to hurt yourself over him. He doesn't deserve it."

She stared up at him, her eyes wide.

He didn't see how any man could call this woman timid. She positively crackled with defiance. He let go of her arm before the fury in her could travel up his hand and consume him. He had enough anger of his own.

"Never mind me," she said. "Apparently I'm not capable of helping myself."

He almost jumped. He wasn't sure how he'd expected her voice to sound—sharp and severe, like her appearance suggested? Perhaps he'd imagined her talking in a high squeak, as if she were the rodent she'd been labeled. But her voice was low, warm, and deeply sensual. It was the kind of voice that made him suddenly aware that she was on her knees before him, her head almost level with his crotch.

Save that for later, too.

"I'm a rodent. All rodents squeal when poked." She punched the sofa once again. She was going to bruise her knuckles if she kept that up. "Are you planning to poke me, too?"

"No." Stray thoughts didn't count, thank God; if they did, all men would burn in hell forever.

"Do you always skulk behind curtains, hoping to overhear intimate conversations?"

Robert felt the tips of his ears burn. "Do you always leap behind sofas when you hear your fiancé coming?"

"Yes," she said defiantly. "Didn't you hear? I'm like a book that has been mislaid. One day, one of his servants will find me covered in dust in the middle of spring-cleaning. 'Ah,' the butler will say. 'That's where Miss Wilhelmina has ended up. I had forgotten all about her.'"

Wilhelmina Pursling? What a dreadful appellation.

She took a deep breath. "Please don't tell anyone. Not about any of this." She shut her eyes and pressed her fingers to her eyes. "Please just go away, whoever you are."

He brushed the curtains to one side and made his way around the sofa. From a few feet away, he couldn't even see her. He could only imagine her curled on the floor, furious to the point of tears.

"Minnie," he said. It wasn't polite to call her by so intimate a name. And yet he wanted to hear it on his tongue.

She didn't respond.

"I'll give you twenty minutes," he said. "If I don't see you downstairs by then, I'll come up for you."

For a few moments, there was no answer. Then: "The beautiful thing about marriage is the right it gives me to monogamy. One man intent on dictating my whereabouts is enough, wouldn't you think?"

He stared at the sofa in confusion before he realized that she thought he'd been threatening to drag her out.

Robert was good at many things. Communicating with women was not one of them.

"That's not what I meant," he muttered. "It's just…" He walked back to the sofa and peered over the leather top. "If a woman I cared about was hiding behind a sofa, I would hope that someone would take the time to make sure she was well."

There was a long pause. Then fabric rustled and she looked up at him. Her hair had begun to slip out of that severe bun; it hung around her face, softening her features, highlighting the pale whiteness of her scar. Not pretty, but…interesting. And he could have listened to her talk all night.

She stared at him in puzzlement. "Oh," she said flatly. "You're attempting to be kind." She sounded as if the possibility had never occurred to her before. She let out a sigh, and gave him a shake of her head. "But your kindness is misplaced. You see, *that*—" she pointed toward the doorway where her near-fiancé had disappeared "—that is the best possible outcome I can hope for. I have wanted just such a thing for years. As soon as I can stomach the thought, I'll be marrying him."

There was no trace of sarcasm in her voice. She stood. With a practiced hand, she smoothed her hair back under the pins and straightened her skirts until she was restored to complete propriety.

Only then did she stoop, patting under the sofa to find where she'd tossed the knight. She examined the chessboard, cocked her head, and then very, very carefully, set the piece back into place.

While he was standing there, watching her, trying to make sense of her words, she walked out the door.

Want to read the rest? *The Duchess War* is available now.

Other Books by Courtney

Author's Note

I'VE DONE MY BEST to make sure that the timing of this story parallels the history of the Reform Act of 1867, which extended the franchise to many (but not all) working-class men in 1867.

The gathering I describe in Hyde Park really did have more than a hundred thousand people attending, and it really did freak out the government—resulting in a much more liberal extension of the franchise than had been previously contemplated. If you'd like to read a surprisingly sarcastic newspaper account of that event from *The Daily News* of May 7, 1867, I've reproduced it on my website at:

http://www.courtneymilan.com/heiresseffect-dailynews.php.

The paper says nothing about a group of women at the park, but it *does* mention a woman in a sailor hat who was said to "harangue" the crowds about equal rights for all. I suspect that any woman who spoke loud enough to be heard in that large a crowd would have been said to "harangue," and so I've assumed that she was as reasonable as the men.

Today we would understand that Emily has epilepsy with partial seizures. At the time, however, epilepsy was very poorly understood. Doctor Russell (who Emily refers to in the book as one of the physicians who treated her) was perhaps the one who best understood the disease; he was one of the first to employ the "numerical method" to epilepsy.

You can read his book on the subject here: http://bit.ly/150aVdY.

In any event, Russell, advanced as he was, believed that it wasn't epilepsy unless there was a lapse of consciousness; hence the reason why Emily claims that her fits are not epilepsy.

If you're ever feeling like you need to be more grateful for modern medicine, consider perusing the above book for a list of treatments that were tried on epileptics. All of the "treatments" that Emily experienced in this book were ones that I found mentioned in various medical texts of around this period.

A brief note on the timing of Anjan's education: In the US today, it would be ridiculous to have someone in school and studying for law examinations in January and then practicing law in May, but it was perfectly possible then. When Anjan says that he is "going out," he means that he's near the end of his time at the University; the final year for students there was not quite a full year. Anjan is studying for the Law Tripos, an examination (or, rather, a set of grueling examinations that would determine whether a student graduated with honors, and what honors those were) that would have been delivered around Easter. Anjan would have to return to Cambridge for commencement, but that was just a formality.

More importantly, he wouldn't have needed a degree to be admitted to the bar. The requirements for bar admission varied, depending upon which bar you were planning to join, but usually required that you get some current members of the bar to vouch for your character, that you passed a basic examination, and that you "kept terms" with the Inn of Court—in other words, you had dinner with a bunch of barristers a number of times. In many cases, you could substitute two years' of Oxbridge education for the part where you ate dinners. Anjan, being a careful planner, would have knocked off the requirements for the bar sometime in the year before.

In terms of trying to accurately portray Anjan's experience, I read a handful of accounts written by Indian students who studied in Britain in the mid-to-late nineteenth century and I've tried to do my best to extrapolate what Anjan's life would have been like. The most famous of those accounts is obviously Mahatma Gandhi's autobiography. But I also drew heavily on a description of life at Cambridge written by S. Satthianadhan, who would have attended Cambridge around the time that my fictional Anjan Bhattacharya would have done so.

Satthianadhan never talked about racism directly, but there were a handful of times when it felt as if he was giving advice out of the corner of his mouth. His praise for the English was over the top, almost as a warning. One passage in particular said (and I paraphrase), "The English might seem like jerks, but that's because they think they're better than us. Pretend that they're right and they'll be nice to you."

I reproduced this passage on my tumblr, for those who want to read it, at http://bit.ly/12j72Ch.

One way in which I've diverged from historical usage is that at the time, Indians in England were often referred to as "blacks." I think that use would be unduly confusing to modern, and particularly American, readers.

One last note about Anjan: Some people might think it over-the-top to have the epilogue for this book mention that Anjan was interested political office in 1874. But the first Indian Member of Parliament, Dadabhai Naoroji, was elected in 1892 at the age of 67. In 1874, Anjan would have been 27—

young enough that if he started working toward that goal, by the time he was in his mid-fifties, that barrier would already have been breached.

Finally, I need to echo what I said in the Author's Note for *The Duchess War:* This series effectively rewrites the scientific history of evolution and genetics. While Mendel's experiments with pea plants were performed in 1830, their import wasn't understood until much later. In the book, I've assumed that having Darwin and a prominent geneticist in the same place and time would accelerate the pace of scientific advancement.

Acknowledgements

I AM DEEPLY INDEBTED to Robin Harders, Megan Records, Rawles Lumumba, Keira Soleore, Leah Wohl-Pollak, Martha Trachtenberg, and Libby Sternberg for various forms of editing and copy-editing, and for putting up with me and my total inability to deliver a book when I say I'm going to deliver it while still handing me extraordinarily thoughtful remarks back in an extraordinarily short period of time. I wouldn't be able to produce books like this without you all, and I'm deeply grateful for your help.

Thanks also go to Kristin Nelson, my agent, for her unstinting support, and to the rest of her agency staff for all the many ways that they help: Angie Hodapp, Lori Bennett, Anita Mumm, and Sara Megibow. I'd like to thank Melissa Jolly for the support she's given me. And finally, Rawles again, for everything she's done in the last few weeks to make my life easier.

Rose Lerner deserves a special thanks for a breakfast in Seattle in January, where we were complaining about…well, everything, including some of the limitations of the subgenre. Anjan is the direct result of that conversation. Thanks, Rose, for pushing me where I needed to be pushed. (If you like historical romances and you didn't get a chance to read Rose's books when they were available from Dorchester, they're all going to be reissued by Samhain Publishing, so keep watching.)

I'm indebted to Rozina Visram for her many books documenting Asians in historical Britain. My sister Tami helped with a few items of research by providing sooper sekrit access to sources that I couldn't get any other way. Sssh, don't tell her university.

There are also my friends, without whom I would have collapsed into a spineless puddle somewhere around month two of this book. Tessa Dare, Leigh LaValle, and Carey Baldwin gave me friendship above and beyond the call of duty, the Loop that Must Not be Named let me complain when I needed to complain and made me write when I needed to write. There are dozens of other people who have answered questions, provided comfort, and otherwise just been awesome on the course of this journey, spread out over publishing loops and individual e-mails: Kris (both Kris+ and Kris 1/a),

Delilah, Rachel, Elisabeth, Elizabeth, Heather, Marie, Tina, Joan, Becky... at this point, I'm realizing that listing people by name is a futile endeavor. If I forgot you, you're awesome and I suck.

And then there is you. You're last but you're never least. Thank you for reading this book. Thank you for telling people about my books, for sharing them with friends. Thank you for reading them silently and enjoying them. Thank you for everything you've done, because without you, there wouldn't be any books at all.

CPSIA information can be obtained at www.ICGtesting.com
Printed in the USA
LVOW11s2237220316

480330LV00001B/102/P